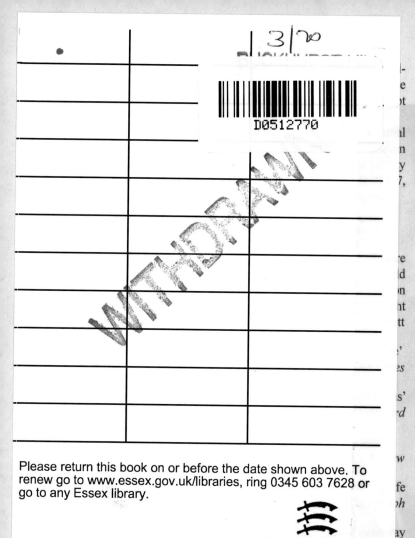

'A brilliant and beguiling heroine. Immensely appealing'

Publishers Weekly

'Tremayne's super-sleuth is a vibrant creation, a woman of wit and courage who wo_____arkle to the wild beauty _____Morgan Llywelyn

By Peter Tremayne and featuring Sister Fidelma

Absolution by Murder
Shroud for the Archbishop
Suffer Little Children
The Subtle Serpent
The Spider's Web
Valley of the Shadow
The Monk who Vanished
Act of Mercy
Hemlock at Vespers
Our Lady of Darkness
Smoke in the Wind
The Haunted Abbot
Badger's Moon
Whispers of the Dead
The Leper's Bell
Master of Souls
A Prayer for the Damned
Dancing with Demons
The Council of the Cursed
The Dove of Death
The Chalice of Blood
Behold a Pale Horse
The Seventh Trumpet
Atonement of Blood
The Devil's Seal
The Second Death
Penance of the Damned
Night of the Lightbringer
Bloodmoon
Blood in Eden

PETER TREMAYNE

BLOOD IN EDEN

HEADLINE

First published in Great Britain in 2019
by HEADLINE PUBLISHING GROUP

First published in Great Britain in paperback in 2020
by HEADLINE PUBLISHING GROUP

1

Cataloguing in Publication Data is available from the British Library

ISBN 978 1 4722 3876 4

Typeset in Times New Roman PS by Palimpsest Book Production Limited,
Falkirk, Stirlingshire

Printed and bound in Great Britain by Clays Ltd, Elcograf S.p.A.

Headline's policy is to use papers that are natural, renewable and recyclable products
and made from wood grown in sustainable forests. The logging and manufacturing
processes are expected to conform to the environmental regulations of the
country of origin.

HEADLINE PUBLISHING GROUP
An Hachette UK Company
Carmelite House
50 Victoria Embankment
London EC4Y 0DZ

www.headline.co.uk
www.hachette.co.uk

For Eleni Triantafillaki
my soul-twin
who encouraged me to accept
nulla vestigia retrorsum –
no footsteps backwards.

Eiecitque Adam et conlocavit ante paradisum voluptatis cherubin et flammeum gladium atque versatilem ad custodiendam viam ligni vitae.

After He drove out Adam, He placed, before the east of the Garden of Eden, cherubim armed and a flaming, whirling sword to guard the way to the Tree of Life.

Genesis 3-24
Vulgate Latin translation of Jerome, 4th century

PRINCIPAL CHARACTERS

Sister Fidelma of Cashel, a *dálaigh* or advocate of the law courts of 7th-century Ireland

Brother Eadulf of Seaxmund's Ham, in the land of the South Folk, her companion

At Cloichín

The victims
Adnán, a farmer
Aoife, his wife
Cainnech, their son
Abél, the second son

The inhabitants
Brother Gadra, a priest
Fethmac, the *bó-aire* or magistrate
Ballgel, his wife
Gobánguss, the blacksmith
Breccnat, his wife
Eórann, mother of Breccnat
Lúbaigh, a farmworker

Fuinche, his wife
Dulbaire, Lúbaigh's brother
Íonait, a milkmaid
Blinne, her mother, a widow
Tadgán, farmer and cousin to Adnán
Taithlech, a merchant
Flannat, his daughter and widow of Díoma, son of Tadgán

The itinerants
Celgaire
Fial, his wife
Ennec, their baby son

At the Abbey of Ard Fhionáin
Abbot Rumann
Brother Solam, *the scholar*
Brother Fechtnach, *rechtaire* or steward

At Cnoc na Faille
Conmaol, a claimant to Adnán's inheritance
Slébíne, his son
Tuama, a shepherd

Enda, a warrior of the *Nasc Niadh*, or Golden Collar, élite body-guard to Colgú, King of Muman

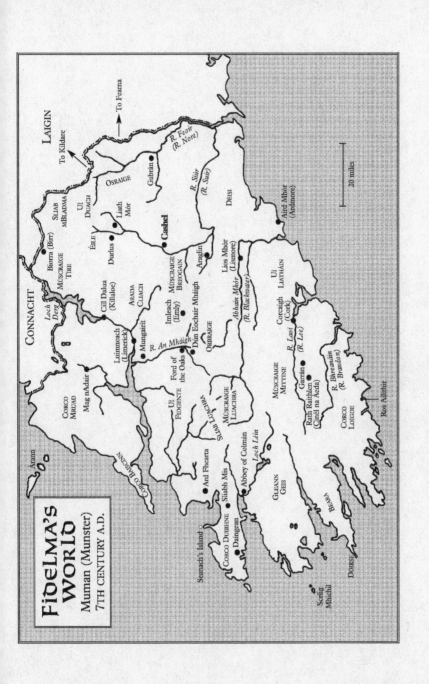

FIDELMA'S WORLD
Muman (Munster)
7TH CENTURY A.D.

CONNACHT

LAIGIN

To Fearna

To Kildare

OSRAIGE

SLIAB MBLADMA

UÍ DUACH

Gabrán

R. Feoir
(R. Nore)

Biorra (Birr)

MUSCRAIGE TÍRE

Liath Mór

Durlus

ÉILE

Cashel

R. Siúir
(R. Suir)

DÉISI

Aird Mhór
(Ardmore)

Loch Derg

Cill Dalua
(Killaloe)

ARADA CLIACH

MUSCRAIGE BREOGÁIN

Araglin

Lios Mhór
(Lismore)

Luimneach
(Limerick)

Imleach
(Emly)

Dún Eochair Mháigh

Abhan Mhór
(R. Blackwater)

UÍ LIATHÁIN

Mungairit

Mag nAdair

CORCO MRUAD

R. An Mháigh

Ford of the Oaks

ORBRAIGE

UÍ FIDGENTE

SLIABH LUACHRA

Corcaigh
(Cork)

R. Laoi
(R. Lee)

MUSCRAIGE LÍACHRA

MUSCRAIGE MITTINE

Garrán

Ráth Raithlen
(Cinél na Áeda)

R. Bhreanáin
(R. Brandon)

Ard Fhearta

Abbey of Colmán

Loch Léin

CORCO LOÍGDE

Ros Ailithir

CORCO BAISCINN

Árann

Seanach's Island

Sliabh Mis

CORCO DUIBHNE

Daingean

GLEANN GEIS

BÉARA

DORSE

Scelig Mhichíl

20 miles

AUTHOR'S NOTE

This story follows chronologically after *Bloodmoon* although it is self-contained. The year is AD 672, the month Mí Faoide (February), regarded in 7th-century Ireland as 'the month of sleep or rest'. There was little to be done in the rural areas during the dark, cold days that preceded the quarter year known as Imbolc, the time of the coming into lamb of the ewes, and whose major festival was dedicated to the ancient Goddess of Fertility, Brigit.

The location is Cloichín (Clogheen), a settlement known as 'the stony place', lying not far from the shadows of the towering Cnoc Mhaoldomhnaigh (Knockmealdown) mountain range situated 32 kilometres to the south of Cashel. The abbey of Ard Fhionáin (Ardfinnan) lies a short distance away to the east. Called 'Finan's Height', it took its name from a religious settlement founded in the early 7th century by Finan the Leper.

It might help readers appreciate the setting to know that the genealogical records of the indigenous Gaelic aristocracy of Ireland are considered to be the most ancient in Europe. Surviving family pedigrees, in written form, date from the 7th century AD; however, the famous Irish scholar Professor Eoin MacNeill (1867–1945) believed that they 'are probably fairly authentic in the main as far back as 200BC'.

We are dealing with an Ireland at a time of social change. New concepts of Christianity being brought in from Rome resulted in conflicts and confusion as ideas on issues such as property owner-ship and inheritance began to be influenced.

The term *derbhfine* (dey-ruv-fin-a), used in this story, refers to a family group of up to four living generations from a common great-grandfather. This was the usual unit for agreement on dynastic succession as there was no primogeniture. Eldest sons did not necessarily succeed fathers, although there was the senior member – the *ádae fine* – who convened the family group. With the concept of *fintiu,* or kin-land, a developing form of private property was recognised. The old tribal land system, over which the *derbhfine* could still make collective decisions, was changing slowly. Another point to remember is that women had the right of inheritance and also retained their own property throughout marriage. In law, they were called *banchomarba* (ban-cho-mar-ba) or female heirs. A good analysis of this can be found in 'The Relationship of Mother and Son, of Father and Daughter, and the Law of Inheritance with Regard to Women' by Professor Myles Dillon, in *Studies in Early Irish Law*, Royal Irish Academy, Dublin, 1936.

Because this is probably the first work of fiction that deals with early medieval Irish law of property and female inheritance, readers will find a number of Old/Middle Irish words and manuscript references. Please do not waste time worrying about correct pronun-ciation. Now and then, some readers have expressed concern that concepts seem so advanced for the 7th century; I believe they suspect I make up the laws as I think fit. This, of course, is not so. *Blood in Eden* may be of help.

CHAPTER ONE

The group of people was a small one but no longer consisted of individual men and women, and the few small, crying children among them. It had coalesced into a frightening mob, moving along the village street as if possessed of one body and one purpose. The noise they made rose like a single discordant sound – an assault on the senses. Even their arms, waving, some bearing cudgels and sticks, appeared as appendages to a single being. A keen-eyed observer could discern that something or someone was being propelled along in their midst. Eventually the body of a man became visible; a man struggling against the rope by which he was being dragged. Through the covering of mud and filth, one thing distinguished him from the mob surrounding him, which was the colour of his skin. It was black.

At the head of the mindless crowd strode a stout figure, now and then turning and shouting encouragement, waving them on as his voice was sometimes lost among their cries and screams of hatred. He wore the black woollen robes of a religieux, with a silver cross hung on a leather thong around his neck. In one hand he carried a curiously carved blackthorn staff.

The mob manhandled their prisoner along the main village street, between dark buildings of poor quality, typical of the many rural settlements of the area. At their doors stood one or two inhabitants looking silently on. As the frenzied group passed one house, the door burst open and a young man, apparently tearing himself away from the restraint of two burly men, pushed his way into the path of the stocky religieux. As he halted, the two muscular men caught up with him and grabbed his arms. The young man, dark haired and handsome, desperately tried to shake off his captors but their grip was tight.

'Brother Gadra!' shouted the young man. 'I order you to stop. Cease this madness!'

The religieux paused in mid-stride and the mob behind him came to an unruly halt, their wild yelling subsiding unevenly.

Brother Gadra turned to the young man, his eyes narrowed, and hissed, 'I am about God's work and the work of justice that *you* should have been about, Fethmac of Cloichín.'

'I am the *bó-aire*, magistrate of this village. It is I who administer the law here,' the young man replied sternly.

Brother Gadra threw back his head and chuckled cynically.

'Magistrate, indeed,' he scoffed. 'You are hardly old enough to shave. What do you know of justice? You are not qualified even in the native law to be a Brehon and command the respect of others. You certainly have no knowledge of the canon laws by which we should all live, placing our trust only in our supreme judge and creator.'

The young man called Fethmac ignored the contemptuous tone in Brother Gadra's voice.

'I know my duties, Brother. I say again, as your magistrate I am the only one here to speak of law and justice. What you are doing is wrong. Release that man.'

He gestured towards the now prone body of the mud-covered victim, the end of the rope held in the hands of his tormentors.

There was a nervous movement among the crowd at the authority in the young magistrate's words.

'You think this . . . this *beast* . . . is a man?' sneered Brother

Gadra. 'You think he has any rights? He is a creature, a mindless animal – and his actions have shown that.'

Fethmac was defiant in front of the confident religieux.

'He is a man under our law and must be heard in his defence. Release him, I say!'

'And *I* say, we will not! Death is his reward,' shouted Brother Gadra. 'Does not the Holy Book of Leviticus say "He that kills any man shall surely be put to death"? He has killed, so he shall die!'

There now rose a muttering in agreement at Brother Gadra's loud declaration.

'Our law demands trial and proof before a man is declared guilty,' cried the magistrate, once more attempting to free himself of those who were forcibly restraining him. 'He has not been judged.'

'We have already judged him,' snapped Brother Gadra. 'As Ezekiel says, "Every person shall die for his own sin." So be it. He shall die now.'

He nodded to the two men holding the young magistrate, and they hauled him from the path. Brother Gadra then turned to the crowd, his eyes aflame with fanaticism, aware that the magistrate's intervention might have weakened their hot-blooded resolve. He held up his silver crucifix for them all to see.

'We are about our Lord's work,' he boomed. 'Do not be turned from the path of righteousness, for the Holy Book says, without qualification, that a killing is punishable by death. God demands it – and is there any among you who will defy God?'

His angry words once more animated the people and once again they became a dangerous mob, baying for blood.

Satisfied, Brother Gadra pointed to the end of the settlement where the track led to a small hillock.

'Let your territorial emblem also signify the means by which those who transgress the laws of God shall receive retribution!'

His outstretched hands pointed towards the tree that grew on top of the mound. It rose, a broad trunk with a spreading crown, an ancient sessile oak with a few obdurate brown leaves, hardy stalk-less acorns, and straight branches sticking outward like signposts to the various points of the landscape. The tree had obviously stood for many centuries, marking the territory of the community, one of the countless rural habitations of the Eóghanacht Glendamnach, in turn one of the largest territories of the Kingdom of Muman. For most of the villagers, it was a sacred tree, for such emblems were used even in the time beyond time, in the time before the New Faith had spread across the land.

The captive was dragged before the tree and stood twisting but secure in the grips of the two village men. He stared up, his eyes white orbs against his black, mud-streaked face, fixing with horror on the gnarled arms of the tree, which seemed to droop ready for the fruit that would soon hang from them.

'Who has the rope?' demanded Brother Gadra.

A man came forward, taking a coiled rope from his shoulder. He was a powerfully built fellow with scowling features.

'I have it here, Brother Gadra.'

'Then secure it to that branch.'

The young magistrate who had tried to stop the mob had managed to drag his two captors closer to the edge of the crowd by sheer willpower.

'Stop! This is wrong!' he screamed over the heads of the crowd. 'You will all be answerable to the law!'

The Brother glanced briefly at him. 'As you will be answerable to God,' he replied. 'Have a care, young magistrate. If you keep interfering, God might require a more immediate answer from you.'

The crowd were hesitant again. After all, Fethmac had authority in the village, and was the dispenser of law. Did Brother Gadra truly have the right to threaten him to the point of death as he appeared to be doing?

Unexpectedly, a young man scarcely out of his teenage years suddenly detached himself from the crowd and moved to the tree with a curious hopping, almost dancing step. From his loosely flapping jacket he took a *fedán,* a reed pipe of the kind many shepherds and cowherders often played. It was no more than a hollow plant stem and he put it to his thin lips. An odd cadence came from it as he stood by the tree shuffling his feet in some frenzied ritual movement. For a few moments, the crowd looked on in silent embarrassment at his performance.

'Dulbaire! Stop that!' An older man came from the crowd and seized the boy's arm while with the other hand he snatched at the whistle. The boy went, protesting loudly.

Brother Gadra had seized the moment and urged the man with the rope to continue his gruesome task. When there was a moment's faltering on his part, Brother Gadra growled: 'If any here be of faint heart, remember whose death we avenge.'

To this there came a low rumble of anger from several throats.

After a quick glance around at his fellows, the designated hangman stepped back and threw the rope towards the tree. It coiled over a branch and fell into his waiting hands, upon which he began to fashion a noose.

'Six men on that end,' instructed the religieux. 'Come on!' he urged when there seemed more dithering.

Self-consciously, reluctantly, some men shuffled forward from the crowd as if impelled by Brother Gadra's terrible, mesmeric gaze. They took hold of the end of the rope as if they were handling a dangerous beast.

At a further nod, the prisoner was shoved forward and the hangman placed the noose over his head then drew it tight.

Brother Gadra stepped close to the sobbing victim.

'God can spare no mercy, for your crime is beyond mercy,' he declared, raising his voice so that the crowd could hear him clearly. 'Do you wish to confess your sins before you meet His terrible vengeance?'

'I did not do this,' the man babbled. 'I am innocent.'

Brother Gadra stepped back and nodded at the men holding the end of the rope.

'Do God's justice . . . now!'

The men began to pull. The noose tightened, choking the man's sobs and he was raised from the ground.

At that moment, a cold feminine voice pierced the silence that had fallen over them all.

'Stop! Stop and release that rope or suffer the anger of your King and the punishment of the law!'

Startled by the unexpected voice of authority, the men at the end of the rope stood stockstill for a moment before letting the rope slide through their hands until the victim's urgently jerking feet found support on the muddy ground again. Everyone seemed shocked into silence. Even Brother Gadra froze in his bloodthirsty exhortations.

As if from behind the oak, although such a thing was impossible, a figure on horseback had emerged. The onlookers gasped at the sight of the rider, the hood of her heavy cloak having become dislodged, showing her mass of untidy red hair. Her face seemed hard as white marble and the eyes were gimlet points of blue-green ice as she looked down on them.

'What now?' demanded Eadulf of Seaxmund's Ham, staring at the burnt-out remains of what had been the tavern where he had often stopped for refreshment while crossing the high pass known as the Way of the Blessed Declan. The pass led through the great forbidding peaks of Cnoc Mhaoldomhnaigh, the bald, brown mountains.

Beside him, Fidelma of Cashel, seated on her Gaulish pony, shook her head and sighed.

'This fire must have only happened recently,' she observed, looking carefully at the charred ruins of the building and not answering his question directly.

They had just spent a few days at the abbey of Lios Mhór to

celebrate the memorial feast in honour of Abbess Gobnait of Muscraige. Despite the fact that the abbess was a century and a half dead, an annual feast in her honour was held at the great abbey even though the link between Abbess Gobnait and Lios Mhór was slight. She had been instrumental in bringing knowledge of bee-keeping to the abbey, using honey for healing purposes and thus preventing a pestilence striking the people there. For this she had been declared a saintly person and duly honoured each year. It was courtesy that a member of the ruling dynasty of the kingdom attended. Fidelma, sister to Colgú, King of Muman, the largest and most south-westerly of the Five Kingdoms of Éireann, had taken the responsibility, accompanied by her husband Eadulf. Now they were on their way back northward to Cashel, the principal palace of the kingdom.

The direct route was not an easy one, twisting up to a height over a thousand metres across the mountain range. Declan, who had been abbot of Ard Mhór on the coast, had reputedly used the mountain pass as his route from his coastal abbey to visit the King at Cashel two centuries before.

Fidelma and Eadulf had crossed the mountains several times and usually halted for refreshment at the small tavern. Now its blackened ruins were a bleak and ominous sight.

'What do you think?' Eadulf prompted after a few moments. 'Is it some deliberate act?'

'It is not unusual for a tavern to catch fire,' Fidelma pointed out. 'Not everything should be interpreted as sinister. Fires from kitchens are frequent – which is why we generally have our kitchens built separately to the main living areas.'

Eadulf continued to examine the charred remains. 'At least there are no signs of bodies.'

'Nor any obvious cause why someone should attack an isolated tavern which so many travellers rely on for food and comfort as they come through this pass. So I would see this as the result of an accident.'

'Accident or not, I was looking forward to some warmth and refreshment,' Eadulf replied wearily. 'This is an inhospitable month. In my language, we call it Solomonath, the month of mud.'

Fidelma raised an eyebrow in query. 'I thought you called it Februa?'

Eadulf shook his head. 'That is Latin, the month of expiation. Latin names are becoming popular now with the advance of the New Faith.'

'Not so much here. Our name for this is Mí Faoide, the month of sleep and rest, and it's still descriptive of what we should be doing during this period; resting for the spring that will soon be upon us.'

Eadulf grimaced tiredly. 'Well, whatever the name, it certainly means that we have to look elsewhere for rest and food.'

As they sat gazing at the ruins, the tinkling of tiny bells caused them to look around. A little further down the slope, a flock of sturdy mountain sheep were strung out. A boy was moving among them with a shepherd's crook, guiding them around rocks that had initially obscured him from Fidelma and Eadulf's vision.

'*Hóigh!*' Eadulf shouted to attract his attention.

The shepherd boy looked up, startled for a moment. Then, to their amazement, he put his head down and carried on with his task.

Eadulf frowned. 'He heard us,' he said. 'Maybe he is frightened of strangers?'

'Sometimes it pays to be cautious of strangers,' intoned a hollow voice from close behind them.

Jolted by surprise, they swung round to find a man seated on a rock on the slope that rose on the far side of the road behind them.

He was a man of middle years, with weather-bronzed skin and greying hair, flowing long and mingling with a beard that almost hid his face. He carried a shepherd's staff, and while his clothes were not out of keeping with the profession of a shepherd there was something about his appearance that did not fit the role. He carried a broad knife in a sheath at one side of his belt, a quiver of arrows at the other and a medium-sized ash bow was strung on his back.

'Why would shepherds be frightened of strangers?' asked Fidelma.

'Oh, there have been assaults and thefts of late along Declan's Way,' the man replied. 'I have taught my boy there,' he indicated where the youth was herding the sheep, 'to be cautious of any strangers along this way.'

'You mean travellers have been held up and robbed?' Eadulf queried.

'They have,' the man agreed easily, rising to his feet and moving down the slope until he was just a few metres below them. There he paused, turning to lean on his staff. His bright eyes narrowed shrewdly as he took in their clothing, especially Fidelma's rich robes of beaver skin that barely hid the golden *torc* which she, as sister to the King of Muman, was allowed to wear as his emissary. Eadulf was clad in the plainer woollen dyed robe of a religious, and his tonsure, cut in the Roman way, proclaimed he was not a member of the native churches of the country.

'I would imagine you are on the road to Cashel?'

'At the moment, we are looking for a place to refresh ourselves on our journey,' replied Fidelma.

'You speak of assaults and thefts.' Eadulf indicated the ruins of the inn. 'Is that what occurred to the tavern there? Were they attacked and robbed? What exactly happened?'

The shepherd said whimsically, 'As you see, stranger, the tavern has burned down.'

Eadulf's brows creased and he was about to respond in annoyance when Fidelma interrupted.

'We knew this was a good place to pause for food and shelter. So how did this tavern burn down when it has stood unharmed for a generation?'

The shepherd gave a sigh. 'Is there not a saying that good care takes the head off bad luck?'

'It is a saying,' Fidelma confirmed, 'but what do you mean by it?'

'The bad luck came one night and that was because there was no good care. A lantern was not extinguished in the kitchen and good care had not been made to place it in a spot where it would do no harm. So harm was made. By the time Béoán, the tavern-keeper, and Cáemell, his wife, awoke, the place was truly alight and they barely escaped with their lives. That is what I heard.'

'So they survived?'

'They did so.'

'There were no guests in the tavern?'

'None. So they had to abandon the place and went for shelter to Béoán's brother on the far side of Cnoc na gCloch.'

Eadulf frowned. 'So there is now no tavern along the mountain pass?'

The shepherd shrugged. 'There is no longer one near here so it depends in what direction you are travelling.'

'To Cashel, of course, as you rightly suggested,' Eadulf replied a little testily.

'Then I know of no place where you might find good hospitality except other than down on the plain at Ard Fhionáin by the River Suir.'

'That is still a fair journey from here,' complained Eadulf.

'The easiest way is to take the path to the east, once you come to the fork not far ahead. The track winds down the hill,' the shepherd advised.

'We know the path,' Fidelma nodded.

They acknowledged the man's help and continued their journey, but were aware of him standing, hands on hips, staring after them.

Once round the shoulder of one of the mountain slopes they came to a place where the track divided into two, one path leading steeply down the mountains to the north-east, which Eadulf already knew was the route to the abbey of Ard Fhionáin. The other path led to the north-west, a route which Eadulf had never explored.

For a few moments Fidelma was content to sit on her horse silently as if waiting for something.

'What's wrong?' Eadulf wanted to know.

'I am not sure. I could not help thinking there was something not quite right about that so-called shepherd.'

Eadulf nodded slightly. 'Yes. I could not help noticing that he was carrying more weapons than usual for an ordinary shepherd.'

'Let's ride on,' Fidelma decided. 'But we will take the track to the north-west.'

'I do not know that route. Is there something wrong with Ard Fhionáin?'

'Nothing wrong with it,' Fidelma said, 'except the route is one most travellers take, as you know. If there are thieves and robbers about, as the shepherd warned us, then that would be the path they are most likely to waylay travellers on. I therefore think we should avoid it.'

'Better the route you know . . . isn't that the old saying?'

'What I am pointing out,' Fidelma said patiently, 'is that it will not add considerably to our journey if we choose to go by the other route.'

'So, do you know where this other path leads? Is there a tavern along the way?'

Fidelma shrugged. 'I recall that there is a small farming settlement at the foot of the mountains – if we take this north-western path. It is many years since I travelled that way, but it descends by a beautiful lake and as we ride down we can look across the great plain towards Cashel. I am sure we can request hospitality in the settlement.'

'What makes you so sure?'

'At the last council of the Brehons I met a young man from the village which stands on the plain below. He had just been appointed magistrate of the village. I forget his name but I am sure he will be aware of his obligations to a visiting *dálaigh*. As I recall, although it was summer when I passed through it, it was a beautiful place . . . just like the mystical Garden of Fand.'

Eadulf could not help chuckling. 'I don't want a detour through the Otherworld to meet a goddess, however beautiful their gardens are. In this cold weather, all I want is shelter, food and a dry bed for the night.'

'I can guarantee you that,' Fidelma smiled.

In spite of their levity, Eadulf was thoughtful as they rode on, thinking about the burned tavern and the curious shepherd.

The way began to drop, almost imperceptibly at first, winding down the side of the hills until coming out in a broad, flat valley in which a deep lake was situated. The stretch of water seemed ominous and dark because of the low clouds that threatened rain. There was little growth hereabouts apart from a few hedges of blackthorns, some rising to the height of small trees with their tough, yellow wood and cruel thorns. Around some of the blackthorn were a few inedible fungi, black with stiff fingers as if to warn passers-by of their poisonous qualities.

The day had grown even colder as they rode down the mountain, due to the fact that they were now in the shadow of the hills – and the presence of the cold lake only added to the chill. Eadulf became aware that Fidelma, riding slightly ahead to lead the way, had halted as she reached the open slope of the hillside. He drew alongside her and saw that a broad vista had opened up. Had the clouds been higher and the sun shining, he realised that he could have seen right across the vast expanse of what must be the great Plain of Femen. Its fertile ground supplied the wealth and power in Colgú's kingdom and was the reason why the Eóghanacht kings had chosen Cashel as their principal fortress, to dominate the plains. He knew this was the site of many tales of the time beyond time, when Bodb Dearg, son of the mighty god The Dagda, made his home there.

Fidelma was pointing downwards. 'That is Cloichín. The track down is easier than it looks,' she promised, aware that Eadulf was not really a comfortable horseman although he had improved over the years. One needed caution to guide a horse down such a precipitous slope.

Eadulf followed the line of her extended arm. Beyond the groups of buildings, across the mighty plain, he could just make out groups of trees and dark lines of what seemed rivers and even stretches of what could have been walls. Far, far beyond were rising dark shadows, but even these were obscured by the swirling rainclouds that were driven across hidden parts of the land before them.

Fidelma saw him frowning as he stared across the distance.

'Sléibhte na gCoillte,' she said, answering his unasked question.

'The Mountains of the Forest?'

She nodded. 'The road to Cashel runs just on the east side.'

'So we are not that far from Cashel?'

'If the weather changes and conditions on the tracks worsen we could be two days crossing the plains to Cashel. Horses can't do more than walk in bad, muddy conditions and a horse's walking pace is little faster than that of a human. So, as your people have named it, Eadulf, this is indeed the month of mud.'

Eadulf sighed. 'From what I can see of it below, the plain is drab; even the greenery seems without colour.'

'It is so at this time of year, though if the sun were shining we would see stretches of carpet-like growth made from rich green lichens, as the weather helps the mosses to make mats upon the earth. When we get down there you will see the countryside change; meadow grass, groundsel, shepherds' purse are all in winter green but soon things will be changing. When the countryside here is in bloom it is like a great verdant garden, speckled with amazing points of colour.'

Fidelma's assessment of the time taken to reach the foot of the mountains soon proved right. It seemed an age of careful riding at less than a walking pace, for the downward path twisted and turned to such a degree that they often had to dismount and lead their beasts over the more difficult places. They finally reached more level ground, and Eadulf could see gorse, waiting to burst forth into a blaze of colour, and spider ferns, although with fronds that were almost like a species of bush. Other than that, the landscape was typical of the month.

As they came to the end of the mountain path, Eadulf was mildly surprised by the number of stone boundary walls he began to see and he remarked on it to Fidelma.

'It is a stony area,' she replied. 'The stones disappear as you get further away from the mountains and begin to cross the plain, but this is why the settlement we are going to is called Cloichín, the stony place. The farmers around it use the stones as boundaries to their territories.'

'Stone boundaries? Isn't that unusual in this part of the kingdom?'

'This is a rich part so far as farms are concerned. The law texts on fencing and boundaries, the *Cóir Anmann*, is very specific on the four types of boundary fencing allowed, and for rich farms stone walls are usual.'

'Then let us hope it augurs well for the richness of the hospitality with which we shall be received,' Eadulf said in a more cheerful frame of mind. Then suddenly, he drew rein and put his head to one side with a frown. 'That sounds like a waterfall,' he said, peering towards a group of trees that hid the landscape ahead.

'That's the River Duthóg which we must ford. It runs south of the settlement.'

Eadulf grimaced. 'I do not like the sound of the water. Doesn't Duthóg mean "the difficult river"?'

Fidelma chuckled. 'Your knowledge surprises me at times, Eadulf. But do not worry. The river runs shallowly over a stony bed and, at this time of year, is therefore quick-flowing and noisy, but not deep. The main village lies just beyond and is actually sited between two rivers, this one, the Duthóg, and to the north, the Teara, which is deeper and full of salmon and brown trout. The two rivers eventually join and run east into the River Suir at Ard Fhionáin.'

They came past the small wood to the bank of the river and Eadulf saw that Fidelma's description of it was accurate. The waters barely came up to their horses' fetlocks as they splashed through. There was an incline on the far side, a hillock with a great oak tree rising on its brow. Fidelma picked her way up the mound first, only to halt suddenly and shout: '*Stop! Stop and release that rope or suffer the anger of your King and the punishment of the law!*'

Startled, Eadulf quickly recovered himself and hastened up to reach her side. He became aware that he was overlooking the buildings of the village, with a crowd of people gathered immediately below them. The crowd stood staring silently up at them, having been silenced by Fidelma's stentorian command. Eadulf registered a man in religieux robes standing at the front of them while, at the base of a tree, he saw some other men, frozen in the act of hauling something up on a jutting branch by a stout rope. The rope was fastened round the neck of a struggling man whose feet swung over the ground. He was choking to death.

CHAPTER TWO

There was a shocked silence for a moment or two and then the religieux, Brother Gadra, was the first to recover. His already red and angry face contorted in fury.

'How dare you interrupt, woman, and give orders in matters that are of no concern to you!' he snarled. Then, turning to the men still loosely holding the rope: 'Proceed as you were told.'

The men did not move.

'Proceed with God's work, I tell you!' Brother Gadra's voice cracked with its vehemence.

The young magistrate, Fethmac, whose arms were still held tightly between the two men on either side, struggled vainly once more in their grasp.

'Lay down that rope! That is the sister of the King.' His voice was shrill. 'That is Sister Fidelma of Cashel!'

One of the men who had been holding the rope let go at once, his eyes wide with alarm as he recognised her name and authority. A nervous muttering began among the crowd. Reluctantly, some of the others released their hold and the half-senseless body of their victim slumped to the ground when the last man was unable to sustain the weight.

'Loosen the rope from his neck and let him breathe,' Fidelma ordered curtly.

'Wait!' cried Brother Gadra. 'You have no authority even though you might be related to the King. Someone here called you Sister Fidelma. Then why do you not wear the robes of a Sister? Have you abandoned your religion? You have no claim to dictate what should be done here. I am your superior in the Faith.'

Fidelma's gaze was like ice as she regarded the excitable man.

'I have left the religious, not the religion,' she responded angrily.

'The same thing,' jeered the Brother. 'You have abandoned the Faith and, because of that, you are the one to be condemned.'

'Brother Gadra,' called Fethmac, 'I am surprised that you have not heard of the Lady Fidelma's authority as a *dálaigh* and of her reputation as legal adviser to Colgú King of Muman. I can only put your ignorance down to the fact that you are newly come to this kingdom and have spent so many years in the Kingdom of Frankia.'

Brother Gadra turned towards the magistrate and for the first time seemed disconcerted. In that moment, Fidelma realised she had control over the crowd.

'Eadulf, see what you can do for that poor man.' She indicated the half-choked prisoner on the ground, who still had the rope tightly around his neck. As Eadulf swung off his horse, Fidelma turned and glared at the crowd. A few stared sullenly back at her while the others guiltily hung their heads, not wishing to meet her gaze.

'See the colour of his skin?' yelled Brother Gadra suddenly. 'He is an animal. He is not one of us. He has no rights among us.'

'All people have rights, wherever they come from,' Fidelma returned angrily. 'If you are a Brother of the New Faith, you should know that.' She addressed the crowd. 'Release your magistrate immediately and go back to your homes while I find out the meaning of this outrage.'

The two men restraining Fethmac immediately released their hold on him as if his touch were somehow unbearable. In twos and threes the crowd began to disperse, all except the young magistrate and the glowering religieux. While Brother Gadra stood his ground, the young man hurried across to Fidelma as she dismounted and introduced himself.

'Lady, I am Fethmac. We met some while ago at a law council. Thank God that you are here.'

Fidelma looked at him and then nodded. 'I recognised you from that council. We were discussing the laws on boundaries at Ard Fhionáin. Tell me why you had no control over the people of your village. Are you not sufficiently qualified? Is that why they do not respect your authority?'

The young man's expression was unhappy.

'Lady, I am qualified and I have completed four years of study on law – but there has been a crime here which has incensed the people to a passion beyond their reason. I could not control their anger.' He paused and indicated the stocky religieux, adding bitterly, 'Brother Gadra, who is newly come among us, condoned their abandonment of the law and thereby encouraged their disobedience of me.'

Fidelma's eyes flashed angrily as she advanced on the religieux, but Eadulf had risen from the side of the victim, who was still lying on the ground finding difficulty in breathing, and he now called for her attention.

'It is best if we get this fellow out of the cold and into somewhere warm. Is his home nearby?'

Fethmac shook his head. 'He has no home here. He is a *ráithech* – a vagrant.'

'Do you have a hostel here?' asked Fidelma.

'There is only the barn next to my house,' the young magistrate replied. 'We can take him there. At least it is dry and warm.'

'Very well.' She glanced at Brother Gadra. 'You will come as well, for I shall want to know the details of all that has happened here and the reasons why a person who claims to preach the Faith is condoning attempted murder.'

Brother Gadra stared defiantly at her.

'I have the authority of the Faith behind me, woman.' His voice was cold and not contrite. 'You will not lecture me on your law. Further, I demand that I should be addressed as Father Gadra, as is my correct title.'

Fidelma smiled thinly, a dangerous sign as Eadulf knew.

'"My law"? I have the authority of the law of the Five Kingdoms behind me, *Brother* Gadra, for that I believe is your name. I hold the degree of *Anruth* and stand next to the Chief Brehon of this kingdom.'

'I care not for your laws but only the laws of God.'

'We shall postpone esoteric debates until a more convenient time. As for your mode of address, we of the New Faith in these kingdoms prefer to be guided by what Holy Scripture says in the matter.' Brother Gadra frowned and so she went on: '*Et patrem nolite vocare vobis super terram unus enim est Pater vester qui in caelis est.* Those are the instructions of Christ according to the text of Matthew. "Call no one on Earth your Father, you have only one Father in heaven".'

Brother Gadra began to splutter. 'How dare you—'

'We are all Brothers and Sisters of the Faith,' Eadulf interrupted sharply. 'Though,' he hastened on, 'some of us, out of respect, will call the head of our religious communities "Abbot", which comes from the Aramaic word *abba*, for Father. However, I am aware that there is a growing custom among the followers of Blessed Benedict of Nursia and his Rules to use the title. But I don't think you are an abbot.'

Brother Gadra was now beyond words.

'Meanwhile, as everyone seems to have disappeared,' Fidelma added impatiently, 'Eadulf will require assistance to carry this poor man to the house or barn of the magistrate.'

'Then it is your task to find someone – *lawyer*.' Brother Gadra folded his arms in a posture of insolence.

For a moment Fidelma was amazed at his attitude. Before she could react, however, Fethmac moved towards Eadulf, saying, 'I will help you and show the way. It is just across there.' He indicated the direction with a nod of his head.

Fidelma decided to say nothing more to the religieux but took the reins of Eadulf's horse with those of her own while Fethmac and Eadulf carried the semi-conscious victim of the near-hanging between them, Brother Gadra following reluctantly behind. Fethmac guided them towards a group of nearby buildings that were part of the settlement. Beside a substantial stone dwelling was a wooden barn whose door was slightly ajar. Fethmac was able to push it further open with his foot so that they could move inside. He and Eadulf laid their burden down on some hay bales while Fidelma secured their horses to one side of the barn.

It was as she was doing so that Fidelma heard a female voice calling for help. Fethmac began moving hurriedly to the house.

'My wife, Ballgel,' he threw over his shoulder. 'They locked her in when they took me prisoner.'

'Prisoner?' Fidelma turned her gaze with a frown towards Brother Gadra.

The religieux sneered. 'The young man had to be restrained for he was interfering with the work of the Lord.'

'You will doubtless teach me the difference between someone being restrained and being made prisoner,' she said dryly. 'Who imprisoned his wife?'

Brother Gadra shrugged indifferently and failed to reply.

Fidelma moved to Eadulf's side; he was still bending over the injured man. 'How is he?'

'There's little to be done except treat the rope burns on his neck and the constrictions in his throat. Honey and hot water should help. Maybe if some marsh-mint was available, what is it called – *cartlann*? What is the man's name?' He looked across to Brother Gadra.

Again the religieux just shrugged.

Fidelma thought she had been surprised enough that day but now she gasped. 'Are you saying you were about to hang a man and didn't even know his name?'

'We were not hanging a name but a murderer,' replied the Brother. 'The devil would not need to know his name to welcome him into the fires of hell!'

Fidelma swallowed, trying to keep her feelings under control.

Fethmac reappeared at that point, followed by a young, attractive girl, who was looking somewhat shaken, but otherwise composed.

'I am all right, lady,' she said, in answer to Fidelma's immediate question. 'The men locked me in a cupboard when I tried to help my husband here. The crowd became crazy after Fethmac tried to prevent them from dragging the stranger, the *doir-fuidir*, to be hanged.'

Fidelma noted the girl used the legal term for a person without rights. However, an itinerant could hire themselves out to work and normally had no limitations on travelling within the territory. Usually, *doir-fuidir* consisted of those who had lost their rights because of fines and moneys owed for compensations which they could not satisfy. They could redeem themselves by the payment of these debts, and were capable of acquiring their own plots of land by agreement with local nobles and by this means returning to their former status with full rights. It was no surprise, Fidelma thought, that Ballgel used legal terms when her husband was the local magistrate.

The girl pointed at Brother Gadra and declared: 'It was he who was responsible for urging the people to disobey the law and lock me in the cupboard.'

'The law! The law!' Brother Gadra growled. 'You cite your pagan law when you should be obeying the laws given you by the New Faith. You smile at the murderers, you forgive them, help them and turn a blind eye to the evil among you. There *is* no law here. I bring you the truth of the New Faith and you will obey the law of God or perish.'

Fidelma ignored him but addressed the magistrate. 'Do you have anyone in the village that you can trust?' she asked.

'Trust?'

'I will want someone to guard this prisoner.' She indicated the semi-conscious man. 'After he has been treated for any injury I shall conduct a court to examine what has gone on here and,' she looked at the religieux, 'it will be carried out under the laws of the Five Kingdoms and not at the ravings of some idea of vengeance.'

Fethmac nodded eagerly. 'Our blacksmith Gobánguss is held in particular esteem in the village. He has a place where the man can be kept.'

'Was the blacksmith part of the crowd?' Fidelma asked. 'I want no one who was involved with this man's attempted murder to act as his guard.'

'He was working on one of the farms by the River Duthóg,' replied Fethmac. 'I shall go and fetch him – it will take me but a short while.'

'Then do so.' When the magistrate had gone, Fidelma asked Ballgel, 'Can you prepare a cup of honey and some mint soaked in hot water? It's for this man. Eadulf and I will also need something to eat and drink and a place to sleep as the day is getting late. I have been told there is no tavern in this village so we must rely on your recommendation.'

'I can offer you the hospitality of our house,' the girl replied immediately. 'It is poor enough but better than nothing.'

'Your hospitality will be much appreciated,' Fidelma acknowledged solemnly. 'And the honey?'

'I shall do that immediately for I have some knowledge of the healing arts because we have no physician in this village.'

After Ballgel hurried away, Fidelma was able to turn her attention to the truculent Brother Gadra.

'From what was said, I gather you have not been long in this kingdom. From your speech, I think I hear the accents of the north.'

Brother Gadra was coming to realise that he could not intimidate this woman as he had the villagers. However, he sniffed to express his disapproval of her. 'It is true that I was originally from Rath Bhoth in the land of the Cenél nEnda.'

'That is Northern Uí Néill territory. It is in the Kingdom of Ulaidh?'

'Your knowledge is good.'

'Yet your knowledge is bad,' she replied waspishly. 'How is it that you think that you can challenge me and the laws of this kingdom?' She lowered her tone to one of disarming mildness. 'Doesn't the law of the Brehons run in all Five Kingdoms?'

Brother Gadra replied impatiently, 'We have embraced the New Faith and now we must embrace the laws of that Faith.'

'You mean the Penitentials?'

'And that which is made clear in the Holy Book of scriptures. This man killed and so he must suffer the punishment. *Qui percusserit et occiderit hominem morte moriatur!*'

'Ah, yes. Leviticus. "He that kills any man shall surely be put to death",' she said sadly. 'The law of retribution.'

Brother Gadra looked surprised at her knowledge. 'It is as God ordained and so He expects His word to be carried out,' he repeated reverently.

'It is not the law of the Five Kingdoms,' Fidelma returned without raising her tone. 'Even in Rome, I would expect such an accused to be allowed to be heard in a trial. And as a man from Rath Bhoth, I would expect you to know the law. What has brought you from Ulaidh to our southerly kingdom?'

'I have come on God's work, to teach the law of the Faith.'

'I ask again, has Ulaidh renounced the laws of the Brehons then?'

'I have been in Frankia these many years,' admitted Brother Gadra stiffly. 'I did not come here straightway. I first went to join

23

the community of Freullen at Fosse in the kingdom of Frankia where they are governed by the Rule of the Blessed Benedict; a place where the laws of God are followed.'

'Freullen?' Eadulf looked up from where he was applying some ointment to the neck of the injured man. 'Ah, Faolán. He became known there by the name Freullen, for the Franks could not pronounce his name properly.'

'That is so,' Brother Gadra conceded stiffly.

'I was taught by Faolán's brother, Fursa, who came to the Kingdom of the East Angles,' Eadulf explained.

Brother Gadra was unimpressed.

'So you are an Angle. I saw that you still wear the tonsure of Rome but doubtless have forgotten her rules. Anyway, Faolán was long dead when I went to Frankia. He was killed by bandits, then his younger brother Ultan became abbot of the community. I have been sent here to the abbey of Lios Mhór to advise on the Rule of Benedict which at the Council of Autun was endorsed by the Holy Father's decree that it should be adopted by all the religious of the True Faith. It was heard that the enlightenment of Benedict had not yet infiltrated the churches in this land.'

Eadulf actually grinned. 'We were at the Council of Autun, my friend, and you can be assured that the Rule and Penitentials are known here and much discussed . . .'

'And widely rejected by most of our religious,' added Fidelma sharply. 'So why were you sent here to this village and not Lios Mhór? Cloichín boasts no abbey and not even a church. What is here that you should come to preach these Roman ideas?'

Brother Gadra said through gritted teeth, 'I was not sent here, to this rural backwoods. I was sent to Lios Mhór where, in their ignorance, they chased me from the place, preferring to remain in idolatry. I merely passed through this village, having determined to pursue my endeavours at some other abbey. However, I discovered that these people stood in need of someone to lead them from their darkness. I have remained during the winter months but when spring comes, I shall seek out an abbey where the word of Rome will be accepted.'

Fidelma gazed thoughtfully at him for a moment before informing him: 'When I investigate this matter and hold a legal court, Gadra of Rath Bhoth, I shall need your presence. You are in the Kingdom of Muman now and you are under jurisdiction of the laws of the Five Kingdoms. In this kingdom, our Chief Bishop is Cuán, Abbot of Imleach. You may well discuss your mission later with him but, I advise you, he respects the law, sitting with our Chief Brehon, our judge, with my brother, Colgú, who is King. I wish to make that clear.'

Brother Gadra shifted his weight a little. 'I hear you, Fidelma of Cashel,' he said. There was a 'but' in his sentence which she decided to ignore.

'I presume you have accommodation here?' she said instead. 'Return to it and I will send for you when I am ready to start my formal inquiry.'

Once more there was a hesitation but then the stocky man turned and swept out of the barn.

Eadulf glanced up at Fidelma and joked, 'Well, I reckon that man would argue even with Paul of Tarsus.'

'What?' Fidelma asked irritably.

'His letter to the Corinthians, remember? "Faith, hope and charity . . . and the greatest of these is charity." Gadra is not possessed of much charity, is he?'

Fidelma did not bother to respond but indicated the victim of the near-lynching, saying, 'How is he?' The man had pushed himself into a semi-seated position and seemed aware of his surroundings. Eadulf had been helping him to sip the cup of honey and hot water which Ballgel had brought while Fidelma had been talking to the religieux.

'He'll be better, by and by,' Eadulf announced in satisfaction.

Fidelma turned her attention fully to the patient, who tried to smile at her. She had only once in her brother's kingdom encountered men whose skin colouring was the same as this man's. She remembered they were from some far-off kingdom called Aksum – a land, they had told her, which was beyond Egypt. They had spoken fluent Greek and so she asked the man if he understood that language. The man looked up at her uncomprehendingly and shook his head.

'I think he understands the language of the Five Kingdoms,' ventured Eadulf.

The man eased himself up further and glanced first at Eadulf and then Fidelma mouthing 'thank you' in turn.

'I think the constriction of his throat has caused a temporary loss of the ability to speak,' Eadulf advised.

Fidelma bent close to the man as he nodded agreement, pointing to his throat.

'Do you understand that I am a *dálaigh* and that it is said that you have murdered someone? No, do not try to say anything,' she admonished as the man struggled to speak. 'I take it that you can follow what is going on here? There will be time to defend yourself for I shall hear the charge and the witnesses and then you will be able to answer. But you shall remain a prisoner until the time I have been able to investigate that matter.'

Once more the man acknowledged her words with a nod.

'Can you at least manage to tell us what your name is?'

The man pointed with one finger to his throat again and shook his head.

'Then can you write it?'

The man shook his head again. It was clear from the motion of his hand that he was without writing skills.

'Never mind. I am going to hand you to the care of the local blacksmith who will have charge of your safety on surety of an oath he shall take. This is not to stop you from running away, for you must know there is nowhere you can run to. It is to stop the villagers doing further harm to you.'

The man nodded rapidly but seemed agitated and was clearly trying to ask a question. His hand made an imploring gesture. Without communication she did not know what to do. Fidelma stared at him for a moment. His age was hard to discern. A thin man, his Adam's apple protruded prominently and moved up and down as he tried to swallow. His neck was scrawny and the burn-mark of the rope showed red against the flesh, in spite of the dark and mud-splattered skin. With his dirty hair in tight curls, his eyes dark and staring from their whites, the man seemed almost like a cornered animal. Fidelma wondered when he had last eaten properly, for he seemed very emaciated.

Eadulf interrupted her thoughts. 'I wonder who he is and where he comes from? I have seen people of his colouring while I was in Rome, and one or two in sea ports working on trading ships.'

'We will know once he is recovered and we can get him to speak,' she replied quietly. 'It is frustrating that I cannot understand why he is so agitated. I hope the young magistrate returns soon. We must find out why the people here suddenly lost all their sense of respect for law. Perhaps it was all due to that belligerent religieux.'

Eadulf sighed deeply. 'Do you know, this is the first time in our travels that I miss being accompanied by one of your brother's warriors of the Golden Collar.'

The élite bodyguard of the Kings of Muman were known as the *Nasc Niadh*, on account of the ancient golden *torc* that they wore around their necks. In view of the fact that Fidelma was sister to the King and Eadulf was her husband, they were often accompanied by at least one of the warriors in their journeys. Fidelma had scoffed at the idea that the comparatively short journey to Lios Mhór warranted a bodyguard.

She was framing a response when Fethmac suddenly returned in the company of a very tall man with wild ginger hair and beard, whose very girth and muscles proclaimed his profession even before Fidelma noticed the leather apron that left one in no doubt that here was a smith.

'Gobánguss,' she greeted him, after he had been introduced. 'Gobánguss, I have a request to ask of you as I am told there is no one else fitted in this village . . .'

'I have already been told by the magistrate, lady. You require me to keep this man under lock and key until you are ready to adjudicate on his crime.'

'I presume you have heard what crime he is charged with?' she asked, judging from his stern tone.

'It is all over the village, lady.'

'Then you will be on your oath to take and protect this man with your life until I have been able to sit in consideration of the accusation against him, for I have not heard the charges nor anything proved against him. Therefore I trust you will remain unbiased until the hearing.'

The tall man drew himself up, facing her with dignity.

'I am Gobánguss, blacksmith of this village. My word is my bond, lady,' he told her. 'I shall have a care of this man no matter how heinous his crime.'

'You say that without knowing the crime?' queried Eadulf, catching the nuance in the man's voice.

'I say it *knowing* of the man's crime,' the smith replied. 'How can I not know it when everyone has come rushing to tell me of it? I had left the village early this morning to shoe some horses at Taithlech's warehouse along the river and did not involve myself until Fethmac came to fetch me.'

'And what were you told?' Fidelma pressed.

'That this *ráithech* has been accused of the vile and senseless slaughter of Taithlech's cousin, Adnán, and his entire family.'

For a moment there was quiet. Then Fidelma said softly, 'I will hear the charges in a proper manner. Meanwhile, you have said you will swear an oath to safeguard this man. You have a place where he may be confined until I am ready to hear the formal charge?'

'I have. There is a stone shed at the back of my smithy which can be barred from the outside. Do you want me to bring his wife and child to my house too? I can put their wagon at the back of my smithy.'

At this, the prisoner uttered some noises and nodded his head up and down.

'A wife and child? Maybe that was what he was trying to tell us,' Eadulf said. The man threw a quick smile at him and nodded vigorously once more.

Fidelma frowned uncertainly. 'Fethmac, you did not mention that the vagrant has a wife and child?'

The magistrate looked apologetic. 'I meant to, lady. When the man was apprehended he was in a wagon with a woman and baby. I was told that she was his wife and that the child belonged to them.'

'And where are they now? I did not see them outside.'

'Lúbaigh and his brother had just brought them in the wagon from the farm where the killings took place and is keeping a watch on them. The wagon is outside and attended to.'

'Lúbaigh? This is complicated and I am tired and hungry,' Fidelma said after a moment. 'We will hear explanations in good time. However, we must do something about the woman and child.' She turned to Gobánguss. 'Are you sure you have room to house the man's wife and baby?'

'I have, lady,' agreed the smith. 'My wife Breccnat can look after them. And as I said, the wagon can be taken there too. It can be put in one of my barns.'

'Thank you. It is better if the woman and child are held separately from this man,' Fidelma added, 'until I have heard all the facts.'

'It will be done, lady,' the smith replied.

'You are aware that oaths are held as sacred? You are aware of the consequence of taking an oath and afterwards denying it?'

'I would never take such an oath if I was likely to break it,' Gobánguss asserted with solemn sincerity. 'Do I not hold a privileged rank in this community? I am a smith. I shall swear this oath by God – and by the battle of my soul.'

Fidelma was impressed that the man understood the new oath, adapted to the needs of the New Faith. She knew that the text on oaths, the *Cáin Domnaig*, had only recently been drafted to make ancient oaths acceptable to the New Faith by inserting the line *forgellat huili o cath anmae* – testifying by the battle of the soul. This was an acknowledgement that the soul must remain without blemish in order to pass to the Otherworld. Even Eadulf was awed by the big man's sense of gravity and knew that smiths were held in high esteem in the Five Kingdoms.

'That is good,' acknowledged Fidelma, 'for I want no more confusion as Brother Gadra seems to have spread enough confusion here. There is only one law in this kingdom and that is the Law of the Brehons.'

Gobánguss looked uncomfortable for a moment but bowed his head in agreement. 'As it was in the time before time, so it is now,' he intoned softly. 'I will take the oath and if this man is fit enough to walk a few paces across to my forge, I will see to it that he is given refreshment and made secure. I have three men who work with me in the smithy if there is any thought of misbehaving.'

The last few words were aimed at the prisoner. The man's injuries had only been confined to his neck and throat, and the short incapacity after that was due to shock and the beating he had received. Apart from the bruising and lacerations, nothing was broken, however, and he was able to rise and, with the help of the smith, was able to walk.

'Where did you say your forge is, Gobánguss?' Fidelma asked.

'My forge and buildings are but a short walk. You can't miss them, for outside is the cauldron plinth that rises above the village.'

'Cauldron plinth?' frowned Fidelma.

'I will explain later,' Fethmac intervened hurriedly. 'Right now I must give orders to Lúbaigh that the man's wagon is to be taken to Gobánguss' forge with the woman and child.'

'Who is Lúbaigh?'

'He is the farmworker who found the bodies and identified the vagrant as the culprit.'

Fidelma stifled a sigh. Night had fallen with the rapidity of the time of year, but she and Eadulf could not rest and eat yet; she would need to speak to this man.

'Very well. Let me see this Lúbaigh before I do anything else.'

She dismissed Gobánguss, who left with his prisoner leaning on his arm. Fethmac soon returned with a man of middle age, and sturdily built. He was weather tanned but showed fair skin where the sun had been excluded by clothing. His eyes were pale blue but held a cold quality that made his smile seem false. There was something about his expression that made Fidelma dislike and distrust the man almost immediately. She tried to put her feelings aside. He was dressed in the manner of a farmworker, she saw; his clothing was made for rough work but their quality showed them to be of good standard.

'This is Lúbaigh, lady,' Fethmac said.

'You have been informed of my authority?' Fidelma asked mildly.

The man indicated that he had. He did not seem nervous in her presence.

'The magistrate has told me that you are the person who identified the vagrant as the killer of the family at the farm where you work. I want to learn what you know – but only briefly, as I shall go to this farm tomorrow and will need to hear the full details then.'

The man frowned. 'Briefly?' he queried, a note of sarcasm in his tone.

'Enough to justify why the man can be held until the case is heard.'

'But he killed Adnán, the farmer I work for. He killed him, as well as his wife and two sons.'

'I am told you are the witness to this. You saw the killings. So let us start with what you saw.'

Lúbaigh looked suddenly uncomfortable. 'I did not actually see the killings but the fact that the vagrant is guilty was obvious to me.'

'Why obvious? You must explain.'

The man indicated Fethmac. 'He knows all there is to know. He is the magistrate.'

'I am asking you,' Fidelma snapped.

At the terseness of her tone, Lúbaigh shrugged. 'Last night the vagrant arrived with his wagon, his wife and child. He claimed he was looking for work and if not work, some food. I was nearby when he spoke to Adnán. There was no work for him and Adnán told him neither was there food to spare in charity's name for the likes of him. But because night was approaching, Adnán said he would allow him to place his wagon by a nearby wood and stream but that he would have to be on his way as soon as it was light.'

'What was the man's attitude at this? I presume Adnán used the phrase "for the likes of him" to mean because the man was obviously a stranger?'

'I would not know about that. I do know there was some argument when the fellow was refused work and food. His attitude was belligerent.'

'Were threats uttered by the stranger?'

'Some harsh words were exchanged but I was out of earshot at the time.'

'The man then left?'

'I believe he drove the wagon to the site indicated. The next morning I found the bodies and saw that the wagon had departed. It was obvious the man came back at night and sought vengeance on Adnán and his family for turning them away.'

Fidelma was frowning. 'We will leave the rest of the details for tomorrow. I will meet you at Adnán's farmstead in the morning with the magistrate. That is all.'

For a few moments she stared after the departing farmworker.

'It is a very slender link,' she said reflectively.

'But the only one,' said Fethmac.

'Hearsay evidence nevertheless. It is not usually admitted in law.'

'Well, Lúbaigh saw him and Adnán arguing,' the magistrate pointed out.

'True, but he did not hear the words. Anyway, I believe we are justified in holding the stranger until a proper hearing.'

Fidelma suddenly realised that they were neglecting their horses and she and Eadulf set about taking off their harnesses and arranging water and feed. Fethmac helped them. Ballgel his wife appeared shortly afterwards and announced that a meal was ready. It was not long before they were able to enter the warm room inside the magistrate's home. He was already pouring drinks of elder wine, mixed with honey and spices. A table had been laid and Ballgel fussed about arranging the dishes.

'We were not expecting guests, so forgive the poorness of our table,' she apologised.

Eadulf was about to say that he had seen poorer, but realised just in time that it was an inappropriate thing to say. This was merely a traditional opening before serving guests. As it turned out, there was fresh-baked oaten bread, a dish of butter, hard-boiled goose eggs and flavoursome bowls of mutton stew, steaming with the aroma of wild garlic and other herbs. In the centre was a bowl of a pottage of herbs whose base was a kind of cabbage called *braisech*, to which was added *folt-chep* of leek. Eadulf noticed side dishes for a sweet course of apples with hazel nuts and honey.

'It is too much,' murmured Fidelma with the proper ritual response. 'You do us much honour with your hospitality.'

Ballgel smiled in appreciation as she waved them to their seats.

'Our only sadness,' began Fethmac, as they started eating, 'is that you have arrived in this usually tranquil village at a time of turmoil.'

Fidelma inclined her head. 'It seems that this Brother Gadra was not helping to calm the anxieties of the people here after the murders,' she replied. 'While he holds strong views I am surprised that he was able to exert such influence over local people to the point that they actually restrained you. Restraining a magistrate and preventing him from performing his duty under law is against all that is respected in our society.'

Fethmac glanced nervously at his wife before responding, 'It is true that his views are not those usually accepted by the people, but he has managed to gain followers here, especially among certain of the women of the village. He holds services in a barn here once a week.'

'You say the local people do not usually share his views,' Fidelma repeated. 'Is that because you generally had no infringement of the law here before this incident?'

There was a pause and then it was Ballgel who replied. 'It is because the victims were our friends and influential among us. This is why the villagers turned on the vagrant as one would a wild animal.'

Fidelma left aside the pedantic point that, under law, the man had to first be proved guilty of the charge. Instead she asked, 'So the victims, Adnán and his wife and sons, were well respected here?'

'They were one of the best-loved and most prominent families of Cloichín,' Ballgel nodded. 'Husband and wife and their two children, all hacked to pieces in the vilest fashion.' She shuddered.

Fidelma glanced quickly at Eadulf. 'I must restrain myself from assuming my role as a *dálaigh* until tomorrow morning, when the day is light enough for me to commence. Just tell me this: I understand the family were killed on their farm. When did this happen?'

'We presume during the night. The bodies were found this morning, as you have been told, by Lúbaigh.'

'Where are the bodies now?'

Fethmac looked nervous. 'Things happened so fast, lady. What with the tracking down of the vagrants and Brother Gadra demanding immediate retribution . . .'

'What are you trying to say?' Fidelma asked coldly.

'I'm trying to say that the bodies remained where they were found for a while. The itinerant was discovered almost immediately and then . . . then Brother Gadra became involved.'

Fidelma looked out at the darkening sky.

'Do you mean that the bodies have been left in the open – prey to wolves, foxes and other scavengers? Do you intend to leave them there all night?'

The young magistrate flushed. 'No, lady. Before the vagrant was discovered, I had ordered Lúbaigh to take the bodies into the barn and secure the doors. I marked in my mind where they had fallen. Adnán, the farmer, was killed before his barn door, one boy in the pigsty and the other nearby. Adnán's wife was in her kitchen where she had been preparing breakfast.' The young man closed his eyes for a moment, reliving the horror, before continuing. 'I had them all placed in the barn, because it is a strong, well-made building. Adnán, as a good farmer, was particular about the security of his barn. Scavengers will not bother their corpses in there.'

Fidelma nodded half-heartedly. She knew that much could be learned by observing the victims in the original situation where they fell. On the other hand it was already dark and pointless going to the farmstead now. It would have to wait until daylight, and at least the bodies had been protected from scavenging animals. Perhaps, too, this young magistrate had more sense than she had allowed him. Perhaps, too, it was not his fault he had lost his authority over his people.

'So no one actually saw the killing?' she said after some thought.

'No one. But it was easy to put two and two together to add up what must have happened.'

'It is still a presumption, and presumptions are prone to error,' Eadulf said.

'It was a reasonable conclusion, but it was not reasonable to dismiss the legal process,' the magistrate replied irritably.

'You mean to follow Brother Gadra's philosophy of an eye for an eye?' queried Eadulf.

'Certainly not. I am a magistrate of the laws of the Brehons, not a Brother of the New Faith and its rules. It was when I tried to stop people obeying Gadra that they turned on me.'

Eadulf had another question. 'What do you know about this Brother Gadra, for he interests me. He is a strange man to encounter in a place like . . .' He halted as he realised his words might sound like an insult.

Fethmac actually grinned. 'Like this isolated village? I am sure you also share this thought, lady,' he said, turning to Fidelma.

'He did tell us that he was an emissary sent to Lios Mhór but was expelled from the abbey there,' pointed out Fidelma.

'Well, why come here?' Fethmac asked rhetorically. 'We do not even have a church here. When we have need of religious comfort we ask one of the brethren from Ard Fhionáin to visit, but we each have our *anam chara*, our soul friend, to talk to about our problems, both personal and religious. We follow the ways of the Faith as it was here before the new ideas that I am told are being brought in from Rome, especially by such as Brother Gadra.'

'So for you, this Gadra was not exactly welcome?'

'You have heard his accent. He is originally a man of Ulaidh who has spent too much time in Frankia. Why did he decide to stay here? Even in the cruellest of winters it is scarcely a day's journey to Ard Fhionáin or some other abbey where he might have sought a role. Why did he not go there?' The young man sighed. 'I would welcome his departure.'

'Who offered him hospitality?' Eadulf asked thoughtfully. 'I presume that a religieux of his persuasion and ego would expect hospitality as of right?'

Ballgel seemed puzzled by Eadulf's critical manner. 'You yourself wear the tonsure of Rome, Brother Eadulf, and are a foreigner like Gadra. Yet you sound disapproving of him.'

Eadulf coloured a little and Fethmac cast a warning glance at his wife, saying, 'It is well known that Brother Eadulf is an Angle from a place I cannot pronounce, and has been the husband of the lady Fidelma for many years. It is his right to approve or disapprove of such matters.'

'His point is a good one,' Fidelma smiled. 'Brother Gadra must be enjoying someone's hospitality here.'

'There's no secret in that. He was offered hospitality with Dulbaire, who has a cabin on the edge of the village.'

'Does Dulbaire hold rank here?'

'Dulbaire?' Fethmac chuckled softly. 'He is Lúbaigh's young brother. He is just a farmworker; a bit retarded. He works as the *bóchaid,* the cowherd, on Adnán's farm. Even his name, which is not his birth-given name, demonstrates his character.'

Eadulf looked blank and Fidelma gave him a quick explanation. 'It means slowness of speech and, as a name, could imply slowness of mind.'

'You have it right, lady,' agreed Fethmac. 'He is a poor half-witted lad. But you should hear him play the *fedán* – why, it is amazing, the sound he can make from a simple hollow reed.'

'So he works on the farm as a cowherd but has his own cabin?' Fidelma repeated. 'And he is able to offer Brother Gadra hospitality?'

Fethmac nodded. 'To be accurate, the cabin belongs to Lúbaigh, his older brother, as it was their father's before them. Dulbaire works with his brother but Lúbaigh's wife refuses to let the boy live with them and her family. So Lúbaigh lets him have the cabin, now shared with Gabra. It is situated not far away on the borders of the farm. So technically it was Lúbaigh who gave hospitality to Brother Gadra, though I suspect at the insistence of his wife Fuinche, who has become a convert of the man.'

Fidelma suddenly sighed and bent to finishing the meal. 'I did not realise that I was so hungry. It seems an age since we broke our fast at Lios Mhór this morning and journeyed over Declan's Pass through the mountains.'

'I thought there was a tavern in the pass where travellers stopped,' Fethmac said, disconcerted by the sudden change of conversation.

'That is true,' agreed Eadulf, 'but it has been burned down. We were told by some shepherd that there had been an accidental fire and now the tavern is closed. So we had to journey on here. It was fortuitous that we arrived when we did, and . . .'

'. . . and are able to partake of your generous hospitality,' interrupted Fidelma. 'We are most grateful and will be more grateful when you show us a cosy bed to sleep in. I fear that tomorrow will be a long and busy day.'

ChAPTER ThREE

The morning was bright but cold. The clouds had vanished overnight and the sky was a mild, translucent blue with the sun hanging like a white orb in the eastern sky. Eadulf was looking out of the window with a smile of satisfaction that there was no wind.

'It looks like a fine day,' he remarked, as Ballgel placed oaten bread, honey and fruits on the table for the first meal of the day. He turned to her and added, 'Let's hope the weather holds and the day gets warmer.'

To his astonishment the girl regarded him with disapproval.

'That is not a good wish for rural folk such as us,' she replied. 'Here we have a saying – "better a world in the cold than fine weather in the month of Faoide".'

Eadulf was surprised and glanced at Fidelma, who had already seated herself at the table.

'Mild weather this month can encourage the growth of crops before the right time, and crops and plants in premature growth can be damaged by frosts that usually begin later,' she explained. 'Rainstorms can cause even more damage. You were obviously never a farmer, Eadulf.'

'Nor did I ever wish to be one,' admitted Eadulf, taking his seat.

Fidelma looked up at Ballgel as she helped herself to fruit. 'Where is your husband?'

'He won't be long. He went across to Gobánguss' forge to check that all was well with the prisoner. He is very conscientious about his position as *bó-aire*, lady. Nothing like yesterday has ever happened before to him and he has been deeply shocked. Until yesterday, the people here have respected him, but that man, Brother Gadra, he seems to have mesmerised the sense out of some of them.'

Fidelma was sympathetic. 'I suppose they were angry if, as you said, the victims were well liked here?'

'Adnán and Aoife were loved by many,' the girl agreed. 'They were known for their charity.'

'In what way?' Eadulf asked mildly.

'It was in their nature to help people. They would be the first to offer it. For instance, if one person lacked the tools to bring in a harvest, Adnán was always ready to loan those from his farm. He and his wife Aoife had one of the biggest and richest farms in this territory.'

At that moment Fethmac entered, exchanging greetings as he sat down at the table.

'The prisoner is well, lady,' he opened before Fidelma could pose the question. 'And his wife and baby are also being well looked after.'

'How is the man's throat?' Eadulf wanted to know. 'Is he now able to speak?'

The magistrate nodded. 'I did not exchange words with him but I am told it is so. I spoke to his wife and learned that his name is Celgaire and he is a *doir-fuidir*, a man without rights. She says they are both exiles from Ulaidh in the north and that they came to this area in search of work as itinerant labourers. The wife is a woman of Ulaidh but she is of a higher rank as a *saer-fuidir*. I thought I had better not ask anything else because, as a *dálaigh*, you will wish to preside over the questioning.'

'That is the correct procedure,' replied Fidelma gravely.

'A *ciardubh* from Ulaidh and married to a woman of that

kingdom?' Eadulf had to think carefully to find the right word which meant a man of dark brown skin.

'The information was given me by the woman herself. Her name is Fial and her baby, a boy, is named Ennec. The baby is not yet a year old. I asked no more.'

Once more, Fidelma inclined her head in approval.

'As I mentioned yesterday,' Fethmac said firmly, 'I studied the law for four years at the abbey of Ard Fhionáin and hold the degree of *Fursaintidh*.'

Fidelma knew this was a degree issued by the ecclesiastical colleges. It actually meant 'illuminator' because, while the young man would be able to pronounce lesser judgements, he would have to answer to those with higher degrees than his and give a clear account of why he had reached his decisions, in order to demonstrate that he understood all the obscurities of the case that he had judged. Had he gone to the bardic colleges, as had Fidelma, and had done the equivalent fourth-year degree, he would have held the degree of *Dos*. Fidelma knew it meant a small growing tree or bush, but she also knew that satirists often made fun because the same word implied inaccurate information.

'You understand,' she said, 'that I hold the degree of *Anruth*?'

'I remember, lady. It is one degree below the highest our colleges can bestow. In Ard Fhionáin your name, linked with that of Brother Eadulf, was much talked about by the students. In fact, it was spoken of with awe, lady. Therefore I would be greatly honoured to be of assistance to you in this investigation.'

Fidelma frowned as she did not enjoy adulation from anyone, even if it was sincere. She had merely wanted to make her position understood.

'Well, you are the magistrate of this village,' she replied roughly, 'so it should be we who are assisting you in this matter.'

'I waive any rights in the matter connected with this case.'

'Very well, we shall proceed.' If truth were known, Fidelma had not expected any protest from Fethmac about her asserting her authority over the case – but she did expect trouble from Brother Gadra. Surely the man had not been sent into the kingdom without any legal authority? Then she comforted herself by the fact that he had been expelled from the abbey of Lios Mhór when he had tried to take over there.

She then realised that Fethmac had asked her a question and apologised.

'I was saying – when do we start?' he repeated.

'We start right away by visiting the place where the victims were found, gathering information about these victims, and finding out the manner of their deaths. Who, where, when and how are always the first questions to be answered in such an investigation. After that we'll come to the prisoner to hear his story,' she assured him.

'I have to say, the woman Fial insists that her husband Celgaire is innocent.'

'I would be surprised had it been otherwise,' Fidelma acknowledged in a slightly caustic tone. 'If we have finished breaking our fast, let us set off for Adnán's farm. Is it far?'

Fethmac answered as they rose from the table. 'It's not far but better to venture into the countryside on horse in this weather.'

Eadulf grimaced. He much preferred walking when he could. Although he had improved over the years, horses had never been his favourite method of transportation. However, once he and Fidelma were seated on their mounts, he was relieved to find that the journey took a comparatively short time. They rode along the western bank of a river that flowed from the north of the village before turning at a right angle towards the east. They could see sparrowhawks diving along its banks with their usual speed and agility, glimpsing their long tails and reddish-brown underparts, scattering a bunch of terrified smaller birds as they searched for their prey.

'That is called the Teara, a good river often replete with salmon and brown trout,' explained the young magistrate. Fidelma was quiet and did not mention that she had already identified these matters to Eadulf on the day before. 'It is different from the river that flows to the south of the village, the Dubhóg. The two rivers join together just east of the village and flow on as one to Ard Fhionáin.'

They approached a wide expanse of undulating countryside consisting of cultivated fields and grazing land. They entered it by means of a large gap in a great wall that rose two metres high – but there was no gate to close the gap. The wall, stretching about twenty metres either way, was constructed of varying shades of sandstone blocks. It was thereafter followed into the distance by a line of wooden fencing.

'The farming lands here look quite fertile,' Eadulf remarked. 'Does Lúbaigh look after all of it?'

'Lúbaigh, his brother Dulbaire and a milkmaid. Lúbaigh was regarded as the steward and I presume he will continue to be so until Tadgán takes over his inheritance.'

'Someone will take over as owner?' queried Fidelma, surprised.

'It is *fintiu* – kin-land, lady,' explained the magistrate.

Ownership of land was changing in many parts of the rural countryside, particularly under the influence of the New Faith, for the majority of abbots and bishops were of the ruling caste, and when setting up their religious foundations had influenced the ruling kings and princes to give them ownership of the land. A *tuath*, or tribe, had initially possessed land in common, but now a family could inherit land with the approval of the *derbhfine*, the council of its kin. An individual in the family could take over the management of the land, although his kinsmen still had technical control over what happened with it. Usually the owner could not dispose of it without permission of his *derbhfine*. The latter could also be responsible for the fencing of the property and have a say if the land was poorly run. On the other hand, the owner had the right, if he was successful, to purchase further land. And if this was successful he could sell one third of the acquired land – if this surplus was gained by his own exertions.

The *derbhfine* usually consisted of living males of the age of choice descending from a common great-grandfather. However, the law still encompassed the rights of women, for it recognised the female heir or *banchomarba* who was entitled to a life inheritance in her father's land. Nevertheless, she could not pass on her inheritance in land to her husband nor to her children, for the land had to revert to her own family – although she could make a legal claim to her husband's land if there were none in his *derbhfine* to challenge her.

For Eadulf, brought up with the simple rule of primogeniture, where the land passed through the eldest surviving male heir, the system had always sounded too convoluted; too cumbersome.

'So I presume the *derbhfine* of the victims will be meeting soon?' Fidelma asked.

'Such as it is,' agreed Fethmac.

'Meaning?'

'Tadgán is now the only male relative, as I recall.'

'Does he live nearby?'

Fethmac pointed to the low stone walls of the surrounding fields. 'Those fields are his. His land borders on Adnán's land.'

'Did you say that stone walls were a sign of a rich farmstead?' Eadulf asked Fidelma. 'If so, these are rich lands.'

'There is a law text called "The Judgements of the Neighbourhood", the *Bretha Comaithchesa*,' she confirmed. 'It stipulates what fencing can be used to mark the boundaries of a farm. On poorer farms, a trench with earth banks is sufficient, while the richer farms are allowed a two-metre-high stone wall of dry masonry, just as you see before you. And from that, Fethmac will inform us that this is a very rich farm.'

The young magistrate smiled. 'Adnán was indeed a wealthy farmer and his land is fine, arable land – the sort that the laws will tell us takes legal precedence in price over all other lands. He was a descendant of the chiefs of the Fir Maige Féne, who in the days before the coming of the New Faith provided the Kings of Cashel with their Druids.'

Fidelma grimaced. 'That, indeed, was a long time ago. I remember that they were not as robust in their loyalty to Cashel in more recent times.'

Eadulf was nodding. 'It was not a year or two back when we encountered the clan during our investigation into Brother Donnchadh's murder in Lios Mhór. They were rather rebellious, as I recall.'

'I know who you mean,' replied Fethmac. 'But they were only distantly related to Adnán's clan.'

'I was told by your wife that Adnán was well liked, even though he was therefore the richest landowner here,' Fidelma said, scanning the fields around her. 'Often someone with wealth is the subject of envy and malice.'

'His fields are well maintained. They produce wheat, barley and oats. He even had a small watermill to grind the corn. Indeed, his farm is a veritable Garden of Eden.'

'He also kept animals?' asked Fidelma.

'He had a herd of cows, as many as ten, I think, and six of them are milking cows and so are valuable. There are oxen for hauling the plough and horses for other duties, along with pigs, some goats and a small flock of sheep. Naturally, Aoife kept several laying hens. As I say, it is a rich farm.'

'Maintained by Lúbaigh and Dulbaire, you said?' Eadulf asked.

Fethmac made an affirmative gesture. 'Of course, Adnán and both his boys worked on the farm as well. Even Aoife did her share.'

Eadulf was thoughtful. 'As you say, Adnán and Aoife seem to have been living in a Garden of Eden,' he observed with a slight irony in his voice. 'Even their names sound appropriate. Surely someone had cause to be jealous of them.'

The young magistrate was adamant. 'Adnán and Aoife might well have been fortunate but they were generous to a fault. Adnán could always be relied on to provide for those who sought his hospitality.'

Fidelma said slowly, 'Yet we are told that this vagrant, Celgaire, came to the farm seeking work and was cruelly turned away with his wife and baby, hungry and cold. Isn't that an argument for a motive?'

Fethmac shrugged. 'That is what Lúbaigh claims. It could be that Adnán simply told him there was no work that he could give him, especially in this month. True, I am surprised that Adnán did not offer the man some food when he allowed him and his family to stay in their wagon nearby overnight. That would be more in keeping with his usual attitude than to flatly turn the man away. But Lúbaigh is witness to this.'

'Lúbaigh is the only witness,' observed Fidelma. 'Do you believe him?'

'Doesn't it seem obvious?'

Fidelma replied sharply: 'So you have already decided what happened. Isn't it a magistrate's job to wait until all the evidence is put forward?'

The young fellow flushed. 'I was only hypothesising,' he protested lamely.

Eadulf made a calming gesture with his hand. 'And not an unreasonable hypothesis,' he said kindly. 'Lúbaigh's brother Dulbaire was the person who came to alert you about the murders, I believe?'

Fethmac sighed, remembering. 'Yes. He came to rouse me, saying his brother had discovered Adnán and his family slaughtered. He also told me that Lúbaigh believed the itinerants, who had called there the previous night, were the culprits and that they were escaping on the northern road. The wagon had been seen on the track to the ford that crosses the River Tonnóg.'

'The marshy area north of here?' Fidelma queried.

'Yes. They had not gone very far and I, together with some others, soon overtook them.'

'Was Brother Gadra with you when you did so?'

'Not then,' Fethmac replied. 'He only became involved when we returned to the village with the prisoner, Celgaire.'

'Where was Lúbaigh at this time? Was he with you?'

'When Dulbaire roused me and I gathered a few companions, we first rode over to the farmstead to ascertain that the report Dulbaire had given us was accurate. Dulbaire is not of the brightest mind, so it was best to check. Lúbaigh was there and showed us the bodies and repeated what Dulbaire had said about the vagrants. Hearing and seeing confirmation, I told Lúbaigh to remain with the bodies and put them in a safe place, out of sight. The young milkmaid, who also worked on the farm, had just arrived and was distressed.'

'Where was Dulbaire at that time? Had he returned with you?'

Fethmac frowned, trying to recall. 'I am not sure. After giving me the news, he seemed to vanish. I don't remember seeing him at the farm when I and my companions arrived.'

'Go on,' she invited, when he hesitated.

'We were all on horseback. We set out after the wagon and soon caught up with it. I told Celgaire that he must return with us. He was driving the wagon with the woman and baby by his side. Naturally, he demanded to know why, and so I told him that the bodies of Adnán and his wife and children had been found. That was when he started shouting his innocence and set the woman screaming and the baby crying. I had to restrain him and one of my companions offered to turn the wagon round and drive it back to the village. My plan was to hold them until I could arrange for the funerals and then to conduct an investigation.'

'So what happened to lead to the scene I witnessed?' Fidelma asked. 'To the attempt to lynch Celgaire?'

'We were on the outskirts of the village when we met Lúbaigh and his brother, and I asked Lúbaigh to take a hand driving the wagon. That was when we encountered several angry villagers led by Brother Gadra. The mob surrounded us. I attempted to shield the murderer . . .' He paused, hearing Fidelma's angry intake of breath. 'I mean, the suspect,' he corrected himself hastily. 'I took him on the back of my horse to try to get him to safety.'

'Then what?'

'News of the killings was already abroad in the village and tempers had gone beyond anger. Adnán and Aoife were well loved, you see.'

'So you have told us,' Fidelma said in a studied tone. 'We know – they were well loved and people were horrified by the news and this aroused their wrath. That is no excuse.'

'Well, the mob stopped my horse and dragged the . . . the suspect off. Things happened so quickly. I dismounted and tried to retrieve my prisoner and then found myself being manhandled and forcibly restrained. I saw my wife trying to reach me but some women took her back into my cabin. Brother Gadra was now leading the mob. I tried to halt them in the name of the law but he started shouting about something he called the *Lex Talionis* . . .'

'The law of retribution,' Eadulf muttered. 'That's what they call Canon Law, the disciplinary rules of the New Faith.'

'I know nothing of this law,' protested Fethmac. 'It is a foreign word.'

'The word is from the Greek *Kanon* meaning rules,' explained Fidelma impatiently, feeling the magistrate should have known. 'It was used to differentiate those laws from the Roman *leges*, civilian law. The *Kanon* were drawn up at Nicea three centuries ago. Some of the religious try to introduce them as Penitentials and claim we should accept them as superior to our laws.'

Fethmac's expression was sour. 'Well, I did not know what he was quoting. Everyone was shouting. The angry crowd was packed around us so tightly that I could barely breathe. Two men held me while the others held the . . . the suspect. I tried to reason with them, saying that the law required a trial and that it was wrong to find Celgaire guilty without hearing what he, as the supposed perpetrator, had to say.'

Fidelma sniffed. 'Exactly.'

The young magistrate flushed. 'I regret that I have let my thoughts slip into my words but I would not impose a penalty without a proper procedure. Brother Gadra told the crowd that the Holy Books of the Faith demanded that killing was punishable by death without any qualification. The Faith required it – and those who disobeyed the word of God faced the eternal punishment of the fires of hell. The Faith demanded an eye for an eye, a tooth for a tooth and . . .'

Fidelma held up her hand to make him pause. 'I know what some say about the Faith but know also that Christ confronted that idea of retaliation. Anyway, you told the people that the guilt of the suspect had first to be demonstrated with clear evidence before that person could be condemned; that it had to be done in a proper legal manner.'

'That's right, but Brother Gadra drowned out my voice, saying that if they did not act it meant that they did not fear the vengeance of God; that they feared the threat of a young lawyer more. He made me into a laughing stock and such was their loss of reason and the greatness of their anger that he was able to stir their wrath to fever pitch. They snatched the suspect from my custody. It was impossible to do anything for I was tightly gripped by the arms. It was as if some madness had caused them to cease to be individuals and they became as one. They dragged the man to the end of the village to the great oak that has always been the totem of this place. Another moment and he would have been hanged – but then you appeared . . .'

At that moment, they arrived at a small patch of woodland comprising mainly of hazel trees, some still with their long, yellow, male catkins while others were shedding their pollen ready for the appearance of their leaves. Among the trees were tough blackthorns in dense clumps. Fethmac waved his hand at the surrounding wood. 'This is where Lúbaigh said the wagon was given permission to stay for the night.'

They realised they had come to the edge of the coppice when a small brook appeared, its rushing waters disappearing down the hillside. Fidelma halted and dismounted.

'What is it?' asked Eadulf, surprised.

'Nothing in particular,' she returned. 'I just thought I should see exactly where Celgaire put his wagon. I presume this track makes its way up from the farmstead?'

'It does,' affirmed Fethmac. 'The farmstead is down in the valley. The track winds a bit because of the elevation but it is a good spot and, as you see, the track leads back southward to the village. There is a branch over there that turns northward and that is where we followed Celgaire's wagon.'

She could see at once the marks of heavy indentation which would indicate the arrival of the wagon and the marks where it had been halted beside a small brook. There was also the circle of burned grass and remains of ash where a fire had been lit. There had been movement around the area, as evidenced by crushed grass and mud.

'I presume the cloven hooves are the oxen that drew the wagon, and the other horses' hooves are where you and your men examined the spot?'

'Just so, lady,' confirmed Fethmac.

For a while, Fidelma walked around the area, watched in silence by her companions. Then she returned to her horse and remounted it.

'What is that building there?' she asked. 'That one almost hidden among those trees?'

Fethmac peered in the direction.

'Oh, that's Lúbaigh's cottage,' he said. 'Dulbaire's cabin is a little way beyond it.'

'Let us ride over and see it before we go to the farmstead,' she suggested.

'But Lúbaigh will be up at the farmstead waiting for us,' Fethmac objected.

'Nevertheless it would help me get my bearings of this land.'

They had hardly reached the low stone cabin when a woman emerged from it and stood, unsmiling, watching their approach. She was a dark-haired and dour-looking woman of middle age. Her dark eyes seemed to lack pupils. The thin lips were a scarlet gash in her sallow cheeks under her beak-like nose. The scowl seemed to fit more easily on her features than a smile. She was scrawny, but her bare, weather-tanned arms, which she now folded under her ample bosom, showed this was a woman used to hard work.

'Greetings, Fuinche,' called Fethmac.

The woman's eyes narrowed as she let them encompass Fidelma and Eadulf.

'My man is not here.' Her tone was uncompromising.

'This is the wife of Lúbaigh,' Fethmac told his companions. Then to the woman: 'I presume he is at the farmstead?'

'Where else would he be, magistrate?' she said rudely. 'He was told to meet you there.'

'We are on our way to see him,' Fidelma intervened. 'I am Fidelma of Cashel. He went to the farm early, then?'

The woman called Fuinche turned her gimlet eyes to Fidelma. 'It is a poor farmworker who does not arise to go to work with the coming of morning light.' Her tone was patronising.

'Of course.' Fidelma forced a smile. 'It must have been a bad morning when your husband found the slaughtered family of his employer.'

'I have known better mornings,' grunted the woman.

'I suppose you were close to Adnán and his family?'

'Close? Adnán was the farmer and we worked his land.' Then the woman tried to soften her tone. 'We are all close in this village.

Adnán and his family were well respected. Indeed, they were generous patrons to those who worked for them. This was always a peaceful place until . . .' She ended with a toss of her head.

'I presume that the deaths came as a shock, not only because you knew the family but we were told there were no deaths in the village until now?' Eadulf said.

'No unnatural deaths, no,' the woman replied, smirking at Eadulf's badly constructed sentence. 'It was a bad day for all of us. When my man told me that the vagrants had arrived seeking work that evening, I told Lúbaigh that he should rouse the magistrate and have a care of them.'

'Lúbaigh told you about the vagrants camping on the land the night before the killings?'

'Of course. My husband always tells me about the events of the day. I was not surprised when, the next day, the bodies were found. It was obvious that the deed was done by that creature.' She shivered. 'I have never seen a man the image of the Evil One before.'

Fidelma's mouth tightened. 'I presume by that you mean Celgaire, the man who was nearly hanged yesterday?'

'If there was any justice, he would have been,' returned Fuinche shortly. 'An evil-looking man, indeed, with skin matching the blackness of his soul.'

'Thankfully, we do have a system of justice and law in this land,' Fidelma said. 'I presume it was Lúbaigh who told you that he felt the vagrants were to blame after he discovered the bodies?'

'*Felt* they were to blame? Was he not a witness? Of course they were to blame! He told me and Taithlech the same.'

Fidelma looked across to the magistrate. 'Taithlech? I believe I have heard the name before.'

'Taithlech is a local merchant,' Fethmac said.

'And a friend of my husband,' added the woman. 'The night before the murders, Taithlech and my husband were here sampling *corma*. They were sampling it a little too freely and to the extent that Taithlech had to spend the night with us. Then Lúbaigh rose and went to the farm. There he made his discovery. When he came back here and told us the news, we urged him to rouse the magistrate and get him to go after the vagrants since we knew, from what he told us the previous night, that they would be to blame. My man sent his brother with a message to you, Fethmac.'

'So this local merchant, Taithlech, was staying with you and Lúbaigh that night?' Fidelma asked.

'Have I not said so?'

'You have. I just want to be sure. Was it usual for him to be here sampling *corma*?'

'Why shouldn't it be? Taithlech and Lúbaigh are old friends. We are a close community in this village.'

'So you consumed a lot of liquor, but that did not stop Lúbaigh from rising at first light to go to the farm to work and that's when he found the bodies?'

'We were shocked when he came back and told us. We were just rising in the early morning light and had been late abed. Taithlech afterwards was ashamed that he had drunk so much that he could not make it back to his own home on the far side of the village.'

'He has the warehouses and house down on the banks of the Duthóg, the southern river,' Fethmac explained quickly.

'Anyway,' Fuinche's voice was suspicious, 'you should be talking to my man about all of this. Not to me.'

'We are going to the farm now,' Fidelma assured her. 'I have several people to question.'

The woman scowled. 'It would have saved a lot of trouble had you not interfered yesterday and stopped the hanging of that evil one.'

'That is not the way of our law, Fuinche,' Fethmac told her sternly.

'What would you know?' she sneered at the magistrate. 'I remember you running through the village in bare feet and rags when you were a child. Just because you went to the school at Ard

Fhionáin you think you are better than everyone else. I tell you, Father Gadra knows the law and we should have obeyed him.'

She thrust out her chin and stared defiantly at Fidelma.

Knowing it would be hopeless to lecture her on the law, Fidelma merely said with emphasis: 'You place a lot of faith in this man, *Brother* Gadra?'

'He is a priest, a *sacradotus.*'

'So you regard him as your village priest?'

'Some of us do,' Fuinche replied. 'Taithlech allows him to conduct services in one of his barns. Maybe we will raise enough support for a proper chapel one day. Like I said, Father Gadra knows the holy law and we should obey *him.*'

Fidelma realised it was pointless carrying on. She thanked the woman for her time then followed Fethmac as he guided the horses away from the cottage. They said nothing until they breasted a small rise in the ground and saw the farmstead before them.

In appearance, the complex was certainly the home of a wealthy farmer. A single storey of limestone construction with a thick thatch was the house of the farmer and his family. Fidelma estimated, from the size of the place, that the building must contain several rooms. To her surprise, smoke was rising from one of the chimneys. She looked round curiously.

Beside the stone farmhouse there were other buildings, most of them clearly barns, tool sheds, enclosures for horses, and a series of pigsties; beyond, were grazing fields for cows and oxen. Chickens flapped freely about the place. Everything proclaimed the prosperity of this place.

A man was standing outside the farmhouse door watching their approach.

'There is Lúbaigh,' Fethmac announced.

They halted before the man and dismounted. He made no move to greet them but returned Fidelma's inquisitive stare with an impertinent one of his own. She realised that her first impression on the previous evening had not changed. There was something sly about Lúbaigh that she most definitely did not like. Eadulf meanwhile found a hitching post and secured their horses.

'We are here so that you can show us how and where you found the bodies and the manner in which you did so,' she said shortly.

Lúbaigh stared at her for a moment more before saying: 'It was early yesterday morning when I came to work that I found them.'

He did not amplify the statement and so she prompted: 'Well, first show us where you found them and in what order, then we will view the bodies. I gather they have been placed together in a shed to protect them from scavengers?'

Lúbaigh pointed to a large barn which had a heavy wooden bar securing it from the outside. 'They were carried to this barn and I have ensured that they have not been disturbed.'

'So, when you came to work yesterday morning, what did you find? Try to be as detailed as you can.'

'I arrived as usual, just after first light. It was dark in the farm-house. Usually there would be a lantern lit in the house as Aoife rises early and starts on her chores. But there was no light. I only thought about that afterwards. I went across to the barn as I could hear that the horses were restless. Again, I thought little about it. I was just outside the barn door when I noticed what I thought was a pile of clothes – until I saw it was a body. It was Adnán. He was lying on the ground, face downwards.'

'You saw that he was dead?'

The man smiled without humour. 'My first thought was that Adnán had taken too much to drink – but then he wasn't usually the kind of man to do that. I bent over him. There was now light enough to see and I saw terrible wounds about the head and neck.'

'Could you see or guess the cause of those wounds?' queried Eadulf.

Lúbaigh shook his head. 'I presumed they'd been done with a heavy axe or something similar.'

'Let us leave the matter of the weapon until later,' Fidelma said. 'First let us hear what else you discovered.'

'Well, I was horrified when I saw Adnán's body. I turned and ran to the farmhouse.'

'Why there?'

'I thought to tell Aoife, to raise the alarm. Also I thought to get the boys – that is, Adnán's sons.'

'But you said there was no light there. Surely that was a warning sign?'

'As I explained, I did not realise what it portended until I found the door wide open and beyond it, the body of Aoife lying on the floor. She lay on her back and I knew immediately that she was dead. There was blood all around her head.'

'You saw all this without a light?'

'I told you – it was getting daylight. My next thought was for the two boys – Cainnech and Abél.'

'How old were they?'

Lúbaigh frowned, thinking for a moment. 'I suppose Cainnech was near seventeen and Abél was twelve.'

Fidelma raised her brows. 'What was Abél doing here at that age? Why was he not still in fosterage?'

For a moment Eadulf was puzzled – and then realised that Fidelma had used the word *ailemain* which was the same word for fosterage and education. Children in the Five Kingdoms were usually sent to be raised and educated by those designated to be their foster parents. This was important in a kin-based society as it strengthened the relationships between families, and prevented hostility towards the families of the ruling caste in particular. Fosterage or education began at age seven and ended at the age of fourteen years for girls and seventeen years for boys.

'Adnán and Aoife were rich farmers, so their children should have been in fosterage. What were they doing at home?' She addressed the question to Fethmac.

'Cainnech had completed his education but I am not sure about Abél. I know he had been away among the Fír Maige Féne but returned some time ago. It did not occur to me to pursue the question, lady.'

'Never mind that for the moment,' she said impatiently. 'Let us continue.' She turned back to Lúbaigh. 'So now you realised that you must find these boys?'

The man nodded, his expression grim. 'That's right. I then found their bodies. Abél was inside the barn. I think the lad had been trying to hide when the killer struck.'

'What gives you that impression?'

'He was behind some bales of hay, almost crouched in a corner. It was light enough to see the blood on his forearms where he had raised them in order to shield himself. His most serious wounds seemed to be in the front and sides of the head.'

'And the older boy?'

'Cainnech's body was lying behind the barn,' Lúbaigh gestured, 'just beyond the place where Íonait milks the cows.'

'Íonait?' queried Eadulf.

'She is a girl from the village who comes to do the milking here. I saw that Cainnech appeared to have been killed with more savagery than the others. There were a lot of blows, aimed at his face. Like the rest he was hacked to death.'

'Grotesque,' muttered Eadulf. 'The person who could do such a thing to an entire family. Lunacy . . .'

'Indeed, someone possessed by the Evil One himself,' Lúbaigh muttered.

'You have been most helpful,' Fidelma told him. 'What did you do then?'

'I was shocked. Confused. I went back to my cottage and told my wife. My friend Taithlech, who had stayed the night, was still there. They urged me to inform the magistrate and so I sent my young brother, Dulbaire, to do that for me.'

'Ah yes – Dulbaire.'

'He looks after the cows here and helps with other things like the sheep and pigs too. Then, as I said, Íonait does the milking. She was late that morning. So, I sent Dulbaire to fetch the magistrate, Fethmac there, and tell him what I had found. I explained carefully so that my brother would not forget. It was not long before Fethmac and a few men arrived here on horseback so that I was able to tell the full story.'

'You told Fethmac that the vagrants were the culprits – that they killed the family?'

'That is so. Who else could it have been? I also alerted the magistrate to the fact that they had left the farmland in their wagon. I knew they had been allowed to park their wagon up in those woods there,' he indicated the hill, 'but he and his wife and baby were gone. I had suspected they would be.'

'Why?'

'To flee the scene of the crime as soon as possible, of course.'

'The tracks of the heavy wagon were easy to see,' Fethmac interrupted. 'My companions and I followed them to the river where they turned along a track that leads north, as I have told you.'

Fidelma ignored him, hiding her irritation, and continued to question Lúbaigh. 'You remained here?'

'For a while. Íonait arrived and I set her to work, milking the cows. As I mentioned earlier, she was late, which was fortunate as it gave me time to hide the bodies in the barn.'

'Did Dulbaire not return with the magistrate?'

'Not at that stage.'

Fidelma frowned. 'What do you mean?'

'My brother came back to tell me that Fethmac had captured the murderers, was bringing them back to the village and wanted me to identify them. I told Íonait to go home after the milking while Dulbaire and I went hurrying off to the village to meet Fethmac.'

'But surely there were still many tasks to be done on the farm.

Life does not stop because of the death of the farmer,' observed Fidelma.

'I felt that those tasks could wait. It was more important to obey the magistrate. We saw Fethmac, the wagon and his men on the track into the village – just as Father Gadra turned up, leading a band of villagers. They were very angry because they had heard what had happened and wanted to take justice into their own hands. It seems Dulbaire had told them and he then joined the villagers. Fethmac suggested I take over driving the wagon while he carried the vagrant to safety on his horse – but of course he was soon stopped. I decided the best thing I could do was drive the wagon to the village, with the woman and child inside.'

'And did you agree with what then happened?' demanded Fidelma.

'My wife and I support Father Gadra, if that is what you mean. He is a great preacher of the New Faith. It was clear the vagrant had killed Adnán and his family, so the Faith prescribes the punishment.'

Fidelma let the matter go unchallenged.

'Was it Fethmac who told you to place the bodies in the barn and secure the doors for safety from scavenger animals?' she asked.

'He did, and I managed to get all four bodies into the barn and barred the door. They are there now.'

'Are you sure no one has tampered with the bodies?'

'No one,' confirmed the man. 'Not even Tadgán, Adnán's cousin, has been near the farm since the bodies were discovered.'

'I am surprised that, being so well loved, as I am told the family was, no one from the village, not even any relatives, came to see what had happened.'

'Adnán is survived by only one close relative,' explained Fethmac. 'That is Tadgán. I can explain about that . . .'

'Later,' Fidelma told him swiftly. 'So let us now go and view the bodies.'

They walked to the barn and Lúbaigh drew back the heavy wooden bar that secured the tall door.

It was a sad sight to see the row of bodies just inside. The tall man, handsome in life; the once pretty and now disfigured woman lying almost tranquil in death; and the pathetic young lads with their faces contorted between fear and pain. The wounds about the head and neck were terrible. Lúbaigh was right. The victims had been literally hacked to death with a fury the like of which Fidelma had never witnessed before. She swallowed hard.

'Take a look, Eadulf,' she asked quietly. 'You might be able to see what I do not.'

Eadulf had spent some time at the great school of healing arts at Tuaim Brecain and while he had left to pursue religious studies in Rome, he prided himself on his knowledge and always carried with him his *les* or medical bag. It had come in useful more than once during the investigations in which he had helped Fidelma. He moved forward, knelt, and carefully examined the corpses, one by one.

'With the exception of the farmer Adnán, the wounds are all to the front and side of the head and neck,' he announced. 'Adnán's wounds are at the back of the head.'

'That means three of the victims were facing the killer?' Fidelma commented.

'It does. Moreover, Aoife, the woman, has wounds to her fore-arms, as if trying to protect herself. The same goes for the two boys. They put up a struggle. Little good it did them. The wounds on the elder boy are particularly savage.' Eadulf asked Lúbaigh to help him turn the body of Adnán face downwards so that he could have a better view of the terrible wounds on the back of the man's head. 'The farmer was definitely struck a heavy blow from behind. That was probably enough to kill him, but the killer continued to hit him several times around the neck and shoulders. Adnán had his back to his assailant and maybe did not even know of the man's presence before the first blow was struck, which rendered him helpless. It was a brutal and merciless attack.'

Eadulf rose to his feet. 'Was a search made for the murder weapon on the vagrant's wagon?' he asked.

'I have not had time to search Celgaire's wagon yet,' mumbled the magistrate, sounding a little nervous.

'Why not?' Fidelma asked in astonishment. 'Did you not search it when you apprehended Celgaire and his family?'

'As I said, there was no time. My immediate thought was to bring them back to the village, and I would have done so – but for the events of yesterday which you yourself witnessed. A search will be carried out as soon as we return.'

Fidelma glanced at Eadulf and rolled her eyes upwards to express her opinion of this lack of essential procedure. Then she turned back to Lúbaigh. 'You say you took over the driving of the wagon when the mob attacked it. Did you stay with it all the time?'

'Most of the time, until I saw my brother, Dulbaire, in the crowd when they were about to hang the vagrant. I thought it better to get him away. He is simple minded and was playing his *fedán*, probably thinking it was a celebration.'

'So the wagon was left unattended?'

'But the woman and infant were there.'

'I saw Lúbaigh drag his brother away,' Fethmac said. 'I recall that. I saw Dulbaire doing a dance and heard him playing at the tree where they were about to hang the man.'

'So the wagon was left with the vagrant's wife?' Fidelma asked heavily.

'For a short time, until I dragged Dulbaire away and returned to it. I then remained with the wagon until Fethmac told me to hand it over, along with the woman and child, into the care of Gobánguss.'

There was a silence. Fidelma was thinking that anything found on the wagon might not be valid as a proof in law, for anyone could have placed it there during the period when Lúbaigh was absent. She suppressed a sigh.

Eadulf had been re-examining the bodies and seemed to be paying special attention to the elder boy.

'There is something very strange here,' he said eventually.

'What do you mean?' Fidelma asked, puzzled by his attitude.

'Either there were two killers involved or the killer, having despatched the farmer, his wife and their son Abél, changed weapons to kill the elder boy, Cainnech.'

CHAPTER FOUR

'Can you be more specific?' Fidelma asked tersely, following the brief silence.

'I am saying that the same weapon could not have inflicted the injuries on all four victims,' replied Eadulf.

Fethmac's brows drew together in bewilderment. 'So there were two killers?'

Eadulf smiled at the young man. 'Or two weapons. It is obvious by examining the wounds.'

'All I see are bodies displaying wounds that have been inflicted with a sharp weapon in such a way as to indicate an uncontrollable fury.'

Lúbaigh was staring at Eadulf with an incredulous expression. 'You did not witness the killings and cannot swear to the weapon that was used. So how can you claim this?'

'It is not a matter of claim. An axe was not the instrument that caused all the deaths,' Eadulf replied firmly without rising to the insult.

'Why are you so certain?' Fethmac put in. 'What magic do you possess that you can be so sure?'

'No magic, Fethmac.' Eadulf's tone remained even. 'Just observation. Examine the wounds on the elder boy. Cainnech's neck is almost severed, and the injury has been inflicted with the edge of a curved blade. That is the weapon we must look for.'

'Sharp and curved?' Fethmac considered. 'That could be something like a short-handled reaping hook.'

Eadulf smiled thinly. 'That would certainly fit the wounds that the poor young lad has sustained. But examine the injuries inflicted on Adnán, his wife and their younger son. None of them are similar to Cainnech's. They consist of heavy, deep cuts, like those a butcher would make with a cleaver. Did you see any sign of another weapon?'

Lúbaigh shook his head slowly.

The young magistrate peered closer at the three bodies as instructed, screwing his features up in distaste.

'I see what you mean,' he acknowledged reluctantly.

Fidelma turned thoughtfully to Lúbaigh. 'I presume there are many such tools in use around the farm that are like an axe or a cleaver in appearance?'

Lúbaigh shrugged. 'I dare say there are.'

'And no one has made a search yet?' Fidelma enquired. Their silence gave her the answer she had feared. 'We should look in the area where the bodies were found first,' she decided.

'Perhaps the vagrant took the murder weapon with him but then found he needed another one to finish the boy,' Lúbaigh offered lamely.

'We shall look,' Fethmac said. 'Show us where you found each victim.'

It was when Lúbaigh showed Eadulf and the magistrate the place where he had found Cainnech's mutilated body that they made the discovery. The reaping hook lay half-hidden in the long grass, a few steps away from the pig pens, close by where the killing took place. Eadulf picked it up carefully. It was a short-handled, sickle-like hook. He could see the dried blood on it.

'I wonder why the change of weapon? It makes no sense,' mused Fethmac.

'I assumed Adnán was first to be attacked,' Lúbaigh said.

'Why do you say that?' asked Fethmac.

'From the way I found the bodies. Had Aoife been the first to be attacked, Adnán would have been running towards the cabin to her rescue and not standing here with his back to the cabin.'

'What if the vagrant struck her before she could make any sound?' frowned Eadulf.

'That could not be so because she died facing her killer, trying to defend herself. She would have had time to scream,' Fidelma, said as they headed towards the farmhouse. 'In fact, I think she was probably the last to die in this carnage.' She glanced at the bewildered magistrate. 'I will explain more later,' she said, before asking Eadulf, 'is there any sign of the main weapon?'

'We'll make another search,' Fethmac said.

Nothing of significance was found. While Eadulf and Fidelma checked the farmhouse, Fethmac and Lúbaigh began an examination of the barn and outbuildings. There were various knives and tools stored ready for use, but nothing that resembled the heavy cleaver which Eadulf said would be powerful enough to inflict the blows that had killed three members of the family.

It was while they were engaged on their search that Lúbaigh's brother, Dulbaire, arrived. They had not noticed him on the previous day. His approach was announced by the sounds of a jaunty air being played on a reed whistle. The young man, whatever his disabilities, certainly had a talent with the crude instrument.

Dulbaire looked to be no more than in his late teens and was thin and ill nourished compared with his sturdy brother. His lank fair hair fell across his features so that every now and again he would jerk his head back in order to sweep it from his eyes. His beard consisted of patchy tufts without mature strength. The young man's eyes were pale and without any sparkle of life in them. He did not look directly at anyone when speaking but kept his gaze upon the ground. His lips were bulbous and constantly parted with a trace of spittle in the corners, for there were gaps in his teeth and those that remained were black.

Fidelma tried to ask him a few questions but he kept his eyes averted when he replied or seemed to focus on things unseen. There was little he could contribute to what she already knew.

As Lúbaigh had reported, Dulbaire had arrived at the farm for his daily work and found his brother Lúbaigh agitated. He saw the bodies and remembered his brother telling him to go to the village and tell the magistrate what he had seen. That he had done. The magistrate had gathered some men and ridden back to the farm with them.

'So you did not return here with the magistrate?' queried Fidelma.

The boy frowned and shook his head.

'When did you return here?' she wanted to know.

'I came back. Work to do. Work or Adnán would scold me. Needed drink first.' He peered up at the sky thoughtfully. 'Went and had a drink. Father did not keep me long.'

'Your father?' Fidelma echoed, plunged into confusion again.

'Father Gadra.'

Fidelma felt irritated that the self-important Brother insisted on this newfound rank which, to her, was contrary to the teaching of the New Faith. And, of course, he was staying at the boy's cabin.

'So you went to your cabin to get a drink.' Fidelma made a guess. 'Gadra was there – so you told him what had happened at the farm?'

'Yes. Told him same message.'

Fidelma looked across to Lúbaigh. 'I would have thought he might have come here today,' she observed tartly. 'There are rituals to be pursued with the dead within the course of the day. So what did *Brother* Gadra do when you gave him the message?'

'He was eating and I had my drink. Said he must go to meet the magistrate and the killer.'

'But you did not go with him?'

The boy smiled happily. 'Later. I went to meet the wagon with Lúbaigh. Everyone greeted us. Whole village. Big celebration. I wanted to play my pipe but . . . but Lúbaigh stopped me and took me away.'

'I see.' Fidelma suddenly remembered the day was progressing and she asked Fethmac: 'Has Brother Gadra made any comment on religious rituals for the dead and preparations for the funerals of the victims?'

The magistrate shook his head. 'After you rebuked him last night, I have seen no more of him. We had no permanent religious here but Brother Gadra seems to be taking that role.'

'I presume he will make arrangements as you say?'

Fethmac looked uncomfortable. 'I don't think Tadgán, Adnán's cousin, is a follower of Brother Gadra. The Brother's services are not to everyone's liking.'

Eadulf smiled thinly. 'Judging from yesterday, I thought he had a strong following.'

Fethmac grimaced. 'Not exactly. What he does have is an ability to play on people's emotions if the time is right. There are still some of us who think his teachings are incompatible with the New Faith as it first came to us. As you have also seen, he talks of replacing our native law with these strange rules from Rome.'

Fidelma sighed. 'Then what of ordinary services? What of funerals and weddings, baptism and the like?' she asked. 'How do you arrange those?'

'As magistrate of the village, I can preside if there is no one else available. If we are in need of strong spiritual advice, then we can send to Ard Fhionáin. It is a distance from here, that is true, but one that can be accomplished easily.'

'Brother Gadra strikes me as the sort who would object if he was unable to conduct all the religious services as are needed here,' Fidelma said.

Fethmac rubbed his chin in a rueful gesture. 'As you know, he has a devoted following among many of the women and some of the men. Perhaps he has already consulted Adnán's cousin.' He glanced uneasily at Lúbaigh.

'So what is intended about the burial of the victims? Bodies are buried usually on the night of the day after death,' Fidelma said sharply.

'You don't have to remind me of the law and custom,' replied the magistrate with a flush of irritation. 'But even if I sent a rider to the abbey at Ard Fhionáin right now, they would not return by tonight. I shall ask Brother Gadra to conduct the ceremony, even if Tadgán objects.'

'Does Tadgán even know what has occurred here?'

'Taithlech has gone to inform him,' Lúbaigh said.

'Taithlech? The merchant whom you mentioned?'

'Yes. His daughter Flannat was married to Tadgán's son Díoma. She is now a widow but still lives at Tadgán's farmstead. She is mother to Tadgán's grandson.'

'I see. Well, I shall leave the matter in your hands. But the law states that the burials must take place tonight and . . .' She broke off as a young girl approached them. 'I presume this is Íonait who is employed as a milkmaid here?'

Fethmac nodded.

The girl was about sixteen or seventeen years old, fair of skin with a hint of freckles and a mass of straw-coloured hair above light grey eyes. Her mouth, Fidelma saw, was a little too wide and her lips too thick for her features. The girl came hesitantly to them when Fethmac summoned her. Íonait could tell Fidelma little for she had not seen the vagrants and only came to the farm well after Lúbaigh had discovered the bodies and removed them to the barn. She had been reluctant to stay at the farm that morning after learning of the terrible slaughter of Adnán and his family, but had done so because of the simple fact that the animals could not take care of themselves.

'There are now two things to do,' Fidelma summed up when the girl had finished.

'Two?' Fethmac enquired.

'The bodies have to be taken to the local burial ground. Fethmac,

I presume you have a *reilic*, a burial place that serves your community?'

'That we do,' he nodded. 'Lúbaigh knows it. It is just on the west side of the village.'

'Then the bodies should be washed, prepared and taken there for burial at midnight tonight, for the customary rituals should be observed. I assume that this Tadgán and his household will come to wash and dress the bodies?'

'I presume so,' Fethmac agreed. 'He is the only relative I know. As I showed you, he has an adjacent farm, just on the other side of the river. He is widowed, but as well as Flannat, there are other women in his household who have performed such acts – although . . .' The young man seemed hesitant.

'Although?' queried Fidelma. 'You said that the merchant Taithlech has gone to tell him.'

'The relationship has not been good between Tadgán and Adnán of late,' the magistrate sighed. 'I was asked to intercede in an argument between them because of the fences that separate their land.'

Fidelma stared at him for a moment. 'I thought you told me that Adnán and Aoife were well regarded by the community and had no enemies here as such?'

Fethmac looked unhappy. 'The dispute was silly . . .'

'A dispute is a dispute and you imply this had led to animosity?'

'Well, it was foolish. It related to the law on conducting water across another's land.'

'The *Coibne Uisci Thoiridne*?' Fidelma named the appropriate law text.

'Just so. Adnán had a water mill constructed on his side of the boundary river and Tadgán claimed it diverted the water from his land. It did not – and that was an easy matter to see and judge. However, Tadgán was not happy with my judgement and refused to speak to me or his cousin, or any of Adnán's family thereafter.'

'You say that Tadgán is the only kin to the family?'

'So far as I know.'

'If this is kin-land then he has a claim on the ownership of the farm now.'

Fethmac shrugged. 'As the senior of the kin, he does, that is true.'

'Well, it will be up to you to see that this Tadgán is informed of his obligations. As *ádae fine*, he and his household must see to the obsequies; to preparing the bodies for the burial and arranging for the burial.'

Fethmac's features were not happy.

Lúbaigh moved forward. 'I can go over to Tadgán's farm,' he offered. 'I know him and also Taithlech is a friend of mine. We are a small village, lady, and everyone knows everyone here. If you wish it, I will go at once.'

After giving her assent, Fidelma asked Fethmac if he thought there would be any dispute about Tadgán's claim to inherit the kin-land.

'Adnán and Aoife were quite clear about their kin,' the magistrate replied. 'Tadgán is clearly the *orbare* or inheritor, being senior kin. This farm is definitely *fintiu*, kin-land, and officially worth fourteen *cumals*.'

'Fourteen *cumals*?' Eadulf almost whistled. 'Why, that is the equivalent to the honour price of a chieftain of a territory or to a bishop . . .'

'. . . and to a Brehon of high status,' Fethmac added with a smile. 'It's the value of forty-two milch cows.'

'And you are sure that when Adnán's *derbhfine* are accounted for, there would be no *banchomarba*, a female heir, in the descent of the four generations that comprise the family group?' Fidelma pressed.

Fethmac shook his head firmly. It was clear that he did not like his word being questioned. 'The *audacht*, the Will, of Adnán was known and, as magistrate, he declared it before me. The farm would have been divided between his two boys, Cainnech and Abél. As they are dead, as this is kin-land, then the only claimant to it is Tadgán. That will make Tadgán one of the most powerful men in this territory.' He paused and a slight frown crossed his brow.

'What is it?' prompted Fidelma.

'Your mention of a *banchomarba* reminds me . . . Tadgán is clearly the inheritor of the kin-land but he has no son now. His son Díoma died, but Díoma's wife Flannat had a son who is still a baby.'

'Well, the daughter-in-law will not inherit when Tadgán dies. She can use the property during her lifetime after Tadgán dies but it must return to her son's family on her death. Of course, if she had property of her own inherited from her family then she retains that. It is simple. I presume, as she is living on Tadgán's farm, she has exercised the right to remain there to bring up his grandson?'

Fethmac agreed but was still worried. 'I seemed to recall something about her being a *banchomarba* because of another matter, but I can't recall it right now. Anyway, for the time being it is Tadgán who takes control of the kin-lands.'

'Very well,' Fidelma acknowledged. 'So let us hope that Tadgán has no problem arising from this argument which you adjudicated. It is said that all arguments should cease at the graveside. So I think we should now return to Gobánguss' forge and examine the wagon before talking with Celgaire and his wife.' She turned to Eadulf. 'Is there anything more that needs to be done here from your viewpoint?'

'I think we have explored everything here,' he replied gravely.

'Then we shall—'

'Lady, lady!' The young girl Íonait came hurrying from the cow pen.

Fidelma turned enquiringly.

'It is the cows, lady. I have finished – but what am I to do with the milk?'

'What do you usually do with it?' Fidelma asked in surprise.

'I take the pails to Aoife. Some she retains and others are exchanged with neighbours.'

'Did you milk the cows yesterday, after the bodies were discovered?' Eadulf asked.

'I did.'

'Then what did you do with yesterday's milk?'

'Oh, Lúbaigh came and took charge but I saw he has now left.'

'He has gone to bring Tadgán here to arrange the funerals,' the young magistrate assured her. 'He will return shortly and I am sure he will take care of it again.'

The girl stood looking at him, wide eyed with sudden apprehension.

'Tadgán? He is coming here?' There was something in her tone that made Fidelma examine her closely.

'You seem to have a problem with that, Íonait. Surely you would know that Tadgán is close kin to Adnán? It has yet to be confirmed legally, but you will be working for Tadgán now that Adnán is dead.'

The girl lowered her head and her cheeks coloured a little.

'But Adnán hated Tadgán!' she blurted out.

'How do you know that?' Fidelma asked.

'I heard them arguing several times and I heard Adnán once say to Aoife that if Tadgán came anywhere near the farmstead, he would kill him.'

Fidelma pursed her lips for a moment. Before she could speak, Fethmac cut in. 'We know all about the dispute between the cousins, Íonait. In such disputes hot words are spoken. But Tadgán will now take over the farm as there appears to be no other heir to this kin-land. So go back to your task and Lúbaigh will return soon with Tadgán. Lúbaigh remains as steward of the farmstead in the meantime.'

'I told you – Adnán *hated* Tadgán,' the girl repeated sullenly. 'Lúbaigh must find another to milk the cows here.'

To their surprise, she then turned and ran off.

Fethmac exchanged a quick glance with Fidelma. 'Out of loyalty to Adnán, no doubt?' He smiled thinly. 'There is no need for you to worry about such things. It is said that changes in circumstance often alter attitudes. I doubt whether the dispute will continue now.'

With nothing else to be done, the three mounted their horses and rode out of the farmstead.

'So, do we go to question Celgaire?' Fethmac asked, after they had ridden some way.

Fidelma replied after a moment's consideration. 'As I said, we will first examine his wagon and then we will question his wife.'

Fethmac tried to disguise his surprise at this and Eadulf, noticing, smiled to himself. He personally had become used to the paths that Fidelma's mind took, and they frequently moved at angles to the path he thought they should be pursuing. Yet, and much to his confusion, they often came up with information that circumvented obscurity and reached the centre of the argument.

'You want to speak with the stranger's wife first?' Fethmac said, as if puzzled.

'First the wagon and then the wife,' Fidelma confirmed with a grin.

The young magistrate flushed in his confusion.

'Have I said something amusing, lady?' he asked sullenly.

'Not at all. I just cannot help thinking the names are appropriate,' she replied. Eadulf, of course, knew that Fidelma liked to amuse herself with the meaning of names. 'The woman, you said, is called Fial. That means one who is modest and faithful. Ennec, the baby, means the innocent one.'

The return journey to the settlement of Cloichín passed mainly in silence. They met few people on the road, usually men hurrying about daily tasks. Some greeted the magistrate and his companions but all seemed conscious of the shameful near-lynching of the previous day. Some, still thinking they had been in the right, held their heads high, while others hung their heads in shame. Only one or two actually greeted the travellers with directness and warmth.

Reaching the village, Fidelma did not have to ask the direction of the smithy, for all they had to do was follow the sounds of the hammer on the anvil. The forge itself was placed in the centre of the settlement but at a respectful distance from the nearest habitations. This was done by law, as flying sparks from a smith's forge could easily set adjacent buildings alight if they were situated too close. What was strange, causing Eadulf to remark on it, was a sight which he initially thought was a symbol of the blacksmith and his trade.

By the track leading into the forge stood three tree-like poles rising to a height of about six or seven metres but close to one of the flat-roofed outbuildings, probably a barn of sorts. On top of these three poles was affixed a small platform and balanced on top of that was the large metal object that had caught Eadulf's eye. It looked like a large bronze polished cauldron.

'Didn't the smith say that he lived by the plinth of the cauldron?' he frowned, recalling Gobánguss' directions.

'He did,' confirmed Fethmac. 'That cauldron is said to have been brought here in the time before time when the Children of the Gael first arrived in this land.'

'Is it a genuine ancient cauldron then?'

'That is so: it is a cauldron of bronze sheets, riveted together to be watertight. Our village is very proud of it,' Fethmac said. 'You can see from here how the rivets run both horizontally and vertically, with two cast-bronze handles attached to the rim.'

'What does it mean? It's not the sign of the smith, surely?' Eadulf was puzzled.

Fethmac chuckled and shook his head.

'You will see that it is kept polished. We take it down for certain ceremonies when the chief of this territory attends. It symbolises his power and wealth and, above all, his pledge to distribute largesse to his people.'

As they nudged their horses forward, Gobánguss set down his hammer by the anvil and, with his *tarngor*, or smith's tongs, he took a piece of yellowing metal from his anvil and placed it back in the fire before turning to greet them. They had dismounted and Fidelma began with an apology.

'We don't want to disturb you, especially when we know that the heat of metal can become unstable in the furnace and what is pliable one moment can be destroyed the next.'

The big man grinned at her. 'Have no fear, lady. I know my metals and will interrupt to attend to it when the time is due. I suppose you have come to interrogate the man, Celgaire?'

'Not immediately. We want to examine his wagon first. Then we wish to speak with the man's wife.'

'The wagon is stationed at the back,' Gobánguss replied. 'The ox that pulled it is in my pen, by the way. The beast is in poor condition. My wife is looking after the woman and her baby. Her husband is locked in the shed yonder,' he indicated the direction with a nod of his head. 'There has been no trouble.'

'We will deal with her in a moment. Let us look at the wagon. So far as you know, nothing has been taken from it? The man and woman have not removed anything from it?'

The smith shook his head. 'It has been left exactly as it was given to me. The man was placed directly in the shed and has not been near it. Neither has his wife. You will excuse me if I don't accompany you,' Gobánguss ended, gesturing to the metal heating in the furnaces.

'Of course.' Fidelma went to leave and then hesitated and turned back. 'Just a thought: what is your opinion of the wagon? You must have seen good and bad workmanship in your time.'

Gobánguss grinned. He lifted the piece of molten metal from the fire and plunged it into a pail of water. As it hissed, he told Fidelma, 'Their wagon is even poorer than the ox that pulled it. It is old but it was well made in its time. It is what we call a *fénae*, lady, built to haul heavy goods. No wonder it found use as an itinerant's home. I would say the hand that made it is two generations dead. Good oak and yew went into it but the wood is rotten in places for lack of upkeep. The newest things are the wheels, which are strong, and those have been better looked after. I think the rims have been replaced not so long ago and with an iron tread. A good smith's hand was at work, for the metal is tight around the rims.'

It was clear the smith knew his profession and Fidelma raised her hand in acknowledgement before allowing Fethmac to lead her and Eadulf towards the place where the wagon was kept. It was pretty much the same type that Fidelma had seen pulling heavy loads on some farms. As the smith had said, it had been well constructed but the passing years and the lack of maintenance had seen deterioration in its condition. A badly constructed frame of alder had been erected on the wagon. This had been covered with linen sheeting, thus forming a tent to keep out the worst of the elements from those who sheltered within.

'So, we are looking for a bloodstained cleaver?' Eadulf asked as he helped Fidelma climb up into the wagon.

'Or something very similar,' she answered cheerfully.

Eadulf had not forgotten how she had rebuked the magistrate for not searching the wagon before.

'The question remains: why did the killer change weapons from cleaver to reaping hook?' Eadulf frowned in thought. 'And do you really think that this man Celgaire would have put one of the murder weapons in his wagon after killing those people – and left the other to be found? He must have known he and the wagon would be searched.'

'Perhaps he thought we would be content with finding one murder weapon,' suggested Fethmac. 'He would not realise that one such as Brother Eadulf could spot the difference between the type of wounds inflicted.'

'That is if he had committed the murders,' Fidelma reminded them.

The interior of the wagon smelled of stale sweat and unwashed clothing. Fidelma observed Eadulf's pained expression and rebuked him.

'What do you expect when a family has lived in this confined space for so long?' she said.

Eadulf sighed and bent to the task with a wrinkled nose.

The magistrate suddenly gave an exclamation. They turned and saw that he was pulling free a small sack at the back of the wagon where cooking pots and wrapped items of foodstuffs, mainly vegetables and herbs, were stored and contributing to the smell inside the vehicle.

'What is it?' Fidelma demanded, going towards him.

'It appears to be a small sack of oats. That would be worth a *miach* in anyone's money.'

Eadulf was surprised, as he had become familiar with the coinage of this land. A *miach* was one of the smallest values of coins, a twelfth of a silver *screpall*, but was still worth having.

Fethmac was smiling with satisfaction. 'How would itinerants be able to afford this sack?'

Fidelma examined it but couldn't see what the fuss was about. 'There is nothing to suggest that they could not, is there?'

'Look at it, lady – that is a fresh sack. The man Celgaire arrives at the farm looking for work. He is sent away – but just happens to have a sack of fresh oats in his wagon. I will lay a wager that he stole this, *and* after the murders, which means . . .'

'Which still means supposition rather than fact,' pointed out Fidelma dryly. 'We have yet to question the man. Now let us carry on with our search.'

Half-heartedly Fethmac and Eadulf returned to the search. It was under some woollen blankets that Eadulf came across an aging flat leather *bolg*, or bag. He peered inside and was surprised to find several sheets of parchment. He immediately called Fidelma's attention to it.

'Why would an illiterate stranger have need of this?' he demanded.

Fidelma glanced through it and her eyes widened. 'Two of them are written in Latin – I think in quite an ancient form. The third is in my language but in the form of the *bérla na filed*.' Observing Eadulf's incomprehension, she added, 'It is the esoteric speech of the poets, another ancient form which some bards preferred to use, when recording important matters. I know something of it but it will take a little time to decipher. We will take the parchments and I will look at them later. Meanwhile, this is not what we are looking for.'

The interior revealed nothing further. As they climbed down from the back of the wagon, however, Eadulf nearly caught himself on some hooks at the back from which a wooden bucket was suspended. In trying to avoid it, he scratched himself on the rough wood. He turned, and was holding the back of his hand to his mouth and sucking to ease the wound when his eyes spotted another hook, from which a sack of apples hung. Stains on the sacking showed that a lot of them were rotting into pulp. There was nothing unusual in such items being carried in that fashion. However, as he was looking at it, he became aware of a sort of shelf just under the tailboard of the wagon, a deep recess that was almost hidden by the hooks and their contents.

Pushing the sack out of the way, he peered inside.

Fidelma caught the movement and teased him: 'Don't tell me that itinerants could not acquire a sack of apples unless they stole them from the farm?'

'No,' returned Eadulf dryly. 'There are plenty of places where one can pick up windfalls along these highways.'

'Well, let us now go and have a word with this woman, Fial.'

However, Eadulf ignored her. He was intent on stretching and reaching into the dark recess. Then he stiffened and let out a muffled exclamation. A moment later, he withdrew his arm and stood up. He had an object in his hand and silently he held it out towards them.

It was a heavy-bladed meat cleaver, a typical *uircenn,* with a strong oak handle. The blade had been honed to a sharp edge, and there were stains on it.

Fethmac, the young magistrate, gave a long low whistle of satisfaction.

ChAPTER FIVE

Had Fial taken a little more care with her personal cleanliness she would have been as attractive as any of the women of higher social status. She was of medium height and well proportioned, with a mass of black curly hair that tumbled in disarray over creamy white skin and a sprinkling of freckles. Her eyes were a deep shade of green. However, at the moment, lack of a recent wash marred her beauty and the full lips had flecks of blood around them where she had been chewing them in agitation. She was dressed in garments that would have been better for a little attention from a needle and thread and a good laundering. She held the small bundle which was her baby son close to her breast, protectively. The child was fast asleep, fortunately, and oblivious to the tension of his surroundings.

Fial stood glowering at them in the *airide* or kitchen and living part of the cottage belonging to Fethmac, the magistrate, where she had been brought from Gobánguss' house. Ballgel had vacated the room to allow Fidelma a private space in which to interrogate the wife of the vagrant. It was clear that Fial had slept little during the night. She stood, eyes fixed on Fidelma, and barely glanced at Eadulf and Fethmac.

Fidelma was saddened as she observed the baby and its age.

'I was not told that your son was so young,' she began. 'I was merely told you had a baby about one year old named Ennec. How old is he?'

'Seven months,' the young woman replied shortly.

'Do you want me to get someone to take care of him while we speak?'

The woman drew the child closer to her, and glared back. 'I will not be parted from him. Do not try to take him.'

Fidelma smiled reassuringly. 'No one will try,' she said. Then she turned to Fethmac. 'A chair for Fial.' She waited for the woman to be seated with her child, then she said more earnestly. 'You realise, Fial, that I am a *dálaigh* and that you must answer all my questions truthfully. I ask you now to swear to the truth of your answers.'

'There are *dálaighs* in the kingdom of Ulaidh as well as in Muman,' Fial snapped. Her origin was made clear by her accent.

The mention of an oath made Fethmac cough nervously. 'Lady, I am told the old *bannoill*, the female oath, is now considered invalid by the amended laws discussed by the Council of Brehons.'

Fidelma glanced at him in annoyance. 'That retrograde step suggested by our reforming Christian brethren has been discussed but not enacted. Who told you about it?'

'Brother Gadra. He says that the New Faith argued that the testimony of women should not be accepted any more because it was rejected by the apostles when the women claimed they had witnessed the resurrection of Christ. He says that only men may testify – and that this has been accepted by the Canon Law.'

'That is the most ridiculous and illogical thing I have ever heard.' Fidelma was aghast. 'If this were the basis, then the apostles should be apologising in shame that they had not believed the women. According to the Faith, the women were proved true in what they had said. In this kingdom, the *Din Techtugad* decrees that the oath and the validity of a woman's testimony are accepted. If not, how could I then be a *dálaigh* and offer judgements in the courts of the Five Kingdoms?'

The magistrate was embarrassed. 'I was only repeating what Brother Gadra said,' he mumbled.

'I will deal with Brother Gadra when I have time,' shot back Fidelma. She turned to Fial. 'Are you willing to swear to tell the truth?'

'I am,' the young woman said. 'I am of Leth Cathail and was born within sight of Rath Celtair, which is now being called Dún Pádraig, where, it is said, the Blessed Patrick was buried. Therefore the Faith has been with us two centuries and we practise it as it originally came to us and *not* with the many changes we have heard of over the years.'

'You are very well informed for a *saer-fuidir*,' Fethmac said sarcastically.

'Is it forbidden that a *saer-fuidir* should be possessed of knowledge?' the woman snapped back.

'Not at all,' Fidelma cut in with a frown of annoyance at the young magistrate. 'So you are now under oath. Let us talk awhile.' Fidelma seated herself before Fial.

'The only thing I need to state is that we are innocent of these accusations,' Fial said firmly.

'Well, there is a little more I need to ask,' Fidelma said coaxingly. 'You have told me where you come from. So let me start with how you became married to the stranger, Celgaire.'

'My husband is neither a stranger to me nor to the people of Leth Cathail,' Fial said proudly. 'He served in the household of the Prince of Dál Fiatach, which is a territory of Ulaidh.'

'How long did he serve him?' asked Fidelma, concealing her surprise. A *sen-cléithe* was of the non-freeman class who were not allowed to leave the territory of the clan in which they were born and served, except by special permission. They were, however, allowed to travel in the clan territory without restrictions. They had rights within the clan, but could not have a voice in clan councils or stand for any office.

'I was told your husband was a *doir-fuidir*, a man without rights,' she said.

'He was the third generation of his family to be a *sen-cléithe* before he decided to lay down his weapons and refused further service. For that act of rebellion he was reduced in social class from *sen-cléithe* to *doir-fuidir*.'

'I see. And where did Celgaire come from?'

'We are both from Leth Cathail.'

'And how long have you been *saer-fuidir*?'

Fial grimaced as if the subject was distasteful. 'I have always been so, serving in the household of Blathmac, the lord of the Dál Fiatach. It was in that household I met Celgaire and so we were given permission to marry . . . that was just before he was proclaimed and exiled.'

'Proclaimed?' Eadulf queried.

It was Fidelma who explained. 'Celgaire would have to be proclaimed to the people, announcing his loss of rights and reduction in status according to law, before he was sent into exile.' She glanced at the still sleeping baby. 'It could be that your son's son, when he becomes of age at seventeen, could automatically be accepted back with full rights in his clan. The law says that the third generation is free of all debts and encumbrances.'

The woman still glowered. 'That does not help us. Being falsely accused of this murder will ensure that we are condemned forever.'

Fidelma sat back and regarded the woman thoughtfully for a few moments.

'Well, I am here to assess whether your husband has been falsely accused or not. So let us start with some facts. What brought you and your husband southwards from the Kingdom of Ulaidh?'

'In search of work, of course. The condition of exile allowed us to travel to seek employment. So we are within our rights to be here. Labour is scarce for the likes of us in the winter.'

'So, you came south seeking work and arrived at the farmstead of Adnán. What made you go there?'

'We went first to the farmstead of a man called Tadgán – a fellow without grace or charity who threatened to set his dogs on us.'

Fidelma glanced at the magistrate, who seemed to agree that it fitted with the man's character. 'Tadgán can certainly be abrasive and he also has hunting dogs that I would not like to meet on a dark night.'

Fidelma turned back to Fial. 'Go on,' she instructed.

'When we left Tadgán's farmstead one of his herdsmen, a kindly man, directed us to another farmstead – the one belonging to this man called Adnán. The herdsman told us that we were more likely to be greeted with sympathy there than anywhere else. We were grateful for it was cold and the daylight was fast merging into night. I remember we turned west and crossed an old bridge across a river and then came to the farmstead.'

'And your husband went to see the farmer, the man called Adnán whom he is now accused of killing, together with Adnán's wife and children?' intervened the magistrate.

Fidelma made clear her displeasure. 'It is better if I conduct this inquiry, Fethmac,' she said coldly before turning to Fial again. 'Did your husband go to speak with Adnán, the farmer?'

'He did.'

'Was anyone else there during that time?'

'Just the farmer's wife. I think there was also another man about the place; perhaps a worker on the farm but I can't remember much about him.'

'Relate to me what took place.'

'Simple,' replied the woman. 'We drew up in our wagon next to the farmhouse. Celgaire climbed down as the farmer and his wife came out. The farmer asked what we wanted and Celgaire told him who we were, and that he was looking for some work as we had no means of surviving the rest of the winter without it.'

'So what answer did you receive?'

'The farmer regretted that it was winter, the month when the earth was dead and people were at rest. There was nothing he could offer my husband. As night was almost upon us, the farmer pointed to a track which led up the hill to a copse. He said it was a good spot to place our wagon for the night as there was a brook close by and we could light a fire and be warm, for there was plenty of dry wood lying around up there.'

'And did you follow his advice?' pressed Fidelma.

'About placing our wagon at that spot? Of course. The track was easy, and firm enough to take our wagon, and we soon found a good berth by the brook.'

'What made you head northwards early the next morning?'

'The farmer had told us that there might be work to the north along a river called the Tonnóg. It was, he said, an area of marsh-land and some of the farmers there needed help during the wet months to maintain dykes or search for livestock that had wandered into the marshes and streams. So, at first light, we set out and while we were on our journey, he and his horsemen . . .'

'He?' Eadulf interrupted for the first time. 'Who do you mean?'

Fial pointed to the magistrate. 'He claimed that we had killed the farmer and his family and would be taken back to the settlement for punishment.'

Fidelma turned a disapproving eye on the young man.

'Is that what you said?' she asked.

Fethmac looked sheepish. 'Perhaps in essence,' he admitted.

Fidelma swung back to the woman. 'And *did* you kill the farmer and his family?' Her voice was a sudden whip-crack.

However, the woman's chin came up immediately and she almost shouted her denial.

'So you had no more dealings with the farmer and his wife? You accepted there was no work and went off to stay where he told you to spend the night. Didn't you find that hard? A rich farm like that and no work?'

'We did not notice that it was a rich farm. We saw only a farm and hoped there was work available.'

'Weren't you angry when the farmer told you there was none?' It was Fethmac who posed the question.

'Why should we be angry?'

'Were you not told there was no work for the likes of you?' the magistrate probed.

'The "likes of us"? You mean because we were seen as vagrants? Those words were not used by the farmer called Adnán but *were* used by the first man we went to – Tadgán. However, in recent months we have become used to the insult.'

'So, let us get this clear,' Fidelma said. 'You are saying that Adnán, while telling you there was no work, suggested that you stay overnight then move the next morning to seek work north along the River Tonnóg. Having said that, you parted company on good terms and did not see them again. All this, in spite of the fact that you were desperate?'

'The farmer and his wife were kind,' Fial insisted. 'The woman, his wife, brought to me a pitcher of milk, fresh from the morning's milking, for little Ennec. She also gave us two bannocks and a piece of cheese for our supper, along with a sack of oats to sustain us which is still in our wagon. We were saving it for the future journey.'

The young woman looked at them and said passionately, 'I have told you the truth. We were very grateful to them. Why should Celgaire then kill the man, let alone his entire family, when all we received was kindness and generosity?'

'You say that you spent the night on the hillside overlooking the farmhouse. I presume you were asleep throughout the night?'

'Not all the time.' Fial looked down at the babe in her arms, still sleeping soundly. 'Babies are fractious creatures. They cry and need attention at the most awkward times.'

'So you were awoken now and then by the baby?'

'That is what I said.'

'And your husband, was he asleep the whole time?'

'Whenever I awoke to tend to Ennec, Celgaire was asleep at my side. Only once did we rouse him. Driving our wagon over the mountains was an exhausting journey and my husband needed the sleep.'

'You were only disturbed by the baby? You heard no other noises?'

'None.'

'You did not hear anyone approach your wagon, for example?'

'Why would they do that? We have nothing that anyone would want to steal.'

'I see. And so you, who were awake on and off during the night, are certain you heard and saw nothing untoward. And Celgaire did not get up for any period during the night?'

'I am certain of it.'

'And your ox – it remained undisturbed? Sometimes wolves or other animals can attack or disturb oxen.'

'For the last time, lady, there was absolutely no disturbance during the night.'

'Very well.' Fidelma addressed Fethmac. 'Take Fial and her baby back to Gobánguss' wife.'

'Can I see my husband?' the young woman asked.

Fidelma shook her head. 'I need to question him before you speak together.'

'To ensure we do not contradict one another?' the woman asked cynically.

'I am sure you understand,' Fidelma replied without emotion. 'I have a job to do. There is no trick in it if you have told us the truth. And if you have done so, then Celgaire will tell us the same truth.'

Fethmac moved forward to take her arm. Reluctantly, Fial rose and accompanied him. The baby in her arms was still sleeping. They were at the door when Fidelma said, as if in afterthought:

'By the way, did your husband or you own a cleaver for meat or wood?'

Fial actually gave a dry laugh. 'If we had, we could have sold it for food.'

After she had left, Fidelma stretched back in her chair with a deep sigh.

'She told a good story,' Eadulf offered.

'You doubt its validity?'

'Oh, I am sure there is a lot of truth in it – but there is one thing that destroys it.'

'Which is?'

'Why, the cleaver hidden in the wagon.'

'Placed under the wagon,' Fidelma corrected. 'But by whom?'

'I understand why you asked whether she had heard anyone near the wagon that night. Unless it was placed there by witchcraft, then she or her husband would have heard it and yet the woman swears she did not hear anything during the night.'

'Perhaps we will learn more when we question Celgaire.'

Eadulf shrugged. 'I say that the meat cleaver is the most damning piece of evidence. You saw me even rub a piece of damp cloth over the blade and what came away was traces of blood, showing it had been used recently for cutting into flesh.'

Fidelma hastened to challenge him. 'Now if I were opposing that evidence I would say – yes, a cleaver was used in the killing of Adnán. Blood was found on this one? Can you prove that the cleaver was used by Celgaire? And if he did use it, why did he kill Cainnech with the reaping hook? And if he did so, why did he not also hide that weapon in his wagon?'

'Well, one thing is for certain, the itinerants had no meat to butcher,' replied Eadulf hotly. 'Therefore, where did the blood on the cleaver come from? Add to that the fact it was hidden in the wagon . . . well, to my mind – *quod erat demonstrandum*.'

Fidelma smiled sadly. 'But Fial denies that they owned a cleaver.

I do not think that we have proved anything. You are astute, Eadulf. Think about it: there were better hiding places if one was serious. We now learn that this Celgaire was a man of some intelligence before he was exiled and dropped in social status. I think he would have hidden the weapon with more care.'

'It is true the recess was open and someone looking, as I was, could have easily found it,' replied Eadulf. 'That is not to say it exonerates Celgaire. Don't forget, we have the evidence of Lúbaigh.'

'I am not forgetting that,' Fidelma returned. 'However, I think you have overlooked something. Let . . .'

The door burst open with an abruptness which startled them. On the threshold stood the scowling figure of Brother Gadra.

'Last night you said you wanted to speak to me further. I am not one who is to be placed at the beck and call of anyone. I am a busy servant of the Lord.'

Fidelma gazed at him thoughtfully without responding for a moment. Only Eadulf noticed the humour in the corner of her mouth.

'I had no idea that you were so busy,' she said solemnly. 'What occupies your valuable time this day?'

'I am to perform the funeral ceremony of the murdered family of Adnán tonight. Taithlech the merchant has asked me to do so. I am more concerned with the fact that you are proving intent on letting the murderer escape just retribution!'

'I am not sure why the procedures of the law should be of concern to you,' replied Fidelma evenly. 'I believe you are a religieux and part of that duty is to perform the rights of the New Faith even though you follow a different path to what is usually followed in the Five Kingdoms. I presume that the surviving family of Adnán, his cousin, has agreed this with you?'

Brother Gadra's scowl increased. 'Tadgán? A rude unbeliever. He has not contacted me but I am told by Taithlech that he speaks for his cousin, the farmer. Tadgán is no supporter of mine nor believer in the true God. However, I respect Taithlech and so I will do it.'

'I am told that you were treated kindly by Adnán when you arrived in this village. That shelter and hospitality were provided by him. I would have thought it was simple courtesy to repay it to the memory of the man and his family.' As a fuming Brother Gadra was summoning up a reply, Fidelma held up her hand. 'Finally, Brother Gadra, I am not intent on letting the murderer of Adnán and his family escape . . . whoever that person may be. Nor am I intent on letting injustice be done. What I am intent on is letting this matter be considered under the law system of the Five Kingdoms.'

'I demand he be punished under the rules and laws of the True God Whom I represent,' snapped Brother Gadra.

'Tell me, Brother Gadra, and I understand you have been absent a long time in Gaul so have probably forgotten the laws of your homeland, what makes you so certain of the facts in this matter? If you have evidence, then it is your duty to present it to me as *dálaigh*. What makes you demand retribution before someone has been tried? Even the laws you claim to represent do not say "execute first and then have a trial afterwards"!'

'*Apud palet conscidisti* . . . what need of a trial when the case is clear cut?'

'Because we have a system of laws – and without laws we have no civilisation.'

Brother Gadra made an explosive noise with his lips. 'The evidence is clear and we should proceed. *De minimis non curat lex.*'

'So you think we waste time and that the law should not concern itself with small matters when everyone is so concerned with retribution for the murder of someone they respected? Tell me, what do you know of our laws? Or do you even remember them?'

'I only know that they are shackles of our pagan past and the sooner they are dispensed with, the better.'

'I ask again for your authority.'

'I am an advocate of the New Faith. I am not without qualification and influence.'

Fidelma returned his belligerent gaze without a change of expression.

'All I know is that you are untutored, or have forgotten the laws of the Five Kingdoms,' she said mildly. 'Your behaviour yesterday was a demonstration of that fact. And now you stand before me trying to defend your actions.'

Brother Gadra's mouth tightened as he attempted to control his anger. 'I am qualified in the law that supersedes all laws.'

'You mean the Canon Laws that some misguided followers of the New Faith have rewritten as what they call the Penitentials?'

Brother Gadra made a cutting gesture with the edge of his right hand.

'In the Five Kingdoms I would hold the sixth grade of the Orders of Wisdom. I am *Saoi Canóine* and have full knowledge of the Canon wisdom of Rome, of the history of the law and faith in the sacred place where it is to be found – in the holy scriptures for all to read as translated by the Blessed Eusebius Hieronymus!'

Fidelma grimaced. 'For all to read? I doubt whether you'll find everyone in the Five Kingdoms able to read the Latin of Eusebius any more than the original Greek texts or even the Aramaic or the Hebrew of the Old Testament. Although those who go to the colleges here are expected to have knowledge of the same.'

Brother Gadra was really angry now.

'My knowledge is based on that of the greatest book available to us, the *Cuilmen*, even to the smallest book called the Ten Words, the Commandments which God gave to Moses. That is all we need to know in life,' he thundered.

Fidelma was now losing patience.

'I suggest you attend to your religious duties, Brother Gadra, and leave the dispensation of the law to those who are appointed to do so. I remind you that, in spite of the arguments from the various councils of bishops and abbots, you still fall under the laws of the Five Kingdoms, as do all the churches and abbeys in this land, for their rights were granted to the religious under the law of the Brehons and *not* under the laws of Rome or from wherever it is you claim your authority. The bishops and abbots are answerable to the Provincial Kings and to the High King for their conduct and for the conduct of their followers. And so, as a *dálaigh* and legal adviser to the King of Muman, my brother, I now tell you to leave well alone or depart from this place, preferably out of this kingdom.'

Eadulf stood amazed as Fidelma delivered this speech in such a cold, incisive way that did not disguise her rising anger. He had never seen her in such a fury. Even Brother Gadra looked shaken. Then, after a moment or two, he composed himself, squaring his shoulders.

'You will have cause to regret this,' he threatened. 'I shall see that your arrogance, lady, is brought to the notice of the Chief Bishop.'

'And you might also see that it is brought before the notice of the Chief Brehon of the Five Kingdoms,' she shot back. 'You will find him at the High King's palace at Tara where I am sure that he, the Chief Bishop and High King will be more than interested in what you have to say, especially after they hear of the events of yesterday. Eadulf, would you show Brother Gadra how to open the door that is behind him?'

Before Eadulf could move, Brother Gadra turned and stormed out, slamming the door behind him.

Eadulf shook his head reprovingly at Fidelma. 'I would say he is a vengeful person,' he commented. 'So take care.'

'Vengeful or not, I know the law,' she replied quietly. 'And I think, from what he has said that I know more of Eusebius Hieronymus' translation of the Holy Book and its meanings than he does. He has little of the spirit of our Old Faith and even less of the New Faith.'

'Let us hope he takes the advice and leaves here,' sighed Eadulf. 'I fear he will continue to be a disruptive influence.'

'Well, let us get back to the matter in hand. We need to continue on and interrogate Celgaire. Has Fethmac returned yet?'

'I thought I saw him speaking with his wife Ballgel outside. I'll go to look.'

'Well, tell them I am now ready to speak with Celgaire.'

When Eadulf returned with Fethmac and the prisoner, Fidelma was seated in her former position on one side of the kitchen table, as she had been when she had interrogated Fial. She indicated for Celgaire to sit in the same chair that his wife had sat in. Eadulf and Fethmac resumed their own seats at the table. There was one difference to Fidelma's previous interrogation. To one side of the table she had now placed a number of inconsequential items as if they had been shifted there to make space for her to use the rest of it for her interrogation purposes. But Eadulf noticed, lying among them, the piece of cloth in which the cleaver found under Celgaire's wagon had been wrapped. Also on the table was the flat leather *bolg*, or satchel, in which were the pieces of parchment they had found.

Eadulf's eyes flickered to Celgaire. The man appeared to stare at the leather satchel in recognition before returning his gaze to Fidelma.

'Now, Celgaire,' she began, 'you realise that I am asking you questions as a *dálaigh* and therefore I wish you to take an oath that you will answer the questions truthfully to the best of your knowledge.'

There was no hesitation before the man replied he would do so. He had regained his voice and now spoke in the strong accents that they associated with Ulaidh. So having dispensed with the formality Fidelma invited him, firstly, to tell her who he was and where he came from. Prompted by her now and again, Celgaire repeated, with only slight variation, the story that his wife had told her.

'I was born and lived my life in Ulaidh and served as a labourer and man-at-arms on the estate of Blathmac, as had my father and his father before him. Being so, I was of the rank of *sen-cléithe.*'

'But now you are reduced in rank to that of *doir-fuidir*. Why?'

'Because I refused to attend the hosting when Blathmac sought to attack the abbey of Magh-Bhile for not paying tribute to the Dál Fiatach, of which he is prince. I was told by my father that it is a tradition in my family to refuse to fight against a Christian institution – to attack those holding the same Faith as us. My refusal to do so caused the reduction of my status and my exile from the Uí Néill kingdom. So I and my wife became wandering labourers seeking work in other kingdoms.'

'But what of your origins? You spoke of a tradition not to fight fellow Christians?'

'My origins?' Celgaire seemed genuinely puzzled.

'You have to admit that a person with your colouring, the darkness of your skin, would indicate that your ancestors must have come to this land from another country?'

Celgaire shrugged. 'The question has been raised before. The story passed down was that my grandfather's father was a young man come ashore from a trading vessel from Armorica. I only know that we always followed the Faith long before it reached these shores.'

'Armorica?' Eadulf could not help but express his surprise. 'I do not think people with your darkness of skin would be natives to Armorica.'

Fidelma tapped the leather satchel. 'Do you know of these documents in here?'

'They were given me by Prince Blathmac's Brehon when my exile was announced. I have no book learning, so cannot read what is there. All I know is that I am of Ulaidh and that must suffice as to my family's origin.'

'Very well. So after your exile was proclaimed, you and your wife journeyed south to this kingdom seeking labouring work. Is that correct?'

'Correct, lady.'

'Tell me whom you first approached when you came here.'

He confirmed the same story that Fial had given about the encounter with the farmer Tadgán and the advice of a farmworker to seek out Adnán. He said that Adnán had not been able to offer him work, but had advised him to go north to the area of the Tonnóg. Celgaire spoke of the gifts of milk and small sack of oats. In fact, he told the self-same story as his wife, including the giving of permission to stay in the area by the copse.

When the man had finished, Fidelma sat back in her chair and stared thoughtfully at him for a few moments. Celgaire did not lower his gaze. It was a frank gaze without apparent guile or cunning.

Fidelma sighed and then said, 'It is all very well, Celgaire, except for one thing.' She reached to one side, took up the cleaver and placed it before her.

Celgaire stared at it for a moment and then raised his eyes to her face in bewilderment.

'I don't understand,' he said.

'Have you not seen it before?' she demanded.

'I have seen cleavers before. But why do you show me this one?'

Fidelma replied almost flatly, 'This is the cleaver with which those attacks were carried out. Have you anything further to say about it?'

There was a horrified look on the man's face as he protested: 'I have told you, lady, that I did not do this thing that I am accused of. I have told you the truth of what happened. I did not kill anyone, and I have never seen this cleaver before.'

Eadulf had long observed that Fidelma liked to use dramatic

pauses to throw witnesses or suspects off-balance. It was a technique she often practised when presenting her cases before the courts. She used the long pause even now.

Then she said: 'Because, Celgaire of Leth Cathail, the cleaver was found in your wagon; hidden where one was not expected to find it.'

There was a moment's silence before Celgaire sprang up, knocking his chair over backwards. His face was contorted.

'Lies! Liar! It is a trick! That cleaver was never mine nor was it ever in my wagon!'

Eadulf and Fethmac had leaped forward and taken a firm grip on his arms, but he was not fighting them. His body was tense but he just stood before Fidelma quivering as if in shock and anger.

'It is a lie to get me to confess to something I did not do! Lies!'

Fidelma stared at him and then said sharply, 'Compose yourself, Celgaire.'

Eadulf felt the tension drain from the man's body and he went suddenly limp. Eadulf just had time to grab the upturned chair and right it, so that the man collapsed back into it rather than dropping to the floor. Even in this state he kept feverishly muttering, 'Tricks! Lies!'

Fidelma leaned forward and tapped the cleaver with her fore-finger.

'Nevertheless, the fact is that this cleaver was found in the recess under your wagon at the back. We came across it this morning when we were searching the wagon. There is no reason why any of us should lie about this.'

Celgaire tried to regain some composure.

'No reason except that you want me to take the blame for something I have not done. Just because I am an itinerant, a *doir-fuidir* without rights, it is easy for you to blame me!'

'In this matter, Celgaire, you have the same rights as anyone else. You are condemned or exonerated only by the evidence: the evidence alone is the arbiter of your fate. That applies had you been king or bishop; it applies to all from freeman to the *fuidir* or unfree classes.'

'But not to me!' Celgaire replied bitterly. 'That's why that religieux tried to hang me yesterday, to get it over with quickly, so that you people would then resume your lives and not be bothered that the real killer has escaped.'

Eadulf felt bound to interrupt. 'You'll remember that it was Fidelma here who saved your life yesterday.'

Celgaire reared up. 'Saved my life for what?' he said ungratefully. 'To add this figment of legal authority to my death?'

'No one is going to die, Celgaire,' Fidelma said coldly. 'You are tried by the Fénechus, the laws of the Five Kingdoms.'

'And you have made up your mind that I am guilty and planted this cleaver in my wagon to satisfy your conscience.'

Fidelma's eyes were by now a steely blue; all the fiery green seemed to have gone out of them.

'Believe me, Celgaire of Leth Cathail, my conscience is only satisfied when I know that the evidence which I hear is the truth.' She sighed, then drummed her fingers on the table for a moment before saying, 'Fethmac, you and Eadulf may take Celgaire back to Gobánguss' shed. He will remain there as a prisoner until I have reached a conclusion on this matter.'

As Celgaire rose, he demanded: 'Where are my wife and baby? What have you done with them? I want to see them.'

'You will remain separated now until a decision is reached. Be assured that they are being well looked after.' She gestured for them to remove him, and then sat alone, frowning in thought, turning matters over. It was a while before Eadulf returned and found her. He was alone.

'I am afraid the magistrate has been intercepted by our friend Brother Gadra.'

Fidelma groaned. 'If only Enda, or one of my brother's bodyguards were here, I would have that malicious influence run out of this kingdom forthwith. I am afraid Brother Gadra needs to remember the advice of the Blessed Aurelius Ambrosius, the Bishop of Milan, three centuries ago.'

Eadulf raised his brow in query.

'Roughly, it translates: when I am in Milan, I do not fast on Saturday; when I am in Rome, I fast on Saturday.'

Eadulf smiled briefly. 'In other words, respect the local laws and customs and do not impose your own on the inhabitants.'

'It is a failing of certain people, to always try to impose on others their way of thinking.'

'Well,' Eadulf said, seating himself, 'it does not influence our situation. It seems the evidence against Celgaire is clear.'

'You think so?'

'Well, we have Lúbaigh's statement and we found that murder weapon in Celgaire's wagon. What else is there to consider?'

'A question of truth,' replied Fidelma. 'What if Celgaire is being honest when he says he did not know the cleaver was there? That recess was open to anyone, remember.'

Eadulf frowned. 'There was no opportunity. His wife said that during the night no one could have approached the wagon without her hearing, so the cleaver could not have been planted at that time. Remember, Lúbaigh said that Aoife was killed while apparently preparing the breakfast, by which time Celgaire and his wife had set off to Tonnóg. There was no opportunity to plant the cleaver by anyone else before the wagon was overtaken.'

'But opportunities were there *after* the wagon was overtaken,' Fidelma pointed out.

'What – you mean that someone broke into Gobánguss' barn and put it there then?'

'Perhaps. There was one other opportunity. When the magistrate and his men brought the wagon back and were attacked by the mob, one person took over the driving of the wagon and remained with it most of the time before he was ordered to give it into Gobánguss' safekeeping.'

Eadulf waited for her to say the name.

'Lúbaigh,' Fidelma murmured softly.

ChAPTER SIX

When Fethmac re-entered the kitchen, he had a broad smile on his face. 'Well, that is that!' he exclaimed triumphantly.

Fidelma raised one eyebrow. 'What do you refer to?' she asked.

'Why, your interrogation of Celgaire. Of course he is guilty. He can't dispute the evidence.'

'I thought that was exactly what he was disputing,' she replied dryly.

The young magistrate seated himself and his confident expression turned into one of uncertainty.

'Oh come now, lady. After that, you cannot say that he has a defence, surely? I thought you would now make the charge official.'

'The evidence must be secure. In other words, there must be no doubts.'

'The evidence *is* there; the cleaver was found in the wagon,' asserted the young man.

'It could have been put there by another hand.'

'Ah, but that claim does not hold water.'

'Unless you can show me that no one else could have placed it there other than Celgaire, then there is still doubt.'

'Such little doubt that we can discount it.'

'But the evidence must be beyond any doubt at all,' Fidelma repeated. 'Are you saying, Fethmac, that you are prepared to find someone guilty of these murders based on dismissal of doubt however big or little?'

The young man looked troubled. 'And are you just prepared to accept Celgaire's word?'

Fidelma shook her head. 'I am prepared to investigate the doubt until it no longer becomes a doubt,' she replied.

'How do you intend to proceed?' Fethmac asked, sounding deflated. 'Are you going to examine those parchments that he had hidden? Surely there is something there? I suppose he stole them from somewhere and intended to sell them. Parchment alone can be costly and I am told some scribes have the ability to clean and reuse them.'

'I have looked at them but cannot be entirely sure of the nuances of the contents,' Fidelma admitted. 'I shall make a trip to the abbey at Ard Fhionáin as soon as I can because I know there is a scholar there named Brother Solam, who can transcribe them. One document I am fairly certain of, since it is written in the *bérla na filed* form of our language. It is the judgement given on Celgaire for refusing to fight on the grounds of his Christian belief. So that part of his story is true.'

'I knew of Brother Solam when I studied at the abbey,' Fethmac revealed. 'Are we to go there now?'

'Not immediately. I want to check the motive of others.'

'What others?' he asked. 'What motives?'

'The main fact that worries me is that I cannot accept the motive that has been offered for Celgaire to slaughter this entire family.'

'We have heard two totally opposing versions of what happened. Lúbaigh's version points the finger at Celgaire,' Eadulf said. 'Yet if one accepts Celgaire and his wife's version, there was no motive at all.'

'So it is Lúbaigh's word against Celgaire's,' Fethmac concluded.

'Exactly.' Fidelma sighed. 'Why would refusal of work be enough to stir someone into such a rage as to slaughter a family in this violent fashion? Celgaire had been refused work in harsher terms from the neighbouring farmer, Tadgán. Why did Celgaire not turn and kill him, if we are saying this motive is valid?'

Fethmac rubbed his face. 'The fact is that he did not,' he eventually replied. 'We are not dealing with what might have been but what is. It was Adnán and his family who were murdered.'

'Both Celgaire and his wife agree that Adnán was regretful about having to turn them away, and that he and Aoife were kind and helpful to them in every way. So where is the motive?'

'That is only if you accept their word for it,' Fethmac grunted. 'Don't forget that even the name Celgaire means "the deceiver".'

'The meaning of names is not evidence.' Fidelma was a little annoyed that her own hobby was being used against her.

'Then if you believe Celgaire and his wife,' the magistrate pondered aloud, 'it means that you do not believe . . .' His eyes widened as he realised the implication.

'It is not that I believe Lúbaigh is lying,' Fidelma said. 'However, someone is. Lúbaigh's version is at odds with that of Celgaire and his wife. So we must question Lúbaigh further and see if there is a way of resolving this anomaly.'

'But why would Lúbaigh lie in this matter?'

Fidelma smiled thinly. 'To answer that is what an investigation is for. Was it not Cicero who declared: *quare; omnia quaestio difficillima* – "why" is the most difficult question of all. If only we could see into the minds of people to ascertain why their behaviour is so aberrant at times . . . Anyway, our task is to pursue the questions until we find acceptable answers. The first question is whether it is Lúbaigh or Celgaire and his wife who are telling the truth.'

Fethmac looked worried. 'I have to say that the people here are in a very volatile state. You saw yesterday how they were demanding justice and would not even listen to me.'

'Justice? They were demanding vengeance, having been whipped into a bloodlust frenzy. Are you saying they have not learned their lesson and calmed down?'

Fethmac shrugged. 'I am saying that Adnán was respected by the people of Cloichín and, having been informed that the vagrant had slaughtered Adnán and his family, they are naturally resentful because there is a delay in his punishment. What's more, we have this Father Gadra . . .'

'Brother Gadra,' corrected Fidelma patiently.

'Whatever,' shrugged Fethmac. 'He is a teacher of the faith, but also he talks much about these new laws from Rome and calls our system pagan and ungodly. That does not help quiet the minds of local people.'

Eadulf frowned at the young magistrate but addressed his remarks to Fidelma. 'If Fethmac is saying that he, as magistrate, cannot control his people, then I would be happier if a *Deirchenborach* of your brother's bodyguards, the Nasc Niadh, were here.'

A company of ten warriors of the Golden Collar, the élite body-guard to the Kings of Cashel, would certainly be an asset for ensuring there were no more outrages such as the one they had witnessed on the previous day.

Fethmac flushed angrily at this criticism of his ability.

'Yesterday was unexpected. I am prepared now,' he said stiffly.

'Even so,' Fidelma smiled thinly, 'I admit that it might make me feel a little more secure.'

'Anyway, do we get Lúbaigh in for an interrogation?' Fethmac spoke brusquely, his annoyance apparent.

'Not immediately,' replied Fidelma. 'First, tell me what you know about him. I presume he was born and raised in this village? Therefore you should know him and his background well.'

'Yes, he was born here as was his younger brother, Dulbaire. Their mother was a local woman who died when she gave birth to Dulbaire. The father was a *ceile*, a clansman of full rights.' He paused abruptly. 'I recall that their father was not of Cloichín but of the Fir Maige Mhór.'

'From where?'

'Oh, somewhere up in the mountains to the south. I did not know him well and he died even before I left for my study at the abbey of Ard Fhionáin. I think I heard he was from around the Hill of Bones on the eastern side of Declan's Way as you travel through the mountains.'

'Why did he come to Cloichín?'

'That I don't know. To marry, perhaps.'

'But he was a *ceile*, a man with full rights?'

'Oh, to be sure. He was a merchant, so I recall, and owned the cabin that Dulbaire now occupies.'

'So how did the sons of a merchant become labourers on Adnán's farm?'

'Lúbaigh, the elder, was not a lucky person. And his younger brother Dulbaire was, as you have seen, a little . . .' He paused, looking for the right word.

'Simple?' suggested Eadulf.

'Let us say that he was not as fast as some and was quite happy herding cows, sheep and pigs. Adnán was generous with both of them.'

'Let us speak about Lúbaigh. Did he resent the change from being the son of a merchant to becoming a farm labourer?'

'I think he was probably happy to avoid having no source of income at all. Anyway, he has been with Adnán for five years and was very content there.'

Eadulf was thoughtful. 'You know,' he ventured, 'having questioned him once of the facts, it will be difficult to question him further without actually accusing him of something. His statement stands in such clear contradiction to Celgaire's that new questions would imply we suspect him of lying. If we do that, it means we are accusing him of the murder.'

Fidelma had already considered the matter.

'You are right, Eadulf. It is annoying but the fact is we will just have to be more surreptitious in eliciting further information out of Lúbaigh.'

'He could have simply made a wrong conclusion,' Fethmac suggested. 'After all, he admits he didn't witness the murders but merely assumed that Celgaire was in the right place at the right time to have carried them out.'

'You are overlooking one point,' Fidelma said. 'That is the motive that he ascribes to Celgaire. He says Adnán refused him a job and they had an angry exchange. Celgaire claims the opposite and he and his wife each say they were given milk and that bag of oats, and advice on where to go to get a likely job. So that is where the differences in evidence lie. It has nothing to do with supposition.'

Eadulf nodded agreement. 'Yet if we accept Celgaire's statement, backed up by his wife – although we can discount the wife's evidence as biased in favour of Celgaire – then . . .'

'There is a point on Lúbaigh's side that must not be overlooked,' Fethmac reminded them both.

'Which is?' Eadulf asked.

'He thought the murder weapon was a reaping hook. Eadulf showed it was only one killing in which a reaping hook was used. The others had been done by a cleaver – the same cleaver that we found in Celgaire's wagon.'

'It is a good point, Fethmac. That question would raise another. If Celgaire is innocent, who put the cleaver in his wagon?'

'But it could also mean Celgaire is guilty,' Fethmac said with a little triumph in his voice. 'That is what I think.'

'It only means there is confusion,' Eadulf ended with a sigh.

'It is our task to remove the confusion,' Fidelma said stoically. 'We still need to talk with Lúbaigh but, as I have said, to do so in a more stealthy way. At the moment the only motive we can identify is an alleged act of madness by Celgaire. I think we must exhaust motives by questioning all those connected with Adnán's farm. So that Lúbaigh will not feel singled out, let us start with his brother Dulbaire and the girl – what was her name – Íonait? What do we know about her?'

At that moment Ballgel, Fethmac's wife, arrived back to reclaim her kitchen.

'Íonait?' she echoed, overhearing the name as she entered. 'Why do you want to know about her?'

'I am trying to learn of her relationship with Adnán's farm,' Fidelma answered as Ballgel placed her basket to one side and took off her *fola*, a heavy woollen shawl, much needed at this cold time of year.

Ballgel sniffed disdainfully, 'Well, she seems to have suffered no ill effects from the events at the farmstead. In fact, I have just seen her and she tells me that Tadgán has already arrived at the farmstead to look over his new property.'

'He hasn't wasted much time,' observed Fethmac sourly. 'And his cousin not yet buried.'

Ballgel had taken her basket to the small *cuile*, the larder, for she had been out to get cuts of meat from a local farm.

'So what do you wish to know about Íonait?' she asked Fidelma.

'What can you tell me? Do you know her well?'

'Everyone knows everyone in a village like this. But why are you particularly interested in her?'

'It is just that she worked on Adnán's farm and I want to get an overall picture of the situation. I thought it might be wise if I knew a little about her. She seemed apprehensive when she heard that Tadgán was going to take over the farm.'

Ballgel grimaced. 'There is no secret to that. She lives with her mother. She is only a year over the age of choice.'

'They live where?' interposed Fidelma.

'A cottage just on the eastern outskirts of the village.'

'Do you know how long she has been working at Adnán's farm?'

'As soon as she was old enough to do so, from the age of fourteen years. Since her father died. That was only a year ago.'

'You said there was no secret why the girl was apprehensive about Tadgán taking over the farm,' Fidelma reminded her.

It was Fethmac who now added further details. 'Her father, Broc, was a *muccaid* – a swineherd. He was killed, having had the misfortune to be attacked and gored by a particularly aggressive boar. Several sows were on heat and Broc got in his way.'

'Usually a trained swineherd would know the dangerous behaviour of bulls and be able to avoid such attacks,' Fidelma observed.

Fethmac shrugged. 'I know the story well. Broc was indeed an experienced Swineherd, but the boar was a new animal and this was the first time Broc had encountered it. He saw the boar coming at him but the ground was muddy and churned up. He slipped as he tried to get out of the way. The enraged boar attacked him as he tried to regain his balance. He didn't stand a chance. A horrible death!'

'This was on Adnán's farm?' queried Eadulf.

'No, he worked for Tadgán,' Fethmac replied. 'Íonait's father, Broc, had worked as swineherd on his farm for many years.'

'Then how did Broc not know the nature of this boar?'

'That is because Tadgán had only just bought the animal from another farmer. He brought it to the farm and placed it in a small field, but had no time to give a warning to Broc.'

'Or so he said,' added Ballgel.

'There is doubt?'

'I was the magistrate who judged the claims for compensation for the death,' Fethmac explained, after giving his wife a frown. 'The claim was the usual honour price for a *saer-fuidir*, which was his social rank. Tadgán claimed that because Broc had acquired unpaid loans from him over the years, he need only offer four *screpalls*. In the end, Broc's wife Blinne was forced to take in mending and washing in order to maintain the rent of the cottage they had and to which Tadgán laid claim. That's why Íonait had to go and work on Adnán's farm.'

'It is interesting that she went to work milking cows for Tadgán's cousin and not for Tadgán – and that maybe explains why she is apprehensive of him.'

Fethmac smiled thinly. 'There was bad blood between Blinne and Tadgán after the compensation was settled. Blinne claimed that there was no such debt but Tadgán presented me with evidence so I could do nothing but judge according to law.'

'What was the evidence?'

'A written document signed and witnessed giving details of the sum to which Broc was in debt.'

'Signed and witnessed?'

'Faced with that, the matter was clear,' the magistrate nodded.

'This was shown to Blinne?'

'She denied it, of course. She pointed out that her husband had no knowledge of writing. That was true. There's no need for a swineherd to possess such knowledge.'

'But you said it was signed and witnessed,' Eadulf objected.

'He signed with a mark, which was duly witnessed. And Tadgán also signed.'

'Who witnessed it?'

'The local merchant, Taithlech.'

'The same Taithlech whose name has been spoken of several times? The friend of Lúbaigh and the father of the wife of Tadgán's son?'

'It is not unusual that people often are prominent in various ways in a village as small as this,' Fethmac said. 'He had known Broc all his life. There was nothing suspicious about it. Taithlech was there when Broc made his mark and the sum was witnessed. In fact, there was no argument. Blinne was lucky to keep the cottage, for the sum of the debt outweighed the sum of any compensation.'

'So Blinne took in washing and her daughter, Íonait, became a milkmaid at Adnán's farm? You told me there was bad blood between Tadgán and Adnán. I suppose Adnán giving support to Blinne's daughter did not help the relationship between the cousins,' Eadulf mused.

'Maybe not,' admitted Fethmac. 'But the main conflict between the cousins started over the matter of borders, as I mentioned before.'

'We started off by hearing that Adnán was so highly regarded that no one wished him harm, but now we learn he had at least one enemy here and that was his own cousin,' Fidelma said.

'But he is not such an enemy to have carried out this senseless slaughter of all his relatives,' protested Fethmac. 'I believe we were right in the first place. The culprit is the vagrant.'

'You may well be right, but as a senior *dálaigh*, I need to verify all aspects before a verdict is pronounced. There is something here that worries me . . .' She paused with a frown. 'We will go to clarify a few facts with Íonait.'

'Well,' interceded Ballgel, 'you must first sit down and partake of the *rith-etir*.'

Eadulf was confused by the term 'middle running'. Fethmac noticed and smiled sympathetically. 'You might not have come across the local term, Brother Eadulf. It is usually called the *eter-shod*, the middle meal of the day.'

Ballgel explained, 'Just something light, for the sun has passed its zenith.' She compressed her lips for a moment. 'I nearly forgot – I met Taithlech and he confirms that the burial will take place tonight at our *reilic*, the burial ground.'

'At what time?' asked Fidelma.

Ballgel shrugged. 'The customary hour of midnight. I expect most of the village will turn out.'

'And we too must attend,' Fethmac added.

'So we must,' Fidelma said softly.

Blinne's cottage lay on a low-lying, very fertile piece of land shaped like an arrow head, with the River Duthóg on the south side and the River Teara to the north. At the tip of the arrow the two rivers joined. The area was fairly secluded, with the cabin surrounded by hardy and durable yew trees. Groundsel and weak straggling chick-weed covered the ground in dull green colours. Eadulf thought it was strange, how noisy and discordant the sound of the rushing waters was of the two rivers, even though the cabin was not right close to where the two streams met before tumbling eastward into the great River Suir below the abbey of Ard Fhionáin. A dog started to bark as they approached the cabin and a woman emerged from the door to chastise it. Catching sight of the visitors, she turned and stood before her door with large fleshy arms folded across her bosom. She had a heavy, almost dumpy figure; her neck had long since descended into layers of double chins, and her eyes were like tiny gimlets sunk into folds. As for her lips, they were a thin line of red underneath a bulbous nose. The whole was topped with dirty grey hair. Uncombed, it spread in wild confusion, shifting this way and that as the slight winds caught it. Those present could see no resemblance between the slight, attractive figure of Íonait and this unkempt woman, whom they now supposed was her mother, Blinne.

'You are not welcome here, Fethmac,' she shouted as they reached her gate, which was set in the wooden fence that surrounded the cottage. The small garden was well tended, which Eadulf saw must be a considerable help, with root vegetables and fruit supplying food during the spring and summer.

'She still blames me for the lack of compensation,' Fethmac muttered to Fidelma before raising his voice, saying, 'we have come to see your daughter, Blinne.'

The woman did not move, and her voice was hostile when she spoke.

'She has gone back to Adnán's farm at the request of its new lord.'

'Then we would like a few words with you, Blinne,' called Fidelma.

The woman glared at Fidelma and Fethmac spoke hurriedly. 'This is Fidelma of Cashel. She is not only a *dálaigh* but . . .'

'I know well who she is! Sister to the King who we never see but who demands tributes from a poor old woman like me or, when my man was alive, would expect him to answer the call to a hosting, if an enemy was attacking. Expecting him to give his life – for what? Oh yes, I have heard what brings Fidelma of Cashel to Cloichín.' Her voice was hard with bitterness. 'It was not to see justice done when my man was killed nor to admit the fault behind his death. Indeed, no one spoke up for him; instead, lies were told about him – a man who never owed a *screpall* in his life. No, this fine lady has come because a rich farmer was killed.'

'You are wrong, Blinne,' Fidelma said firmly. 'I was passing here when I found this community about to lynch a man, and I stayed to reassert the law.'

'The law for the rich farmer and not for my man,' snapped the woman.

'For your man also, if he was the victim of injustice under the law.'

'Ah, that is a clever twist of words, lady. You can do much with that word "if". I say my man was a victim both in his physical death and the death of his reputation.'

'Did you appeal when you disagreed with the verdict that the magistrate delivered based on the evidence before him?'

The woman frowned and then the sardonic tone came back into her voice.

'Appeal? Who would I appeal to? He is the judge.' She jerked her head towards Fethmac.

Fidelma glanced at the magistrate who was now red faced with embarrassment.

'I presume you did explain this matter of appeal?' she asked.

'I did, but—'

Fidelma cut him short. 'The situation is that the magistrate, who is the judge who decides a case in law, must deposit a sum to the value of five ounces of silver, as a surety in case of dispute about his judgement. If the litigant, that is yourself, is dissatisfied with his judgement and wishes to get the case re-examined by a judge of higher rank, then they may do so.'

She turned back to Fethmac. 'I hope you did make that pledge, for you know that if you did not, then you become debarred from further practice in the territory.'

'I did everything according to the law,' protested the young man.

'Then that is good. However, I see no reason why I should not re-examine this matter, as part of my current investigation here – and if I come to a judgement then I shall also be bound by a similar pledge if you appeal against me, Blinne.'

Even Eadulf was amazed at this but presumed that these were words to win the belligerent woman over. However, Blinne was watching her with suspicion.

'I have no five ounces of silver, lady,' she said slowly.

'You will not need them. For the moment, I require you to answer some questions and I suggest that it might be more comfortable for all of us to seek the warmth of your cabin, rather than stand out here in the cold.'

Blinne hesitated and then shrugged her large shoulders, unfolded her arms and stood aside.

'You are welcome to come in,' she said, although the words were hardly those of a convivial host.

They entered and were thankful to feel the comforting warmth of the wood fire blazing in the hearth. There were not seats enough for all to sit so Fethmac and Eadulf remained standing while Fidelma sat and motioned the woman to be seated before her.

'Before anything,' Fidelma began, 'I want to know how your daughter is after the shock of the discovery of her murdered employers. I would like to question her about the matter.'

'She fares well enough.'

'I hear she has been the milkmaid at the farm for a year.'

'A good year and happy at her work until recently.'

'Until recently?'

'I will allow her to tell you. The fact is, she was intending to leave and seek work elsewhere.'

'Tadgán has already gone to take over the farm,' Fidelma went on. 'I suppose that is not an inducement for her to stay?'

Blinne sniffed. 'No inducement at all but the opposite. Anyway, my daughter would have left before. They are all the same, that family!'

'You dislike both Tadgán and his cousin Adnán?'

When there was no answer, Fidelma pressed on: 'Where is your daughter now?'

'At the farm.'

'Why has she gone there now? The cows had been milked this morning when I saw her.'

'Lúbaigh felt she should go there, as well as Dulbaire, his brother, when he heard Tadgán was coming to take over the place, so they could all hear what Tadgán intended. But it will make no difference now, even if he wants to keep her on as milkmaid.'

'I am not sure that I follow you.'

'I mean that Íonait does not want to continue to work there, especially after the way Tadgán treated us after her father was killed.'

'I can understand your dislike for him, but you also expressed a dislike for Adnán. And yet I am told that everyone, except Tadgán, liked and respected him.'

The woman snorted. 'That family were all spawned from the same womb, each as bad as the other. There is corruption and evil throughout that entire family.'

'I understand your antipathy towards Tadgán but surely, Adnán gave your daughter employment?' intervened Fethmac. 'Why are you angry towards someone to whom you should be grateful?'

'Why should I be grateful for that? He had his reasons,' Blinne said darkly. 'All I say is – a widow's curse on him, and may hell's seventeen demons make a ladder of his spine and splinters from his legs!'

Fidelma's eyes widened at the intensity of the old curse and then shook her head at the magistrate as he was about to respond. Here was a secret hate which needed to be coaxed out rather than confronted – but now was not the time to do it. She changed the subject.

'Regarding your disagreement with Tadgán, how can you be sure that your husband was not in debt?'

For a moment Blinne glowered at her before saying, 'We had no secrets between us. Broc took pride that he was never in debt and he would rather us go without if the fish were not running in that stream or if the ground here did not provide enough of its fruits. Unlike some, he never asked for oats or grains or anything from Tadgán's farm other than what was due in payment for his labour.'

'Yet I am told that a friend of his, Taithlech, was Tadgán's principal witness for this debt and Taithlech swore to it, witnessing the debt and your husband's mark in agreement.'

'All I can say is that Taithlech was a liar.'

'That is hard to prove,' Fethmac interposed. 'I had to warn you before that if you continued to repeat that statement, you were liable to severe fines.'

Fidelma turned to the young magistrate. 'What Blinne tells me, in response to my questions, is privileged. She is putting her side of the argument during my re-evaluation of your judgement.'

Fethmac was clearly annoyed, however. 'I resent having my judgement challenged.'

'You should have learned by now that a lawyer is not entitled to the egocentricity of resentment when his word is challenged,' she observed coldly.

'This matter is over a year old!' he protested. 'No one has challenged it until you did.'

'I did not challenge it,' Fidelma told him in an even tone. 'I only pointed out to Blinne that it had been, and still is, her right to express her dissatisfaction with the judgement.'

'She did not challenge it—'

'That's a lie!' the woman said hotly. 'I protested.'

'But you did not legally challenge it,' Fethmac replied.

Fidelma shook her head sadly. 'Fethmac, let us put this matter in perspective. Blinne here protested at your judgement. That is her right. She does not seem aware that she should have been provided with advice on how to make her protest into a legal one and find another arbiter to assess your judgement.'

'It is not my task to challenge my own judgements,' Fethmac replied sullenly.

'But it is the task of all under the law we acknowledge to advise litigants how the law stands and how they should respond. I presume that this village is regularly visited on a circuit by a member of the Council of Brehons of the kingdom? In which case, during their visit, Blinne should have been able to present her case.'

Fethmac seemed about to respond, thought better of it and shrugged. He realised that Fidelma had full authority over him in law. In other circumstances he knew that he would have been flattered that she was working with him. On her part, she was well aware that a young man's vanity often proved a barrier to logic and so hoped he would not pursue the matter.

'I will have a talk with Taithlech,' Fidelma assured Blinne. 'We will see whether there are any concerns that need to be raised over this matter. His name has cropped up several times.'

'It is not surprising since we are a small rural community,' interposed Fethmac.

Blinne made an ugly grimace. 'Then remember, at the same time as Taithlech proclaimed his friendship for my husband Broc, his daughter, Flannat, had married Tadgán's son. He would never put at risk his position, or his daughter's position. He bore false witness because he needed to ingratiate himself with Tadgán.'

'This was an argument Blinne put forward at the time,' Fethmac said before Fidelma could make a comment. 'For her own sake, I dismissed it immediately.'

'Why would you do that?' Fidelma wondered.

'I know the *Bretha Nemed Déidenach,* the law on these things. Publicising an untrue story about another person is a verbal assault and must be treated with utmost gravity: it requires payment of the victim's honour price. In Taithlech's position that would be a fine of the equivalent to eight cows. I did it for her daughter's sake as much as finding the correct judgement.'

'For Íonait's sake? I presume that you mean if Blinne lost her case and became destitute, she and Íonait would have no shelter over their heads? I also presume that you did enquire into whether personal gain prompted Taithlech's involvement?'

'What was there to enquire into? Taithlech's word of honour was accepted. Everyone knew that his daughter, Flannat, had married Tadgán's son, Díoma. Unfortunately, Díoma died of fever a few years ago, leaving a young son. Tadgán looked after Flannat and the boy. So he and Taithlech were no strangers. Everyone knows that Taithlech did business with Tadgán. Taithlech had been a friend of Broc as well and so his input was a neutral one.'

Blinne muttered something under her breath.

'Did Taithlech also do business with Adnán?' Fidelma asked, feeling that the interrogation was getting out of hand.

The magistrate hesitated. 'Not as far as I am aware.'

Blinne gave a short, sharp laugh.

'Adnán would never do business with him, not after the argument they had.'

Fidelma's eyes narrowed. 'An argument?'

'Yes, a vicious one. Íonait told me. She had witnessed the last moments of it. She heard raised voices when she came from milking the cows, and at the corner of the stables she saw Adnán waving his fists at Taithlech and heard the merchant shouting as he mounted his horse and rode away.'

'What was he shouting?'

Blinne grimaced. 'Only that he would kill Adnán if the farmer tried to stop his trade.'

There was a silence for some time. Then Fidelma glanced at Fethmac and said, 'It looks as though your Garden of Eden begins to fill with snakes. The more I hear, it seems that not everyone loved Adnán as you and others have tried to persuade me.'

The young magistrate scowled. 'What people say in anger over business is not pertinent to the facts of this matter.'

'No? Perhaps. But I believe it to be something that should be considered in the case. I will do so later. In the matter of Broc, however, I would say that it is *not* publicising an untrue story unless you have endorsed it by proclaiming it as fact. Are you saying that you did so?'

'I could not allow Blinne to say as much during the official hearing, for she would be proclaiming it in law.'

'Not so, my young colleague. And even if she had publicised it and it were found to be untrue, she could always make a public retraction which I am sure, when faced with paying compensation to the value of eight cows, she would have done.'

Fethmac had reddened with mortification.

'At most,' Fidelma commented with a sigh, 'it makes the testimony of Taithlech a little less watertight than the testimony of a person who was a long-term friend of Broc. Yes, we will have a word with Taithlech about his motivations.'

Blinne was looking at Fidelma with a little more respect now.

'The sky is darkening, lady,' she ventured in a tone that had become polite. 'Can I offer you a cup of dandelion wine? I make it myself.'

Fidelma shook her head. 'Another time, perhaps.' She rose from the chair. 'As you remark, the daylight is fast fading. It has been a long, tiring day, and I, for one, will need some rest before the funeral ceremony at midnight. I presume we shall see you and Íonait then?'

Blinne almost exploded. 'What? Not I! Nor will you see my daughter.'

'Your hatred of Tadgán is such that it encompasses Adnán – the man who gave your daughter work?' Eadulf asked, repeating Fethmac's remark of earlier.

'Have I not said that they are spawns of the same sow? A sow who did not know the boar of her kindred.' She ran a hand through her tangled grey hair and hissed: 'May they all suffer the red diarrhoea and may six ox wagons of graveyard clay cover all and each one of them. I have already given their souls to the devil!'

Eadulf had never heard such vehemence expressed before and was surprised that it came from the mouth of a woman.

'I have come to understand your hatred to some extent, Blinne,' Fidelma said, as they prepared to leave the cabin, 'but I cannot see why your daughter should not attend this funeral, save that she owes loyalty to you. After all, as I have said, Adnán and his family gave your daughter employment milking their cows.'

The response shocked them. Blinne started to laugh, harshly at first, the tone rising into an hysterical screaming. The unearthly sound was still ringing in their ears as they left the cabin, even drowning out the rushing waters of the rivers' confluence as the three visitors made their way back to the village along the darkening path.

CHAPTER SEVEN

'Aren't you being a little harsh with young Fethmac?' Eadulf asked as he and Fidelma sat resting before the funeral in the room Ballgel had given them. 'After all, we are guests in his home and he is your fellow lawyer.'

Fidelma turned to him with an expression that held both amusement and rebuke.

'I should remind you that hospitality is an obligation in this country, and certainly not one that imposes requirements of a *dálaigh* to overlook any professional action that they might find questionable. I should also remind you that Fethmac only holds the degree of *Fursaintidh*, having studied law for only four years at Ard Fhionáin . . .'

'I know, I know,' interrupted Eadulf wearily. 'You hold the degree of *Anruth*, only one below the highest degree one can obtain in this land, having studied eight years at Brehon Morann's law school at Tara. I have heard that enough times.'

'I was going to say that unless young Fethmac is prepared to take some instruction from someone of greater experience and knowledge, then he will be a failure in his profession,' Fidelma added, irritated by his monotone addition.

Eadulf persisted. 'Fidelma, it is not what you tell him but the manner in which he is told.'

Her brow darkened further. 'You are questioning my manner?'

He knew how to defuse her threatening look, saying gently, 'I know that you are aware of your faults. You admit that you can often be severe with people. By all means point out where you disagree with Fethmac, but do it as a mother guides a child, just as you do with our son Alchú, when he goes astray. You do not do that in a dictatorial way.'

Fidelma did not relax her expression immediately but as Eadulf smiled infectiously at her, she eventually smiled back, a little ruefully.

'All right. I shall be more considerate. He is inexperienced and in need of guidance, but I shall try not to upset him.'

Eadulf detected a hint of mockery in the last few words.

'If you were correcting him in law,' he went on, 'I was surprised that you didn't raise the matter of "The Right of Corpses" in this case. I know it is there to save the family of a dead man from destitution in case he died in debt. Wouldn't that apply in Broc's case? Even if her man was in debt when he was killed, Blinne should have been given something to sustain her.'

Fidelma regarded him in surprise. 'What do you know of "The Right of Corpses"?'

'Old Brother Conchobhar at Cashel introduced it to me. Doesn't it say that every dead body has its right to a cow, a horse, and a garment and the furniture of its bed – and that these shall not be paid in satisfaction of his debts because they are the special property of his body?'

Fidelma gazed at him fondly. 'You are certainly learning some of the laws of the Five Kingdoms, Eadulf. But you overlook one thing: this rule applies only to the higher ranks in our society, the *flaith*, the noble, and the *céile,* the full-citizen. Poor Broc was a *saer-fuidir* and thus the law did not apply to him.'

'That is unfair.'

'Of course, it is unfair. That is the nature of most societies that

I have encountered. But do the slaves among your own people, the Angles or the Saxons, have any rights at all? They have no *wergild*, as you call it – no worth.'

'That is true. Anyway,' went on Eadulf, changing the subject slightly, 'you have taken over the investigation of this multiple murder. For that, Fethmac seems grateful for he did not have enough authority to face down Brother Gadra. I think the young man's heart is in the right place so I cannot see why you had to criticise him in front of that crazy woman.'

'In front of Blinne? Perhaps she is a little crazy. However, the situation was that I needed to get some information from her, regarding her dislike of Tadgán but especially about Adnán. I felt that by saying that I would re-examine the case she lost against Tadgán, and pointing certain things out, to get her on my side, it would make her relax sufficiently to tell me.'

'You mean that you made up those criticisms of Fethmac's conduct of the case merely to win Blinne round – to make her believe that you were her friend and get her to tell you what you wanted to know?' Eadulf was aghast.

'Eadulf, surely you know me better than that! Those were genuine points that needed raising. Otherwise I would not have done so.'

'Well, I think you should have done it in some other way; a more diplomatic way. In the end, it did not seem to help much, did it!'

'On the contrary,' Fidelma returned, 'I think it has opened some new facets to this case.'

'It only told us why she disliked Tadgán. What else emerged? Anything of relevance to do with the murders?'

'It told us that she hated Adnán and his family – but *why*? Her daughter had worked for that family for a year. Why did this hatred suddenly erupt now? Why did her daughter decide to leave her job at the farm just at the time of the murders? Or was there a grievance that was festering for a long time?'

Eadulf stretched back on the bed, hands behind his head. 'Blinne was certainly vehement about both Tadgán and his cousin Adnán,' he conceded. 'I have never heard such curses uttered before.'

'Well, young Fethmac wasn't able to enlighten us on our return here, was he?'

Fidelma had taken the opportunity, after they left Blinne's cabin, to ask the young magistrate if he knew any reason why the woman hated Adnán as well as Tadgán. Fethmac had confessed to total ignorance. Indeed, he said that, apparently, Blinne had previously expressed gratitude to Adnán for giving her daughter a job milking his small herd. At that time, there appeared no animosity at all. Fethmac had been just as shocked as Fidelma and Eadulf when the woman had exploded with her expressions of hatred.

'He too felt that this hatred was a recent change in the woman,' Eadulf agreed. 'But what caused that change?'

'The only person who can tell us that will be Íonait herself,' Fidelma concluded. 'No doubt it is directly linked with why the girl decided to leave Adnán's employment.'

'At least we have proved one thing,' Eadulf sighed.

'Which is?'

'That Fethmac, our young magistrate friend, has told us something that is patently untrue.'

'Explain.'

'According to him, Adnán and his family were universally loved and respected by everyone in this place.'

'I would have thought that much was obvious by the fact that they were all brutally killed,' Fidelma replied with quiet irony.

At that moment there was knock on the door and, after a moment, Fethmac entered.

'I am told the grave diggers have finished their task and soon the mourners will be gathering for the traditional *uath-fecht*, the grave walk,' he announced solemnly.

'So soon?' queried Fidelma.

'Tadgán has dispensed with the *fled cro-lige* – the funeral feast

– and it is obvious that he feels no need for the period of watching the corpses, due to the circumstances of the deaths.'

Eadulf knew it was a custom for members of a family to spend a day or a night watching over their dead relative before burial.

'What of the proclamation of the *audacht*, the Will?' he asked.

Fethmac made a gesture with his shoulder; a half shrug. 'It will be a simple formality to announce it at the graveside. As I have said, Tadgán is the only inheritor of the kin-land, so it is a straight-forward matter.'

'I presume Tadgán and his family will escort the bodies to the grave?'

'That's right. They will bring them from the farmstead on a wagon hauled by oxen. Because of that, only Tadgán and his family will escort the wagon. Will you and Brother Eadulf come now, lady? The people are gathering.'

She glanced at Eadulf and her expression showed that she did not approve of the truncated procedure of the burial. While Fidelma did not believe in elaborate ceremonial, she did believe in the legal rituals. Ritual was paramount in society and each ritual, such as the watching, the funeral feast, the escort to the grave followed by mourners – all had their place and everyone had their role to play in the obsequies as they followed the traditions handed down from the time beyond time. In some things, Eadulf noted, Fidelma was a confirmed traditionalist.

Outside, the night sky was dark. The clouds were thickly bunched, obscuring any hope of light that the moon and stars could provide, but all over the village, torches and braziers were alight, offsetting the cold of the night, and people were gathering in small groups. Fidelma and Eadulf had joined Fethmac and his wife as they moved into the central square where a crowd had assembled. The flickering light of the torches distorted faces, so it was hard to recognise any individuals. A tall, sturdy figure came forward to greet them. It seemed that Gobánguss, the smith, had been given the task of marshalling the mourners.

Fidelma's first question was to the welfare of the prisoners.

'Have no fear, lady,' replied the smith. 'Celgaire is locked in the shed and my wife has decided to stay with our children, as they are young, but also to keep an eye on the woman and her baby. All is in order.'

Fidelma looked around for any sign of Íonait but could not spot her.

From far off, there came the sound of a handbell. Its summons was slow and evenly paced. Fethmac listened for a moment.

'That's the death bell,' he told them. 'That means Tadgán is approaching the burial site with the bodies.'

Gobánguss had meanwhile turned to address those gathered.

'The death bell is sounding. Let us go forward to the graves to bury our beloved friends.'

The women formed a double line, two abreast, and started the traditional slow clapping of hands, the *lám-comairt*, moving in measured steps towards the traditional burial place of the village. The men followed, heads bowed, each holding aloft a brand torch and walking with the same, deliberate paces. Then a woman started up the ancient *cáinind*, a high cry of lamentation; the wailing dirge for the lost souls of the dead. Although Eadulf had heard it many times since he had come to live among the people of the Five Kingdoms, it still raised a curious tingle in the base of his neck.

Fidelma herself had separated from Eadulf, for it was tradition that the *uath-fecht*, the grave walk, which was the name given to this ceremony, should separate the sexes. She had placed herself at the end of the line of women. As Fethmac had said, the graveyard was but a short walk to the north of the village – but it was hard in the darkness, even with the torches, for her to follow exactly where they were, except that they left the road and entered a moss-covered field.

Another, smaller group with torches was standing waiting for them. In spite of the distortions of the light, Fidelma had no difficulty in recognising the rotund figure of Brother Gadra, for it was he who held the bell of office in his hand and now ceased to ring it as the villagers approached. Behind him was a cart or wagon and she knew what its load would be.

The procession spread around the dark hole that was now illuminated by the light of the encircling torches. It seemed that Adnán and his family were to be consigned to a single, large grave. Brother Gadra raised his hand, the lamentations stopped and an eerie quiet descended. Fidelma presumed that the tall, dark man standing alongside Brother Gadra was Tadgán. He now turned to the men around him and issued a quiet instruction. To her surprise, she saw that one of these men was Lúbaigh. Four of them moved to the wagon with its patiently waiting oxen. They took from it two long objects wrapped in the white linen *racholl* of winding sheets. This also surprised Fidelma, for while poor people were often buried in similar fashion, those who possessed any degree of wealth would usually be buried in coffins of varying wood, depending on that wealth.

The two larger bodies were lowered into the grave first. Then the other two shroud-covered bodies were extracted from the wagon and lowered into the grave next to them. As the bell gave another sharp note, the women raised their voices in a strange musical chorus called the *écnaire* or requiem. This was followed by prayers from Brother Gadra, the meaning of which, as he intoned them in Latin, was lost on most of the villagers.

Then the man Fidelma identified as Tadgán stepped forward. His thin, shadowy figure was matched by a voice that was too highly pitched to instil confidence in anyone.

Fidelma knew this should be the moment of the *Nuall-guba*, the address in honour of the dead, in praise of their accomplishments and sorrow at their passing.

'There is no need for me to say anything,' Tadgán began, which caused an intake of breath from most of the mourners. She saw Fethmac take a step forward and whisper to him. 'I mean,' the farmer continued hurriedly, almost petulantly, 'that you all knew my cousin, his wife and two boys. There is little need for me to praise them. They were murdered by the vagrants and they will be avenged. It should have been sooner rather than later.'

Fidelma's mouth tightened at the statement but many of those present muttered agreement and there was a feeling of tension in the air.

However, Brother Gadra had started to sum up the proceedings. 'It is well spoken and we hope the magistrate will reassert his authority over the strangers who have come among us to intervene in our law and custom. Let us have judgement before another sun sets. No strangers should come into our midst to either commit murder or tell us what the law is in response to it.'

Fidelma found herself almost speechless at the affront to her and to Eadulf, not to mention the assumption of Celgaire's guilt before trial. The words were insulting and disrespectful. She was about to take the unusual step of intervening in protest but Fethmac had already taken charge.

'As magistrate I am forced to make two points of correction,' he said loudly, having obviously found new courage. 'I should remind you that under law, the vagrant Celgaire has yet to be tried in due legal form – and only if sufficient evidence is found for him to answer the charge. The investigation, in which *I* am involved, is yet to be concluded.'

A silence followed his statement . . . followed by a murmur of anger.

'Shame!' cried a woman's voice. 'This is a hallowed place and no one has the right to interrupt the address in honour of the dead.'

To their surprise, Fethmac insisted on continuing, his voice growing stronger with every word. 'I have heard little in the way of an address in honour of the dead. I have heard only criticism of the living and information that is false. I must tell you all that Fidelma of Cashel is sister and legal adviser to our King, Colgú.

She is no stranger in any area of this kingdom, for she is a *dálaigh* of the degree of *Anruth*, which gives her total legal jurisdiction here. I therefore welcome her intervention and accept her guidance in pursuit of the perpetrator, or perpetrators, of this heinous crime. This matter is conducted under the laws of this kingdom.'

Fidelma felt a mixture of emotions as the young man finished, especially because she had already taken to heart Eadulf's criticism of her behaviour towards him. Maybe she had been too severe on the young magistrate.

It was Brother Gadra who responded, his voice sour. 'I speak as I see. When I see a bull, I do not pretend it is a goat. There is little else to say . . .'

However, Fethmac stood his ground. 'Things will be done by the law,' he insisted. 'And by the law of this kingdom only.'

Brother Gadra stood hesitantly and then decided not to pursue matters. 'Then there is but one other task to perform before the final prayer at this graveside,' he announced. He lowered his voice and said something to Tadgán. The farmer seemed annoyed but then he shrugged and spoke aloud to all those present.

'I am told it is customary that you should hear the *audacht*, the Will, of my cousin Adnán. He and his family, his sons, are all dead. I am sure there will be no surprise to learn that I am now the owner of all that Adnán once owned.'

He was about to turn away when Fethmac raised his voice again. 'It is also customary, when proclaiming a Will, to ask whether there are, among you, anyone who makes a legal challenge to Tadgán on this matter? It is a legal requirement.'

Tadgán rounded on him angrily. 'The matter is clear!' he snapped. 'I am the only heir.'

'Whether clear or not,' replied Fethmac, unmoved, 'the ritual should be fulfilled. Is there a reason why you should object to legal requirements?'

As Tadgán did not respond, Fethmac continued: 'Very well,

Tadgán. Your silence is consent.' Fethmac then produced a small scroll of *caitirne*, or specially prepared membrane of calfskin. A person able to write their Will on vellum was obviously someone of rank and wealth. Fethmac held it up in the torchlight. 'This is the *audacht* of Adnán, given and witnessed by me. I hold this for examination in accordance with the legal requirement. I can confirm that it was to his sons that Adnán left his farm and properties and for the use of his wife, Aoife, during her life time. However, as wife and sons are dead and Adnán did not specify further bequests, also bearing in mind that this is kin property, then the inheritor is deemed by law to be of senior male descent among three generations from the common ancestor of Adnán.'

There was nothing surprising in this for Eadulf had learned that three generations constituted the *derbhfine* of a family through which common kin-land passed.

Tadgán snorted impatiently. 'And since there *is* no other senior male descendant except for myself, the kin-land automatically passes to me,' he said. 'There is no need for this waste of time.'

'It is the ritual under law,' Fethmac repeated pedantically, 'and it is my duty to proclaim it in this manner. I have to formally ask if there is any challenger to the ownership of this kin-land? As there is no challenge . . .'

'I challenge it!'

The voice cracked like a whip through the darkness. There was a moment of stunned silence before a collective gasp of amazement went through the gathering. Heads turned in the semi-darkness, trying, by the light of the burning brand torches, to see who had spoken. For several long moments no one said anything. Then Tadgán, squinting into the darkness, cried angrily: 'Who are you, who dares challenge my rights?'

'I am your senior cousin, Tadgán,' replied the voice.

By now, they had all identified the speaker as a dark figure on horseback who had approached unnoticed to the edge of the crowd.

He sat very still astride his mount, appearing almost like a shadow. They could not see the man's face nor make out anything much as he was clad in a long, dark riding cloak with a hood.

'Get down and identify yourself,' called Fethmac.

'I shall not get down, young lawyer,' replied the voice. 'I value my life too much and have no wish to find a cleaver buried in the back of my skull.'

The gathering gasped again as if of one voice.

Brother Gadra motioned someone to come nearer with a lantern and hold it up. The light revealed hardly anything more, except that the cloak and hood were the type associated with mountain men, and often worn by shepherds and goatherds.

'Step down if you respect the dead and fear God!' thundered Brother Gadra. 'You have no right to profane this assembly with accusations.'

The figure chuckled without humour.

'I thought that the right was given when the young lawyer asked for a challenge. I merely answered that challenge.'

Fidelma had moved closer, and now she spoke.

'I am Fidelma of Cashel, a *dálaigh*, and I suggest you get down and identify yourself so that we may know who challenges this Will and on what grounds. Otherwise, your challenge cannot be assessed.'

The rider did not seem to be disturbed by her presence.

'The King's sister? Your reputation precedes you, Fidelma of Cashel. You are here at a most propitious time to witness my challenge. I am Conmaol, of Cnoc na Faille, and I challenge Tadgán's right to be *ádae fine* and senior heir male to Adnán. I am the eldest surviving descendant of Ágach Ágmar the Warlike, and therefore senior to Tadgán.'

'You can prove this?'

'I can and I will do so. I came here tonight to obey the ritual procedure that the young magistrate is so concerned with. Having asserted my claim I will not delay here for I respect my life and do not want it to end prematurely, as Adnán's did.'

'You were free with the term cleaver just now,' Fidelma observed. 'How did you know that the victims were struck down that way?'

'Words spread from mouth to mouth more swiftly than the raven flies, lady, you must know that,' mocked the man. 'Now I have made my challenge known I shall go to fetch proof of the *cráeb* of our *derbhfine* – the indisputable genealogy that shows I am who I say I am. I shall return shortly.' He then raised his voice to Tadgán. 'Do not make yourself too comfortable on the farm that is not yours. You are not the only one in Cloichín who has seen the genealogy of our family. I shall need an accounting of everything.'

With an abruptness that surprised even Fidelma, the man called Conmaol swung his horse around and rode headlong into the night leaving an excited and talkative crowd behind.

Tadgán was clearly in a rage. 'The man is a liar. I know of no other branches of my *derbhfine*. He was playing some trick here, using my cousin's burial to create some ill will against me.'

'But why?' queried Fethmac. 'If the claim cannot be substantiated, why should he come here and make it?'

'Where did he say he was from?' Eadulf asked.

'Cnoc na Faille, the Hill of the Cliff,' replied Fethmac. 'That is up in the mountains south of us. It has been pointed out to me on journeys to Lios Mhór. For the news of what has happened here to reach it in this amount of time would, by the way, be impossible.'

Fidelma glanced at Fethmac. 'Do you know this man?'

'I can't say that I have ever heard of any Conmaol before, but he certainly looked, and sounded, as if he was much more than a mere shepherd or herdsman from the hills. The only person I know who makes regular trips up there is Taithlech. We could ask him.'

Fidelma stiffened. 'Taithlech again.'

'He is a local merchant and therefore has contacts everywhere.'

'Point him out to me if you can see him in this darkness.'

'I do not see him,' Fethmac confessed. 'Perhaps we should go and visit him.'

'In good time,' Fidelma sighed. 'It is too late now, anyway.'

'I wonder if Conmaol's claim is as accurate as his information that Adnán was killed with a cleaver,' Eadulf said quietly.

'Indeed, it is interesting that he knew about that,' Fethmac conceded. 'What, exactly, is he doing here? Apart from creating a dispute with Tadgán by claiming the kin-land, what else could his purpose be?'

'We have found yet another person who would have a vested interest in the death of Adnán and his sons,' Fidelma pointed out. 'What's more, if this Hill of the Cliff is so remote, it means Conmaol must have been in this vicinity to learn the news and details of the murders so quickly.'

Eadulf smiled grimly. 'Perhaps we have found another suspect.'

'I would certainly like to talk further with this Conmaol,' Fidelma stated. 'He said that news travels fast – but not that fast.'

Quiet had been restored on the restless crowd and Brother Gadra had uttered the final blessing over the grave. The villagers now began to disperse, but as they went Tadgán still seemed to be arguing with one or two people by his wagon, while members of his family were climbing aboard. The few men who had helped carry the bodies to the grave were busy laying branches of broom over the corpses, both as a protective layer for when the graves were filled in the next morning, and also it was a practice originating from the days of the old religion, meant to prevent the souls from rising before Donn, the God of Death, was ready to gather them for transport to his island in the west for their voyage to Hy-Brasil, the Land of the Ever Living Ones.

Fidelma moved over to join Tadgán. The farmer's features, in the flickering light of the brand torches, plainly showed his anger. Fidelma made to introduce herself but the farmer cut her short.

'I know well who you are, lady. I have seen you before, when I was part of the hosting called by your brother, the King, when he went to defend Osraige against the invasion by the warriors of

Laighin. I saw you at your brother's side.' He paused to glance at Eadulf, who had followed her. 'I saw the Saxon there, too.'

Eadulf quickly corrected: 'Angle, not Saxon.' But no one seemed to hear him.

'I object to your interference in the matter of the death of my cousin and his family,' the man went on. 'I am assured by Lúbaigh and Brother Gadra that everything was clear until you intervened.'

Fidelma met his gaze with a steely mask of her own.

'Murder was about to be committed,' she said. 'And this village would have had to pay for its folly when the facts found their way to the Chief Brehon. So now I am helping your magistrate, Fethmac, in this matter. For that I do not expect gratitude but only respect.'

Tadgán made a dismissive gesture with his hand. 'I cannot understand why there is a delay. From what Lúbaigh says, the matter is clear cut, in spite of what Fethmac here has said. If there is need for a formal hearing then the quicker it is done and the vagrant punished, the better.'

'The law will take its course, Tadgán, and I hope to come to talk formally with you tomorrow.'

The farmer frowned. 'I fail to see what I can add to the knowledge of how Adnán met his death.'

'We will leave that for the moment. For the time being, I am interested in this man Conmaol who has challenged your right to the kin-land and also claims that he is your cousin. What do you know of him?'

Tadgán swore. 'He's no cousin of mine, nor is he part of my *derbhfine* – let alone senior male heir.'

'You have never seen him before?'

'Not only have I never seen him but I've never even heard of him. What would one of my kin be doing up in the remote mountains anyway? Turning up here, trying to claim our kin-land – it's nothing more than a blatant attempt at theft.'

'Yet isn't it strange that he would come and challenge you in this manner if he had no proof of his claim?'

'Where's his proof? All I heard was his words. If he does return . . . well, then we will see that he is a liar – and a fool.'

'Was he correct in saying that your ancestor was Ágach Ágmar?'

Tadgán nodded his head. 'Ágach Ágmar the Warlike was of the line of the kings of the Fír Maige Féne. That was in the days when our people were hereditary Druids to the Cashel Kings. Ágach Ágmar came to these lands under the shadow of the mountains and settled here. For three generations from him, we have farmed these lands.'

'Three generations is a long time to produce so few male descendants,' Eadulf observed.

Tadgán sniffed. 'I am the senior surviving male heir of Ágach Ágmar, that is, apart from my own grandson.'

It was Fethmac, who had been respectfully silent during this time, who decided to explain.

'We had many deaths here, not so long ago. The Yellow Plague took many lives. Your own cousin, King Cathal Cú-cen-mathair, died of that plague and thus your brother, Colgú, became king.'

Fidelma had no need of a reminder of the devastation that the terrible plague had wreaked, having cast its shadow from far away in the east, crossing Gaul, then Britain until it reached the Five Kingdoms, carrying off kings, princes and abbots together with entire populations without distinction.

'We lost many in our family,' Tadgán said gruffly. 'The irony was that Ágach Ágmar had come to this place to escape the famine of one hundred years ago and all went well until the time of the great solar eclipse. The mystics claimed that it foretold of disasters to come. We should have listened.'

'The plague had arrived long before the eclipse,' Fidelma corrected him, annoyed. 'I was in Hilda's abbey at Streonshalh, attending the council called by King Osiu of Northumbria when the eclipse happened. The plague had already been raging long before that time.'

'Nevertheless, the plague came and most of the men who would have constituted the *derbhfine* of our family had perished,' asserted Tadgán.

'Who kept your genealogies?' Each *derbhfine* or kin group had one person who rigorously maintained the genealogy of the group. This was usually the person who came forward at a burial or an inauguration of a chieftain, or even to the rank of the High King himself, to recite the *forsundud,* the recitation of the ancestral line. Fidelma had noted that such a person had not been evident at the funeral of Adnán.

Tadgán shrugged. 'It would have been Brother Ágach Ágmar, named after our ancestor. He took up the religious life and went as a scribe to the abbey of Ard Fhionáin. He was the last to keep the *Genelach* of our family, the genealogy. There has been no one else since.'

'Until what time did he keep these records?'

'Until his death from disease ten years ago. It was reported that he died of the *teine-buirr.*'

'The fire of swelling?' Fidelma did not know the disease.

'An infectious disease but not the plague,' Eadulf quickly explained. 'It's an inflammation of the sensitive parts of the skin which induces fever. It is often fatal.' Eadulf continued to take an interest in the healing arts and had often been essential in assisting Fidelma in her cases.

'Was anyone else appointed to keep your *Genelach* after him?' she asked.

'There was no one.'

'Did he record them by oral tradition?'

Tadgán shook his head. 'Brother Ágach Ágmar was a scribe and prided himself on producing written records.'

'So the *Genelach* exists in written form?'

'I should imagine the records are in the *tech screpta*, the library of Ard Fhionáin. But why such questions?' His eyes narrowed. 'Are you saying that this Conmaol is worthy of being taken seriously?' Tadgán's voice had a dangerous inflection.

'What I am saying is that the man claims he has proof. If he returns here, the magistrate must be prepared to consider his evidence in order to decide whether Conmaol's claims are valid or a lie. That being so, if there is a written genealogy, then he needs to know about it.'

Tadgán's expression became hard. 'I know what I know and I say that I am now the only male heir descendant of Ágach Ágmar who came here a hundred years ago. If the genealogy still exists in the abbey, then it would demonstrate that fact. My word would not be questioned.'

'Nevertheless, if this man Conmaol claims he has a proof, where would he get it except from that same genealogy?'

Tadgán reflected for a moment. 'I accept that there is no other source. Questioning our ancestry has never arisen before.' And then he smiled broadly, declaring, 'I recall that Taithlech once told me that he had been in the scriptorium of the abbey at Ard Fhionáin and had seen the genealogy – because it was when his daughter was to wed my son Díoma. So it exists.'

'Therefore, if Conmaol turns up with a written genealogy from the library of Ard Fhionáin, you would have to accept it?' Fidelma asked the magistrate.

Fethmac's eyes opened wide as he realised what she meant.

'You think that is where he has gone? He has ridden off to Ard Fhionáin to get this genealogy?'

'It's a strong possibility,' replied Fidelma. 'At least you are aware of its existence and you will have to examine it carefully.' Then she turned to Tadgán. 'It grows late, and your womenfolk are getting cold, sitting upon the wagon. You may expect me sometime tomorrow.'

Fethmac followed her with Eadulf as she moved away from the

now deserted graveside, leaving the farmer with no time to protest. The three began to make their way back to the village centre.

'This matter grows complicated, lady,' he said in a woeful tone.

'Do not worry, it should not be too complicated,' she reassured him. 'It should be easy to see if the record of the late Adnán has been tampered with.'

A figure suddenly loomed out of the darkness before them. It was a distraught woman of middle age.

'Fethmac!' she cried when she saw the young magistrate. 'Bad news . . . bad news . . .' Her voice was high pitched, her panic obvious.

'Calm yourself, Breccnat,' the young man soothed her. He introduced her to Fidelma: 'This is the wife of Gobánguss, the smith.'

A tingle of anticipation ran through Fidelma as she examined the woman. 'Tell us what your news is,' she said softly.

'It is . . . it is the vagrant. He has broken out of the shed and escaped!'

CHAPTER EIGHT

'Well, there is your proof positive, lady,' Fethmac observed dryly. 'An innocent man would not try to escape.'

'Where is your husband?' Fidelma asked Beccnat, ignoring Fethmac.

'He has not returned home yet. He was at the funeral – did you not see him?'

'You were supposed to be looking after the itinerant's wife and baby. Where are they?'

'I have left them safely locked in my house. I thought I heard noises at the forge and went to investigate. When I got outside I saw the shed door open – the shed where my husband had put the vagrant.'

'Let us get back to the forge immediately and check if the woman and her child are still in your cottage. Oh, and have you told anyone else?'

The smith's wife shook her head. 'With Gobánguss not back yet, my first duty was to find the magistrate. People should be warned lest we all be murdered in our beds.'

'Then keep this news to yourself.' Fidelma turned to Eadulf. 'Would you mind going back to the cemetery to find out why Gobánguss has been delayed? Fethmac and I will go to see how Celgaire has managed to break out of the shed.'

'Celgaire has clearly shown his guilt, lady,' the young magistrate observed as they set off for the forge.

'I recall the smith saying that it was fairly secure and locked from the outside.' Once again Fidelma did not respond to his comment but addressed her remark to Breccnat.

'Yes, the lock was on the outside, as well as a strong bolt, and the door opened inwards. There are no windows. I would have thought it impossible to break out, yet the door was smashed open.'

With Gobánguss' wife scurrying ahead of them, they followed until they came to the forge where a couple of lanterns blazed. The village was silent now and night had enveloped most of it. Fidelma was thankful for the lanterns to guide them. The shed was a separate construction behind the smithy. There was room enough for a tall man to stand carrying a young boy on his shoulders, and adequate space for him to lie down within it. It was, as she could see by the lantern that Fethmac had taken from Gobánguss' wife, constructed of strong, thick timbers, both posts and boards. The door hung to one side, as if it had been wrenched almost loose from its hinges.

Leaving the door for the moment, Fidelma entered, taking the lantern from Fethmac and peering round. Breccnat had been right. There were no windows or openings saving the door. The sheepskins lay on the floor next to a wooden box on which a half-burned but extinguished candle was placed. Everything looked secured. She turned out of the shed and began to examine the lopsided door before standing back and handing the lantern to Fethmac.

'Have a look and tell me what you think,' she instructed the young magistrate.

Fethmac went inside and made a swift examination. Then he moved to the side to which the door had been fixed before standing back with a frown.

'Well?' prompted Fidelma.

'The bolt was drawn open but the lock is still intact and the wood around it is splintered. The force against the door was also enough to shatter one of the hinges. My conclusion is that the door was smashed inwards. Someone from outside broke it open and released Celgaire.'

They turned as the figure of Breccnat reappeared out of the darkness.

'The vagrant's wife and baby are still secure in the room where I left them. My own *becán*, my little one, is also safe.'

'Are you sure that the woman has not left your house without you knowing?' pressed Fethmac.

'There is no way she could have done so and returned.'

'If she had managed to get out and release her husband, she would have gone with him,' Fidelma pointed out.

At that moment, Eadulf came hurrying back. 'The cemetery is now deserted and there is no sign of Gobánguss.'

Fidelma asked Breccnat, 'Your husband did not return early from the funeral?'

The woman shook her head. 'I know that he went to it and left me looking after the prisoners. Sometimes he is called away by an emergency and he has no time to warn me.'

'We need to speak to him as soon as he returns,' Fidelma said, turning back to the smashed shed door which Eadulf had now been examining.

'Whichever way you look at it, Celgaire was helped to escape by someone. He had an accomplice,' Eadulf said.

'I had already reached that conclusion.' Fidelma turned to Breccnat. 'You said that you heard a noise earlier. I am surprised that the sound of the shed door smashing did not alarm you.'

'The babies were crying. Fial's baby as well as my own little one.'

'And no one else heard the noise?'

'The forge is isolated from the rest of the village for the usual reasons – the fire is a danger to surrounding buildings,' Fethmac explained pedantically. 'And the shed is behind the forge, so it's even further away.'

Fidelma closed her eyes briefly in frustration. She knew well enough that smiths were required to build their forges a good distance away from domestic buildings.

'But you were saying that you did hear something earlier?' she pressed Breccnat. 'Can you describe it?'

'Earlier I had heard horsemen arriving as well as folk in wagons. I presumed they were on their way to the funeral. Sometime later I heard several horsemen.'

'Several horsemen?' repeated Eadulf in surprise. 'But only a single horseman came to the funeral later and he was that curious man Conmaol.'

Breccnat frowned. 'I know of no one here called Conmaol.'

'Neither do I. He was a man from the mountains who claimed to be Adnán's cousin and a cousin of Tadgán.'

Breccnat looked puzzled. 'I have lived here all my life and I have never heard of a cousin of that name.'

'This Conmaol challenged Tadgán, claiming to be senior in the *derbhfine* of Ágach Ágmar's kin,' explained Fethmac.

The woman was surprised and said so.

'So was Tadgán,' Fethmac said with irony.

'Didn't you think it was unusual for a band of horsemen to arrive after the funeral had begun?' interrupted Fidelma, impatient to get back to the subject in hand.

'Why should she?' the young magistrate countered. 'This is a rural place, lady, and folk could still have been riding in from the surrounding farms, though on reflection, I think most of them had already arrived, with family, on wagons. Well, whoever it was,' he went on, 'Celgaire had help and seemed to have no compunction in abandoning his wife and baby in order to escape. It is too late now, but at first light we should make a search.'

'A search?' queried Eadulf.

'Of course,' Fethmac declared. 'We have some good trackers among the villagers. Good huntsmen who should pick up the vagrant's trail whether he went on foot or—'

'Let's not involve too many people at this time. The fewer who know about this the better,' Fidelma advised. An idea suddenly struck her. 'Let us see if his wagon is still in the barn.'

Even before they reached it they saw the doors standing wide open and knew the wagon would be gone.

'The ox has not been taken,' Fethmac reported, after he and Breccnat had investigated the stables.

'But one of my husband's best wagon horses is missing,' she announced angrily.

'Understandable,' commented Fidelma. 'The quickest way to escape with a wagon would be using a horse rather than oxen. But this presents an even greater mystery. If you need to flee quickly, why not take a horse, mount it and ride off? Why take a cart horse and hitch it to a heavy wagon? Breccnat, how can it be, that none of this activity disturbed you?'

'I told you, as soon as I heard something, I went to investigate.'

'The man won't get far,' Fethmac said. 'We can easily track him down. In the darkness, he could have passed as one of the mourners come in from the country, but in daylight . . .'

'Remember, he is not alone,' Eadulf reminded the magistrate. 'His wife and baby son are still here.'

'There is much that I do not understand.' Fidelma felt frustrated. 'His rescuer, or rescuers, took him on his wagon, so as you say, Fethmac, that should be easy to follow.'

'The problem is, there were several wagons carrying mourners to the funeral. It might be hard to identify the tracks of the wagon we are seeking,' Eadulf pointed out.

'We shall have to wait for first light, anyway.' Fidelma felt exhausted. 'It is late now so I think we should have a few hours of sleep before considering further. Let us hope your husband, Gobánguss, will have returned by them. Good night, Breccnat.'

It was later, in their darkened room at the magistrate's house, that Eadulf raised himself in the bed and said to Fidelma: 'You have been tossing and turning for some while now. Isn't it time that you shared your thoughts with me?'

He heard her sigh, before she answered. 'There is a flaw in this matter,' she said quietly.

'In Celgaire's escape?'

'Yes. Fethmac does not seem to attach any significance to the fact that someone helped him to escape.'

'I thought that was peculiar,' Eadulf agreed. 'Celgaire is a vagrant. He arrives here with his wife and baby, supposedly looking for employment. He is refused work by Tadgán and directed to Adnán's farmstead where, again, he is turned away – albeit kindly. This is said to be the reason why he goes berserk and slaughters the entire family. He is pursued and made prisoner. Someone then releases him. How did he have an accomplice, apart from his wife who, according to Breccnat, never left the cabin? And nothing was heard, in spite of the door being smashed in, and then all the business of the theft of the horse, hitching it to the wagon and then driving off into the night with Celgaire.'

'Well,' replied Fidelma, 'with two babies screaming loudly, it is just about possible to have missed all that going on outside.' She hesitated. 'Possible – but unlikely. Although as Euripides once observed, *deus ex machina*. Sorry, I know the Latin better than the original Greek.'

'I don't understand. God out of a machine?'

'It means an unlikely event on which things depend. When something impossible happens, people refer to the drama of the Ancient Greeks in which, in order to resolve the impossible, a god is sent onstage by a mechanical device, like a crane, as if he is descending from the sky. The god then sorts things out by a proclamation of a miracle, gods being able to do anything – hence the words "god out of a machine".'

'Well, we are not talking of gods now, Fidelma,' Eadulf said rather irascibly.

She then said, 'One thought has occurred to me: perhaps the rescuer was not an accomplice at all.'

'I am not sure what you mean?' Eadulf frowned in the darkness.

'Let us play the "what if" game. As you know, I'm far from satisfied that Celgaire is guilty of the murders. What if I am right?'

'Then if you are right and Celgaire is innocent, what reason would someone have for effecting his escape?'

'There is, of course, one very good reason.'

Eadulf suddenly caught onto her train of thought.

'The real murderer wanted Celgaire to escape as a distraction, so that we would believe what everyone else believes – that Celgaire is guilty.'

Fidelma nodded. 'That means, too, that the murderer hopes we might catch up with Celgaire shortly and turn a deaf ear to his defence.'

'There is another meaning.' Eadulf's voice was suddenly toneless. 'The escape was purposely staged so that Celgaire is killed.'

'Or that this "accomplice" has already killed him.' Fidelma hoped she was wrong. 'As Fethmac believed, the escape was evidence of the man's guilt and his death would be accepted as such and the case closed.'

'There is nothing to be done before first light,' Eadulf reminded her. 'We should be up and ready to make sure that young Fethmac gives the right instructions to these trackers he is going to unleash. We don't want another try at lynching Celgaire.'

After washing and dressing the couple found Fethmac already up and having breakfast, served to him by Ballgel, who greeted them with a nervous smile. Obviously she was aware that Fidelma and her husband did not see eye to eye and was doing her best to be the cordial hostess.

Fidelma lost no time in putting forward their thoughts on Celgaire's escape. Predictably, Fethmac did not seem impressed.

'There is some illogic in your arguments, lady,' he replied at once.

Eadulf looked at her, hoping she would read his warning not to rise to this young fellow's rudeness. Fortunately, Fidelma was still bearing in mind his advice of earlier.

'Illogic? I am open to your counter-argument, Fethmac,' she said pleasantly.

'If Celgaire was helped to escape, I have conceded that he could only have done so with outside help. In which case it is illogical that it was the murderer of Adnán and his family who did this. And that is presuming that Celgaire was innocent. Why would the murderer thus reveal his guilt? All he had to do was keep silent and allow Celgaire to rot in his prison, and not draw attention to there being someone else involved.'

'It is a good argument,' acknowledged Fidelma. 'Yet what if the murderer was panicked by the fact that Brother Gadra's attempt to have Celgaire hanged was thwarted and we,' she emphasised the 'we' for the young man's benefit, 'had started asking questions rather than merely condemning Celgaire on the evidence? What if that panicked the person into some immediate action?'

'If Celgaire escaped, it would be a good way to have his guilt confirmed to everyone and we would have to condemn him,' Eadulf put in. 'But the one drawback to the scheme was that he had been put in that shed where it could only be broken into and not broken out of.'

'This is why it is possible that Celgaire may already be found dead or will be placed in such a position that it is hoped he will be killed during an effort to recapture him,' Fidelma went on.

'I don't see how. I suggest we take Fedach, a woodsman, as tracker. He is good with a bow if Celgaire, or his accomplice, put up a fight. I want to take Celgaire alive as much as anyone so that he can pay for the slaughter of Adnán's family.'

'So you remain convinced of his guilt?' queried Eadulf.

The young man flushed. 'What else will it take to convince *you*?' he retorted stubbornly.

Fidelma lost patience. 'Evidence that is unquestionable,' she snapped. 'That's what it will take. The circumstances call for clear evidence and that should be your concern as well as mine.'

Before Fethmac could respond there was a knock on the door and Gobánguss marched in before anyone had time to call out an invitation. The big smith looked troubled.

'I am sorry I was not at home last night, lady. My wife told me what happened. I was called away by a relative of mine at the funeral. There was a task he needed help with, and it couldn't wait.'

'So late at night?' queried Fethmac, puzzled.

'Disaster can strike at any time. Anyway, you had only just gone when I returned and Breccnat told me the news. It was Taithlech again who needed something fixing urgently. I apologise for my absence, lady. But I have some important news.'

'Taithlech?' The name kept cropping up. 'What is your important news, Gobánguss?' she prompted.

The smith stood hesitantly as if wondering how to articulate it.

'A lad came to my forge this morning – just a short while ago, in fact. He brought my horse that was taken last night. He told me he found it wandering in the oat fields north of the River Teara.'

'How did the boy know to bring it to you?' Fidelma asked at once.

'He recognised my markings on the beast. He is a local lad, his father has a cottage by the river and fishes the salmon and trout there.'

'In whose oat fields did he find the animal?' Eadulf asked.

'That is not important.' Gobánguss was clearly distracted over something and was trying to think of a way to explain it.

'What is it?' Fidelma urged, trying to contain her impatience.

The smith's jaw tightened a little. 'The horse had most of its harness on and it was unharmed. What concerns me is that the traces and the lines – the long leather straps to guide the animal—'

'We know about harnesses. What was wrong with them?'

'The ends had been burned. They had been severed . . . by fire.'

'Fire?' Fidelma suddenly rose to her feet. She did not wait for the smith to reply. 'We want our horses ready at once. It looks as if our theory might be right. Celgaire was not meant to survive his so-called escape. Where did you say the horse was found – the oat fields along by this River Teara?'

Fethmac had also risen. He flushed a little, apparently in recognition that he had dismissed Fidelma's theory. 'It is the route we took yesterday morning,' he said humbly. 'We turned west to Adnán's farmstead. It's farmland along both banks of the river there.'

'So in whose oat field was the horse found? Did the boy say?'

Gobánguss nodded. 'That would be Tadgán's oat fields along the eastern bank.'

Fidelma exchanged a quick glance with Eadulf but made no comment. 'We will leave immediately,' she repeated.

'It will take time to fetch Fedach the woodsman,' protested Fethmac. 'You should have let me send for him last night.'

'I don't think we will have need for him,' Fidelma returned brusquely. 'I believe the wagon will be located near where the horse was found.' She turned to Ballgel. 'Say nothing of these things to anyone.'

The young woman was offended. 'I have plenty of work to do without spending time gossiping with neighbours,' she replied.

Fidelma shrugged. She could have put the matter more diplomatically, but she didn't want the villagers to begin a search for Celgaire and run amok with fear and hatred as they had previously.

It was but a short time later they were cantering towards the wooden bridge to the north of the village where the River Teara made an almost right-angled turn to the east. Beyond the bridge lay the fields and the farmstead of Tadgán. Gobánguss had accompanied them, at his own insistence. He declared he was responsible, having been in charge of the prisoner when the escape had happened.

With Fethmac riding ahead and Eadulf and Gobánguss behind, they saw only the occasional farmworker moving in the fields during the cold early morning. Other than the tilled fields awaiting the emergence of early crops, most of the area they passed through was of dull winter green. The mosses had spread their mats on the earth and on lime-rock areas. Fethmac led the way, keeping to the track along the river. The waters showed their occasional inhabitants such as an otter, with short powerful legs, long back and powerful rudder-like tail pushing purposefully across the current. Sparrowhawks were diving along the banks in search of breakfast, scattering the few wrens trying to remain inconspicuous with their tiny, reddish-brown and buff-coloured bodies but, now and then, letting forth their explosive cry of 'tit-tit-tit' in alarm as they darted to avoid the speed and agility of the deadly predators.

Finally Gobánguss waved his arm to an area of open field to their right, clearly planted with oats for early spring harvesting. It was easy to see why the emerging crop would have attracted the attention of the horse and allowed the boy to grab hold and take charge of it. A large section of woodland spread to the north of where they were. It was mainly thick with birch and elm, and with hazels reverting to almost shrub-like levels under the high canopy. Other than that, elsewhere the land was fairly bare and open.

'No sign of a burned-out wagon,' observed Fethmac heavily. 'Maybe the horse galloped a distance. This is where Fedach would have been useful in picking up the tracks.'

'If there are tracks to be found, I myself can find them in this soft ground,' Gobánguss objected. 'I know the shoes of my own horse – for did I not put them on myself? I can see them plain . . . here and here.' The smith was pointing to the ground before him. 'You can see where the oat plants are broken because the beast stood there chewing at them.'

Fidelma, however, was scanning the fields that spread over the undulating ground.

'I can see smoke!' she exclaimed.

'Where?' cried Eadulf.

She pointed to where a thin plume of smoke was rising from some hidden defile in the hills.

To their surprise, Fethmac chuckled slightly.

'Well, that's no burning wagon,' he almost sneered. 'That's Tadgán's farmstead.'

'So close?' Fidelma commented. 'I see. In that case, since we are here, we may as well have the meeting I promised him last night.'

Fethmac was surprised. 'I thought we were looking for the wagon?'

'There is nothing to say that we cannot do both.' She turned to Gobánguss. 'I suggest we leave you to look for any signs of the wagon tracks or horse tracks around here while we go and have a talk with Tadgán.'

'I'll do what I can, lady,' the smith acknowledged.

'Good. We will see what Tadgán has to say.'

'Might I remind you, lady,' protested Fethmac, 'that Tadgán and his family and some of the farmworkers were at the funeral. So they could not have known of Celgaire's escape.'

'Who is saying that they did? But it is his land. That is his farmstead across the hill. As you will recall, I promised him that I would ask him a few questions today, so what better time?'

'Yes, but . . .'

There was little difference to Tadgán's farmstead from his late cousin's complex of farmhouse, barns and outbuildings. On a green hill beyond, they could see a small flock of sheep being tended. A noisy group of animals was enclosed in a large pen some distance east of the main buildings. They were the long-snouted, thin but muscular and active pigs still confined in their winter *muc-fóil* or sty. Nearby, in his own pen, was a bad-tempered boar testing the confines of his pen with great vigour. The pigs seemed to know

that it was close to the time when they would be let out to run wild
in the surrounding woods, where they would gorge themselves on
mes – a combination of woodland nuts such as beechnuts, acorns,
chestnuts and whatever else came their way. With pork being the
most popular meat in the country, eaten by nobles down to those
of lesser rank, pigs were seen by farmers as the cheapest and easiest
animals to breed. Only during the winter months were they rounded
up by the *muccaid*, or swineherd, and then penned until the spring
before being released into the forests to fend for themselves. There
they often had to compete with the wild boars and pigs that no one
claimed and which were often not such good eating. Eadulf recalled
that the *Book of Ailill*, which Fidelma often quoted to him, contained
numerous regulations about compensation for injuries inflicted by
pigs. He was therefore glad to see a *muccaid* standing with a short
blackthorn staff watching the activities with an impassive eye.

Tadgán's farmstead was thriving. As well as some calves, oxen
and horses, there were the sheep and pigs, and a great many poultry
in evidence. They could see a few workers occupied in tasks. The
main group of buildings was actually surrounded by a small ditch,
almost like a *rath*. Unlike Adnán's farmstead, the dwelling house
was large, with a separate kitchen and even a separate pantry or
storehouse. Beyond was a kiln for drying corn. Most of the buildings were the usual round-shaped wicker-style houses with a conical
roof, apart from one building, obviously a barn, which was oblong.

A dog started to bark at their approach.

Fidelma was surprised by the size of the farmhouse for she had
assumed that Tadgán was less wealthy than his cousin. Immediately
this thought occurred to her, she rebuked herself. She had jumped
to the conclusion that the alacrity with which Tadgán had taken
charge of his cousin's farmstead was a matter of greed, She realised
now that a farmer might have other concerns. In spite of Lúbaigh
being the steward there, a caring farmer might have been concerned
for the animals and the need to have Adnán and his family buried

in the traditional form before midnight. She told herself to be careful not to make any more assumptions.

They had not reached the farmhouse before the tall, thin man she recognised as Tadgán emerged to greet them. He stood, hands on hips, watching their approach. She had only seen him in shadow and flickering torchlight at the funeral on the previous night. Now, in daylight, Fidelma saw that his skin was sallow and he was badly in need of a shave. The blackness of his hair and eyebrows was mirrored by the dark orbs of his eyes, which appeared to be without pupils. His lips twisted into what was supposed to be a smile but looked more like a sneer.

'Welcome, lady,' he said in his irritating high-pitched voice as she dismounted. 'You told me that you wanted to have words with me but I did not expect you to come so soon.'

He ignored both Eadulf and Fethmac as the two men dismounted.

'Will you come inside to the fire and warmth? I can only offer you cider from our apple orchard.'

Fidelma smiled and shook her head. 'Let us sit on that log,' she suggested, pointing. 'I fear that going inside in the warmth and then having to return to this chilly air will cause discomfort rather than comfort. We have but recently broken our fast, so require nothing.'

Tadgán appeared relieved. He walked to where a short cut log was placed and stood waiting until she had seated herself before doing likewise. Eadulf had taken charge of her horse and stood holding their two mounts a short distance away. Fethmac, taking the hint, stood by him with his horse but was scowling at being excluded like this. However, they could hear everything that was said.

Fidelma began by asking: 'I presume you have heard no more from the man who challenged your rights to inheritance last night – Conmaol of Cnoc na Faille?'

Tadgán gave a snort. 'No, nor do I want to, since he is a liar – a so-called cousin that I have never seen nor heard of before. Well,

I know my rights although I gather the bastard is trying to carry out his threat.'

'His threat?'

'Of seeking proof that he is senior in the *derbhfine*.'

'How do you know this?'

'One of the mountain men came down this morning to see about a ram he wanted to purchase from my stock. He told me that this Conmaol is well known in the high peaks. He also knew that Conmaol had set out for the abbey at Ard Fhionáin to research the genealogies they keep there. Presumably the *Genelach* of our family is kept there too.'

'In these circumstances, do you have no wish to go to the abbey and examine it yourself?'

Tadgán sniffed. 'I am no scholar but I know who my father was, and his father and his father's father. I say, let the red pox descend on all so-called cousins!'

'Speaking of cousins,' Fidelma went on quietly, 'I gather that you were not well disposed to your cousin and neighbour, Adnán?'

The farmer was quiet for a moment and then replied: 'There is no law that says relatives and neighbours must always be in harmony with each other.'

'True enough. What was your dispute about?'

Tadgán gestured to Fethmac and said with gritted teeth, 'He will tell you all about it. After all, he was the arbiter on the matter – and found in favour of my cousin.'

'Let us hear about this from you – and why you thought it was an unjust decision.'

The farmer shrugged. 'It is not complicated. The river is the boundary between our two farms. It is clearly marked not only by the river itself but by a number of *coirthe*, boundary stones, as prescribed by law, which had been raised on either bank. Recently, Adnán constructed a watermill to help irrigate his arable land as well as to grind corn. It was built opposite a part of my land where rocky protrusions prevented the natural flow of water from the river and streams anyway. Once the watermill was erected the situation became far worse. There was no way I could divert the flow of water back to my lands and I knew that my crops would wither and die. The course of the river itself was altered by his work. I protested. When he refused to change things, I took the matter to law.'

Fethmac stirred uncomfortably beneath Tadgán's malignant gaze. 'The law is the law,' he said uneasily.

'Your law,' snapped the farmer. 'It was my belief that to change the flow of the river to make the current strong for his watermill to the detriment of his neighbour was unlawful. Adnán had rocks planted in the riverbed which diverted the flow from my side of the river, changing the course towards his side, making it impossible for me to siphon water with the strength needed to irrigate my field. The only way to bring water to it was by hand, bucket by bucket. It was not practical.'

Fidelma was thoughtful. 'And this was the argument you presented to the magistrate?'

Tadgán glowered at Fethmac. 'It was.'

'Did you investigate that?' Fidelma asked the young magistrate.

'Of course I did,' Fethmac replied hotly. 'I am sure you know the law on "The Rights of Water". It was clear that Adnán could construct the mill, but only if he shared the benefits with his neighbour – that is, his cousin here. Therefore I found in favour of Tadgán's claim.'

'In favour?' Fidelma was surprised at this apparent contradiction. 'So what is your problem with this, Tadgán?'

'The compensation was one cow and the use of the mill when I wanted grain to be ground.'

'Wasn't that fair enough?'

'Not when that point of the river had been best situated for bringing water to my barley field. The offer of a cow and the grinding of grain – provided I sought my cousin's permission well beforehand – was not nearly compensation enough. The rocks that Adnán placed in the riverbed were clearly an illegal act.'

'You investigated this as well, of course, Fethmac?' Fidelma asked.

The young magistrate was vigorous in his affirmation.

'I examined the rocks – but who could tell when they first appeared there? Adnán claimed that they had always been there. Tadgán took a contrary view. A judgement had to be made.'

'Rubbish!' ground out the farmer.

'It was Adnán's word against Tadgán's,' protested Fethmac. 'I had to make a choice.'

'And why was Adnán's word more respected than mine?' Tadgán's voice was bitter.

'It was because I found it impossible to believe that he would resort to such subterfuge as to bribe men to carry rocks into the river to divert its currents. Why would he do that – and against his own cousin with whom, until then, he had had a good relationship?'

'Well, the answer to that is because it benefited him,' Fidelma replied shortly. 'It is, of course, a valid question that Tadgán has posed, and which is not about benefit to his cousin or to himself. It is a matter of legality. What were your legal criteria in making the judgement?'

Fethmac fidgeted.

'Legal? The river flowed between the two properties and the boundary stones were clear. So it came down to the matter of the current, the flow of the river being diverted. I found no good evidence that it had been. True, the flow was more prevalent on Adnán's side as there were fewer obstructions there, but Tadgán could still access the water. No one could prove whether the rocks on the riverbed had been placed there recently or hundreds of years before.'

Seeing the scowl on Tadgán's face deepen, Fidelma leaned towards him with a smile.

'Surely the question is superfluous now, isn't it? You stand to take over the kin-land, so you will now control both sides of the river?'

'That was not the point.' Tadgán was still upset.

'You took this argument with your cousin very seriously?'

'Of course I did.'

'So seriously that you broke off communication with him and his family?'

'Everyone knew that.'

'It did not seem such a major dispute as to rip a family apart,' Eadulf observed, making a contribution to the conversation for the first time.

Tadgán scowled at him. 'Families have been split for less,' he said sourly. 'Blood feuds are not so uncommon here.'

'A blood feud?' Fidelma pretended to be shocked. 'Is that what it came to between your families?'

Tadgán suddenly realised he was moving into dangerous legal ground. Blood feuds in families in a kin-based society were considered the most heinous of all crimes; the equivalent to *fingal* or kin-slaying if anyone was killed or injured. Even Eadulf knew that.

'It was an argument, by which it was decided to part company. No more than that,' he averred.

'Difficult when you are neighbours as well as cousins,' reflected Fidelma. She suddenly pretended to be looking around for the first time in search of someone. 'Which one of those women is your wife? I do not know her name.'

'That is because I no longer have a wife,' replied the farmer sullenly. 'She died.'

'Ah, then who were the women that accompanied you to the funeral?'

'Flannat, the widow of my son Díoma, and women who work on the farm.' He scowled again at the magistrate. 'And before you hear it from another source,' he looked at Fethmac meaningfully, 'I was due to marry someone else before I married the mother of my son, Díoma.'

Fidelma was intrigued at this offer of information. When she said nothing, he continued, 'I was due to be married to Aoife.'

Fidelma let out a soft breath. 'That would be the same Aoife who became your cousin's wife?'

'It is no secret. The marriage contract was arranged. Aoife was from another village and our marriage had been arranged between myself and her father, who had paid me the *coibche*, the principal bride-payment. Adnán and I were friends then and it was my ill fortune that it was he who was nominated to go to her village and escort her back to Cloichín for our wedding. It was doubly my misfortune that Adnán enticed Aoife into going with him. It was an illicit union.'

Fidelma was thoughtful. 'Even if it was the union of what we call an "abducted woman", the marriage laws are clear. Aoife would retain all her legal rights and neither she nor her offspring are ignored under the law. But the *coibche* that was paid to you . . .?'

'I did return it.'

'But it could hardly have put Adnán in good standing with you,' Eadulf observed.

'I choose my friends,' Tadgán replied tartly. 'I did not choose my relative.'

'True enough. But there must have been an existing antagonism between you, apart from the argument over borders?' Fidelma suggested.

'We lived our own lives and had no called to trespass upon one another.'

'You had no intercourse with one another? You did not visit his farm and he did not visit your farm. You had no contact with Aoife or her two boys.'

'We did not speak even on market days when need impelled me to come to sell livestock.'

Just then, the boar crashed against the side of his pen, causing them all to turn their heads in his direction, thinking that the wood of the construction must surely have shattered.

'A powerful animal,' commented Fidelma.

'But a fine sire for the herd,' replied Tadgán.

'It is not the same boar that a year ago gored one of your workers?'

'You mean Broc? No. That boar had to be put down for the swineherd was killed. This is a new boar and I had to spend much to obtain him.'

'And much in compensation to the dead swineherd?'

Tadgán glanced towards Fethmac with a suspicious expression.

'If you have not heard, I will tell you that Broc was a feckless individual. He was known to gamble and he became indebted to me. Oh, the magistrate will tell you that the matter was done legally, a document made and signed and witnessed in proper form. When he died, Broc owed me so much, that when it was deducted, I owed his kin nothing. In fact, the debt outweighed any compensation. But I am a fair man. He had a widow and a daughter. They had their own cottage outside the village. So I allowed them to retain it without having to sell it to reimburse the man's debts.'

'I heard it said there is a tradition that every dead man killed his own liabilities,' Eadulf remarked softly.

The farmer ignored him and Fidelma continued, 'I understand that Íonait, the milkmaid at your cousin's farm, was the man's daughter and went to work there after her father was killed.'

'So I have been told.'

'Will she continue once the farm is confirmed as yours?'

'I have no idea. I have only a few milch cows and my own milkmaid is adequate for the task. It all depends. Lúbaigh, who was my cousin's steward, has been helpful. He will continue in his job and make recommendations to me about the farm. And now, lady, time passes and I do have this farm to run, as well as looking after my new inheritance.'

Fidelma rose and smiled. 'Indeed. I thank you for your time. Let us hope the matter of Conmaol's claim is speedily clarified.'

'I still think that the matter is as clear as ever it will be. The sooner you make your pronouncement of guilt on the vagrant we will all rest at night.'

'If only life was as simple as that,' Fidelma said evenly. 'But the law is a hard taskmaster and requires proof positive. Still, we are moving towards the truth. I am sure it will not be long before we can make the pronouncement on whoever is the guilty one who so brutally killed your cousin and his family.'

'Well, I knew the vagrant was a bad lot the moment I saw him. You know he came here looking for work? I did not trust him and told him to clear off.'

'Ah yes, so he said. That's why he went on to seek work on your cousin's farm instead.'

'Whatever happened there, that is the fault of Adnán. He should have chased the vagrants off instead of allowing them to stay overnight on the land. Trespassers are certainly not welcome on my land. Making camps, building fires – they cause more trouble than if the territory was invaded by an alien army.'

'So you have had trouble from itinerants before? They make camps and build fires without permission?'

Tadgán had risen and was nodding. 'I've had fields and even a barn destroyed by illegal fires over the years.'

'Was there a fire in this area last night? I think someone reported seeing a blaze.'

Eadulf could not help admiring the subtle way that Fidelma had manipulated the conversation into asking for news of the missing wagon belonging to Celgaire. If it had been set on fire as they suspected and the horse had escaped from it, then it would surely have been seen and reported to Tadgán. However, there was no mistaking the genuinely puzzled look on his sallow face.

'A fire? Not that I have seen, nor have any of my workers reported such a thing to me.'

They rode back in silence towards the field where Gobánguss' horse had been found. It could be true that the fire had not been seen, if the wagon had been set alight, because of the hill being in the way and, of course, the time of the fire. At the moment, the only evidence that the wagon had been fired at all was the horse's harness with its tell-tale burnmarks.

'What now?' Fethmac asked, as they crossed the oat field. He was still short of temper and obviously still felt Fidelma's criticism strongly.

'Now we look for Gobánguss,' she reminded him. 'We'll ride northward for a while for that is the only direction in which he could go.'

It seemed an age before they spotted the burly form of the smith riding on horseback out of the stretch of woodland to their right. He saw them, halted and eagerly waved his hand.

'He's found something,' grunted Eadulf. Indeed, it was Eadulf who had already noticed the crushed areas of green anemones and primrose leaves waiting to flower in the next few weeks. It was obvious that a heavy vehicle had driven off the main track running alongside the river and headed into the woods from which Gobánguss had appeared.

'This way,' the smith called, his face sombre. There was no need to ask him to explain further.

The young magistrate urged his horse forward immediately, ignoring Fidelma's warning cry to be careful. She and Eadulf knew what was waiting ahead and chose to follow the young man at a more controlled pace.

It was strange. The trees had a way of masking odours, for they did not notice anything until they crossed the grass border from the trackway and then entered the woods, which was when the distinctive smell of charred wood enveloped them.

'We shall soon know the reason for the burned traces and lines on that horse,' Fidelma said to Eadulf. 'I am afraid it will be as Gobánguss feared.'

She had barely spoken when the voice of Fethmac was heard shouting just ahead of them through the trees. His tone was high pitched and the words were just inarticulate sounds.

A moment later they emerged into a small clearing alongside him and saw what it was that was causing him such emotion.

CHAPTER NINE

There was enough left of the burnt woodwork to recognise Celgaire's wagon. The iron-rimmed wheels and some of the spokes had remained untouched by flames. The bolsters supporting the width of the frame and the timber oar pole, from the front of the vehicle to which the oxen or horses were attached, were also scarcely torched. Other than that, it seemed a great conflagration had rendered the vehicle into an almost-skeleton of charcoal. The fact that the grass around it was not only scorched but burned to the earth showed how intense the flames had been. Even the trees around the edges of the clearing were charred and blackened. It was amazing, so Fidelma thought, that the intensity of the inferno had not set the entire woodland alight. Had it been a dry summer, there was no question that the blaze would have spread.

They sat in silence awhile, gazing with a peculiar fascination at the scene.

It was Eadulf who spoke first.

'We should check the remains,' he said, dismounting.

No one asked what he would be checking for. They sat on their horses in silence, watching him as he approached the vehicle and began to sift through the ashes. He made a thorough examination before he turned back to them.

'No sign of a body,' he reported.

Fethmac was shaking his head. 'The vagrant is stupid!' he exclaimed.

Eadulf frowned at him. 'Stupid?' he echoed.

'It is obvious that he set fire to the wagon to disguise his escape. Where does he think he will escape to on foot? At least if he had kept Gobánguss' horse, he could have used that to travel across country. Why set fire to the wagon, allow the horse to wander into the field and then set off on foot? And where would he be heading to?'

'You are forgetting again, Fethmac, that he was not alone,' Eadulf said heavily. 'His rescuer must have accompanied him.'

'Before we begin that discussion, we must make a search of these woods.' Fidelma's tone was dry. 'Whoever released Celgaire from Gobánguss' shed had it planned. They came here and knew how and where to continue their journey. Let's get started.'

They all dismounted and, on Fidelma's instructions, began to spread out in a circle around the clearing.

It was barely a moment or two before Gobánguss shouted, 'I have him! I have found the vagrant!'

They rushed to join the smith. He was standing over the prone form of a man. The first thing they saw was the scorched back, barely covered by burnt and tattered clothes. The only sign that the man was still alive was the limbs twitching and the occasional moan.

'He must have escaped from the fire,' Fethmac admitted begrudgingly.

'That much is obvious,' Fidelma tutted. 'How badly is he burned?'

'It looks pretty bad,' Eadulf said. He went down on one knee beside the semi-conscious man and began trying to lift away pieces of the clothing from his back. While he did so, Fidelma instructed Fethmac and Gobánguss to continue to search as far as they were able. It was no use wasting time just watching Eadulf.

However, it was not long before Eadulf stood up and went to take his *les*, the medical bag, from his horse.

'He has extensive burns on his back, but with the right medical treatment, he can recover. There are no injuries to his front.'

'If the burns are not so bad, why is he groaning and in a semi-conscious state?' Fidelma queried.

'Because there are bruises and contusions at the back of his skull and neck. I would say he was hit a couple of times with something heavy.' Eadulf paused. 'There is something else,' he added quietly.

'What do you mean?'

Eadulf pointed to the man's wrists. 'You see those marks? They were not caused by fire. They are the burnmarks of rope. His wrists were tightly bound and, I would say, bound behind him.'

Fidelma was not entirely surprised. Whoever had 'rescued' him, had brought him here bound, set the wagon on fire and left him to die in the flames.

Eadulf was now kneeling once more by the side of the wounded man, applying some medications from his bag and carefully binding his head. Celgaire did not seem able to recognise any of them and was mumbling words that made no sense.

'There is no one else in the vicinity.' It was Fethmac returning. 'And no sign of anything else.'

A moment later Gobánguss joined them from the other side of the clearing. 'Nothing to report, lady.'

Fidelma looked from one to another, before saying: 'I am now positive that Celgaire was used by the real murderer in this matter. His escape was engineered so that we would think he had fled for the obvious reasons, as the guilty party. The murderer bludgeons the man then, having tied his hands together, he leaves him in the wagon, to which he sets fire, hoping the body will be reduced to ashes, along with the wagon.'

Fethmac still looked dubious. 'So you believe he was unconscious with hands tied behind him, yet still he managed to escape from the burning wagon?'

'People can do some extraordinary things when driven to save their lives,' Eadulf pointed out.

Fidelma was harder. 'You saw the evidence for yourself and I hope I do not have to remind you of it. Gobánguss' shed was forced from the outside, which showed . . .'

'Only that he had an accomplice,' Fethmac muttered sullenly.

'From where did this accomplice miraculously appear?' Fidelma challenged him. 'Think carefully. If you will not be guided by me, you have the right to protest to the Council of Brehons or to my brother's Chief Brehon. Until then I have taken charge of this matter and trust you will accept my guidance.'

The young magistrate's mouth tightened for a moment and then he inclined his head in silent acceptance.

'Good. The situation is clear.' Fidelma then stopped and put her head to one side, thinking for a moment. 'Who knew that Celgaire had escaped from Gobánguss' shed, apart from us?'

'My wife did and, I presume, so did Gobánguss' wife,' Fethmac answered.

'What about the boy who brought the horse to you?' Fidelma asked, glancing at the smith.

'As far as he was concerned, he just found the horse wandering loose and knew it belonged to me. He did not know anything else.'

'Then we must make sure that it stays that way. Not a word of the man's escape, far less that we have recovered him. We must not alert the person who did this that we have found Celgaire and that he is still alive.'

'Why?' Fethmac asked.

'Because this was an attempt on Celgaire's life,' she replied patiently. 'What was done once can be done again. I think Celgaire's life is in danger because he was meant to take the blame for the slaughter of Adnán and his family.'

'So what do you suggest be done now?'

'We must return him to a place where he can be nursed and recover from this attack.'

'Nursed?' The word came as a protest from Eadulf. 'You forget that I am the only one here who seems to know about the healing arts, and won't it look strange if I suddenly disappear to look after someone? People would soon become suspicious.'

'I suppose they would,' Fidelma replied reluctantly.

'You really think he was freed by someone in the village, who then left him in this state and meant him to die?' Gobánguss asked slowly, still reflecting on the implications of what she had said.

'I believe that to be so.'

'If we can get him back to my place in the village, without anyone seeing us, we could return him to the shed and I can easily repair the locks,' he offered.

'No, it was broken into once. So it seems we must hide him from the murderer as well as from the anger of the crowd,' Eadulf replied.

'There is a space in the hayloft at the back of my barn,' suggested Fethmac, 'and there is a door there which we can use. In the loft, surrounded by hay bales, no one will find him. Eadulf can move in and out at will.'

'Someone will see us going back to the village with him,' Gobánguss said gloomily. 'It's morning and there will be people on the road who are bound to notice us transporting the unconscious man. Even if we hide his features, they will know who he is. One of them will gossip and that will soon spread.'

'Well, he needs attention immediately and it will take time for his recovery,' Eadulf said. 'Having received that blow on the back of the head, I would say the less we move him, the better. And, of course, the sooner those burns are attended to . . . well, they could become infected and I don't have the right medications with me.'

'What is it you need?' Fethmac asked.

'Ideally, I need a salve of elder blossom, yarrow and red clover simmered in wheatgerm oil. Dried chestnut leaves also, if some can be found.'

'My wife can supply those for she is sometimes called upon to treat the local children as we have no physician in the village.'

Fidelma was thinking hard. 'The main problem is where to take him. Gobánguss is right. Someone will see us if we take him back to the village. Also, we can't move him far without doing his injuries further damage.'

Fethmac spoke up then, and it was clear that an idea had occurred to him.

'You realise that the nearest building to here is but a short distance across the river?'

'Across the river?' Fidelma frowned. 'That would be on Adnán's farmstead?'

'A little to the north and on the river itself is the watermill. At least it is sheltered and warm. Thanks to the rocks that Tadgán was on about, there is an easy ford there,' Fethmac said.

'I know the place well,' Gobánguss declared. 'I could take you there while Fethmac rides back to the village to get the healing herbs from his wife that Brother Eadulf requires.'

Fidelma was hesitant but it seemed that Fethmac knew exactly what was passing through her mind.

'Lady, you can trust me,' he declared. 'I question some of your deductions but I will follow you in your position as senior to me. However, I will reserve the right to make my protest to the Chief Brehon if you are proved wrong.'

Fidelma stared thoughtfully at him for a moment. He returned her gaze without flinching. She suddenly smiled. 'Very well. You know what Eadulf needs. As soon as Celgaire is fit enough to travel we will see about taking him somewhere that is more secure than the watermill.'

After Fethmac departed on his errand, Gobánguss, as the more experienced horseman other than Fidelma, decided that he would carry the injured man across the river. This was done by placing Celgaire on his stomach across the back of the horse in front of the smith, who steadied the body. Fidelma and Eadulf rode anxiously behind the burly fellow and his semi-conscious passenger. Fortunately, they did not encounter anyone en route.

They saw the watermill on the far side of the bank as they came round a bend in the river. Mills of varying sizes had been common in Ireland for centuries although the Uí Néill genealogists claimed that it was the High King Cormac Mac Art who introduced them in the country three hundred years before. It was a claim that Fidelma knew was firmly disputed. The drying and grinding of corn was known in the time before time. The dark oak watermill, which Adnán had constructed beside the river, was one of the more common smaller mills.

Gobánguss halted at the bank of the river and regarded it carefully.

'I see the ford,' he called out. 'I don't think it is very deep.'

Silently, Eadulf hoped that the smith was right. The race, as the river approached the mill, was certainly faster than the usual steady current he had seen as they rode along the water.

'Shall I go first?' Fidelma asked. 'You have Celgaire to weigh you down and so I am lighter than you.'

Gobánguss looked doubtful but Eadulf knew that Fidelma was an excellent horsewoman and he had no concerns as she nudged her horse further along the bank and then entered the river. Indeed, at times, the water barely swept above her mount's higher hock joints and it was easy for her to reach the far bank. Gobánguss went next without problems and Eadulf gave free rein to his placid cob who, sure footed, easily conveyed him across.

The watermill was strongly constructed for all its simplicity. There were openings that provided both light and ventilation. The place was deserted as they had expected it to be, not only because of the circumstances of Adnán's death and lack of work on the farm but because the grinding season had passed so there was little enough work to do. They dismounted, hitching their horses to a bar designed for the purpose, and then helped Gobánguss carry Celgaire into the interior. There was plenty of room away from the working part of the mill where the sacks of grain would be stacked before and after the grinding process. It was here they laid Celgaire down and Eadulf bent to check on his condition.

In spite of the openings for light, some extra illumination was needed to examine Celgaire and it was Gobánguss who found a lamp and the means to ignite it. While Eadulf then went to fetch his medical bag from his horse, Fidelma stood back and surveyed the interior of the watermill.

Its construction was simple. Fidelma had seen several mills of this kind in which the shaft stood vertically with the wheel horizontal at the lower end of it. She knew it to be an inexpensive mill and one that did not call for much skill to operate, for the two millstones were hardly bigger than querns, placed horizontally on top of the shaft. The bottom one was fixed while the top one could be turned and the adjustable height between the two allowed the miller to grind coarse or fine grain. She wondered if Tadgán was right to be unhappy about Fethmac's judgement. It was true that he could still take water from the river, but not at so convenient a point to his field. She tried to remember the details of the law text called 'The Rights of Water' that dealt with this matter, but it was a long time since she had consulted it.

She turned her attention back to the immediate problem.

'How is he?' she asked Eadulf, who had returned having also refilled the leather water bag he usually carried. He finished bathing the man's forehead with a cloth, before replying.

'If I can get the herbs to make the salve, there will be no problem with the burns healing. It is the blow on his head that I am worried about. I cannot do much about that except treat the contusion. I worry that he has had no lucid moment since we found him.'

'We need him to identify the man who released him,' Fidelma said, almost feeling guilty as she said it.

Eadulf made a face. 'Are you so sure it was a man?' He was remembering the times when Fidelma used to point out that one should never presume a killer was a male as opposed to female.

She did not rise to the bait.

'One thing is now certain,' she replied. 'There is a killer on the loose and we have hardly begun the task of investigation. All that we have clarified at the moment is that the prime suspect, Celgaire here, appears to have been deemed guilty by prejudice alone.'

'And that the farmer Adnán was not the innocent champion of good that we were first told. Some people disliked him intensely,' Eadulf added.

'There are certainly several people that I would like to question before we are capable of even assessing the facts.'

'You have yet to question Taithlech, the man who was witness to the dead swineherd's will,' Eadulf reminded her. 'His name seems to come up in everything we have heard.'

They were interrupted by a piteous moan from Celgaire. Eadulf turned back to his patient.

'I think he might be coming to,' he declared excitedly after a moment or two examining the man.

Gobánguss moved forward. 'Is there anything I can do to help?'

Eadulf shook his head without looking up. He took a cloth and bathed Celgaire's head again. The man had turned on his side and then encountered the discomfort of his back. He groaned aloud. Then he peered up towards Eadulf and blinked several times as if trying to regain his focus. He showed no sign of recognition . . . and gave a gasp and tried to struggle to sit up. Gently Eadulf pressed him back.

Celgaire's voice was distorted as he attempted to speak. Eadulf allowed him to take some sips of water.

'You are among friends. Rest easy,' he instructed quietly. 'Do you remember your name?'

The man coughed a little, clearing his throat and speaking hoarsely. 'I am Celgaire. I seem to know you.'

'I am Eadulf – Eadulf of Seaxmund's Ham. Do you remember me?'

It seemed the man's memories were flooding back, the expressions on his features changing as they did so.

Fidelma bent forward at Eadulf's side. 'And do you remember me, Celgaire?' she said.

'I do, lady. What has happened to me?'

'I was rather hoping that you would tell me that,' she replied.

When the man hesitated, Eadulf asked: 'What was the last thing you remember?'

Celgaire frowned as if trying to summon up the memory. 'I was a prisoner in a shed. It was dark. Then . . . then I heard a bolt scraping and I stood up as someone was trying to open it.'

Fidelma and Eadulf exchanged a quick frown.

'Go on,' she prompted when Celgaire hesitated. 'Who was it?'

'I do not know. A voice ordered me to stand away from the door. Then it was smashed in. I suppose there was a lock on it as well as a bolt. A figure then stood in the shadows but before I could do anything further, something hit me. That was the last clear thing I remember.'

'You did not recognise the figure?'

'A black shadow, that was all.'

'Nothing else?'

'Some disjointed memories.' He gave a grunt. 'My back is painful.'

'You have been burned. Try not to put pressure on it. I will treat it as soon as I have my salve.'

'Burned?' Then Celgaire gave a moan.

'You remember something else?'

'It is all so confusing,' he said.

'Tell us whatever you can recall.'

'I think I was back in my wagon. The smell and shadows seemed the same. I thought I was dreaming. I realised my hands were tied behind my back. The wagon was moving and then . . . then I think I passed out again.'

'Do you remember anything else?'

'The burning. It doesn't make any sense at all.'

'Just tell us what you can,' encouraged Fidelma.

'I came to and was still on the wagon floor. I knew that. But my hands were no longer tied. There was smoke everywhere. I felt I could not breathe. And the heat . . . Although I couldn't understand it, I knew that I had to get out. I had to escape. My head throbbed. I felt I was going to pass out but the fear in me made me strong; it told me that if I did so, I would die. I crawled towards the back of the wagon – by instinct more than anything else, and fell off onto the ground. I recall the ice-cold air, although I could still smell smoke. And then I was crawling through mud and grass. It was cold but the cold was like a balm. Then I blacked out again. And that is all – until I awoke just now.'

Fidelma and Eadulf were silent as they absorbed his story. Then Fidelma stood up.

'Try not to worry about anything. You are safe now and Eadulf will tend to your burns as soon as he is able.'

'Where am I, lady?' asked the man.

'For the moment, you are in a safe place some way from the village.'

'But my wife, my child . . . were they, were they in the wagon?' There was a sudden shock in his voice as if he had just realised the possibility.

'Your wife and child are still safe in the village and are being looked after. You were the only one taken in your wagon.'

Celgaire let out a gasp of relief. Then another thought occurred to him.

'My wagon, lady. Is it really burned? Is that memory a true one? Is it completely destroyed?'

'It is,' she confirmed.

'It was our only home,' Celgaire said dully. 'Our only means of transport with all our belongings.'

'Do not worry about that for the moment,' Eadulf said gently. 'Things can be replaced. Our concern is to get you better. So lie down and rest, but keep off your back for the time being.'

Celgaire nodded wearily, his eyes closing and, stretched on his side, was immediately asleep.

Fidelma turned to Gobánguss who had remained standing anxiously by.

'Can you take a look to see if there is any sign of Fethmac returning?'

The big smith nodded and left the mill. Fidelma went to a box at one side and sat down. Lost in thought, she absently watched Eadulf trying to make the injured man more comfortable. When he came to join her, she was looking perplexed.

'This is getting complicated, Eadulf.'

'It always was,' he returned dryly. 'But it confirms what you thought. That someone released Celgaire, took him as a prisoner in his own wagon, having rendered him unconscious with his hands tied behind him then, that same person brought him to the woodland across the river and set fire to the wagon.'

'Having ensured he was still unconscious and removing the bonds, thinking he would be dead in a short time.'

'Yes – and it was thought that, like fools, we would be lured into believing that Celgaire, our main suspect for the slaughter of Adnán's family, had been released by a confederate and perished in a fire accident.'

'Yes, we were taken for fools. Young Fethmac certainly was happy to follow that pattern of thought.'

Eadulf raised a brow at the reference to the magistrate.

'You still seem unhappy with the way Fethmac is conducting himself.'

Fidelma shrugged. 'I know he is immature and inexperienced, but he is responsible as a magistrate in this area. He should know better when evaluating certain things.' She raised a hand. 'I know, I know. You think I am too hard on him. But if I do not correct him or try to teach him, who else will he learn from? I do not want to have to report him to Fíthel.'

Eadulf was surprised. 'You'd report him to the Chief Brehon?'

'I am doing my best for him. The judgement of compensation for this watermill is another thing. My opinion is that the compensation he felt Tadgán was entitled to was so derisory he might just as well have not given it. The value of one cow and free use of grinding corn – when it could be arranged and without a specific time given? That as compensation for the loss of water to irrigate his barley field? The laws are strict about those who change watercourses.'

'But Fethmac said that it was impossible to say when the rocks were placed on the riverbed.'

'Why, there are plenty of local people who would have known if the flow of the water had been changed!'

'Perhaps – plenty of people who supported Tadgán and plenty of others who would have supported Adnán. What was it that you said? That this was a little Garden of Eden?'

'I said it was like entering the Garden of Fand,' she corrected. 'I passed through it once in summer with the flowers and greenery and it seemed to me to be a place of Otherworldly beauty.'

Eadulf sniffed. 'If I recall aright, for all her Otherworldly beauty Fand was a weak and helpless person, intriguing with her lover against her husband. There was death and evil in Fand's Garden, just as in this one. A Garden of Eden it is not.'

Fidelma smiled thinly. 'Well, even the Garden of Eden had its evil serpent.'

'I can't say that this is the most pleasant place I have ever been in,' Eadulf told her. 'To my mind everyone seems to feel a degree of animosity towards everyone else.'

'That is what makes our task hard but, on the other hand, it makes me more determined to discover the truth. It takes a diabolical mind to arrange the escape of the suspect when it must have become known that I had doubts about his guilt. A diabolical mind to plan Celgaire's death so that he would perish during his escape in a burning wagon and thus everyone would be satisfied the guilty had been punished and further investigation would be stopped.'

'Except that it would not have stopped,' Eadulf demurred, 'because the diabolical mind, as you put it, does not know your character. You could not have given up once you had that suspicion in your mind.'

Fidelma grimaced without humour. 'That's just it, Eadulf. The murderer does not know my mind. And as I said, there are still people I want to question.'

'I presume that you are thinking of that stranger's arrival at the funeral. What was his name, Conmaol? He would make a good suspect for the killing of his cousin, especially if he has legitimate claim to the kin-land.'

'At the moment we only have his word that he was not here when the event took place. He was certainly near enough to hear the news and be able to arrive at the funeral so quickly. So maybe he was near enough to have committed the actual murders.'

'And there is Taithlech, whose name keeps appearing in almost every conversation,' Eadulf said. 'Taithlech, who suddenly had that urgent task for Gobánguss to perform last night after the funeral.' He paused. 'We may be overlooking the obvious,' he added quietly.

'The obvious?' Fidelma queried. 'What is being overlooked?'

'Have you considered how big Celgaire's wagon is? That it is heavy, a cumbersome vehicle.'

'And your point?'

'That to move it takes skill to harness and drive it quietly away.'

'The sort of skill that would come to a merchant often used to driving heavy wagons of goods?' smiled Fidelma. 'I have already noted that this Taithlech was not seen at the funeral.'

'I am sure Gobánguss' wife heard more than she was letting on.'

'It is one thing being sure but in law, Eadulf, you have to prove it. It is hard to believe that Gobánguss' wife would become involved in this matter to the point of lying. The fact is that we have information but not enough facts to make any sense out of it all.'

There came a moan from the injured man and Eadulf left Fidelma to go and tend to the man and wet his dry lips.

'It shouldn't be long now before we get that medication and your pain will be eased,' he promised Celgaire with a comforting smile.

The words were barely out of his mouth when he heard Gobánguss cry out from outside the mill.

'There's a rider coming.' There was a hesitation. 'From the direction of the village but . . . but it is not Fethmac!'

CHAPTER TEN

T he rider turned out to be Ballgel, Fethmac's wife.

'My husband is delayed,' she explained as she swung down from her horse. 'A dispute in the village has required his attention.'

'A dispute?' frowned Fidelma. 'To do with this matter?'

The magistrate's wife shook her head. 'No, it was not related to the murders. It was some sort of dispute about sharing honey between two neighbours. A simple matter but one that needed arbitration from Fethmac.'

Bees were considered of high value and important, and the law texts were full of the regulations pertaining to both wild and domestic hives. An individual keeping hives for honey had to share the honey with neighbours, on the basis that the bees gathered their nectar from neighbouring lands as well as the land where the hives were situated.

Ballgel took down her saddlebag and turned to Eadulf.

'I have brought the items you requested. I have a jar of a salve made from elder blossoms, and yellow clover which has been simmered in wheatgerm. I made this last year and it can be applied directly. Does the man have a headache or fever? I have brought dried elderberry, nettle and valerian, any of which I could use to make an infusion.'

Eadulf nodded approvingly. 'That is good. So you know something of the healing arts?'

Ballgel explained, 'I learned things from my mother, who learned from her mother. You know that we have no permanent physician in the village, so I am often called upon to use what knowledge I have to help in these matters. Is there anything more I can do?'

Eadulf thanked her, and added: 'I think I can do everything that needs to be done now.'

He disappeared inside the mill to attend to Celgaire while Fidelma asked if Fethmac would be following after he had resolved the dispute.

'He said he would come as soon as possible,' Ballgel answered. 'He told me that the problem for you will be to return the murderer to the village without anyone knowing.'

Fidelma raised her eyebrows at the woman's use of the word.

'Don't forget the man is yet to be judged,' she reminded her sharply. Then, before Ballgel could respond she turned to Gobánguss who had joined them, saying, 'You had better resume your watch on the road.' Then she gestured for Ballgel to follow her into the slightly warmer atmosphere of the mill house.

Fidelma was glad of the opportunity to speak to Ballgel without her husband's presence. There were questions on her mind but she decided that she should approach them carefully.

'I suppose you have lived here all your life?' she opened, as they seated themselves on the far side of the mill from where Eadulf was now bending over the distraught figure of Celgaire and applying the medications.

Ballgel loosened her riding cloak, a little annoyed at Fidelma's rebuke.

'I have. My mother was an *étidach,* a professional dressmaker, and my father was a merchant, taking the clothing that she made to Árd Fhionáin, or to Cathair and even to Cashel itself.'

'And do they live in the village here?'

A look of sadness crossed the girl's features. She shook her head.

'No, they were taken off by the Yellow Plague. That was some years before I met Fethmac, when he returned from his law studies.'

'So you know most people in the area?'

'I know that the only deaths that have occurred within living memory have been natural ones or those visited on us by the Yellow Plague or other pestilences. The murders of Adnán and his family are the first of their kind. We once had a physician who was also carried off by the plague and, as I said, now we have no permanent physician here. There are few ills so serious that I cannot handle them.'

'That is not what I asked,' Fidelma said mildly.

'I think I understand your meaning. Violence has only come to us in the form of outsiders. We were a peaceful community until the vagrants came.'

Fidelma sighed impatiently.

'Married to a magistrate, you should know something of the law, Ballgel. The matter of the murders must be proved beyond question. I have several questions. I presume your views reflect those of Fethmac? Otherwise, not being privy to the investigation, you would merely be expressing a personal prejudice without knowledge.'

The girl's jaw tightened.

'Everyone knows that it could only have been the vagrant who slaughtered Adnán and Aoife and their boys.'

'The knowledge of everyone is often not entirely correct,' Fidelma replied.

'Fethmac believes in the guilt of the vagrant. It's just that he has become confused by . . .'

'Let us hope his confusion has merely come about as he has learned more from the evidence and not because he is unwilling to follow my guidance on how an investigation should be properly run.'

The girl said disdainfully, 'It is up to my husband to tell you what he thinks. I speak for myself.'

'Quite rightly so,' agreed Fidelma, not without irony. 'Belief out of loyalty to your husband is certainly not conclusive. However, it is of you that I wish to ask some questions.'

'Such as?' The girl's tone was suspicious.

'About your views of people in the village. People that you obviously know. For example, I am sure that you know the woman Blinne.'

'Íonait's mother? Of course – I know them both. But I thought my husband took you to see Blinne?'

'That is so. I was interested in her situation and her relationship with Tadgán, Adnán's cousin.'

Ballgel snorted, 'You mean the lack of it! It was her husband Broc who worked for Tadgán and when he was gored to death, Tadgán refused to pay compensation on the grounds that Broc was in debt to him.'

'Your husband told me of the case and said that evidence was presented which he could not dispute.'

'There was a witness to the debt,' Ballgel agreed.

'The merchant Taithlech? He seems a prominent inhabitant of this village, though I have not met him yet. He was the witness to that debt. I understand he is a merchant like your father was, so—'

Ballgel's jaw raised a fraction. 'Not like my father was!' she retorted. 'No one likes Taithlech. He's a mean-minded man in spite of being successful in his trade. He deals in corn, oats and wheat, selling mostly to the mountain folk.' She gestured with her head to the southern peaks. Fidelma knew that growing sustainable grain crops in the high peaks was not an option so an enterprising merchant could trade for the produce of the hills.

'It seems odd that Taithlech, being a merchant, claimed to be a close friend of Broc, who was a worker on Tadgán's farm, as well as Lúbaigh, a worker on Adnán's farm,' reflected Fidelma.

'No,' Ballgel disagreed. 'It's not so unusual in a small rural hamlet like this. Everyone knows everyone to a greater or lesser extent. However, he was more a friend of Tadgán. It was the grain crops that he bought from Tadgán that he took and sold in the mountains. You must have been told that Taithlech's daughter, Flannat, married Tadgán's son, Díoma, who is now dead. Flannat and her baby live at Tadgán's farm as is their right.'

Fidelma acknowledged the fact. She mentally reminded herself that she had promised to speak with Taithlech about his witness to Broc's statement. However, she was more concerned with the murders at the moment.

'How does Tadgán get on with the father of his late son's wife?' she asked. 'Could his witness have been biased?'

Ballgel's shrugged. 'One cannot choose one's relatives.'

'He doesn't like him? But he does business with him?'

'I doubt you will find many in the village who would own to liking Taithlech,' she responded. 'Probably not even his own daughter.'

'Yet it was considered that his witness to Tadgán's claim against Broc was valid?'

'My husband judged it so,' the girl said defensively.

Fidelma waited a moment and then asked: 'Do you know Íonait, Blinne's daughter?'

'Of course. Poor girl.'

'Why do you refer to Íonait as "poor"? Because of her mother's position after Broc was killed?'

'Blinne manages well enough. No, it's because I felt that Íonait was a vulnerable girl, even though she has now passed the age of choice. She seems to need protection.'

'In what way?'

'Oh, it's nothing specific. It is just something I feel. A few days ago I met her returning home from Adnán's farm. She was dishevelled and crying.'

'Did you ask her what the matter was?'

'I did. All I could get out of her was that she had decided to quit the farm.'

'Did she tell you why?'

'She did not.'

'Yet because she decided to stop working there, you say she was vulnerable? I do not understand.'

'I felt there was more to it.'

'What more?'

Ballgel sighed. 'Well, if you must know, that young brother of Lúbaigh might have the mind of a child, but he is at the onset of manhood. I am sure you know what I mean.'

'You think something happened with Íonait?'

'The girl would say nothing. But twice, I myself have seen Dulbaire staring at her. You know the look – he was mooning after her. I think he has begun to pester her. I cannot say further.'

'But you have no proof? She did not say anything?'

'Of course not. Would a young girl wish to confess to the attentions of an imbecile? Her distress was plain enough. I hoped she might have told her mother.'

'A rider and two horses coming!' Gobánguss' cry from outside caused both women to rise to their feet and go to the door of the mill, to stare anxiously across the river.

'It's my husband!' cried Ballgel.

It was indeed the young magistrate, leading a packhorse.

'I thought, if the vagrant was well enough, we could wrap him in a blanket and put him across the packhorse, so that no one could see to identify him. Then we could ride back to the village and head straight into our barn,' Fethmac explained when he had dismounted and exchanged greetings.

Eadulf had joined them. 'If we take it easy, Celgaire might be able to make it. I am still concerned about the head injury but the burns, while unpleasant, should not cause him too much discomfort.'

'We will ask him how he feels about that,' Fidelma said, after consideration. 'I don't suppose there is any chance of him being able to identify whoever it was released him from the shed?'

'Not a chance. As you know, he did not see the man . . .'

'Or woman,' Fidelma added ironically, remembering Eadulf's wit.

Ballgel did not understand the humour. She gasped. 'You mean the wife of the vagrant released him?'

It was Fethmac who corrected his wife. 'The woman was under the custody of Gobánguss' wife at that time. The lady Fidelma is merely stressing that we do not know who released him, man or woman. The vagrant was knocked unconscious before he glimpsed his rescuer. Anyway, if he can be moved, I suggest we do not waste the day further.'

Fidelma cast him an irritated glance. She felt she should remind him that 'the vagrant' had a name. Celgaire. Also, she did not feel that she had wasted the day. Eadulf had gone inside the mill to have a word with Celgaire. Although still confused and in pain, it turned out that Celgaire was willing to undertake the journey. He wanted to be close to his wife and son.

Fidelma had agreed it would draw attention if they all rode back in a single body. It was decided that she and Ballgel would ride to the village first. Ballgel could then prepare to receive the injured man in their barn. Fethmac and Eadulf would escort him there after a short interval, with Celgaire shrouded in the blanket that Fethmac had brought. Gobánguss would make his own way back.

As they were preparing the packhorse so that Celgaire could be conveyed on it in reasonable comfort, Eadulf asked Fidelma quietly, 'Are you not coming with us?'

Fidelma smiled briefly. 'We have seen that Eden is inhabited by more than one serpent. I shall ride on to the village because I am going to visit one of them.' She chuckled when she saw Eadulf's frown of bewilderment and added, 'I think it is about time I met this Taithlech.'

'Shouldn't I come with you?' Eadulf was concerned.

'I'd rather you made sure that Celgaire reaches Fethmac's barn in safety and that he will be secure and comfortable there. Whoever released him will try to kill him again if they find out he survived. So be careful whom you trust and keep a careful watch.'

Eadulf looked a little disconcerted but shrugged acceptance of the task.

Taithlech's house and grainstores lay to the west of the village by the north bank of the Dubhóg. Fidelma was directed there by a young boy. She saw at once that the merchant had an affluent home compared even to the magistrate, but dominating the buildings was the large, oblong barn in which he stored his grain. It stood on a north–south axis with one side open and a roof supported on posts. This type of barn was called a *sabhall* and it was said that when the Blessed Patrick was preaching in the northern lands he held his services in such barns, so that the word *sabhall* became the first word used for Christian chapels or churches. That Taithlech was successful and prosperous could be seen by the number of workers about even now in the winter months, and there were several donkey carts on which grain was being loaded or offloaded.

One of the men paused in his work to direct her to the house where, she was told, she would find the merchant.

As she dismounted in front of the house and was hitching her horse to the post, a large dark-haired man emerged at the main door and stood, feet wide apart, hands on hips, regarding her with suspicion. Her immediate feeling was one of dislike as she gazed at his moon-shaped features and tiny, gimlet eyes, black and expressionless as if they were just marble stones. If the eyes were windows to the soul, as the saying went, then this man's soul was lost in the black pit of the Netherworld. The white fleshy skin contrasted starkly against his jet-black hair, which seemed well tended and combed, but the line of it across his forehead made a sort of Devil's peak. The eyebrows were also black in colour and yet – and what was strange – Fidelma saw no trace of stubble on the man's cheeks, jaw or above the upper lip.

His clothing was all black, both trousers and linen jacket. He wore a black silk shirt underneath. Gold was the predominant colour of his necklet and of the brooch that fastened his black woollen riding cloak around his slightly bent shoulders. Indeed, there was nothing about his appearance that inspired a good feeling. Fidelma found herself thinking that if ever a person had been wrongly named it was this man, for his name meant 'he who pacifies or placates'.

'I presume that you are Taithlech,' she said as she came towards him.

'You presume correctly, Fidelma of Cashel.' His voice was uncompromising as he remained without moving his stance.

'You know me?'

'The entire village has been speaking of you since your arrival.'

'Therefore you know of my position as a *dálaigh*?'

'I have been told that you have put yourself in charge of the investigation into the deaths of Adnán and Aoife and their sons. I cannot help you in that investigation because I know nothing about the matter.'

Fidelma raised an eyebrow in surprise.

'I think you pre-empt my questions. Yet your name occurs several times during my inquiries.'

There was no change of expression on the merchant's face. 'I fail to see in what way,' he countered.

'I understand that you were staying with Lúbaigh and his wife on the night of the murders.'

'I know Lúbaigh and Fuinche and have often cracked a jug of *corma* with them.'

'Did you stay overnight and when Lúbaigh left the next morning, you were not stirring? So when he came back to report finding the bodies, you were there.'

The merchant sniffed. 'I do not mind admitting that I had imbibed too much of the spirit. So I had to stay all night and had only just woken when he returned, excited and shouting about the murders.'

'What happened?'

'Fuinche told her husband to fetch the magistrate. I stayed long enough to recover my wits, for I had to go to deliver goods to a client up in the mountains. If you are here to seek information on the murders then I cannot provide it.'

'I am told that you are a merchant, specialising in selling grain and oats to the mountain people. Adnán ran one of the biggest farms here. Did you have business with him? Would you not be alarmed at the news of his death?'

His mouth twisted a little as he said, 'I had no business with Adnán and no need to have business. As to knowing him and his family, this is a small community but I had no cause to socialise with them.'

'Why was that?'

'Why not?'

Fidelma hid her impulse to tell the man to stop answering her questions with a question. She wondered how she was going to get round his defensive wall.

'Did you socialise with Broc, a swineherd?' she asked quickly.

'He's dead,' the man replied. She was pleased to see a slight look of perplexity at her change of subject.

'He is – but I am told that you were a lifelong friend of his.'

'Fethmac, the magistrate, knows that well enough.'

'You were witness that Broc had borrowed a large sum of money from Tadgán because of which, when Broc's widow sought compensation for his death, she received nothing.'

'I witnessed the document, signed by Broc, accepting the loan and promising to repay it.'

'Signed by Broc?' Fidelma repeated, questioning the word.

Taithlech's smile was condescending. 'I meant Broc made his mark and I witnessed it. I did not make the law which resulted from it. Why am I being asked this? Is it argued that I should have lied to get money for Blinne and her daughter?'

'I ask for a simple statement of truth and not your interpretation of why the question was asked,' Fidelma replied sharply. 'However, it is interesting that Blinne claims you were never the friend of her husband. Moreover, that you *were* the friend of Tadgán. That being so, was your signature above bias?'

'Since when has friendship been exclusive? I cannot help what Blinne claims. Broc allowed himself to get in debt to Tadgán. It would be natural for Blinne to claim bias against me being a witness. And since when is it wrong for a merchant to be friends with someone with whom he does business?'

'Your answers are logical,' Fidelma agreed. 'Indeed, you do a lot of business with Tadgán.'

'As I do with others. Tadgán has a large farm and you must already have been told that my daughter, Flannat, was married to his son, Díoma.'

'So you traded with Tadgán and not his cousin, Adnán?'

'Have I not already said so?'

'Why would that be?'

'I am a merchant. It is my choice whom I do business with.'

'But Adnán owned one of the richest farms here,' Fidelma persevered.

'That is irrelevant,' the man said stubbornly.

'Was it something to do with the argument that I hear you had with him?'

Taithlech's eyes widened. 'Who told you that?' Then he huffed. 'I suppose it was Lúbaigh?'

Fidelma thought rapidly. So Íonait was not the only witness to the argument between Adnán and Taithlech. Instead she asked: 'Why would Lúbaigh tell me about such an argument?'

'Because he was there.'

'So he heard the argument?'

'Of course. He was standing next to Adnán and heard it all.'

'Did he hear you threaten to kill Adnán?'

The merchant stared. 'He would not say that!' he asserted.

'The point is – did you do so?' pressed Fidelma.

Taithlech shrugged expressively after a moment's thought. 'I will not deny it. Adnán was a stubborn fool.'

'Stubborn? About what?'

'I discovered that he was trying to supply one of my regular customers of his own volition. Trying to undercut my prices. I went to tell him that I did not take kindly to it and ordered him to desist.'

'Surely he was free to supply his produce to whomever he liked?'

'I have my living to earn,' protested the merchant.

Fidelma stared about the buildings. 'And it seems that you do it very well,' she noted sardonically.

'I do it very well because I allow no one to interfere with my business, not even relatives. If Adnán wanted to sell to me I would have had no objections. But his aim was to cut me out and deal directly with this customer.'

'I was under the impression that you dealt with the folk in the southern mountains while Adnán sold his grain and stock to the townships in the north of this territory.'

'True. It was when Adnán started selling to a customer of mine in the mountains that I went to see him.'

'A customer in the mountains?' Fidelma repeated.

'That is so. In the Pass of Declan.'

Fidelma regarded him with sudden interest. 'Your customer would not be Béoán and Cáemell, the tavernkeepers in the pass?' she asked abruptly.

'It is no secret. Béoán and his wife Cáemell have long kept their tavern up in the Pass. It is the only place where hospitality is served between here and Lios Mhór, so they were my very good customers for the grains and the stock that I could provide. It is hard to grow grain up there in the mountains,' he added unnecessarily.

'I don't doubt it,' Fidelma agreed. 'So you are saying that Adnán tried to cut you out of dealing with Béoán and Cáemell?'

'I warned him that they were my clients.'

'I suppose Adnán refused to stop supplying them? Is that why you threatened him?'

Taithlech moved uncomfortably. 'I made the threat in temper only. I simply meant to make my point.'

'Tell me, if Béoán and Cáemell were such good, long-standing customers of yours, why did they do business with Adnán?'

'It had been a harsh winter and Adnán took advantage of the fact that he knew I had delayed gathering my goods from Tadgán. So he took a wagon up the mountain pass and sold the grain to Béoán directly. By the time I got there, the deal had been done and Béoán could not buy my goods. Nor could he pay me what he owed me on previous orders. He tried to tell me that Adnán had told him that I would not be coming.'

'I suppose it is business but I agree it was not an ethical thing to do,' Fidelma said. 'How did you leave things with the tavern-keeper?'

'Leave things?'

'When you told him that Adnán had trespassed in your territory? Also, you say, he could not pay you for previous goods he owed to you.'

Taithlech shrugged. 'What could I do? A debt is a debt and an example had to be made to those who decided to deal with Adnán and not me.'

Fidelma's eyes narrowed as she realised what this meant. 'So you burned down Béoán's tavern and did so as an example?'

'I was in my rights under the law of debt, the law of *ainfiach*.'

'On our way here, travelling through the Pass of Declan, we found Béoán's tavern razed to the ground.'

Taithlech said grumpily, 'They are safe, staying with a relative at Cnoc na gCloch. As I say, I have the right to recover debt.'

'But you must have hated Adnán for his underhand business dealings?'

When Taithlech spoke again, his voice was heavy with irony.

'You can rest assured, *dálaigh*, that I had the right to set fire to the tavern when I was denied the debt owed me. But I did not slaughter Adnán and his family, if that is what you are thinking. I am a merchant and I cannot conduct business without general good will. As I said, I have business dealings with Tadgán and others. I did not need to trade with Adnán. He was free to do as he would – so long as he kept out of my territory.'

Fidelma was quickly absorbing this new information. According to the young milkmaid, there had been another argument. She felt unable to pursue this, however, until she had questioned the girl further. Finally, she said: 'These other farmers you traded with . . . tell me about them.'

'Why should I?' The merchant was annoyed.

'Because it is a *dálaigh* who asks the question,' Fidelma replied mildly.

'It has no relevance to the matter of Adnán's death, so I shall refuse.'

'And if I say that it *is* of relevance as I judge it, do you repudiate that by *fris-toing*, swearing oath against it?'

A frown crossed his features as Fidelma used the legal term to repudiate or forswear. 'I do not understand.'

'To refuse to answer truthfully the questions of a *dálaigh* related to the inquiry into the murder of a person, involves the taking of an oath by the person being questioned. This is a form of renouncing the relevance of the question, and it is called *fris-toing*. The oath is accepted, of course. But if, at the end of the matter, it is found that the question was relevant, then a punishment may be imposed on the one who refused to answer. So now – do you swear an oath that the question is not relevant?'

Taithlech looked bewildered.

'How do I know if you intend to make it relevant?' he argued.

'What I am concerned about is your relationship with Adnán.'

'Isn't it irrelevant, when Adnán is dead and Tadgán now owns Adnán's farm?' he responded sourly.

'That does not make it irrelevant. I am enquiring into Adnán's murder and the motive behind it. You say that Adnán was not the only farmer you refused to trade with. Who *did* you trade with?'

'I am a merchant. I traded with many people.'

'As an example, did you ever trade with Conmaol?'

Taithlech did not respond immediately to the name.

'It is true that I trade grain with many of the hill farmers in the southern mountains. My grain comes from Tadgán as well as smaller farmers in this district. Adnán was the exception. He always took his grain to the towns to the north of this plain, as I have said.'

'Are you telling me that you have never heard of Conmaol?'

'It is a familiar name.'

'I am sure you have heard that it was Conmaol who has challenged the right of Tadgán to claim the kin-land of Adnán?' pressed Fidelma.

'Do you claim that I told this Conmaol the news so that he could come and make his claim of the kin-land here?'

'Well, did you?'

'Why would I, when Tadgán was my friend and my daughter was married to his son, who is now dead?'

'I found it interesting that Conmaol, claiming to be a cousin of Adnán and Tadgán, who lives up in the high peaks, learned so quickly about Adnán's murder and Tadgán's takeover of his farm; so quickly that Conmaol suddenly arrives at the funeral to make his own claim.'

Taithlech's piggy eyes widened a little. 'Are you accusing me . . .?'

'You have just told me that you trade in the southern peaks,' Fidelma replied calmly. 'I just wondered if you knew that Conmaol was a cousin of Adnán and Tadgán and had the right to claim seniority, being a member of their *derbhfine*. Do you know Conmaol, did you trade with him and inform him of the events here?'

'I would argue that we are probably all descendants of Ágach Ágmar the Warlike. It was only Adnán who was arrogant enough to think it made him better than anyone else; that it gave him the right to his farmland and territory,' snapped the chubby merchant. Then he seemed to catch himself and breathed deeply for a moment. 'I trade in the southern peaks. I do not recall the name of all the people I trade and speak with. I will admit that I did trade with Conmaol. I trade in news as well as goods. But I will ask *you* a question now, lady. Do you think that in the short time that has elapsed since Adnán's murder and the man's appearance at the funeral, that I could have taken my wagon up the precipitous paths to the southern peaks, passed on this information and given time for this Conmaol to arrive and challenge Tadgán to ownership of the kin-land?'

Fidelma pursed her lips for a moment. She acknowledged that Taithlech was a formidable person to question. But behind his obstructing she had learned that some of her suspicions were correct. She now believed two things about the merchant. Firstly, that he had lied about Broc so that Tadgán did not have to pay Blinne any compensation over her husband's death. Secondly, that he had known Conmaol, although at first he had tried to deny it. She was also sure that the mysterious cousin had learned of the death of Adnán from him – but how could that fit in with the timeframe? Perhaps it would just work if Taithlech had abandoned his wagon and ridden up into the high peaks on a strong horse instead. The question now was whether the merchant had any involvement in the violent and disturbing slaughter of Adnán and Aoife and their sons.

It was time to leave. With a brief word of thanks, she turned and mounted her horse, leaving the unsettled merchant still standing, looking after her.

She rode in the direction of the village, passing one or two inquisitive workers along the trackway. However, she barely noticed them, as her mind was still busy considering what she had learned from the merchant. She realised it would not be the last time she would have to question him, and must devise a way of getting through his technique of blocking her questions by other questions. Before doing anything further, however, she would go to Fethmac's barn to find out whether there had been any problems in getting Celgaire back to the village. She hoped Eadulf had been able to attend to the man's injuries without complications.

Her mind quickly passed on to what she had to do next. Her priority was to question Íonait, for not only was the girl a partial witness to that argument but Fidelma also needed to know why she had suddenly decided to quit her job at the farm the day before the slaughter of the family there.

The village was quiet now as she rode through it. In fact, the early dusk of the winter's day was already descending. The day had turned chill. It was icy where the wind caressed her cheeks and she pulled her robe and hood closely around her. She was coming to the forge and saw that the furnace was dark and unlit. It seemed as though the smith, after their early morning adventure to find the itinerants' wagon, had not returned to relight his fire. The whole place was in darkness and she pulled rein by the three poles supporting the ancient symbolic cauldron of the village.

She sat a moment wondering whether she should call in and enquire whether all was well, since Beccnat, the smith's wife, was still in charge of Celgaire's wife and child. The house beyond the forge seemed quiet but there were lights. Even if Gobánguss had not returned, Fidelma decided to just have a quick word with Beccnat and so nudged her horse forward.

At that very moment, there was a curious scraping sound which preceded a crash that startled even her placid horse, causing it to shy and make a whinny of protest. The shock made Fidelma's heart thump madly for a few seconds before she reacted, urging the horse to stillness with soft, reassuring tones. He had shied a length or so from where she had halted. Ensuring he was calm, she turned in her saddle to see what the cause of the noise had been.

In the very spot where she had stopped her horse outside the blacksmith's forge lay the great bronze cauldron. Its rim was some fifty centimetres in diameter and the weight was shown by the indentation in the soft earth of the track. It was heavy enough to disable a horse, and kill a human, had it fallen on her.

She sat staring at it, almost disbelievingly. Then she gazed upwards to the platform on top of the three poles. It was still intact. Somehow the cauldron had been pushed off its plinth. Coldly she realised that this was no accident; there was no way the cauldron could have fallen onto the path by accident. Someone had pushed it off while she was underneath. And that someone had intended to kill her.

CHAPTER ELEVEN

A door opened and Gobánguss the smith came hurrying out of his house beyond the forge.

'Whatever was that colossal noise?' he demanded, before he saw Fidelma there. 'What was it, lady?'

She pointed wordlessly to the cauldron.

Gobánguss stared at it, bewildered. Then he raised his eyes and saw the supporting poles and platform still intact.

'How on earth could that have happened?' he gasped, his face gone pale. 'The cauldron has never fallen from the platform before.'

'What's going on?' Breccnat had appeared in the cottage doorway.

'Someone tried to kill me,' Fidelma said simply.

The smith was still very shocked. Finally he said, 'By your leave, lady, what you say is impossible. You would have seen someone climb up to the small platform using a ladder. But there *is* no ladder there at present and no one can balance on top of that platform as there is not enough room. The nearest building is my barn and there is no way anyone could reach the top of the platform from that. There is a gap of nearly two metres.'

'Nevertheless, the cauldron could not have fallen of its own accord. I had halted under it for some moments and had just begun to move off when it fell.'

Gobánguss shook his head. 'If it were deliberate, then who would know you were passing here and that you would pause in such a position for them to achieve the impossible of getting the cauldron to fall?'

Fidelma had to admit the smith made a good point. Nevertheless, she felt the impossible *had* been achieved. But how?

'Do you have a lantern?' she asked, for dusk was now rapidly descending.

'There is one in my barn.'

'Good. It is the barn, or rather the roof, I wish to explore. It has a flat roof and it comes nearest to the cauldron's platform.'

'But as I said, there is a space of two metres between the barn roof and the platform. You would have seen if someone had managed to span that impossible space. They would need a plank.'

'Let us go to the roof and see,' she replied firmly. Then she asked as an afterthought, 'Didn't Fethmac tell me that the cauldron is taken down for certain ceremonies?'

'It is taken down to be polished and used when the chief of the territory visits to attend the ceremonies. That is once every nine years.'

'How is that done?'

Gobánguss shrugged. 'I keep a tall ladder in my barn. It is placed against the poles and one man goes up with a rope. Another goes up on the roof of the barn. The man on the ladder feeds one end of the rope between the cauldron's handles and then he throws the other end to the man on the barn roof. Holding the ends of the rope and paying it out carefully, the cauldron is eased off the platform and slowly lowered to the ground.'

'Why only once in nine years?' Fidelma was curious.

'It is said that when Crimthann Srem became lord of this territory he went to the Well of Knowledge. The Well was a mystical place of crystal-clear water surrounded by nine tall hazel trees which dropped their fruit into the waters, in which swam nine salmon who fed on the nuts. Whoever ate of the salmon would be possessed of all the knowledge they needed to rule wisely and well. Thus when Crimthann Srem was among us, or, indeed, his progeny, a salmon is cooked in the great cauldron every nine years.'

Fidelma sighed impatiently. 'A similar story is told in every one of the Five Kingdoms.'

Gobánguss had lit a lamp and now led the way to a fixed ladder in the barn which led upwards to the roof.

'Who has access to the barn?' called Fidelma as they climbed up using the fixed ladder.

'The barn is open all the time so anyone can come and go as they please. Nothing of great value is stored here. The tools and implements found here can be shared among the village.'

'And the tall ladder used to get to the top of the three poles?'

'That is here in the barn where it always is. I noticed it was still there when we entered.'

They emerged onto the flat roof. It was dark and Fidelma was thankful for the lantern, for the roof was without any barrier and someone could easily miss their footing if they stood too near the edge. In fact, she did trip – only to be steadied by the muscular arm of the smith. His lantern showed the cause.

A long pole of around eight feet lay on the roof.

Fidelma regarded it with a grim expression.

'So that is how the impossible was achieved. All that had to be done was to place the pole across the intervening space and push the cauldron off its plinth.'

Gobánguss sighed. 'You said "all", lady. It would also require some muscle.'

'Muscle is not lacking in such a place as this village,' Fidelma said. 'The rest was easily done. While I was moving my horse and looking to see what had nearly crashed down on me, the perpetrator would have had time to leave the roof, go down the ladder and exit the barn into the gloom.'

'It still doesn't explain why he would be on the roof of the barn just when you happened to come along and halted beneath the cauldron,' objected the smith.

'That is true. But perhaps there is an easier explanation than looking at it as a well-conceived plot.'

'Which is?'

'Events are not always premeditated. In fact, actions are more likely to be made when one seizes an opportunity.'

Gobánguss shook his head, saying, 'This is my roof, the roof of my barn. Even given the notion that this was just an opportunity seized, who would be up here in the first place and be doing . . . what?'

That was certainly a mystery she could not answer yet.

'It's too dark now to see anything. I'll come back to examine this roof when it is light tomorrow,' she said. 'Now I think we should descend. The answer to one question is sufficient for today and I realise that I have not eaten since morning.'

Fidelma was unusually quiet when, later, she sat at the table with Eadulf and Fethmac, picking at the meal that Ballgel had prepared. Her mind was clearly not on the food and twice the magistrate's wife asked her pointedly if she did not like the dishes she had prepared. The second time, and hearing the irritation in Ballgel's tone, Fidelma drew herself together to apologise and concentrate on the plate before her. Then she paused again and told her companions about the cauldron, saying that she considered it had been an attempt on her life.

Fethmac was swift to respond; his comments, perhaps naturally, were supportive of what Gobánguss had said. That it was impossible for anyone to have made a planned attack on Fidelma in such a haphazard fashion. There were too many 'ifs' to make it viable.

Eadulf agreed reluctantly that it could not have been premeditated.

Fidelma was still stubborn about her suspicion although she knew the others were being logical.

'I think the one thing I am learning is that there is something more complicated to this matter than the slaughter of Adnán and his family by a vengeful vagrant.'

After the meal, Fidelma said she wanted to have a word with Celgaire. Eadulf went with her to check how his balms and medications were working. The injured man had been placed in a corner of Fethmac's hayloft, inside a small partitioned room which had been built for some purpose and which was almost disguised by the hay bales in front of it. Celgaire lay on a makeshift bed of straw, and seemed easier than when she had last seen him.

'How is your head?' she asked when Eadulf had ascertained that the burns were healing well.

'It still hurts, lady,' replied the man.

'It is to be expected,' Eadulf said kindly. 'You have bruises there which will heal, but thankfully there is no damage to the skull.'

'I was wondering whether you could remember anything more about the attack?' Fidelma asked, sitting down beside Celgaire.

'It is as I first told you, lady. I did not see my attacker and was immediately rendered unconscious until I awoke in that blazing wagon.'

'A pity,' she sighed. 'Also, I was wondering whether you could tell me a little more about yourself. I have looked at the parchments you carried with you and I am afraid my learning is not sufficient to understand everything – apart from the fact that you are the third generation to serve the ruler of Dál Fiatach in the northern kingdom. Yet it seems you can tell me nothing about the origin of your family?'

'Nothing other than what I have told you.'

'I would like to take the parchments to the abbey of Ard Fhionáin to see a scholar there. I think these would cast some light on your background. Would you object?'

For a moment the man looked surprised. 'Why would you ask me if I object, lady? No one has asked me that before because I am not a man of rank.'

'You still have rights,' Fidelma said reprovingly. 'Have you not heard of the law text *Senbriathra Fúthail* which states that even the unfree are entitled to their rights? No? No matter. Rest assured, your rights will be protected.'

'All I can say, lady, is that the right that most concerns me is the right to have my wife and child safe, and the right to proclaim my innocence of false accusations. I did *not* kill the farmer and his family. I have never taken the life of another human being.'

'Your first concern now must be to regain your health. Mine is to resolve these mysteries and to find who was responsible for the murders, whoever they are.'

Later that night, Eadulf asked: 'I can't see where we go from here. No one seems to have any ideas other than to blame Celgaire and his family as the guilty ones. They were the only people in the right place at the right time.'

'Yet the motive for such a violent slaughter is so weak,' Fidelma replied. 'And we still haven't found out why two different weapons were involved.'

'I put it down to the killer setting down one weapon, then being confronted by his last victim and grasping anything sharp that was near at hand.'

'So, in your opinion, the older brother, Cainnech, was the last to be killed?'

'I think so, as the reaping hook is not a perfect weapon to kill with.'

'Perhaps you are right, Eadulf. But there are things here that do not seem logical.'

Eadulf pursed his lips. 'Who says any murder is based on logic?'

Fidelma smiled briefly. 'A good point, husband. But whether we call it logic or a pattern, we still have to follow it.'

'When will you be taking the parchments to Ard Fhionáin? Tomorrow?'

'No, I thought I should question Blinne's daughter next. But first, some sleep is necessary.'

The next morning, Fidelma found that Fethmac had been called away to settle some dispute about fishing rights along the southern river, An Dubhóg, and so she decided that she and Eadulf would go back to Blinne's cabin to find Íonait. She remembered the way from the time Fethmac had taken them.

It was as they were coming to the small patch of woodland on the hillock overlooking Blinne's cabin at the fork of the river that they heard the soft wailing tones of a *fedán*. The reed pipe was playing a curious lament. Eadulf edged his horse near to Fidelma's mount.

'Up in the tree to your left,' he called softly.

Fidelma glanced up. A figure was perched in a fork of the branches about five metres above the ground. The young man was bending forward slightly as if in concentration, apparently staring towards Blinne's cabin while, at the same time, the pipe was at his lips, uttering its strange dirge. Fidelma halted as she recognised the figure.

'Good morning, Dulbaire,' she called up.

The lament stopped abruptly and the youth stared down at them.

'I am not doing any harm,' he replied almost in a whine.

'I am sure that you are not,' Fidelma returned with a smile. 'Is it a good view from up there?'

The young man was frowning. 'I was just playing. Just playing my pipe.'

'We heard you,' agreed Fidelma. 'You play well.'

Dulbaire sniffed. 'You won't take it away?'

'Take away your pipe? Why should I?'

'Some people want to. They don't like it when I play.'

'Who would want to take it from you?'

The youth gestured towards Blinne's cabin. 'Her,' he said shortly. 'She doesn't like me playing.'

Fidelma regarded him thoughtfully.

'Then why are you playing here, so near to her cabin?'

'I'm not playing for her,' Dulbaire said sulkily.

'I thought your cabin was further over on Adnán's farmland?'

'Adnán? Cainnech is dead. I know he is dead,' asserted Dulbaire. 'Adnán is dead. They are all dead.'

'Indeed, they are all dead. But your cabin is quite a way from here, so why come and play here if Blinne doesn't like it?'

'Not playing for her,' repeated the boy. 'Playing for Íonait.'

'I see. You like to play for her? You like her?'

'Not doing any harm.' He was suspicious and defensive again. 'Not doing anything wrong.'

'Of course you are not. But maybe you should play for her somewhere it won't annoy her mother.'

'Not playing for Blinne. Only Íonait.'

'But . . .' Fidelma stopped herself trying to explain. Maybe it was a hard concept for the boy to understand. Instead she said: 'Well, aren't you working at the farm today?'

'Íonait is not there,' asserted the youth.

'I know. I was told that she was no longer milking the cows on that farm. But isn't your brother now in charge of the work on Adnán's farm?'

'Adnán is dead,' the boy repeated stubbornly.

'But your brother Lúbaigh is there. Won't he expect you to be working there?'

'Lúbaigh? He's at the farm.'

'Exactly. So I think you should go to see him. We will come and visit you later.'

Fidelma and Eadulf rode on towards Blinne's cottage after bidding farewell to Dulbaire, who had climbed down and reluctantly gone on his way. They dismounted as Blinne came out and watched them with a scowl.

'I thought it was that crazy boy making that infernal noise. I was told you saw Taithlech last night. Did he confess that he lied about his witness?'

'I am afraid not,' began Fidelma but the woman interrupted, her voice belligerent.

'If you came here to tell me that, there is nothing else to say.'

'I came for a different matter.'

'Well, what do you want?'

'I was going to speak with your daughter,' Fidelma reminded her. 'Is she here?'

'She is not. And tell that stupid boy to stop hanging around and giving me a headache. That awful racket is the last thing I need.'

'Where is Íonait?' Fidelma persisted.

'Gone looking for work, I hope.'

'You told me that she did not like working on Adnán's farm. Do you know why?'

The woman's eyes narrowed suspiciously. 'You would have to ask her.'

'So you are not sure where your daughter is at the moment?'

'So long as she stays away from that idiot.' The woman gestured towards the trees. 'He is dangerous.'

'In what way?' Fidelma frowned. 'He is a little simple perhaps, but dangerous?'

'I told you that he had been mooning over my daughter. I suspect that he is the reason why she decided to leave the farm. I have told Lúbaigh to have a care of his brother, but he takes no notice, that one.'

'I have heard that your daughter doesn't, if fact, bear any animosity towards the boy,' Fidelma pointed out.

'All I know is that one day, something happened to her and she came home in tears. I saw the condition of her clothes. I am not stupid.' The woman folded her arms.

Fidelma examined her quietly for a few moments. 'Are you saying that you believe that your daughter was raped? Are you accusing Dulbaire?'

'I know that one day she was a virgin and the next day she was not,' Blinne said defiantly.

'That is a serious charge. You are also saying that, if your daughter was raped, and has not said anything, she has concealed the fact after the rape happened. In that case, according to the law, she is one of the seven grades of women who cannot have compensation levied on their behalf for such an assault. The perpetrator then goes free.'

'I know nothing of law. I know what I know.'

'If you claim that this is the reason why she made up her mind to leave Adnán's farm, as I said, it is a very serious charge.'

'The facts speak for themselves, don't they? But I cannot afford to make charges when the judgement is given by that idiot of a magistrate.'

'So far, I have heard no facts but only accusations,' Fidelma replied. 'If I hear facts, they will be acted on, Blinne. Therefore, I will continue my search for Íonait and get this matter cleared up.'

'And tell the imbecile that I will not be responsible for my actions if I catch him making a noise near here in the future.'

For a moment, Fidelma thought the woman was referring to the magistrate – and then she realised she meant the boy, Dulbaire.

'The point to remember, Blinne, is that we are all responsible for our actions in law,' Fidelma warned. 'So be careful what you declare. Now – are you sure you have no idea where your daughter has gone?'

'If she is looking for work, you may find her at any one of the many farms around here.'

'When did she go?'

'I have no idea. I was late rising. It was after first light and she was not here then.'

'When did you last see her then? Last night?'

'Indeed, when she went to bed. I am a heavy sleeper so, as I said, I was not disturbed when she left this morning.'

'Very well.'

After they mounted their horses and rode away, Eadulf said: 'I have to admit, I do not like that woman.'

'She is a rough woman, to be sure,' replied Fidelma, 'but then what do you expect among folk who exist in these conditions? They hardly have the refinements of higher social castes.'

'It's not just her manners,' Eadulf said.

'She has come from a harsh life. Don't forget that her husband was a swineherd who was killed and she was, I believe, cheated out of her just compensation.'

'I'll try not to be prejudiced,' Eadulf responded. 'It's just that I would not like her to be my mother.' He suddenly glanced up at the trees. 'Well, at least our musician has disappeared. Do you really think he would be guilty of rape, as Blinne is suggesting?'

'I suppose all men are potentially guilty,' Fidelma replied.

Eadulf at once protested.

'What I am saying,' Fidelma intervened for clarity, 'is that biology is a powerful force.'

'But that youth has the mind of a child.'

'Ah, but he has the body of a man. Anyway, we shall find out if Blinne's fears are well founded. The thing is, where shall we start looking?'

'There is the very man to help us!' declared Eadulf.

Fethmac, on horseback, had appeared abruptly on the track ahead of them.

'When I heard you had gone to Blinne's I came in search of you,' Fethmac said. 'As you know from our first visit she is a difficult woman to handle.'

'We thought you were tied up with a fishing dispute,' Eadulf commented.

'It was easy to resolve. Where are you off to now?'

'We are looking for young Íonait. Any ideas where she may be? Her mother thinks she is looking for work.'

'As a milkmaid? Well, there are not so many farms that have herds with cows enough to warrant the cost of hiring someone to milk them.'

They rode back through the village, as Fethmac suggested they might start looking at the farms that bordered the south-western area just beyond the Taithlech's storehouses. There were a few smaller farmsteads there where the girl might seek work. However, they had not ridden far when they suddenly came across a group of women who were apparently crowding round as if in dispute with one another. Some were shouting and others wailing, and some voices even rose to a scream. The three riders drew their horses to a halt. They could make neither head nor tail of the hubbub.

'This village seems to contain a lot of excitable people,' Eadulf muttered. 'First they form a mob to hang a man and now the womenfolk are apparently rioting.'

Fidelma glanced at Eadulf with disapproval before she nudged her horse forward to join Fethmac, who was now calling for the women to calm down and asking for someone to explain the cause of the uproar.

After a moment or two a gaunt-looking woman pushed her way forward, declaring, 'I am Fuinche, the wife of Lúbaigh!' Her attitude was menacing and she actually waved her fist at Fethmac, shouting, 'You are not worthy to be our magistrate. You allow that woman there to dictate what you should and should not do. She released a maniac to kill again. Then you allow her to go and insult a man of religion and argue with him.' Her voice rose. 'Where is the killer? Bring him out, because if the men of this village can't hang him we, the women, will.'

There was a chorus of support from the women around her.

Fethmac held up his hand and tried to silence them.

'What are you saying? You are not making any sense. The suspect is held in safe custody until the lady Fidelma who, I must remind you, is a *dálaigh*, legally my superior as well as being the sister of your King, makes a decision in accordance with the evidence.'

Jeers and laughter combined with anger greeted this statement.

Fidelma now moved forward, letting her horse nudge a passage to take her into the middle of the crowd.

'Disperse to your homes and I will forget this behaviour,' she called in a stentorian tone. 'You will obey the law, and if you do not think the law acts for your interests, then you have recourse to complaining to the Chief Brehon of this kingdom.'

Her words had no effect on them at all. Again the pandemonium rose around her.

Not for the first time did Eadulf wish they had at least one of the King's élite warriors of the Golden Collar with them to maintain order.

'You will regret not obeying the sister of your King!' he roared. 'You may think you will be treated leniently by disobeying a lawyer, but I can assure you that if you disrespect the sister of your King, then his warriors will fall on this place in retribution and there will be nothing left of it.'

Because this was the culture of his own people he put sincerity into his voice and that caused their voices to die away. As they hesitated, Eadulf shouted again.

'You know the tales of the warriors of the Golden Collar; you have heard of their victories and how they are pledged to defend the Eóghanacht of Cashel. Think on it, if you disobey or harm the sister of their King. Think hard, my friends. Then go silently to your homes and let a spokesperson come forward and explain your complaint.'

The women started to look to each other for support or reassurance. Some whispered ominously but generally they had fallen silent and a few, at the outer edges of the crowd, began to slowly move away.

'The nearest garrison of the warriors of the Golden Collar is no great distance from here,' Eadulf called again. 'It is less than a morning's ride. So don't think that distance is your protection! Shall we ride for the local commander to bring his warriors here to restore order by *torching the entire village*?'

Now the group began to disperse more rapidly.

As Fidelma moved her horse back close to Eadulf, she wore a faint smile.

'Now should I start calling you Brother Brécaire?' she asked. The term meant one who was frugal with the truth. 'You know well that the warriors of the Golden Collar would never do what you suggested even in extreme cases.'

Eadulf shrugged. 'Well, the women did not know that. It was a quick way to stop their hysteria from spilling over into any rash action.'

Fethmac was seated silently on his horse. Fuinche, Lúbaigh's wife, now stood alone in front of him. Her features were contorted; she had lost none of her fury.

'And so, Fuinche, you are the spokesman of this group?' Fidelma asked sternly.

The woman glared back malignantly. 'I shall speak for the women,' she hissed.

'So what is the cause of all this uproar?' Fidelma demanded. 'You well know that the death of Adnán and his family must be properly investigated and the facts of the matter heard before you can start accusing people of their deaths, let alone punishing them as that misguided mob tried to do the other day. Why have you started to stir these people up again?'

There was a snarl on Fuinche's lips.

'How many deaths must we see before you punish the guilty?' she responded.

'How many? The killer of Adnán and his family will be found and punished,' she assured the woman.

'I have just come from Dulbaire's cabin,' Fuinche said, her voice strangely harsh.

'Something has happened there?' queried Eadulf, catching the nuances in her voice. 'Something has happened to Dulbaire?' It was only a short while since the young man had left them outside Blinne's cottage – surely not enough time for him to return home on foot.

'Something?' Fuinche paused. 'Oh yes, something has happened. Murder has happened.'

'Who has died?' Fidelma asked quietly, after some moments absorbing the shock.

'Íonait,' Fuinche replied, her voice accusing. 'The poor girl has been hacked to death.'

CHAPTER TWELVE

There was another silence while the news registered. Then Fidelma asked: 'How do you know this?'

'I was passing Dulbaire's cottage and thought I would call in to see if Father Gadra needed anything. I usually stop by to make sure the boy is feeding himself but now also to ensure that the good Father has everything he needs, and sometimes I will take his washing.'

Fidelma suppressed her irritation, remembering that Fuinche was a 'follower' of Brother Gadra.

'Please explain what you discovered.'

'I called out at the door. There was no answer and so I went inside. I saw the girl's body immediately. There was blood all over her head. I could see that she was dead. This is the result of saving the vagrant the other day, Fethmac,' she spat, rounding on the young magistrate. 'As I said, you are not fit to administer the law here.'

Fethmac regarded the woman coldly. 'I fail to see the connection you are making.'

'I heard the animal escaped from Gobánguss' shed. It is obvious that he has done this.'

'You are wrong, Fuinche,' he snapped. 'Celgaire is safe in our custody and there was no way he could have escaped to kill Íonait this morning.'

Fuinche blinked at this news and the force with which Fethmac delivered it.

'But I thought . . .' she began, and then seemed to catch herself.

'Thinking does not become you,' Fethmac sneered. It was unusual for the young man to show his anger.

Fidelma decided to intervene. 'You say you found the girl this morning?'

'It was but a short time ago,' Fuinche replied sullenly.

'So why did you come here?' Fidelma asked. 'Wouldn't it be nearer to return to your husband to raise the alarm or go direct to the magistrate?'

'Lúbaigh was already at Adnán's farm. I thought it pointless to tell *him*,' she jerked a thumb at Fethmac, 'because he would defend the vagrant. So I came here and met some friends. We were discussing the murder when you arrived.'

'Discussing?' Fethmac echoed with disgust.

'There was no sign of Gadra at the cottage? *Brother* Gadra,' Fidelma said.

'The cottage was empty. There was no sign of Dulbaire or Father Gadra. Just the girl lying on the floor of the kitchen, her head smashed in.' The woman paused. 'But if the vagrant was in your custody, it means . . .'

'We should get to the cottage immediately,' Fethmac suggested nervously. He looked hard at Fuinche. 'From now on, woman, make sure of your facts before you start stirring up a mob to vengeance.'

The woman's face stiffened but she made no reply as they turned their horses and left her.

Dulbaire's cottage was no more than a cabin on the north edge of the village. The single-storey stone building with a thatched roof was set at the side of a track, with a small wood at the rear. Fidelma recognised the area as being close to Lúbaigh's house. Fethmac explained that beyond this was where Adnán's farmland started.

Apart from the patch of ground in which vegetables had been

cultivated and now ran wild, the surroundings were overgrown. The cottage seemed quite deserted and silent although the woodland was alive with the sound of birdsong. Near the cottage they could only make out the dark brown of the female blackbirds searching for grubs and worms on the ground before leaping back into the cover of the shrugs and bushes which were their home. A few wrens flitted here and there. It seemed that Dulbaire did not tend his garden much, Eadulf thought as he noticed the new leaves of wild garlic appearing in clumps here and there, while the chick-weed's first flowers were evident among clusters of dandelions and nettles.

They dismounted and secured their horses to the bushes before approaching the cabin door which stood wide open, presumably left like that by Fuinche when she fled from the scene. Thankfully, the time of year excluded flies from the body of the girl which lay just inside the door. Eadulf immediately bent and examined the bloodied head.

'As you see, the back of her skull has been smashed in with some force,' he said, standing up.

'What sort of weapon was used?' asked Fidelma.

'Not a blunt one, like a piece of wood,' returned Eadulf. 'More likely an axe or a . . .'

'. . . cleaver?' she asked pointedly. 'Like the one we recovered from Celgaire's wagon?'

'Something like that,' Eadulf sighed.

Fethmac was frowning at her. 'You are not suggesting the same weapon was used as killed Adnán's family?'

'Obviously not. Cleavers are in common use in rural areas.'

They heard a noise at the gate and turned to see the lugubrious face of Brother Gadra staring at them. He was clad in his usual black woollen robes with his silver cross on the leather thong around his neck. He still carried the ornately carved blackthorn staff. He had halted as he saw them at the open door of the cottage.

'What's this?' he demanded, his eyes like angry shining dots.

Fidelma moved forward. 'At what time did you leave this cottage?' she asked sharply, ignoring his question.

Brother Gadra blinked. It seemed that he was about to refuse to answer. Fidelma saw the tensing of his shoulders.

'After first light,' he replied, adding insultingly, 'if it is any business of yours.'

'As you know well enough by now, it certainly is my business,' she replied coldly. 'Where have you been?'

Brother Gadra shifted his weight from one foot to the other.

'Why am I being questioned?' he wanted to know. Then he saw the look on the faces of her companions and muttered, 'I have been to pray at the *reilic*, the burial place of this village. Then I went to visit some of the farmsteads that lie to the east of here, preaching the Word of the True God.'

'Who was here when you left?'

'The boy, Dulbaire.'

'There was no one else here?'

'Why would there be anyone else?'

'The young milkmaid called Íonait – was she here?'

'She was not. Why do you ask such questions?'

Fidelma stood aside so that he could see the body lying on the floor. There was no doubting the shock and the startled intake of breath it produced.

'Is she . . .?' he began.

'She is,' Eadulf affirmed.

Brother Gadra turned to Fidelma. 'Who did it? Was it the boy – the half-wit, Dulbaire?'

'Why do you think that?'

Brother Gadra said bitterly, 'I would have thought that much was obvious, because he lives here, and because he is always following her. Always following, like a sheep everywhere she went. I even heard a rumour that he molested the girl.'

The thoughts of the religieux obviously ran on the same lines as the girl's mother Blinne.

'Why would it mean that he killed her?' Fidelma pressed.

'She was a normal girl. And he . . . well, you have seen him.'

'I presume you are saying that his attentions were not reciprocated and this angered him to the point of murder?' Fethmac summed up.

'Exactly so,' Brother Gadra agreed.

'As obvious as Celgaire slaughtering Adnán and his family?' Fidelma could not help the riposte.

The fleshy religieux scowled. 'That is still to be proved one way or the other. Do not think I have forgotten either your behaviour or your lack of respect towards a member of the Holy Church, Fidelma of Cashel. I shall be taking it up with the Chief Bishop at Imleach as soon as I am allowed to leave here.'

'You are welcome to do so and may leave as soon as my investigation is over,' replied Fidelma. 'When I no longer need you here in my investigation, especially in the murder of Íonait – found in the cabin where you are staying – then you shall be free to go. Right now, you are a witness in this matter as well.'

There was a silence for a moment or two before Fidelma addressed Fethmac.

'Doubtless Fuinche has spread the story of the killing. I wish we could let Blinne know in a more gentle form, but I presume the news will have already travelled more quickly than we can. The girl's body will have to be taken to her home for washing and preparing for burial. Can you see to that, Fethmac?'

'What will you do?' demanded the young magistrate.

'Eadulf and I will go in search of Dulbaire. He needs to be questioned and taken into safety, especially if there are many in the village who hold the views of Brother Gadra here.'

The tall religieux scowled. 'Not my views but the Word of the Holy Book!' he rasped.

'I will fetch Gobánguss,' Fethmac spoke over him, 'and use his wagon to take the body to Blinne's house. It is best if I go with him and the body and speak with Blinne.'

Fidelma gave a curt nod. 'Keep a sharp lookout. We saw Dulbaire earlier outside Blinne's cottage. He might still be there. We shall try the farm.'

Fethmac was surprised, for she had not mentioned this to him before.

'He was there at Blinne's?'

'Up in a tree, watching the cottage and playing his whistle to Íonait,' Eadulf explained. 'He had gone, however, by the time we finished speaking to Blinne.'

'The boy is insane,' muttered Brother Gadra. 'That I have been made to sleep here at nights in the same place with a murderer is an insult. I will demand compensation for this threat to my life.'

'What threat!' Fidelma exclaimed. 'You are always too quick to form judgements. The boy has not been charged with anything.'

'It is no thanks to you that I do not feel safe in this place!' Brother Gadra admonished. 'This community is not safe. What recourse do we have but to take matters for our protection into our own hands?'

Fidelma's eyes narrowed. 'I would not advise you to take that course. You barely escaped the retribution of the law last time and, thankfully, no lasting harm was inflicted on Celgaire. But remember this, Gadra, being a religieux does not place you above the law of this land. I have yet to consider whether Celgaire, as a *drúth,* is entitled to compensation . . .' She stopped herself from revealing that Celgaire would also be entitled to the value of his wagon and goods lost in the fire.

Brother Gadra wisely kept his feelings to himself but his look at her was full of spite.

Fidelma made for the door, saying, 'If you can attend to what is necessary, Fethmac, Eadulf and I will see if we can find the boy.'

'If you do find him, where will you take him?' Fethmac called after them.

'I'll bring him to your place,' Fidelma returned as she mounted her horse.

'Where do we commence looking?' Eadulf asked as he followed her from the cottage.

'I thought that we should try Lúbaigh's place first as it is on the way to Adnán's farmstead. After all, Lúbaigh is his brother and the boy worked with him.'

'I have a feeling that you don't think the boy did this. Do you believe that all these killings are connected?'

'Remember what I always say?'

'No speculation without information?' Eadulf sighed. 'Yes, but it seems odd we arrive in a village where there has been no violent crime in living memory. Well, there are now enough bodies for me to think they must all be connected.'

'I have said many times that suspicion is one thing. Proof is quite another. As much as I dislike him, Brother Gadra could easily be right. The boy could have killed Íonait. For example, remember Blinne's suspicion that she had been raped? That she wanted to leave the farmstead? And yet . . .' Her voice trailed off.

'The boy was in love with her,' Eadulf said.

'It is a sad fact that young men sometimes respond with violence when they are rejected by a woman, rather than the other way about.'

'I would have thought all rejection has consequences.'

'Love is a powerful emotion. Accepting rejection and merely walking away is not usually an option. Yet it is often said, and I presume it is said by men, that a woman, when rejected, can be more extreme in her response. Even the Old Testament, as translated by Eusebius, claims that a woman, in spite of her wisdom, when rejected says, *Quia vocavi et rennuistis extendi manum meam et non fiut qui aspiceret . . .*'

Eadulf chuckled as he recognised the words from Proverbs: 'But since you rejected me when I called and no man gave heed when I stretched out my hand . . . I will also laugh at your disaster. I will mock when calamity overtakes you, when disaster sweeps over you like a whirlwind, and distress and anguish overtake you . . .'

After he had finished, Fidelma smiled wanly. 'I never thought of it that way before, Eadulf. What I am saying is that violence after rejection is found more commonly in young males than in women. As much as Dulbaire is regarded as backward and an imbecile, he is still a male. So there is a suspicion.'

'I find it difficult to think that Dulbaire raped her as her mother claims,' Eadulf argued. 'If there was proof that she was raped, and that was why she was leaving the farm, was that Dulbaire's doing – or was it down to someone else?'

Fidelma shrugged. 'We still need facts, and now we need to see Dulbaire and not be hesitant in putting certain questions to him.

'If he did kill the girl, then he might have fled somewhere we can't find him.'

Eadulf objected, 'For someone about to kill the girl, why was he then seated up a tree, looking at Blinne's house and playing his *fedán* to Íonait?'

'You must remember that we are dealing with someone whose logic is not the same as a normal person's logic,' Fidelma said.

They fell silent for a while as they skirted the woodland along the fields which they presumed formed the southern borders of Adnán's farmlands. In a corner, partially shielded by a copse of birches, was the familiar stone cottage where they had first met Lúbaigh's wife Fuinche. At first they thought it was deserted until the echoing sound of wood being chopped somewhere close by came to their ears. Behind the cabin Lúbaigh, stripped to the waist, was splitting logs with a large axe. He paused and rested on the handle of the axe as they approached, greeting them with a quick smile.

'Good morning, lady. What service can I render?'

Fidelma swung off her horse. 'I am afraid that we have come with some bad news, Lúbaigh.'

'Bad news? What is it now? Is my wife safe?'

Fidelma frowned for a moment. 'Why do you ask about your wife?'

The man did not hesitate. 'She had gone to see Brother Gadra. However, I always feel a little nervous because that means going to Dulbaire's cottage. My brother is not quite right in the head, as you have seen.'

'It is not about your wife that we have come. It is, in fact, about your brother.'

'What has Dulbaire been up to now?'

'So far as we know, nothing. We just need to ask him questions.'

That seemed to perplex Lúbaigh. 'I do not understand. Questions about what?'

'About the girl, Íonait.'

'She has been murdered,' Eadulf could not help adding, to Fidelma's annoyance.

Lúbaigh stared silently at them for a moment or two.

'Are you saying he killed her?'

'I did not say that.'

'Well, it is a natural conclusion,' Lúbaigh said, mopping his brow. 'The boy was always drooling after the lass. Composing tunes on that damned whistle of his. Following her about everywhere.'

'No reason to think that he killed her,' Eadulf said, trying to make amends for his slip.

'We are just asking if you know where your brother is?' asked Fidelma.

'My brother is insane and it is obvious you suspect him, which is why you want to question him over the death of the girl. Where was she found?'

'In his cottage.'

It seemed for a moment that Lúbaigh actually smiled – but the expression was gone before Fidelma could be sure.

'Then I was right,' he said. 'But my wife went down to his cabin first thing this morning. Are you sure she is safe?'

'She is well. We met her in the village, where she told us that she had discovered Íonait's murdered body. So we went straight to the cottage, of course. The religieux Gadra was there.'

'Father Gadra?' The man seemed surprised. 'He was there?'

'No, he turned up after we arrived. We have left Fethmac to take the girl's body back to Blinne and make the necessary arrangements.'

'And you are now looking for Dulbaire.' Lúbaigh sighed. 'Well, you won't find him here. If he is not mooning around outside Blinne's cottage then there is a small waterfall near an island in the Duthóg River to the south-west of here. It's just a short ride.'

'Why should we go there?' Fidelma wanted to know.

'It's where he and the girl sometimes met. A lot of people did not know that, but I . . .' Lúbaigh suddenly fell silent as if he realised he had said more than he should.

Fidelma shot a glance at Eadulf, just to warn him in case he was about to make some remark before she replied, 'Very well, we shall look for him there.'

'You said Blinne does not yet know about . . . about her daughter?' Lúbaigh asked.

'Fethmac has gone to tell her,' Fidelma assured him.

'It was something my wife feared.' Lúbaigh closed his eyes. 'We were too good and helpful to the boy. I knew that something bad was bound to happen one day. He is going to cost us a fortune and destroy us!'

Fidelma found her dislike of Lúbaigh increasing.

'Do you know the legal status of your brother?' she asked coldly.

'According to Fethmac, he is classed as a *drúth*.'

'Which means?'

'Which means that he is classed as mentally retarded,' Lúbaigh replied confidently.

'So as a *drúth* the right of the insane takes precedent over all other rights,' Fidelma pointed out. 'That means he is not held accountable for any crimes. It means that Dulbaire is not responsible to the full extent of the law; that is, to the payment of fines or compensation. However, under the *Do Brethaib Gaire*, which lists the rights of a person of unsound mind, it means that the kin of the person is obliged to care for them and see that they are protected.'

Lúbaigh was now looking worried, declaring, 'But I have always looked after him! I made sure he had a decent place to live and a job – or at least, he had a job on Adnán's farm.'

'That might not have been enough. Anyway, I think you should go and find your wife. Since it was she who first discovered the girl's body, I think she might need some comfort from you. We will see if we can find your brother.'

They left Lúbaigh looking at a loss and turned in the direction that he had suggested. The track here was barely more than a narrow path beaten by people's feet over the ages, with scarcely room for a single person, taking them first through grain fields and then through winter woods, copses of bare trees with only patches of green here and there. Eventually they became aware of buildings to their left on the far side of the trees.

'Those are the warehouses belonging to Taithlech,' Fidelma called over her shoulder to Eadulf. 'The river should be just ahead of us.'

Eadulf had no time to reply before the river itself appeared, flowing smoothly along in a broad passage. It was lined with trees along both banks, mainly alder trees that thrived in the wet soil. The pathway abruptly ended and they came on a stony area with some large flat grey rocks.

That was when they heard the mournful sounds of the *fedán* from some distance in spite of the rushing waters of the river. It was high and clearly a lament. The boy was sitting cross-legged on one of the larger boulders with the reed pipe to his lips. He must have seen them; seen or heard the heavy approach of their horses as they entered this curious stony spot by the riverbank, but he took no notice and the music continued its sorrowful tune. Fidelma slid quietly from her horse, securing her reins to a tough bush, and then she walked to a rock near the lonely player and seated herself.

Eadulf then dismounted from his placid cob and stood awkwardly by, not sure what to do.

The music all of a sudden rose to a crescendo – then there was silence.

Dulbaire seemed to finally focus on Fidelma, expressing neither surprise nor any change of expression.

'She used to sit there,' he said finally.

Fidelma smiled softly. 'This was your favourite spot?'

'Came here often. No one knew.'

'No one?'

The boy shrugged. 'Maybe my brother. But no one else. Our special place.'

'You loved Íonait?'

Dulbaire raised his head defiantly. 'We were one but they hated us.'

'They?'

'All of them. We came here and they did not know. They hated us.'

'Who killed her?'

'Dead? She is not dead. She will be here soon.'

Fidelma hesitated, unsure how to proceed.

'Where is she now?' she tried.

The boy frowned for a moment. 'Just sleeping.'

'I see. Is she . . . is she sleeping in your cottage?'

'In my cottage? Yes.'

'Her mother is very concerned. So you must come with us and tell us if . . . if you caused her to sleep.'

The boy was shaking his head. 'Found her asleep. Her mother hated me. Told you this morning.'

Fidelma paused. 'Did you do anything to make Íonait sleep?'

'I played my *fedán*. Used to enjoy that. Good sleepy airs. But she is sleeping soundly now.'

'Did you do anything to her?' Fidelma tried to form some link to the boy's way of thinking.

Dulbaire held his head to one side. 'You mean bad? A bad thing?'

'Yes. A bad thing.'

'No. Cainnech did that.'

'Cainnech?' Fidelma tried to hide her surprise. 'Adnán's elder son did a bad thing to her?'

The boy nodded. 'He caused the blood. He pushed her to the ground and lay on top of her and Íonait cried but he would not let her up. Finally she rose. There was blood on her dress. She screamed and then ran home.'

Fidelma tried to control herself as she realised what she was hearing.

'You saw this very bad thing?'

'I was in the barn. It was a very bad thing.'

'What did you do?'

'I did not know what to do.'

'Did you speak to Íonait?'

'Had to talk to Íonait. Came here. This is our special place.'

'When did you come here?'

The boy shrugged.

'The same day?' pressed Fidelma.

The boy shook his head. 'She told me not to tell. I did not tell.'

Fidelma was now beginning to see some sense in the events.

'Who did the bad thing to Cainnech? Was that in revenge? Was it you?'

'Cainnech did it to her. I told you. I . . . I protected her after she did it to him.'

Fidelma sat back and stared at him, trying to work out what he was saying.

'You said she did the bad thing to him?' she prompted.

He smiled. 'She made him sleep. I saw. Gave her the sickle to help her. He was bad.'

There was a silence. 'What happened after she made Cainnech sleep? What did you do?'

Dulbaire frowned, as if thinking. 'We went away.'

'Who made Adnán and the rest of his family sleep?'

The boy shrugged.

'Wasn't us. We went to the woods. Íonait cried. Then I heard shouting. My brother was shouting my name. So I left Íonait and went to him. Lúbaigh was near the farm building. Told me to run to magistrate. Asked me to memorise message. I told you that. I told you that before.'

'He told you to tell . . . what? That the vagrant had killed the family and escaped on the northern road?'

'He told me that.'

'You did not tell your brother about the bad thing that Íonait did to Cainnech?'

The boy smiled again. 'That was Íonait and my secret.'

Fidelma compressed her lips for a moment. 'And you have remained silent about this. Why have you told me now?'

'Because I saw Fuinche and she told me that Íonait had left the village and I would never see her again. She said I was responsible and soon the men would come and make me sleep too.'

Fidelma was aghast. 'When did Fuinche tell you this?' The woman had certainly left this out of her story.

'This morning.'

'And you are sure that you did nothing bad to Íonait, no bad thing to hurt her or to make her sleep?'

The boy whispered, 'No!' – and then all of a sudden his whole frame trembled and he curled up on the rock in a foetal position, his body wracked by sobs.

Fidelma rose awkwardly and looked towards Eadulf who was still standing by the horses but had heard everything.

'Did you understand what the boy was saying?' she asked him.

'I did. But how does it fit in?'

'I begin to see some light but it presents us with even greater problems.'

'Why?'

'Because the boy is a *drúth*, not of sound mind and therefore an *anteist* or untrustworthy witness. He is someone who cannot give evidence.'

'At least we can begin to see what happened.'

'Yet it is still confusing.'

'I don't see how. Adnán's elder son raped the girl Íonait. She then took the sickle, which Dulbaire gave her, and killed him. They left the farm and went into the woods. We had suspected something was not quite clear when we saw that Cainnech was killed with a reaping hook while the others were killed with a cleaver. What the boy says fits. The only confusing thing is, who killed the rest of the family with a cleaver?'

'Then Lúbaigh arrives, discovers the bodies and tells his brother to find Fethmac and report that the vagrants had done the deed.'

'Just think about what you have said, Eadulf.'

'I know . . . between the killing of Cainnech and the time Lúbaigh discovered all the bodies, the murderer came to the farm. We now have an explanation as to why two weapons were used. The reaping hook and the cleaver, which miraculously found its way onto the wagon of Celgaire. I admit that there is still a great deal to be discovered.'

Fidelma glanced at the still sobbing boy.

'If we can trust his words. Oh, I believe what he is saying; the problem is, fitting it into a timeframe. When did the rape of the girl take place? And when did Lúbaigh discover the bodies? Everything seems to fit except for the spaces in between.'

Eadulf looked disappointed. 'I thought it made things clearer.'

'It could still be argued that the others were killed by Celgaire, although unlikely given what else has happened. And the fact that the boy cannot bear witness means that in legal terms we are no further on.'

'So what shall we do now?'

'The boy will have to be held in a secure place. We will have to take him to Fethmac's home for it is now the only safe place I know.'

'I still wish we had a few men from your brother's bodyguard with us,' sighed Eadulf. 'I am uneasy about the volatility of these people and this so-called quiet little Eden. I can understand they might have been stirred up against Celgaire as a stranger who is easily identifiable from them, but it horrifies me that those village women could unite against one of their own who is but a poor, simple boy.'

They helped the distraught boy rise to his feet, having a little difficulty uncurling him from his position. He was clinging fiercely to his reed pipe as if it was some talisman against the evils of the world. As Fidelma was the more experienced horsewoman and her mount, Aonbharr, was the stronger of their two horses, Dulbaire was placed behind her and told to cling tightly. Then with Eadulf riding behind in case of accidents, Fidelma set off back to the village.

Fethmac had returned to his cottage by the time they reached it. He was there with Ballgel discussing the latest events. They were stunned when they saw who Fidelma and Eadulf had with them.

'The boy must be kept safe,' Fidelma told them. 'Now I know you already have Celgaire in your safekeeping but you must find another space for Dulbaire. If certain women of this place get their hands on him, his life will be in danger.'

'This place was not built to keep prisoners,' protested Ballgel.

'You would rather we let the boy run wild?' Fidelma asked. 'At the moment I am putting my trust in you both. It is no use asking Gobánguss after Celgaire was taken from him.'

'You really think people would harm an idiot boy?' Ballgel demurred.

'Your husband saw the mob led by Fuinche. I think you can believe it. And there is obviously someone else to have a care of. The person who tried to kill Celgaire.'

'Are you saying that the person who did that would be interested in the boy? Surely the two matters are entirely separate?' Fethmac queried. 'For what reason would they harm Dulbaire?'

'Perhaps for the same reason. It turns out that he is an important witness.'

Fethmac and Ballgel stared at her in astonishment.

'The boy is a *drúth* – and therefore an untrustworthy witness,' the young magistrate said eventually.

'Even so, what he has been able to tell us is of great importance. I will explain it to you later. For the moment, I need to know that he is secure until I have sorted matters out.'

Fethmac thought for a moment or two. 'If it is only for a short while then we can put him in a shed behind the barn.'

Ballgel reluctantly agreed with her husband. 'I cannot watch him the whole time as I have to tend to the burns and other injuries sustained by Celgaire. I have followed Brother Eadulf's instructions but it is a slow process.'

'Thank you. I hope it should not be for long,' Fidelma reassured her.

Fethmac took charge of the boy, who seemed to have sunk into his own world, muttering and weeping. Fidelma wanted to clarify some points with Ballgel.

'There is no one who is close to him other than his own brother?'

Ballgel was cynical. 'Possibly not even his own brother is close to him. Oh, certainly Lúbaigh did what was right by him but I think he was always embarrassed by the lad. As you know, from the argument between Tadgán and that man from the mountains, people are proud of their genealogies in our society where ancestry matters so much. Even for folk like Lúbaigh, who ranks as only an *ócaire,* a freeman but just a herdsman, with an honour price of only three *sets,* I believe that even he was ashamed of having a retarded brother.'

'I suppose that is natural,' Eadulf observed quietly, having worked out that the honour price of Lúbaigh, by which social grading was judged, was equivalent to the value of one-and-a-half milch cows.

'When you say that Lúbaigh was embarrassed by his brother . . .' began Fidelma.

'Oh, don't get me wrong,' intervened the magistrate's wife quickly. 'As I said, I am sure he does all that is required by law.'

'Sometimes that is not enough. The support of one relative to another who needs help should be total in an ideal society.'

'Well, if the truth were known,' Ballgel began, her head held to one side as if self-conscious, 'I think Fuinche has a lot to do with Lúbaigh's attitude to his brother.'

'In what way?'

'Well, after she and Lúbaigh were married, she insisted that the boy live elsewhere. Luckily, Lúbaigh and Dulbaire's father had left a cottage and so the boy was sent to live there.'

'So Fuinche was not close to the boy at all?'

She was surprised when Ballgel replied with a chuckle, 'I can't say that Fuinche ever pretended to be close to the boy. She never had any time for him.'

'But I am told that she often went to his cottage to ensure he had things to eat?'

Ballgel grimaced. 'Huh! That is the first I've heard of it. She only started to go there after the religieux Brother Gadra moved in. She is among several in the village who have fallen under his spell; people – mainly women, I admit – became impressed with him and his preaching. That was why he was able to whip people into a frenzy about hanging that man Celgaire. They would not have followed most strangers, but Brother Gadra is regarded as a *deorad Dé.*'

The term caused Eadulf to wince slightly. It was the legal term used of his own position – an exile of God – recognising his role as a foreign religieux but one who had been given special status and privileges.

Fidelma, who had not noticed his discomfiture, continued: 'So I can discount any fraternal feelings between Lúbaigh and the boy?'

'Lúbaigh secured work at Adnán's farm for Dulbaire. As for food, why, various village women took pity on him and gave him meals, otherwise I doubt the boy could fend for himself.'

'Would you say that Íonait was one of those who took him meals and looked after him?'

'I have heard stories to that effect,' affirmed the woman. 'Of course, Íonait's mother hated Dulbaire. There were stories of an unnatural relationship between the two young ones.'

'Unnatural?' queried Eadulf.

'That they were . . . Well, lovers.'

Fidelma suppressed a sigh. 'That is unnatural?'

'It's what people thought, but it was just gossip. The boy being an imbecile and Íonait being an attractive and normal young girl, their pairing would be hard to accept.'

'Now, are you absolutely sure there is no one else in the village who is close to the boy?' Fidelma asked again.

'No one.' Then Ballgel suddenly paused and screwed up her eyes in thought. 'Yes, there is. There's old Eórann. She has always been very close to Dulbaire.'

CHAPTER THIRTEEN

'Yes, old Eórann is the one to talk to,' repeated Ballgel. 'She is like a mother to Dulbaire.'

'Who is she?' queried Fidelma.

'She is the mother of Breccnat, the wife of Gobánguss, the smith. She often looked after the boy when he was younger because his mother died when he was born.'

Fidelma was surprised. 'Where does she live – with her daughter and the smith?'

'You'll find she has her own cottage about fifty metres from their place, on the road behind. She is still very independent,' Ballgel replied.

'Good,' Fidelma said firmly. 'We will have a word with her and then there are a few more questions I need to ask of Lúbaigh.'

In a short time, after leaving the magistrate and his wife and passing behind the forge, they came to a small stone cabin and found an old woman on her knees, pulling weeds in the patch of ground before it. As they halted and dismounted, the woman rose to her feet. Albeit elderly, with straggly grey hair blown this way and that in the wind, she had pleasant features, somewhat reminiscent of her daughter Breccnat. She looked like a person used to the outdoor life, and her skin was tanned almost nut-brown.

'Greetings, lady,' she said, rising to her feet, showing her suppleness in spite of her years.

'You know who I am?' Fidelma returned her smile of greeting.

'I have heard much about you and Brother Eadulf there since you arrived in our village. Subjects of gossip are few and far between here, and we have had much to gossip about these past days.' The woman chuckled. 'You think because I am old that I know nothing? I may be aged but my mind is still as clear and inquisitive as when I was a young girl.'

'That is good, Eórann, because we have come seeking knowledge.'

'I did not think you had come to talk about the weather, lady. You are welcome to what knowledge I can give you. Come inside and take some elderflower wine with me. I make it myself.'

They followed her into the small but comfortable cabin and took the seats she indicated by the open fire while she poured the drinks.

'What would you have me tell you?' the old woman queried as she handed the cups to them. 'I have been hearing stories about you from my daughter.'

'Then I shall come straight to the point. I would like to ask you about Dulbaire.'

The woman's face seemed to soften. 'Poor boy. The result of a bad birth in which his mother died. He emerged into this world feet first and from that moment all has been backward for him. I was called to help when his mother succumbed to the difficulties. When his father died it was left to Dulbaire's brother Lúbaigh to raise him. I do not blame Lúbaigh but a brother is no compensation for a mother or father. So it often fell to me to care for him.'

'Have you seen Dulbaire much recently?'

'Bless you, of course. I often give him a meal here. Especially since Brother Gadra went to stay at his cottage.' The old woman grimaced in disgust. 'Lúbaigh was wrong to let that man stay there. Dulbaire is scared of him.'

'Who gave Gadra this hospitality?'

'It was Lúbaigh's wife, Fuinche, who offered the man the use of Dulbaire's cottage. As I said, the boy was scared of Brother Gadra and spent as much time out of it as he did inside it. I am of the old ways and do not trust this man who insists that everyone should call him "Father".'

'So Dulbaire spent much time here?'

'He did.'

'You could communicate with him?'

'Naturally. He might not articulate as others do but he is easy to understand. I have looked after him since birth, so know his ways.'

'Lots of people here appear to be prejudiced against him.'

'That's because lots of people here are prejudiced.' The old woman sniffed in disapproval.

'What can you tell me about Íonait and her relationship with Dulbaire?'

Eórann's eyes narrowed a little. 'Have you been speaking to Blinne?'

'We have.'

'Her prejudice is the worst of all. I have heard her claim that Dulbaire was unnaturally pursuing her daughter.'

'And was he?'

'Not unnaturally,' the old lady corrected at once. 'Dulbaire was just a boy in love and, if truth were known, the girl cared for him for she saw beyond his disability. They were the best of friends and often came here to eat and speak with me.'

'So when Blinne intimates that Dulbaire raped her daughter, what is your response?'

Eórann's face was shocked. 'Is that what she claims? He would never do so. I have seen them together. They were a loving pair. Innocent and loving.'

'You will hear this claim before long, Eórann. I am afraid I must tell you bad news.'

The old woman stared at her, trying to read her expression.

There was no easy way to say it. 'It is claimed that Dulbaire not only raped Íonait but killed her. Her body was found in his cottage this morning by Fuinche.'

For moment it looked as if Eórann was about to pass out. Eadulf sprang forward to take the cup from her shaking hand and help her back into her chair. The woman let out a long low moan; almost a wailing sound.

'Never, never, never!' she mumbled. 'They loved one another too well. Find the boy and ask him . . . ask him . . .'

Fidelma leaned forward and laid a hand on the elderly woman's arm.

'I have found him, Eórann. He is in safe custody. I have placed him so for his own protection for there are many who now wish him harm. If I have interpreted his words correctly, he claims that he did not do it.'

'It is not in his nature,' the old woman said with a sob. 'I tell you, he and Íonait were like my own children. I would know.'

Fidelma smiled with gentle reassurance. 'You have confirmed what I needed to know,' she said. 'For that, much thanks.'

'Can I go to him? Where is he?'

'It would be helpful,' Fidelma said. 'But have a care that no one else knows where he is. I do not want a repeat of what happened with the man, Celgaire, when a mob nearly lynched him. Dulbaire is being hidden by the magistrate. Perhaps you could give me a while before you go to see him. I need to make some further inquiries and then we might go to see him together, for I am sure you will be able to help with some interpretation.'

'I will do as you request, lady. But I hate to think what will happen when this news gets around.'

'I am afraid the news will already have been spread from Fuinche and from Blinne. But I don't think anyone saw us take him to Fethmac's place.'

She was about to rise when another thought struck her.

'Do you know much about Adnán and his family?'

Eórann stared at her for a moment, trying to adjust her shocked mind to the sudden change of subject.

'This is a small village, lady. You should know how those in rural communities live on top of one another.'

'That is why I ask the question.'

Eórann gathered her thoughts and spoke frankly.

'Adnán was a proud and arrogant man. He was also ambitious. Ambition is an essential quality in all of us, for without it we cannot progress individually or as communities. But with Adnán came the desire for power. He was proud of his inheritance from Ágach Ágmar the Warlike who founded this very community, or so it is said. Yet his progeny were weak and eventually, as I suspect you have been told, there was the presence of his cousin Tadgán. I was informed of some relatives who had taken to the mountains a few generations ago and I heard that one of them – Conmaol – apparently came to Adnán's funeral to make a claim.'

'You did not have a high opinion of Adnán? I had the impression he was well respected.'

Eórann shrugged. 'Only by those who sought his patronage. Ambition had made him ruthless, and he was without feeling for any of us. In fact, he expected some sort of deference from us! Had he not been checked by the claims of his cousin Tadgán, I believe Adnán would have tried to make himself chieftain of the area and demanded tribute from everyone in the territory.'

'The Eóghanacht Glendamnach might have had something to say about that,' Fidelma mused. 'Or the Déisi to the south-east. Between them they would have seen off any challenge.'

'You did not know the strength of Adnán's ambition,' replied Eórann.

'Well, since he is dead, I suppose the question no longer arises. But I was wondering whether his elder son, Cainnech, shared his father's arrogance and ruthlessness?'

Eórann replied without hesitation. 'There is a saying, lady, like father, like son. The boy was in need of a father's guidance, but unfortunately, Adnán was too caught up in his schemes to be a father. The boy ran wild. Anything he wanted was given to him – and if it was not, then he simply took it.'

'For example?'

'He forced other boys to do his bidding.'

'Dulbaire, for example?'

'Dulbaire was an immediate victim for he worked on Adnán's farm and Cainnech could order him around with impunity. Thankfully, Dulbaire could not fight back and so his placidity did not provide the entertainment that Cainnech craved. In a strange way it was his very simplicity that saved him. Those who did fight Cainnech soon learned how he harboured grudges when crossed. Even long afterwards, those who had challenged him would be made to suffer. Oh yes, that boy had a long memory for grudges.'

'In short, Cainnech was a bully?'

'He was a shameless bully, lady.'

Fidelma rose, saying, 'You have been most helpful, Eórann. As soon as I have completed the other inquiries I need to make, I will let you know and we can have a good talk together with Dulbaire.'

As they rode away, Eadulf remarked, 'So a pattern is emerging. What the old woman says about Cainnech's character fits in with the sort of person who could rape the girl.'

'Also what she says about the relationship between Íonait and Dulbaire supports that there was something more between them than the girl's mother would have us believe.'

'It is certainly plausible that events unfolded in the way the boy told us.'

'With the exception of why the other members of Adnán's family were killed after Cainnech was despatched,' Fidelma reminded him.

'Or why Celgaire was abducted from Gobánguss' shed and the attempt made to murder him,' Eadulf added.

'One thing is certain,' Fidelma said, 'if the girl killed Cainnech and was helped by Dulbaire, they would have no reason to release Celgaire and attempt to kill him. He was the pawn to be blamed by the murderer for all the killings.'

Eadulf was thoughtful. 'Perhaps whoever killed the rest of the family – accepting that Íonait and Dulbaire only killed Cainnech – discovered that we were beginning to suspect that Celgaire was as innocent as he claimed, and therefore staged the escape from the shed in order to re-establish his guilt.'

'A good point, Eadulf,' replied Fidelma. 'The killer arranged this escape, thinking also to silence Celgaire in an accident, so that we would accept him as the killer once and for all.'

'There is much still to be sorted out, if we are to prove that.'

'And I fear that we have only just started.'

As they approached Lúbaigh's cabin, Eadulf suddenly drew rein and called softly to Fidelma: 'Hold a moment.'

She halted and turned towards him. 'What is it?'

'I don't recognise that man leaving the cabin.'

Fidelma turned in time to see a dark figure on horseback disappearing behind the copse at the back of the cottage.

'That was the merchant, Taithlech,' she told Eadulf.

They did not see Lúbaigh immediately but some movement attracted their attention and they found him saddling a horse behind his cabin.

Lúbaigh seemed startled when they appeared.

'My wife has gone to offer Blinne comfort,' he said.

'I know what Blinne thinks of your brother,' Fidelma said. 'So why would she accept comfort from other members of the family?'

Lúbaigh gave a short bark of laughter without humour.

'I am afraid that Blinne and my wife share the same opinion of Dulbaire. Anyway, we are a close community here, lady. It is natural for Fuinche to go to see Blinne.'

Fidelma watched him tightening the girth and asked, 'Are you going to join her?'

Lúbaigh frowned uncertainly.

'I presume you are preparing to go somewhere?'

'Oh yes. Some business – I have to consult Tadgán. After all, he is in control of Adnán's farm now and I am still steward there.'

'Ah, and he is allowing you the use of his horses?'

'I need to get about quickly.'

'Indeed. Presumably Tadgán does not believe that Conmaol will succeed in presenting proof of his claim?'

'It is nothing to do with me,' the man said roughly.

'Since you are employed on the farm, I would think it has much to do with you,' replied Fidelma. 'By the way, I saw your friend leaving just now.'

'My friend?'

'Your wife and you yourself told me that Taithlech was a friend and that you often drank together.'

Lúbaigh shrugged. 'Oh, that. Everyone knows Taithlech.'

'But not everyone likes him. Adnán didn't like him or do business with him.'

'What of that? I choose my own friends.'

'And Tadgán certainly does business with him. So if Tadgán takes over the farm there will be no problems arising.'

Lúbaigh was silent and suspicious. When no more was said, he added grumpily, 'Taithlech had heard about Dulbaire and so came to see what he could do for me.'

'I have to tell you that your brother is being held in custody of the magistrate while I am investigating matters.'

'You are investigating – not Fethmac?'

She ignored the question. 'I just wanted to clarify a few things with you.'

The steward looked trapped. 'How can I help?'

'Firstly, why are you here? I would have thought, given the news, you would be searching for Dulbaire.'

'You just told me that he was in custody.'

'I did. But you were not concerned enough about him to go and search.'

Lúbaigh scowled. 'Listen, lady, so far as I was concerned, Dulbaire does not wander far. I was sure that you would find him at the spot that I told you to go to. I presume that *is* where you found him? If he was not there, I was sure he would come home. So this is where I stayed.'

'That seems quite reasonable,' Eadulf said.

Fidelma apparently agreed for she continued, 'With regard to the morning that you found the bodies of Adnán and his family . . .' she paused and then went on '. . . you came to the farm at what time? Was it still dark or was it after dawn?'

'It was just after first light,' the man said. 'As I told you the first time. But generally still dark.'

'How then did you spot the body of Adnán? I think you said he was the first body you saw?'

'That is so. As I explained, it was not so dark. The night was above the distant hills. I think I mentioned that I saw the farmhouse in darkness but the door opened. I spotted what I thought was a bundle of clothes which turned out to be Adnán. I ran back to the farmhouse and found Aoife. Then afterwards, I found the bodies of Abél and then finally, Cainnech. By which time it was first light.'

'And you said that your brother arrived about then?'

'Not long after, but long enough for me to see that the vagrants' wagon had gone from the spot.'

Fidelma pursed her lips thoughtfully.

'Is something wrong, lady?'

'Just a matter of fitting in with the time,' she replied. 'Tell me, when was the last time you saw Cainnech alive?'

Lúbaigh raised a hand and massaged the back of his neck thought-fully.

'I suppose it was the previous evening. Why?'

'What did you think of him?'

'Of the boy?' Lúbaigh frowned. 'He was just the son of the boss.'

'He treated you well?'

'A bit arrogantly. He liked folk to know who his father was. But he did not interfere with me or me with him.'

'And you are sure that he was the last body you found?'

'I have said so several times. And I still maintain, whatever the itinerant says, that he killed Adnán and his family.'

'You are very adamant, Lúbaigh.'

'I am entitled to my views.'

'I am not questioning your entitlement or even your views, but the fact that you are so adamant. What would you say if your brother said that he was a witness to Cainnech being killed, that he and the girl, Íonait, left the farm before the others were killed and that this was after dawn?'

Lúbaigh stared at her. It took him some time to gather his thoughts and then he said calmly and clearly, 'I would say that the boy is a liar.'

'You see, if he were telling the truth, there are several other questions to be raised.'

'The only question to be raised is what possessed the boy to say what he did. It must have something to do with the girl, Íonait. Maybe that is why he killed her.'

'Well, one thing that needs to be established beyond doubt is whether you came before or after it was light,' Fidelma said. 'Perhaps if you arrived later that morning, when it was full light, then it could be as Dulbaire says. It means that the boy and girl were here at first light; that Cainnech was killed at the time Dulbaire says, and that the two had left before you arrived. It also means that the other family members were killed after Íonait and your brother fled.'

Lúbaigh stared belligerently at her for a moment or two then gave a shrug.

'Maybe it was lighter than I thought,' he replied gruffly. 'Even so, I found the bodies in the order I said that I did. If the others were killed as you are now claiming, then the vagrant would have had time to do so.'

'So what time are you now saying that you arrived at the farm?'

'Perhaps an hour after first light. My wife and I told you we were drinking late with Taithlech that night. So perhaps I was a little later than my usual time in getting to the farmstead.'

'That would make more sense,' Fidelma agreed solemnly. 'For that would have given Celgaire, the vagrant as you call him, time to have broken camp and moved his wagon. I was worried about that as the timescale did not seem to fit.'

Eadulf glanced at Fidelma. He was puzzled that she was not pressing the man.

Lúbaigh had kept glancing at the position of the sun several times during the conversation.

'I suppose so,' he said hurriedly. 'Look, I do have to go to see Tadgán, lady. I am answerable to him about the farm. If that is all . . .'

'Ah well, you have resolved the question of time. There is no need to delay you further. Obviously, your brother will be taken care of until all these things can be settled.'

Lúbaigh was looking relieved when they mounted their horses and started back towards the village. He finished adjusting the saddle and then he too mounted his horse and moved off.

Fidelma and Eadulf were some distance from the outskirts of the village when a dishevelled figure stumbled into their path, causing their horses to shy and almost throwing Eadulf. It was a woman, her clothes and hair disordered. It took a moment or two to recognise Ballgel, the magistrate's wife.

'Lady, lady.' She was sobbing and clinging to Fidelma's stirrup for support.

'What is it?' called Fidelma in concern, about to dismount.

'Get to the village, quickly! They have attacked Fethmac. They have taken Dulbaire. They are going to hang him. Hurry! Please hurry!'

Without a second's hesitation, Fidelma dug her heels into the sides of her horse and her animal broke into an immediate gallop. Eadulf stirred his more placid cob after her. By the time they reached the centre of the village they became aware of people running in all directions towards their homes and slamming their doors behind them. She quickly realised that they were fleeing from her approach. Dread filled her as she saw they were coming from the general direction of the hillock – the hillock on which the great oak stood.

Without a word to Eadulf she cantered on and when she reached the hillock the crowd had vanished. There was only one person standing there, hands on hips, looking up at the tree. It was Brother Gadra. Her eyes followed his gaze and the breath caught in her throat.

Hanging by a rope from a low branch was the body of Dulbaire.

Eadulf had already dismounted and was hacking at the rope with his knife. The body fell, crumpled in a heap, while Eadulf tried to loosen the knot around his neck. Fidelma quickly dismounted and joined him, staring down at the mottled features of the young boy.

'Is he dead?' she asked unnecessarily.

'He is,' Eadulf replied, gently laying the boy's head back on the turf.

Eadulf rose as they both turned to look at the unmoving Brother Gadra. His face showed no expression.

'You have finally succeeded in hanging someone.' It was Fidelma who broke the silence. 'I trust you are pleased with yourself.'

Brother Gadra blinked several times and then drew himself together with a touch of his old belligerence.

'You should address me as Father Gadra,' he replied coldly.

'You are neither a Father nor a Brother of any Faith that I know,' she told him. 'The person that I now address is one who is a *guinid,* a killer and, as such, you will now be answerable to the law.'

The man shook himself angrily. 'I need no words from you, woman. I am only answerable to the law of God!'

'You have used that excuse before to hide behind and conceal your true nature. If there is evil here, it is of your creation. Here you are answerable only to the law of the Five Kingdoms. You have committed and participated in an illegal killing. For this you will be held until your defence is heard.'

Brother Gadra answered her with a sneer. 'You have annoyed me long enough, woman. I am not answerable to you. Nor am I answerable to your pagan law. Try to hold me? What are you going to do – set *him* on me?' He gestured towards Eadulf.

Fidelma looked at Gadra in disgust. Out of the corner of her eye she had seen Gobánguss and a rather shaky-looking Fethmac approaching and she turned to address the burly form of the smith.

'So, Gobánguss, you have heard what has happened here? Where do you stand? I need you to hold another prisoner. This man,' she indicated Gadra, 'who calls himself a religieux.'

Gobánguss looked nervous and then, to her surprise, he refused, saying, 'Leave me out of this, lady.'

She stared at him, her gaze hard. 'Will you obey the law of the Five Kingdoms? You took oath to do so the other day.'

'I have always obeyed the law of the Brehons, lady, but this matter is not as simple as that.'

Fidelma looked at him in surprise. 'It is very simple,' she said. 'I am a *dálaigh* and I now ask you to place this man under constraint.'

The big smith looked apologetic. 'My wife and I are devotees to the New Faith, lady.'

Fidelma was puzzled for the moment and said so.

'Father Gadra is a priest of the New Faith,' Gobánguss responded. 'He has taught that the servants of God stand outside the law of the Five Kingdoms because they are servants of the laws of God. My wife and I hear him preach regularly at Taithlech's barn.'

'So your mind is filled with the new ideas from Rome? You support these rules that are now being imposed in the western churches. You adhere to them rather than the original teachings?'

The man shrugged. 'All I know is that I must obey these laws given by God.'

Brother Gadra was smiling triumphantly. 'Do you see now, woman? I am here to do God's work. Your pagan ways have no effect on me.'

Fidelma saw the fanatical gleam in his eyes. She was shocked that she had not been able to persuade Gobánguss and his wife to disobey the priest. Only a few days ago, the smith had had no problem in being entrusted to take charge of Celgaire, nor did his wife Breccnat object to looking after the vagrant's wife and child. She could not understand it. But then . . . then she remembered that Celgaire had been released from Gobánguss' imprisonment and her mind started to race.

It was Eadulf who interrupted her thoughts.

'There is no need to place Gadra into custody,' he said. 'I do not think he will try to escape justice.'

Brother Gadra smirked. 'I will run towards God's justice willingly. I am proud to be His servant.' Then he turned and simply walked quickly away.

Fidelma whirled on the smith with an angry expression.

'Just when did you suddenly become a convert of Brother Gadra? Are you also proud of yourself that because of him, you attacked your own magistrate and took a poor, helpless imbecile and killed him?'

The big man looked pained. 'I assure you, lady, I had no part in this. I only knew about it when Fethmac came to my place. He told me he had been bound by villagers led by Father Gadra – by a mob who had dragged Dulbaire to be hanged here. Fethmac's wife had just managed to release him. He came for my support and we both came on here. I do not like the deed, but Father Gadra says—'

'I do not recognise that title – for even the New Faith says there is only one person who should be called Father and that is God.'

'But he says—'

'I do not require your services any more, Gobánguss, except that you may have to answer for this shameful matter later on.'

The big smith hesitated, reluctant to go. 'But my wife, lady,' he mumbled.

She cut him short. 'You must take responsibility for your decision, Gobánguss, just as your wife is answerable for her decision. You may go – for now!'

Downcast, he turned and began to walk slowly away.

Fidelma now addressed Fethmac. 'You will be needed to identify those who attacked and imprisoned you while this murder was committed.' She gestured towards the body of the boy. 'I trust you have taken all proper precautions for the safety of your other prisoner? Are Celgaire and his wife and baby all unharmed?'

'They are safe, lady, for once the mob found the boy, they did not search further.'

'You must now doubly ensure their safety. It seems we can no longer rely on the loyalty of even such as Gobánguss.'

Fethmac was scratching his head in bewilderment as he glanced after the smith, who was plodding off towards his forge.

'I have no understanding of this. I knew that Breccnat was one of those who had become fascinated by Brother Gadra and his rantings about the new interpretations from Rome. But Gobánguss was never one for such things. All he is interested in usually is his work. It is strange that he should offer his wife's influence as an excuse.'

'Has anyone gone to tell Lúbaigh about his brother?' Fidelma asked. 'We left him a short time ago heading to Tadgán's farm.'

'I will fetch him to come and take care of the body of his brother and see to the burial arrangements,' offered Fethmac.

'No. Your task is to ensure the safety of Celgaire and his family. Gadra nearly succeeded in hanging him once, and now, having succeeded with the boy, he will probably try again,' Fidelma said. 'Especially if he can now exert such a hold on people, even someone responsible like Gobánguss.'

Fethmac was about to say something when they saw several elderly women approach. They were led by an old woman, whose face was hard, as if carved in granite. It was Eórann.

'I have been told,' she said grimly as she halted before them. 'Great shame has been brought upon us, lady. Great shame – and I grieve that an innocent boy has been murdered with the complicity that reflects on us all. I grieve for the child, for I was fond of him. I grieve for the evil that has come upon this village in the form of a stranger preaching a religion that has turned the thoughts of our people to acts of violence. Lady, I cared for that boy. There are a few people in this village who are still of sane mind, so let us take the body, wash and prepare it for burial as is our ancient custom. I cannot guarantee that Fuinche and Lúbaigh will do so.'

Fidelma saw the dignity and sorrow in the elderly woman and inclined her head slowly in sympathy. She turned to Fethmac.

'You are magistrate here, Fethmac. It is you who must give permission to Eórann in case Lúbaigh does object. Certainly I have no objection.'

'Then I have no objection either,' Fethmac replied. 'You may arrange to take Dulbaire's body and prepare it for burial.'

'Thank you,' Eórann returned solemnly, and the thanks were echoed by her companions.

That evening, there was a chill atmosphere in the house of the young magistrate. Fethmac and Ballgel avoided eye contact and spoke only in monosyllables. Fidelma and Eadulf could see that Fethmac now realised he had lost total control over the villagers. He seemed a broken man, staring into space and not speaking. It was clear that his power as a magistrate had been supplanted by the force of the priest. He had lost face and would never regain his dignity nor the respect he had once commanded.

It was only later, in their room, that Eadulf spoke his mind to Fidelma. 'We must either bring this matter to a conclusion now or return to Cashel and wash our hands of it.'

'If I surrender now, I may as well give up law entirely, for then I will have to accept that what this man Gadra says is more powerful in the people's minds than a millennium of our law and culture.'

'Accept it. There is nothing to be done,' protested Eadulf.

'There is always something to be done – right or wrong. There is still one thing that disturbs me . . . and I think that may be the Gordian knot.'

Eadulf cast a bewildered look at her.

Fidelma explained. 'The ancient Greek legend goes that when Gordias of Phrygia tied a knot, an oracle revealed that only the future master of the East would be able to untie it. When Alexander of Macedonia could not untie it, he drew his sword and cut it. To be confronted with a Gordian knot is to face a perplexing problem but one that, if severed, leads to the solution.'

'And just what is your Gordian knot?' Eadulf enquired, intrigued.

'I think it is in the *Genelach* of Adnán's family at Ard Fhionáin.'

ChAPTER FOURTEEN

It had not taken them long to traverse the ten or so kilometres between the village and the abbey of Ard Fhionáin. Once they had left the banks of the River Teafa, the track rose and fell over undulating ground and led in and out of stretches of forest. Even so, Fidelma regretted having delayed the journey until the afternoon for now she realised they would probably have to stay overnight in the abbey as darkness would have fallen by the time they could return. However, she had spent a busy morning making sure that everything was secure before leaving, especially with regard to Celgaire, his wife and child, ensuring they were in safe hands and that Gadra and the other hotheads of the village knew what would happen to them if harm befell her prisoners.

As they crested the hill, the familiar outline of the abbey of Ard Fhionáin stood before them on the far side of the River Siúr. It lay at the eastern side of a new bridge which, when they had last been here a few years ago, had caused Eadulf some concern about its safety. Then its timbers were hardly seasoned and he distrusted the building work of the members of the community. The abbey had initially stood by a natural ford across the river, where a small settlement had sprung up under the shadows of Rath Ard, the fortress of the local prince. At that time, there were few other habitations in the area apart from a tavern perched fortuitously at the end of the bridge.

Ard Fhionáin had quickly become a major township on the river for, as well as a good location in pleasant scenery, it provided a base for traders coming upriver from the seaports. Here they could transfer their goods to smaller barges or pack animals in order to access the distant areas of the kingdom. The ford had always presented problems, however, for the currents were strong. The abbey had been built to provide a 'watcher by the ford' to ensure that no accident went unobserved. A bell hung ready to summon help if needed. But now the ford was practically abandoned after the abbot and the community had built the strong new bridge.

Fidelma and Eadulf guided their horses across it, the hooves echoing on the wooden planking. They passed the small tavern designed for travellers who did not wish to go to the abbey but to travel on along the main road to Cashel. They had stopped there once during a hot summer day. Eadulf recalled grimly that it was the same day they were ambushed while on their way to the mountain track that was an alternative route to Lios Mhór. He shuddered at the memory of how near death had come to them.

They guided their horses up the small incline which led to the gates of the abbey. Their approach had been seen and the wooden gates had been opened. A member of the community hurried forward and greeted them in the traditional form before introducing himself as Brother Fechtnach, the *rechtaire* or steward of the abbey. It was clear that he had recognised who Fidelma was and had guessed the identity of Eadulf. They dismounted and the steward signalled for one of the brethren to come forward and take their horses to the stables.

'We wish to see the abbot,' Fidelma explained, first extracting the bag with the precious parchments from her horse.

'Of course,' Brother Fechtnach replied warmly. 'Abbot Rumann is expecting you.'

Fidelma exchanged a glance of surprise with Eadulf.

'Expecting us?'

The steward smiled and nodded. 'Follow me, lady, and I will take you to him immediately.'

He turned and rapidly led the way into the building. Fidelma did not bother to question the man further as it was clear that the abbot would provide any explanation needed. As they were shown into a small chamber and announced, the abbot – a middle-aged, nondescript man, but whose pleasant greeting seemed genuine enough – rose from his chair and came forward. He held both hands outstretched and was smiling warmly.

'Welcome, welcome, Fidelma. Welcome also, Brother Eadulf.'

'We are honoured by your welcome, Abbot Rumann,' responded Fidelma on behalf of both of them. 'I am sure we have not met before but I am told you were expecting us?'

'One of the brethren saw you crossing the bridge, recognised you and sent word to my steward. I was not surprised that you were at the gates and knew you would be coming to see me.'

The abbot saw that she was still perplexed and his smile broadened.

'It's easily explained,' Abbot Rumann told them. 'The abbey has recently received a visit from Conmaol of Cnoc na Faille, who told us of the events at Cloichín. He spoke of your attendance there as *dálaigh*. I felt sure that you would come here in person to learn from our librarian's own mouth about Conmaol's claims.'

Fidelma had been right when she deduced that Conmaol would have gone to the abbey to consult the same scholar that she had in mind about the *Genelach*, or genealogy text. 'Yes, it was about the claim of Conmaol – that he was of the *derbhfine* of Adnán and Tadgán?'

'Yes, yes, yes,' nodded the abbot quickly. 'Your meticulousness is a by-word in this kingdom and so I knew that you would want to check out his claim at first hand. He was most upset at what we had to tell him, and I wondered if he would attempt to argue his case before you. However, he is *not* the senior member of his *derbhfine*.'

Fidelma was cautious and just inclined her head in response.

'Yes, yes,' went on the abbot. 'You may set your mind at rest about that matter. Conmaol is a very enthusiastic young man but, alas, one whose enthusiasm can lead him astray. It is true that his clan was vanishing and there were not many who claimed descent from their famous progenitor, Ágach Ágmar the Warlike. As you know, our abbey has a reputation for keeping genealogical records, especially of the local clans. That is why he came to consult us. We told him that he is certainly a member of his *derbhfine* – but equally certainly, not senior.'

'Really?' The news surprised Fidelma, who recalled the assertiveness of the man at the funeral of Adnán's family.

The abbot nodded complacently. 'The genealogies of Ágach Ágmar the Warlike and his ancestors have long been held at the library of this abbey. Our genealogists and scribes have authenticated it and they do not make mistakes. Ágach Ágmar was descended from Aed Flann Cathrach, son of Crimthann Srem, fifth in line . . .'

Fidelma broke into the recitation, asking pointedly: 'So Conmaol has no claim or authority over the kin-land at Cloichín?'

'None at all. I am aware of the death of Adnán and his sons, but his kin-land goes to . . .' He paused, trying to recall a name. 'I am sorry, I have forgotten the name but it was an inhabitant of Cloichín. You may consult our records on this. Our archivist, Brother Solam, is in charge of them.'

'Brother Solam? I know of him and it is he whom we wish to consult on another matter,' Fidelma said gently. 'You say that Conmaol was disappointed at the news that you told him about his ancestry?'

The abbot spread his hands and replied sadly, 'I do not exaggerate when I say that he was actually outraged. In fact he almost refused to believe our records. I have never seen a man so angry.'

Fidelma was thoughtful. 'I can understand disappointment – but you used the word "outraged"?'

'I understood that he had been assured by someone in Cloichín that he was correct in his claim for seniority. This person had encouraged him to make the claim over the matter of kin-land.'

'Who would that be?' she asked suspiciously. 'Only the local magistrate would be competent to have that knowledge in order to give advice.'

'You mean young Fethmac?' The abbot shook his head. 'Do you know that he studied law here? I doubt that he would be competent to advise in such matters anyway without access to the *Genelach*. It was apparently someone else – but again, I cannot recall.'

'So this person, whoever it was, persuaded Conmaol to make his claim . . . Is Conmaol still here in the abbey?'

'No. He left and should already be back at Cloichín. That is where he said he was going, to confront his adviser. I gave him a special letter to present to any legal judge, authenticating that genealogy which we hold. Anyway, he left a full day ago.'

'A full day? He had not returned by the time we left Cloichín. But I am interested to know that his claim is not genuine. However, as I say, it is another matter entirely that has brought us here.'

'Ah yes. You said you wish to consult with Brother Solam?' Abbot Rumann seemed curious.

'I came because I had heard of Brother Solam and his abilities.' Fidelma decided to appease the abbot's curiosity with an explanation. 'He has a reputation as a Latin scholar, and his old colleague, Brother Conchobhar, who was my mentor at Cashel, often spoke of him.'

Abbot Rumann smiled. 'I have met Brother Conchobhar a few times at council. He must be of a great age now. Is he still alive?'

'He is,' Fidelma confirmed. 'And is Brother Solam well? I have some documents that I wish to show him. I need his opinion. May I consult with him?'

'You shall,' the abbot beamed. 'He is one of our finest scholars. But first there are matters of etiquette to be observed. Allow me to offer you both our hospitality, albeit belatedly. You will, of course, stay overnight with us as I presume you will want to discuss matters with Brother Solam after he has had time to study the parchments. Night is fast approaching. So, after you have tasted of the wine which we distil from elderflowers, you may wash, refresh yourselves and then join us for the evening meal. After that, Brother Solam may be able to provide you with the opinions that you need. If you find all well, then you will have daylight in which to return to resolve these matters at Cloichín.'

'We shall gladly accept your hospitality,' Fidelma confirmed. In spite of her gracious tone, Eadulf knew that she was chafing at having to accept the inevitable rituals of hospitality.

'Excellent. And you must tell me all the news from your brother's capital. Indeed, if you have news from Imleach, of Cúan, the Chief Bishop, then that will be most welcome. In truth, I have not met Bishop Cúan so you will find me all attention.'

The abbot picked up a small brass bell and shook it. Brother Fechtnach entered almost immediately and the parchments were handed to him.

'What is it you want me to ask Brother Solam?' Fechtnacht enquired.

'I would like him to cast his eyes over these documents and tell me what he thinks, especially of the older text whose Latin is so archaic that I am unsure of the nuances. The second text is in bad Latin and so I am likewise in need of someone's opinion to confirm the translation. The third text is in our own tongue, therefore easy to read, but I would like him to see it in the context of the other texts in case there is any contradiction.'

Brother Fechtnach nodded, saying, 'I shall take them straightway to Brother Solam and will convey your message. He may have time to prepare so that you could consult him after the evening meal.'

It was, indeed, following the meal that Brother Fechtnach came to conduct them to see Brother Solam, who was still at work by candlelight in the gloomy *scriptorium*. As Fidelma and Eadulf entered the darkened library, an elderly man rose to greet them. He had long white hair and his bent shoulders spoke of years of devoted study at a desk rather than the outdoor life.

'Fidelma of Cashel?' His whispering voice came almost like a wheeze.

'I am – and this is Brother Eadulf. I have heard much of your scholarship on ancient texts from Brother Conchobhar of Cashel. He holds you in high regard. That is why I brought the parchments to you for your advice.'

The old man sniffed disparagingly. 'So old Conchobhar is still of this world? He could have earned a great reputation for deciphering the ancient records instead of playing with his herbs and spices and seeking the secrets of the stars at night.'

Fidelma hid her amusement at the old scholar's thoughts on Conchobhar for, as well as welcoming her into his apothecary in Cashel, he had taught her the rudiments of reading the portents from the night sky.

Brother Rumann went on: 'Anyway, you do me too much honour, lady. I know that you have knowledge of Latin, some Greek and Hebrew as, indeed, most scholars are taught in our places of learning these days. Therefore I am sure you need little advice from me in construing such documents.' He gestured to the parchments which lay on the table before him.

'You are very kind, Brother Solam. But my ability with languages is not the ability of a scholar. I have some knowledge of Latin but not always of the gradations and shades that permeate the language – the subtle changes from old forms to modern forms. The language of the first text is too archaic for me so I have little understanding,' confessed Fidelma. 'Have you had time to examine that which I have brought you?'

'Brother Fechtnach told me that you wanted me to look at the parchments in order to tell their veracity, one against the other.

Come and be seated.' He waved to some chairs by the table and then bent over it to smooth the parchments out.

'Well,' the old scholar said, seating himself. 'The first is a fascinating historical document. May I ask what is its provenance? Where did you acquire it?'

Fidelma exchanged an uneasy glance with Eadulf.

'I am afraid that I have to use my authority as a *dálaigh* to decline to answer you specifically. Let us say, the documents were found in a wagon driven by a vagrant, exiled from his own territory.'

Brother Solam pursed his lips thoughtfully. 'Forgive me for pressing. Was this vagrant a man whose skin was of dark complexion?'

Fidelma's surprise was enough to answer the scholar's question without her verbal reply.

'Then it makes sense.' The old man sighed. 'Well, unless you want a detailed translation, I can tell you roughly what they say.'

'A rough outline is all I need at this time,' Fidelma assented eagerly.

'Very well. The first archaic document is a copy of a letter written by Bishop Eucherius of Lugdunum. The original letter would be nearly three centuries old but this copy is more recently made. I would say it is still over one hundred years old.'

'A century?' Eadulf sounded impressed. 'But how do you know that the original is three centuries old?'

Brother Solam tapped the parchment with his forefinger. 'That was the time when Bishop Eucherius lived. Moreover, the person who made this copy was careful to replicate the same spellings and phraseology and even lettering of the original. Having seen many such documents of the period, I can say it was written in the Latin of that period and not in more modern form.'

'You were saying it is a letter from a Bishop Eucherius?' prompted Fidelma.

'The name of the writer is clear. Eucherius of Lugdunum. That is a town in Gaul. It is addressed to a Bishop Salvius. Eucherius is known to us scholars for he wrote some philosophical discourses and letters. When I was a young pilgrim, I saw them in the abbey of the Blessed Mauricius where I stayed on my way to Bobbium.'

'Indeed,' Fidelma said a little impatiently. She knew the abbey of Bobbium well for, returning from Rome, she had stayed there. The abbey had been founded by Columbanus in the Trebbia Valley. It was there she had solved the murder of one of her teachers, Brother Ruadán, who had joined the community there. However, she had not heard of the abbey of Mauricius.

'So what has this Eucherius to say?' asked Eadulf.

'Have you ever heard of the Martyrs of Agaunum?'

'Never.' Fidelma's reply was immediate, and Eadulf was also shaking his head.

'Agaunum is where the abbey of the Blessed Mauricius is now located,' explained the old man. 'It is high in the mountains that form a natural barrier between the southern parts of Gaul and what the Romans called Cisalpine Gaul. It is in those high peaks where Hannibal and his Carthaginians ventured to launch their war on Rome.'

'Very well; and you say this place is called Agaunum?'

'It was so in Roman times. In this document Eucherius relates how the Martyrs of Agaunum met their deaths. He tells the story of the Theban Legion of the Roman Army. Do you know the story of the Legion and the Blessed Mauricius?'

Again Fidelma looked bemused.

'What period are we talking about?' Eadulf asked, seeking clarity.

'It was nearly four centuries ago,' replied the old scholar. 'The story, as Eucherius explains, starts when Mauricius, who was from Thebes in the southern lands of Egypt, and a follower of Christ, joined the Roman army. He rose through the ranks to become the Legate and commander of the Theban Legion. It was a legion that was recruited in southern Egypt so all the legion was as dark skinned as Mauricius himself.'

Fidelma's eyes widened. She was now beginning to see some hint of a connection.

'This was four centuries ago?'

Brother Solam nodded solemnly. 'The Roman Emperor of that time was Maximianus. He was not a Christian, of course. But the story was that the entire Theban Legion had converted to the Christian faith. It was, perhaps, the only Christian Legion in the Roman Army because most Roman soldiers usually worshipped the god Mithras.' He paused but then became aware of Fidelma's impatience and went on: 'Maximianus spent most of his time as Emperor putting down revolts against Rome. Often he did not trust troops from areas close to Rome, or from the places where the unrest was, and so he called upon legions that were raised from the periphery of the empire.'

'Such as these Egyptian troops from Thebes?' Eadulf deduced.

'Just so. The emperor ordered Mauricius and his Theban legion to Gaul where one of the Gaulish tribes called the Bagaudae – I am told that it is a Gaulish word that simply means "fighters" – were in revolt. When Mauricius and his legion arrived, they discovered that they were being ordered to attack people and annihilate them simply because they were Christian. Mauricius and his legion, over six thousand men, refused to carry out the order to massacre fellow Christians. They explained to the emperor that they, too, were also Christians. Maximianus was furious and ordered the legion be punished by decimation.'

Fidelma frowned and asked what it meant.

'It is from the Latin *decem*, meaning ten,' the old man replied pedantically. 'It meant that every tenth man of the legion was picked out and executed. Polybius and Livius both described how legions were punished. General Marcus Licinius Crassus did it while fighting the slave general Spartacus. This was not an uncommon punishment among the Romans. It is thought that this was what happened to the Ninth Hispania Legion in Britain when they refused an order. In fact, Julius Caesar had threatened the Ninth Legion with decimation as a punishment earlier during the civil war against Pompeius.'

'Go on,' urged Eadulf, when the elderly scholar paused.

'The Theban Legion were again ordered to attack Christian villages and again refused. Mauricius himself led the mutiny. So this time Maximianus ordered them all to be disarmed and annihilated, including Mauricius. We are told that this is what happened. However . . .' Brother Solam paused tantalisingly.

'However?' pressed Eadulf.

'Well, when Emperor Constantine recognised the Christian faith and ordered the empire to convert to it, an abbey rose on the site of the massacre and it was dedicated to the Blessed Mauricius.'

'But you said "however", as if there was some significance,' protested Eadulf.

Brother Solam shrugged apologetically and tapped the parchment with his forefinger.

'I meant to say that in this account, Bishop Eucherius writes that a few of the Theban legionaries escaped and were hidden by fellow Christians despite the different colour of their skins, which had made it easy for the Praetorian Guards of the Emperor Maximianus to identify them. Eucherius further adds that several of these survivors were smuggled to Naoned in Armorica and were hidden by the Christian sons of the chief magistrate of the city. The sons were called Donatian and Rogation. Maximianus discovered what the magistrate's sons had done and had them executed. Eucherius says that some of the legionaries escaped again and made their way to the peninsula of Kraozon where the Romans could not follow them, as that part of Armorica still clung to its independence and Rome could not exert control.'

The old man fell silent once more as if gathering his thoughts.

'And then?' prompted Fidelma.

'Eucherius writes no more.'

'We brought you three documents,' Fidelma reminded him.

Brother Solam sighed and nodded. 'The other two are not as interesting as the first and oldest one.'

'But what does the second text say?' asked Eadulf.

'Well, the next document is written in very bad Latin. It dates from the time when Báetán mac Ninnedo was High King of Ireland – because it says so.'

'And that was about one hundred years ago?' Fidelma queried.

'That is so. It states briefly that the writer was a merchant and owner of a trading vessel. His name was Drago, and he was owner of the *Louarn* sailing out of Kraozon in Armorica.'

'Kraozon – the place where Eucherius says some of the Theban legionaries went for sanctuary,' Eadulf recalled.

'The *Louarn* means the Fox and was apparently a trading vessel,' the old man confirmed. 'Drago is writing this in a place called Magh Inis, in Ulaidh. He says he is writing to announce that he is freeing one of his sailors and making him a freeman in reward for his courage serving in dangerous tempests and saving the ship from foundering on the voyage to Ulaidh. Further, this Drago states that the man's family, father to son, have served his people for several generations and thus this man is deserving of his freedom – and so free he shall be from then on.'

'He does not mention the man's name?' Eadulf asked.

'He refers to him in Latin *et milites Thebanos*.'

'The Theban soldier?'

'That is the translation,' confirmed Brother Solam.

Eadulf gave a slow whistle, causing the old scholar to look at him disapprovingly.

'So Celgaire is a descendant of the original Theban survivors of the legion annihilated by the Emperor Maximianus?' Eadulf turned to Fidelma excitedly.

Fidelma did not appear to mirror his excitement. She asked: 'And the third paper?'

'That was the easiest to read of the three, seeing that it is written in our own language so I am sure you have read it, lady. Although it is in the *berla fine*, the ancient tongue of the poets, the form is still used for official documents.'

'I have read it,' agreed Fidelma, 'but it is good to have a second opinion of the archaic forms in relationship to the previous texts.'

'It is written by the Brehon of Cathal, Prince of Ulaidh, at his fortress at Leth Cathail. It is only a few years old. It merely says that the Prince's assembly has proclaimed the warrior Celgaire who, having served the Uí Néill, as had his father and his father's father before him, as being absolved from all duties to the family; and that he is no longer held in the rank of *sen-cléithe*, in spite of serving the Uí Néill for three generations. Refusal to serve them in war, is the reason that he is now recognised as a *doir-fuidir* in rank, without an honour-price, and without the right to enter into any legal contract. Further, he is exiled from the territories of the Uí Néill. It adds that his wife Fial, in choosing to accompany him into exile, simply retains her rank as *saer-fuidir*.'

Fidelma sat back and suppressed a sigh. 'It seems that Celgaire and his ancestors have a sad history,' she remarked.

'And an exciting one,' Eadulf reminded her. 'Celgaire was exiled by Cathal of Ulaidh. Isn't it unusual to exile someone?'

'No, not that unusual. The exile, or *deorad*, can be proclaimed before an assembly and then be exiled from a territory in the hope of being taken on as a servant in another territory. The law allows that the exile might even re-establish themselves as a legally recognised member of the new territorial chieftain.'

'I wonder why Celgaire refused to serve Cathal of Ulaidh in war? I thought that was a duty of all members of the territory.'

'Well, we can now ask him,' Fidelma said firmly. She rose, as did Eadulf. 'Thank you for sharing your knowledge in this matter, Brother Solam.'

'It is my pleasure to examine such a document as the letter of the Blessed Bishop Eucherius, whose work is spoken of highly by members of the Faith. I would ask a favour, that at some point a scribe may be permitted to copy it so that we may lodge it in our library here.'

Fidelma smiled. 'I will ensure that it is so. Is it so valuable, then?'

'There are few references to the Theban Legion – a legion annihilated by the Roman Emperor for disobedience and a legion of Christians, as well as men whose skins were black. Any of those three reasons might be enough to cause some people to wish to erase the facts from history. I fear it is already being expunged from our records as well as those of Rome.'

'Then, rest assured, I will see a copy is made for you,' confirmed Fidelma, taking the documents from him.

They were about to leave when she added, 'Forgive me, Brother Solam. There is something else I would like to see in your archive. We heard that you have the genealogy of Ágach Ágmar the Warlike.'

'Ah yes. I almost forgot that. The abbot had suggested that you might want to see it for yourself. It was only a day or so ago that Conmaol of Cnoc na Faille came here to ask to see it.' The old man grimaced. 'He was a descendant of Ágach and claimed to be the senior of the *derbhfine* since Adnán of Cloichín and his sons were no more. He was most disappointed to find that he was not a senior surviving member. It is all there in the genealogy, authenticated by the scribes of this abbey.'

'May we see it?' asked Eadulf respectfully.

'Of course, of course.' The elderly man took a candle and turned to the shelves. They waited patiently as he peered along. It seemed to take a time but he finally stopped and muttered, 'This is strange. It is not in its usual place. I distinctly remember putting it back after I showed it to him.'

'The abbot said he had to write something to give to Conmaol to take with him, and which endorsed the finding that he was not the senior of the *derbhfine*. Could the abbot not have kept it?'

'No, the abbot wrote that note here.' Brother Solam gestured to his table. 'He did so in the presence of Conmaol and myself. I took the *Genelach* to replace it on the shelf only after the abbot had finished writing.'

'Conmaol was here and saw you do this?'

'Yes, as I have said,' agreed the scriptor. 'Do you imply that he would have removed it? But why? I know the man was upset that it did not prove his claim, but why take it? The document was of little use to him. Anyway, the abbot and I would have seen . . .' The old man paused again.

'What?' asked Eadulf.

'I have a vague memory . . . some months ago, someone else wanted to see the genealogy. But that's irrelevant because it was still here yesterday when Conmaol saw it.'

'Someone wanted to see the genealogy of Ágach Ágmar the Warlike?'

The old scholar nodded. 'They came and made some notes. I remember now.'

'Who was it? Not Conmaol?'

'Oh no. It was a person other than Conmaol. I do recall they also came from Cloichín.'

Fidelma stared thoughtfully at Brother Solam.

'It was not a farmer called Tadgán, by any chance?'

The old man frowned in thought.

'I don't recall the name. However, I am sure he was no farmer. He wore a leather jerkin and trousers and a short apron, making him look more like a blacksmith. The curious thing was, he also wore a black shirt and I could swear it was made of silk – quite at odds with the rest of his appearance. I am afraid I can no longer retain a clear picture of who he was, but I do know he was an officious kind of fellow who said it was important that he learn the precedent of the descent. He was able to read the text himself. That I recall.'

Fidelma exhaled slowly. 'A pity it has gone missing,' was all she said.

'Anyway,' Eadulf put in, 'perhaps Conmaol could have taken the genealogy when you were not looking.'

'But why, when he knew he was not the heir? It doesn't make sense.' Brother Solam raised a hand to massage his brow as if it would bring back some memory. Then he shrugged. 'After I put the text back, the abbot had to leave, and I went with him to the door of the scriptorium. In view of Conmaol's angry outburst, the abbot wanted to tell me quietly that he would send Brother Fechtnach along to ensure that Conmael left the abbey with no further trouble.'

'So, for a moment, Conmaol was unobserved and could have taken it from the shelf. Did he have somewhere to hide it?' Eadulf wanted to know.

'It was not a large item for it only recounted the genealogy of Ágach Ágmar's descendants – four generations – encompassed in a couple of sheets of vellum. An additional sheet went to the descent of Crimthann Srem and his line. He could have thrust it under his shirt and we'd be none the wiser. But I still don't understand why he would take it,' the scriptor echoed again. 'It would have served him no purpose, for it did not support his claim.'

Fidelma asked him, 'I don't suppose you recall the name of the person who *was* senior in the *derbhfine* – I mean after Adnán?'

'I deal with so many of these *Genelach* with so many names that it's impossible to remember them all. I can only repeat that it was someone from Cloichín. Conmaol had brought the news of the death of Adnán, so it was not he. I was going to mark off Adnán's name later that evening. He had sons, of course, but only one of the age of choice. I am so sorry that I cannot recall the boy's name.'

'The son was Cainnech and he, too, is dead.' Fidelma rose suddenly. 'You have been more than helpful, Brother Solam. Don't worry. If I see Conmaol, I will ensure he returns this genealogy.'

'It is most upsetting,' the old scholar sighed. 'Of all the things that cannot be replaced, information in the manner of documents is the most valuable. I suppose we are fortunate in that things can be restored to a certain extent.'

'What do you mean?'

'A genealogy has many branches and often, each senior member of the branch will have his genealogy drawn up so that the family trees running parallel can intertwine and thus the genealogy can be restored. I think the grandfather of Conmaol had his own branch drawn up a long time ago. Of course, it was all covered in the genealogy I showed Conmaol. But we have the original somewhere, although it might take me a day or so to find it.'

'That might help, but it is not urgent if we can get the main genealogy from Conmaol.'

'Well, let me know if you do, otherwise it will take some work for our scribes to draw it up again.'

It was early the next morning that Fidelma and Eadulf found themselves on the road back to Cloichín. They had not talked much after their meeting with Brother Solam. In fact, Eadulf could not see what they had gained towards resolving the murder of Adnán and his family. True, they had learned that Conmaol had no claim as a senior member of the family and therefore no claim to the kin-land of Adnán. That simply meant the kin-land would go to Tadgán without dispute. For Eadulf, he was also pleased to have learned some of the exciting background of the man they had thought of as a poor vagrant.

The track they were following led south-west towards the River Teara, running west to east. It was fairly good arable land along the river but crowded forest land around the track. Again, it was the sort of short journey that Eadulf could enjoy, especially as the weather was not excessively cold. He and Fidelma could relax and allow their mounts to amble at their own pace.

Eadulf was deep in thought when Fidelma suddenly stifled an

exclamation. He glanced up to see her guiding her horse to where a small path left the main track on the left-hand side, heading into the trees towards the river.

'What is it?' he called.

'The movement of our horses disturbed something in the undergrowth,' she called back.

Eadulf was aware of a couple of long grey bodies crashing off through the shrubbery as if in alarm at the horses' movement.

'Careful!' he cried as he realised they were wolves. He knew that wolves usually avoided human contact but, if hungry or threatened, they had no fear of attacking.

Fidelma paid no heed to his warning but urged her horse forward.

'What is it?' Eadulf demanded again when Fidelma halted and stared at something half hidden in the undergrowth.

'I am not sure,' her voice came back.

'Do you need help?'

'I don't think so.' Then he heard her sudden gasp. 'I do not think that anyone can help now,' she said, her voice sombre.

'What do you see?' he said as he moved his horse to join her.

'It is the body of Conmaol.'

ChAPTER FIFTEEN

The body of the man that they had seen at the funeral of Adnán and his family lay slumped in the undergrowth. It was more by his dark, mountain-style cloak and hood that they recognised him, for much of the body was torn and covered in blood. It was clear that the wolves had begun their feast, or perhaps had the intent to drag the remains to their lair.

Eadulf stared down with a horrified expression.

'How could a strong man, as Conmaol undoubtedly was, have allowed himself to be attacked like this?'

'Is it possible to examine the body and tell me?' Fidelma asked.

Eadulf was reluctant, not because of the state of the corpse but thinking that the wolves might return any moment. Nevertheless, he dismounted and bent over to scrutinise the body. As it lay face down, he immediately saw something that made him blow out a breath.

'The wolves reached him after he was dead,' he announced firmly.

'After?'

'Yes. There is a wound in his back which would have been almost immediately fatal.' He pulled aside part of the cloak. The weapon, a small axe, was still embedded in the wound. Eadulf took the handle and gave a quick tug before he turned to her and held it up.

Fidelma stared at it for a moment. It was an axe but not a battle-axe, which was little used by warriors who preferred to do their fighting with spear, sword and shield. This was a *biail*, a common axe for chopping wood or felling minor trees. It had a metal head, fixed to a short oak handle.

Eadulf stood up. There was no point in examining the body further. He peered around.

'His horse might still be in the vicinity, for I think the young man was attacked on his way back to Cloichín.'

'If he was killed on his return from Ard Fhionáin yesterday or even the day before, how did we not see him on our journey there?' Fidelma asked.

'He could have made a detour or have seen us and hidden until we passed by. Anyway, he was probably ambushed and killed immediately. The weapon was obviously thrown with force by the killer from behind, and from the way it smashed into Conmaol's back, biting deep into the spine below the neck, it was thrown at an upward angle.'

'You mean that Conmaol was on horseback and the killer was on foot?'

'That seems logical,' Eadulf nodded. 'Bandits, do you think?'

Fidelma reached down, took the axe from Eadulf and turned it over in her hands.

'Not bandits. This is a woodsman's weapon. It seems axes are turning out to be a favourite murder weapon in these parts!'

'It could belong to anyone, not necessarily a woodsman, for these axes are common about the farmsteads here,' Eadulf pointed out.

Fidelma put the axe in her saddlebag and asked him if he had found anything else.

'I noticed a silver ring on his finger,' replied Eadulf. Wincing, he took the dead hand in his, using the other to pull the heavy silver ring from the finger. 'It has some emblem on it. Curiously enough, it looks like a fish's head.'

'It might be a signet ring,' Fidelma said, taking it and putting it in her *marsupium*.

'What would a mountain man need a silver signet ring for?' wondered Eadulf.

'To claim he was senior head of his *derbhfine*,' replied Fidelma.

It was so obvious an explanation in context that Eadulf gave an inward groan for not having thought of it before. He returned to checking whether there was anything else on the body, then uttered a profanity in his own language.

'You have found something?' Fidelma asked.

'I nearly missed it. There was something hidden under the back of his cloak.' It was a square leather pouch, a *bossán* or wallet-like affair. Eadulf peered inside and then handed it up to Fidelma. 'There's a piece of vellum within,' he said.

Fidelma drew it out and glanced at it.

'It's only a torn scrap, and not what we wanted. It seems to be part of the letter the abbot wrote. There is nothing else on the body?'

Eadulf shook his head.

'So the pouch was empty except for that scrap and there is nothing lying about . . . Then what of the abbot's letter and the genealogy from the abbey? The contents must have been torn out of the *bossán* before the wolves started their work on the body. Either Conmaol took out the rest, tearing it in the process or—'

'Or someone else did and it was certainly no wolf. What does the fragment say?' Eadulf asked.

'It is only a corner piece with a few words. "Descent of Ágach Ágmar the Warlike . . ." and "his *derbhfine*" and "senior". That's about all.'

From somewhere close at hand they suddenly heard a howl. It was clear the wolves had summoned courage again and were inviting the pack to join the feasting.

Fidelma thrust the wallet in her *marsupium* alongside the ring and cast an anxious eye about.

'Well, we cannot remove the body in this state. We'll have to leave this unfortunate fellow to his fate.'

'We must stop at the first stream we come to,' called Eadulf, regarding his bloodied hands with distaste, as he mounted his horse.

'Let us put a safe distance between us and the scavengers first,' Fidelma retorted, urging her horse into a canter.

After a short time they came on a small stream and halted. Eadulf immediately dismounted and plunged his hands in the cold running waters, washing off the blood. He urged Fidelma to do the same even though she had not touched the body – but she had touched the axe, the ring and the leather wallet. She respected Eadulf's knowledge in such matters so raised no objection. After a while he went to his medical bag, found the little bottle he sought and ordered Fidelma to cup her hands. He poured a few drops of the liquid inside, instructing her to rub it over her hands. He did the same to his own hands.

'What is it?' she asked.

'It is distillation of golden rod with comfrey and yarrow,' he replied. 'Together it is a strong antiseptic and should prevent any diseases coming from the wounds on the body. There are too many diseases to be caught that way.' He hesitated and said, 'When you commented on the axe, were you saying we are dealing with the same killer who slaughtered Adnán's family?'

She was looking around her and failed to answer. 'How far do you think we are from Cloichín?' was all she said.

For a moment Eadulf thought she was changing the subject. Then he understood. 'It should be on the other side of that hill, beyond the forest line, so far as I can judge from our outward journey to Ard Fhionáin.'

'And wouldn't this be on the extremities of Tadgán's farm?'

Eadulf frowned. 'You think Tadgán . . .?'

'Not necessarily in person, but . . .' She shrugged. 'As you remarked, that axe is a common object, especially on a farm. What you asked is a possibility, even though one should not spring to judgement. I am always aware of Cicero's question *cui bono* – who will benefit? Who would stand to gain from Conmaol's death?'

Eadulf did not look entirely convinced as he replied, 'So far as I can see, only Tadgán benefits as there is no one now who can challenge his claim to the kin-land. Conmaol certainly had no legitimate claim.'

'What if everyone still believed that he had such a claim?' Fidelma seemed struck by an idea.

Eadulf stared at her in amazement. 'You think that he might have been murdered because . . . but surely that is too obvious.'

'Sometimes the obvious should not be dismissed. After all, Conmaol made a serious challenge to Tadgán for Adnán's kin-land. What if it was thought that he was returning with the proof that he was senior member of the *derbhfine* and could prevent Tadgán from becoming the largest and most powerful landowner in this area? With Tadgán's character and ambition I am wondering what he would do in the circumstances.'

'Then having killed him, he would have seized the contents of the *bossán* – and then he would have learned the truth – that the murder had been unnecessary. If we are going with the kin-land as the motive, that makes Tadgán the murderer.'

Fidelma smiled and shook her head. 'It might be a little more complicated than that, Eadulf. Anyway, we cannot dally here long. Let's get back to Fethmac's house and inform him of the new problems that face us – or rather, ask him if he has let anything happen in our absence.'

'You don't have much faith in him, do you?' Eadulf observed.

'True enough. I am just hoping that he still has Celgaire and his family in protection. If Fethmac has allowed Celgaire to be taken out of his custody then we could be looking at a second hanging. This is a rural community and emotions are easily whipped up by fear, especially when you have such a person as Gadra as a catalyst. But remember it is to Tadgán's advantage to create as much fear as possible simply because the stranger has a different skin colour to us. And now I don't even trust Gobánguss and his wife to be without prejudice in this matter.'

Fidelma suddenly stood up. She had been staring at the mountains to the south of them.

'What is it?' demanded Eadulf.

'I have just realised that there is one place I think I need to visit before we return to Cloichín. But I am afraid it will put another day or so on our journey.'

Eadulf followed her gaze. 'Where to?' he asked, already knowing the answer.

'Cnoc na Faille.'

'I know that's where Conmaol came from – but who do you expect to see there?

'It's an instinct,' she explained briefly. 'Are you with me, or do you wish to return to Cloichín?'

Eadulf shrugged. 'You need someone to look after you,' he said dryly.

Across the river, as a crow flew, the distance to Cnoc na Faille from where they were was the same distance as from An Cloichín to Ard Fhionáin, except they weren't crows. They had to make their way up to the tall peaks, some of which rose almost vertically. Fidelma vaguely knew the direction, having crossed the mountains to Lios Mhór several times. She remembered a path alongside a fast-flowing rivulet called Glengalla. It rose in the mountains and descended onto the plain. The river was long, and there were hidden dangers among the wet, slippery rocks. Several times, Fidelma had to suggest that they dismount and lead their horses.

'There must be an easier way,' grumbled Eadulf.

Fidelma could not suppress a chuckle. 'Not from where we were.'

The steep path took them much longer than Fidelma had anticipated as they climbed slowly upwards into the towering peaks, where the settlement was named after the mountain. The river itself which dominated the high valley was a white-water stretch falling precipitously from the point in the mountains where it rose. Fidelma found a safe ford which crossed it onto a small mule track that led upwards to a small valley between two peaks.

She pointed to the far peak. 'That's Cnoc na Faille,' she called.

'I hope the name does not mean what it says,' responded Eadulf.

Fidelma chuckled again. 'The Neglected Mountain? You are getting a good grasp of the language, Eadulf.'

They rode further into the valley, a small, dark cleft squashed between the surrounding mountain peaks. Now they could see several stone cabins of the type shepherds used and indeed, the surrounding hillsides were speckled with the white fleeces of many sheep and lambs. Higher up, snow lay draped across the peaks. But the whole area was shadowy and cold. Eadulf glanced anxiously at the sky.

'Whatever we do,' he said, 'we will have to find a place to stay the night.'

'Let us first locate the cabin of Conmaol.'

'Who do you expect to find there?' he queried. 'We know he is dead.'

'If my instinct is right, we might learn something.'

They rode on towards the habitations. Outside one, a heavily built woman was turning a spit over a fire. The smell of roasting pork rose in the air around them.

Fidelma called a greeting. The woman stopped a moment and regarded her with a suspicious look.

'Which is the cabin of Conmaol?' Fidelma called.

'He is not here,' the woman replied uncompromisingly, eyes narrowed.

'But I presume his cabin is?' Fidelma said tartly.

The woman looked confused as to whether Fidelma was being serious or making fun of her. Finally she pointed to a series of cabins further along the valley.

'Conmaol dwells there. But he is gone down to the plains below. I told you, he is not at home.'

Fidelma simply thanked her and rode on. As they came closer, they noticed there were several mules tethered outside one of the cabins. Nearby was a fair-sized wagon. Two men were carrying filled sacks from the wagon to a stone-built storehouse.

Fidelma and Eadulf drew rein and Fidelma called, 'Is this the dwelling of Conmaol?'

The two men turned in surprise and glanced at each other without speaking. Then one of them replied, 'If you are looking for Conmaol, he is not here. He has gone down to the plain, to the abbey of Ard Fhionáin.'

'I am Fidelma of Cashel,' Fidelma said. 'And you are . . .?'

The man shuffled uncomfortably as he recognised the form of address and knew this was a woman of noble bearing.

'I am called Tuama, lady. I am a shepherd.'

'Does Conmaol have a family here?'

As the man turned and pointed to a large stone cabin behind them, a youth had just emerged from it. He halted and regarded her warily.

The man called Tuama addressed him. 'This is Fidelma of Cashel,' he announced. 'She is looking for your father.'

'He is not here,' the young man said coldly.

'To be honest, I know he is not,' Fidelma replied, dismounting. Eadulf followed her example. 'I am afraid we have come to ask you some questions.'

'What do you seek here?' the young man replied. There was no welcome in his tone.

Fidelma regarded him. He was about seventeen years in age, tall, with a mop of curly fair hair. A muscular young man whose tanned skin and outlook proclaimed him as a mountain man.

'We will speak of it later.' She felt in no mood to be sympathetic. 'Firstly, I would say that I seek the hospitality due to all travellers and which the folk of these mountains claim to be known for. Secondly, I seek the respect due to the sister of the King of Muman. Thirdly, I seek the obedience that is due to a *dálaigh*. Is that clear enough, boy?' Her voice was never raised but the sharp tones penetrated as she stared at him.

It was the youth who dropped his eyes first and he shrugged.

'I am Slébíne, son of Conmaol. I bid you welcome to my father's house. Enter freely and enjoy what hospitality I can provide and tell me how I can serve you before you continue your journey in safety.'

'Then I thank you, son of Conmaol. This is Brother Eadulf.'

The boy was still suspicious. 'I have heard of you both. My father spoke of you as being in Cloichín. You are investigating the murder of distant cousins. What brings you here?'

'It is a story that may be long in the telling,' she said quietly.

The youth eventually stood aside and motioned the visitors into the warmth of the cottage. It was dark inside but a fire was already lit and a lantern burning above a rough wood table. Slébíne indicated a wooden bench by the fire.

'I have nothing to offer you except *corma* – the drink of the people here. It is brewed locally and is rough, but it keeps the mountain chill from our chests.'

They accepted the spirit which turned out be as strong as the youth implied it was. Eadulf ended up coughing for a few moments, much to their host's open amusement. Then he turned to Fidelma.

'Lady, you have not answered my question. What brings you here? I am above the age of choice, so that I hope for the courtesy of an answer.'

She glanced back at him with a sympathetic smile. She did not wish to tell him of the fate of his father until she had had a chance to question him on other matters.

'When we are young we always wish to be older,' she began, and felt sad that she would soon have to tell him that he was now the elder of his family. 'When we are older, we always wish to be younger. If we knew what responsibilities we were rushing to embrace, I think we would remain forever young.'

Slébíne was frowning, sensing she was saying something which he could not yet fully understand.

'Lady? Is it something to do with your investigation into the death of the cousins in Cloichín?'

'Can you tell me how your father was so speedily informed of the deaths of his cousin Adnán and his family? For he came to the funeral and challenged another cousin, claiming he was the senior of the *derbhfine*.'

'My father was so speedily informed because he had gone down to the plain in order to negotiate some business with Taithlech the merchant.'

'Ah, so Taithlech told him?'

'He did not get to see Taithlech. My father arrived to learn that Taithlech was absent – and then he was given the news about Adnán. He was told that you were there investigating matters. It was too late for my father to ride back here. So when he left the funeral he spent the night with a shepherd on the lower slopes and returned the next morning. He told me that he had issued the ritual challenge at the funeral and seemed very pleased with himself. I was disgusted with the whole thing. I did not support my father in this matter.'

Fidelma exchanged a quick look of surprise with Eadulf.

'I do not understand what you mean,' she said gently.

'I was raised in these mountains. I did not know of any relations on the plains until my father recently told me. He was interested in his family line and even considered himself the senior of the *derbhfine* descending from Ágach Ágmar the Warlike. It was a weakness of vanity on his part.' The young man took a sip of his drink. 'We may be three or four generations removed but we have always lived here in the mountains with only our flocks and goat-herds. What good did it do us to look in envy at folk living more comfortable lives on the plain, while claiming ancestry that did not mean anything in real terms?'

'So you say that you do not share your father's claims about the family of Ágach Ágmar the Warlike?'

'It was just a dream but my father enjoys it.'

'When your father returned here that morning I presume he told you all about his challenge. Do you know what made him make that challenge in the first place? Who suggested that he claim the kin-lands of his cousin?'

'Later that day, the day he rode back from Cloichín, the merchant Taithlech came here. We frequently do business with him. He and my father talked things over. I think it was Taithlech all along who told him that he knew these cousins were possessed of *fintiu* or kin-lands. Lands, as you know, that could be inherited under the permission of the *derbhfine*. My father thought this over and real-ised that under law, if he were eldest of the *derbhfine*, he could make a claim to inherit those lands.'

'How did Taithlech know about your father being senior in the *derbhfine* of Ágach Ágmar?'

The boy shrugged. 'My father told him. It was something that was a favourite topic between him and Taithlech. They were good business friends. As I say, Taithlech was a regular visitor and often he and my father cracked a jug together and spoke of this and that. Taithlech traded regularly with us in this valley. We took his grain and he took our sheep in exchange.'

'What then?'

'My father saw the idea of a farm on the plains below as a way to escape from life in the mountains.'

'Is your mother still living?' Fidelma asked at that point.

The boy shook his head. 'She died several years back during a winter's cold that carried off many in this valley. She was of the mountain people and would have dissuaded my father from the idea.

But when she died, he began to become more and more obsessed about pursuing it.'

'So, although this might have been of benefit to you, you were not supportive of your father wanting to claim this kin-land,' Fidelma noted. 'Doesn't the idea of farming on the plain below appeal to you?'

The boy thrust out his chin belligerently, saying, 'I was born here, under the shadow of Cnoc na Faille. I am content here, and what's more, I believe in the old ways. Land is not owned by us: we are owned by the land. We are born to use it for a while and then . . . that is all.'

'That is an interesting philosophy.'

'I believe it was what the Brehons originally taught and it is only due to recent influences from the strangers from the east that we have developed the idea that property is ours, and ours alone, to hold power over. I do not believe in kin-land and that is why I disagree with my father. I had some education at Lios Mhór, just across the mountains here, and found that even the Faith in its early times did not accept such things until the Roman emperors started to pervert the teachings.'

Fidelma stared at the youth for a long moment, surprisd by his wisdom and maturity at so early an age.

'You seem to have learned much in your youth,' she smiled approvingly.

'I learned enough to disagree with my father's attitude. I also learned that many of the teachings of the Faith that are now being thrust upon us have nothing to do with the original teachings.'

Eadulf too was nodding. 'I think you would be a good foil for Brother Gadra, despite your youth,' he commented.

'I do not know of a Brother Gadra,' snapped Slébíne. 'And age has no sole prerogative of speaking wisdom.'

'I suspect you are a poet, Slébíne,' Fidelma observed.

'Am I to be condemned for that?' The youth coloured.

'Not unless you are a bad poet.'

'Well,' he was defensive, 'I am, indeed, a *filé*.'

Eadulf knew that the word meant he had been trained in the art of the ancient and intellectual poetry of the country. Had he used the word *bard* it would have meant he was a mere rhymer, a purveyor of doggerel.

The youth must have caught the look of surprise on Eadulf's features, for he went on: 'I am qualified to the level of *fochlocán*.'

This revealed that he had studied his art for two years; the name literally meant a sprig of brook lime from which great things could grow.

'Did your father agree with your chosen path?'

'Whether he does or not, I am the one who must tread it. I am happy here in the mountains with my sheep, my friends and neighbours, and my verse and thoughts to keep me comfort.'

Fidelma was beginning to like the lad.

'So you were two years studying at Lios Mhór. What else did you learn there that would make you disagree with your father?'

'In the abbey you learn much about the New Faith, even when one is not specifically studying it. I learned that when the *Cunctos populos*, the Edict of Thessalonica, was issued towards the end of the fourth century by the three Roman Emperors, Theodosius, Gratian and Valetinian, it was ordered that Christianity become the official religion of the Roman Empire. Moreover, it was the Nicene philosophy of Christianity. It was decreed that all other creeds and religions were to be suppressed and temples destroyed. The church leaders then became temporal princes; they owned private property and they even owned slaves – slaves who fought to their deaths as gladiators in arenas of the empire to make money for their owners. They possessed great wealth, these new Christian leaders.'

Eadulf stirred uncomfortably, for he had seen such wealth in Rome in the households of cardinals, abbots and bishops.

'What are you saying, Slébíne?' Fidelma asked softly.

'Before Rome took over the Faith, the Faith was the Faith of the poor, the slaves and the hope of their progress. But the Roman overlords, seeing they could not suppress the Faith, simply made it their own – a Faith in which they were still in charge. Before that, Tertullinus of Carthage, one of the first Christian philosophers, had mocked the idea that Christians should not share property in common. Basil of Caesarea had said that property was theft. Then Aurelius Ambrosius declared that only unjust usurpation had created the right of private property and—'

'We have heard enough,' Eadulf intervened at this point. 'You may believe what you believe. That is not what we have come for.'

Fidelma frowned at the interruption for she was fascinated by the lad's youthful vehemence. Then she sighed and accepted that she had a difficult task to fulfil.

'There is much in what you say, Slébíne,' she said to mollify the boy. 'Indeed,' she glanced at Eadulf almost apologetically, 'I have heard these words spoken of before. And it is true that absolutely private property is becoming a new concept in this kingdom. We have already introduced the concept of kin-land, as you say, and that is now enshrined in our law. The important point is that you say you are at odds with your father on his claim to kin-land – and is it on the grounds of what these early philosophers of the New Faith taught?'

'It is. Not just what they said but what the Old Faith here taught.'

'So you would not be unhappy if it were shown that your father had no entitlement under the law and was not a senior member of the *derbhfine*?' Fidelma continued.

'I would be sad for my father, having fostered this dream only to be shown that dreams have little substance. Anyway, two days ago he left for the abbey of Ard Fhionáin to consult the official *Genelach*, the genealogy that they hold of the family of Ágach Ágmar. So we await his return on that.'

'When and where did he learn the abbey held such a document?'

'I think he may have discovered that from one of our old folk. I heard him discuss it with Taithlech.'

'And then he set off? Who else knew about his visit there?'

The boy chuckled. 'Practically everyone he met. It was no secret.'

Fidelma realised the time had come to reveal the truth to the boy.

'Slébíne, I need to inform you that the document at the abbey showed that your father was not the *ádae fine*, senior of his *derbhfine,* and had no claim on the kin-land.'

Slébíne did not appear surprised. In fact, a smile spread over his features.

'So now we can return to some reality.' Then he frowned. 'But why has he not returned to tell me? Is he ashamed?'

Eadulf glanced at Fidelma. He knew that she had held back from telling the young man about his father's death so she could learn more about Slébíne and ascertain whether he was part of his father's plans. Eadulf had seen Fidelma use the technique before in order to extract information. At his silent, questioning look, she gave a quick nod.

'We bring bad tidings,' Eadulf then said starkly.

The boy turned to him, sensing trouble.

'Slébíne, your father is dead.' Fidelma spoke quietly, wishing there was some other way of saying it, of delivering such devastating news.

CHAPTER SIXTEEN

Slébíne registered a momentary shock before he made a visible attempt to pull his shoulders back and take in this news. His eyes asked the question.

'We found him on the trail from the abbey heading back to Cloichín,' explained Fidelma. 'I am afraid to say your father had been murdered. He had received a blow on the back of the head and his body had been left to be mauled by wolves. We could do nothing but leave his body where we found it.'

'He was murdered?' the boy asked hollowly. 'By whom? And why?'

'We don't know . . . yet,' Fidelma replied with emphasis. 'As to "whom", that I shall find out. As to the "why", I believe it is connected to the murders of your distant kinsmen.'

There was a silence.

'Are you saying it was because he tried to claim the kin-lands?' the boy asked incredulously.

'He had left the abbey with the genealogy of Ágach Ágmar the Warlike, as well as a statement from the abbot, revealing that he was not the senior member of the *derbhfine* of the family. The genealogy had the name of the real heir to the kin-land on it. That was stolen from the body. Some torn pieces that remained showed what they had been.'

For a moment or two the boy was obviously struggling between shock and grief and his bewilderment.

'I do not understand,' he finally said. 'If the documents showed he had no claim on the kin-land, why were they destroyed? Had they showed he had a claim, then I would understand why he was killed and the papers were taken. If they did not support his claim, then why . . .?'

'As I said, I think the *Genelach* had the name of the killer on it,' Fidelma repeated quietly.

The boy stared at her, and comprehension slowly dawned in his eyes.

'You mean there is a genuine senior member of the *derbhfine* who can claim the kin-lands and wanted to ensure that claim?'

'We are sorry to bring you the news of your father's death and apologise for having to ask your position on these matters first.' Fidelma did not reply to his question. She moved to her saddlebag and took the silver ring from it. 'He still had this on his finger. It belongs to you.'

The boy took it and examined it without expression. Then he said: 'This ring has been passed down in our family since the days of Ágach. It was my father's treasured possession.'

'Now it is yours. The murder of Conmaol, following that of his cousin Adnán, could indicate that the motive was possession of the kin-land.'

Slébíne sighed deeply and raised a pain-stricken face to her.

'As much as I disliked his philosophy, or what he was trying to do by making this claim, he was still my father. I might have rejected his attitudes and ambitions but I loved him. But this ring and the claims to kin-land are a curse and I shall have nothing to do with them.'

She leaned forward and placed a hand on his arm.

'I believe you. Keep the ring for his sake. Remember, there is someone who thought Conmaol's death and the loss of those documents would benefit them. But who? That is what we must discover.'

'I will help you, though I cannot think how.'

The winter skies had darkened, portending the long, dark night ahead.

'May we trespass on your hospitality for this night,' Fidelma asked, 'for it is pointless to chance our lives in descending the mountain until tomorrow. We hate to intrude on you in the circumstances.'

The youth smiled wanly. 'You are welcome, although in other circumstances, lady, I would have been pleased to discourse on those subjects that I have heard you are interested in. Even in these mountains we have learned of your defence of our native faith and laws.'

He stood up abruptly. 'Tomorrow, I shall take men from the village and go to find my father's remains so we may give him a traditional burial. But night is upon us and, as you said, one should not put people's lives in danger to descend the mountain passes in the darkness and icy cold.'

'A wise decision,' agreed Fidelma. 'In the morning, we will go by the main route back to Cloichín but leave you with guidance to where we found the body.'

The boy seemed to have taken on a new authority as he realised that he had been precipitated into a new role in life.

'I will ask Tuama to see to you and your horses. There is space in the barn to keep them from the chill mountain air. Tonight there was to be feasting in the barn of Óenu, who is senior among our valley community here. He is our chief, if you like. It was to be a celebration of the coming into lamb of the ewes, but now it will be a celebration for my father. I hope you will both attend.'

Eadulf looked a little shocked. 'We have brought you news of your father's murder. Is this an appropriate cause to celebrate?'

Slébíne's smile held a little whimsical sadness.

'We mountain folk celebrate death as is the ancient custom of our people.' Then, seeing that Eadulf was still puzzled, he added: 'Before the coming of the New Faith, we believed there were two worlds. We believed that when someone died in this world, they were reborn in the next. When someone died in the Otherworld, they were reborn in this. Therefore, no one ever really dies.'

Eadulf nodded thoughtfully. 'I know that you believed in the immortality of the soul long before you accepted the New Faith. But celebrating the death . . .?'

'We celebrate death in this world because it means a soul has been newborn in the Otherworld. We mourn birth in this world because it means a soul has died in the Otherworld. That is our way, up in these mountains. We believe in the old ways, which is why I never wanted to escape to the plains as my father did. So I hope he will achieve what he wishes in the Otherworld.'

Slébíne left them to make his arrangements.

Eadulf looked at Fidelma and raised his brows. 'Well, what do you think? Have we moved any closer towards finding a resolution? I have to admit that I can't see how these things are as interconnected as you say.'

'I think I am beginning to see connections. Perhaps even with the deaths of poor Íonait and Dulbaire.'

'I have to say, I find this lad Slébíne strange for one who has just been told of his father's death.'

'Perhaps it is not so strange. The belief system he told you about is still widely held. It is true that the new ways are encroaching, but in the mountains these beliefs not only linger but are reinforced as a defence against people like Gadra who seeks to make all people the same. Let us hope the day never comes when we all think, behave and speak alike.'

Eadulf sighed and was about to respond when Slébíne returned. He was carrying their saddlebags.

'Tuama is seeing to your horses and will make sure they are fed well.' He placed the saddlebags down. 'I have asked him to guide you in the morning to the head of a pass by which you may make an easier descent of the mountains to Cloichín. It will be a more gradual path down than the one you came up by, for it will connect you with the Way of Declan as it is called.'

Eadulf looked nervous. 'We passed along that path a few days ago and saw the burned-out tavern of Béoán and Cáemell.'

Slébíne sniffed. 'The work of bandits or hired thugs. I have heard stories about them. Thankfully Béoán and Cáemell escaped the flames and sought refuge elsewhere. Although he was a friend of my father, there are many stories connected to Taithlech the merchant, and it is said he has a ruthless way of conducting his business.'

'So you have heard that story too?' Fidelma asked.

Slébíne stared at her for a moment and then smiled. 'I suppose there is little that escapes your attention. It is said that they refused to do business with him and because of that he ordered certain of his men to burn them out. The mountain people would be willing to point the way if ever the King at Cashel were inclined to send a battalion of his warriors to help flush the bandits out.'

Fidelma looked at him for a moment and said softly, 'That might be arranged. Taithlech should not be allowed to go unpunished either.'

'That is good. And now, if you are not too exhausted, let me take you down to Óenu's barn where you will join in the merriment of the mountain people.'

Outside, the area had become alight with flickering brand torches. In the distance they could see people moving towards a wooden barn. The noise of their conversation rose and there was the odour of roasting meat in the air. The sounds of merry music reached them. Inside, the feasting and dancing had already begun. In a corner a fiddler was flanked by a *cuisig* player, not just playing a *bodhrán,* a goatskin drum, but other instruments of timpani, while another man was a *cnamh-fhir*, or bone man, who used animal bones to beat out rhythms, and there was a traditional piper whose air bag was inflated by the pumping motion of his elbow.

Slébíne introduced his guests to various people whose names Fidelma and Eadulf promptly forgot if ever the names registered above the laughter, music and high-pitched talking. In a moment of quiet, someone called for all to stand in silence. Slébíne was beckoned forward and then announced the death of his father. It was a simple, dignified speech in which heads were bowed in acknowledgement, and an old man came forward. In the days before the New Faith, Fidelma would have recognised him as a Druid, a spiritual leader of the people. Perhaps he was still a Druid. Fidelma was not troubled by names. The old man spoke in a high voice.

'Donn, God of the Dead, has gathered the soul of Conmaol, the wolf-warrior, for safe transportation to the Otherworld. We rejoice in the rebirth of Conmaol in the Otherworld. May he be long and happy dwelling in the place of the Ever Young.'

At this, the company began a curious clapping of the hands, slow and rhythmic accompanied at regular intervals by the stamping of their feet. It was unlike anything Eadulf had heard before. It seemed curious, wild and pagan. Finally, as if at a hidden signal, it stopped. There was no warning. It left a silence that was almost unnerving.

Then the old man turned to Slébíne and laid his hands on the young man's bowed head as if bestowing a blessing.

'What's going on?' whispered Eadulf.

'These mountain folk have their own ancient customs as I mentioned,' Fidelma murmured.

The young son of Conmaol turned to those gathered and began a strange wailing chant, an ancient form with rhythms not only at the end of the lines but two or even three within the lines them-selves. Eadulf had not heard the form in all the years he had travelled the country.

'The wolf-warrior is gone from us.
No longer will he count the ages of the Moon.
Not in our lifetime will he call his sheep.
among the high peaks, in the echoing valleys.
Silence has fallen as he crosses the Plain of Mists.
The descendant of Ágach Ágmar the Warlike
Has left us to commence his westerly journey.
He is wrapped in the protective cloak of Donn.
He has ridden the seven green waves.
Soon he will thrive in the Land of the Ever Young.
In the Hy-Brasil, in the Land of Promise.

The dirge, for that is what Eadulf presumed it was, ended as abruptly as it began. There was a moment of silence and then the fiddler took up his bow. He was a small man, his features tanned almost nut-brown by the outdoor life. His fellow musicians gathered around him. He played a single note and looked round, whereupon his fellows nodded as if in answer to his unspoken question. Then he started in earnest playing a tune that seemed infectious to Eadulf. It did not last long but by the time it ended, men and women, old and young, had gathered in two lines, facing one another, in the centre of the barn.

The fiddler repeated his opening and was then reinforced with a loud accompaniment on the goatskin drum. At the first stroke on the drum the males began to move. They performed their movements before the women who stood in an attitude of repose. The male dancers held their hands loosely at their sides, faces immobile, allowing the movement of their bodies, the masculine vigour, and the exhilaration of being alive, express itself through the dexterity and quickness of movement of their feet; a movement that did not let a note pass by without a complementary answer.

When the music paused and the males stopped, it was the turn of their female partners to come forward but they did not entirely copy or repeat the movement of the males. They began with hands clasped in front of them and with steps that seemed higher than their male partners. There was a lightness and grace in their movements that both harmonised and supplemented their partners'. Unlike the males, who expressed their emotions with their feet, the women smiled and allowed their faces as well as their bodies to betray their pleasure at life, love and the music.

Then the dancers were twisting and turning as they changed positions, moving with an uncanny assured choreography as if someone was directing them; the men with their heavy virile steps, the women with their softer, flowing movements but the interchange of both genders agile and fluid. It seemed to Eadulf that dance succeeded dance until the musicians were exhausted first before the dancers.

It was then that an elderly woman came placing plates of food and more drinks before them. Fidelma and Eadulf did justice to the dishes. How long they stayed with these mountain folk, Eadulf was not sure. But he was falling asleep when Fidelma nudged him and they started to offer their excuses to seek their bed.

Slébíne escorted them back to his cabin and showed them where they were to sleep.

'You have seen how we mountain folk greet death, lady,' he said solemnly. 'There is joy in all things and we seek that joy. We seize the hour. That is our philosophy. Take what the hour brings without yearning for tomorrow.'

She smiled in return. It was almost as Quintus Horatius Flaccus had written it: *carpe diem, quam minimum credula postero* – enjoy today, trusting little in tomorrow.

The next morning, the pale sun was above the eastern peaks when Tuama, their guide, halted on the top of a steep downward track and pointed.

'All you have to do is follow this track downwards and it will intersect with a larger track which is the way you want. Turn to the north and you will recognise the route. There are no hidden obstacles along the track and your horses should have no problems.'

Fidelma turned to the old mountain man.

'That is good to know, Tuama. Are there any other obstacles that we should know about?'

'You mean the story of bandits?' asked Tuama with a toothless grin. 'Well, they should not bother the likes of you. I have heard they only look for rich merchants.'

Tuama raised his hand in a gesture of farewell and turned back, leaving her and Eadulf to start their way down the path. As the more experienced rider she nudged her Gaulish pony down the track first with Eadulf following behind on his cob.

It was a chilly morning in spite of the high sun and lack of clouds. The day was quiet, with the occasional cry of a chough: the excited 'keeaar, keeaar' cry was unmistakable. Now and then they saw the bird, with its black plumage, take off to do acrobatics in the sky above them.

'I found last night unusual,' Eadulf called after a while.

'In what way?' asked Fidelma over her shoulder.

'I did not know you could have two cultures in the same kingdom. I thought I knew this land well by now, yet I have never felt such a foreign traveller until last night.'

Fidelma chuckled in response. 'Even to the people of the plains, the mountain folk are different. It seems that they maintain their traditions from the time before time, ancient and inalterable. Their music, poetry and ways of looking at the world are those that were old even before the children of Gáidheal Glas came and wrested these shores from the ancient folk.'

Eadulf was about to comment when something made him glance up at the mountain above them. He blinked a moment and stared again. His eyes first moved to the high black speck of a peregrine circling in the pale blue sky. Then they alighted on the peaks above to their left.

'Fidelma!' Eadulf's call was quiet and urgent.

She looked back at him in surprise at his change of tone. 'What is it?'

'I've just seen a number of riders on the track to the left and just above us.'

'Riders?' She glanced quickly upwards in the direction he had mentioned but could see nothing.

'I only saw their movement as they passed between two outcrops of rock. They are moving down the mountain. They looked like armed men. If this path intercepts the path they are on, then we would meet with them lower down this slope.'

Fidelma had halted and was looking thoughtful. 'Armed men, you say?'

'I saw some reflection on shields. Men do not carry shields unless they also carry weapons.'

'Armed men . . .' she repeated.

'Perhaps these are the bandits that we have heard of?' he suggested. 'If so, for all that is said, they would not have any respect for the King's sister, let alone a *dálaigh*.'

Fidelma stared upwards. There was nothing she could see but the mountain was very rocky and the rocks often hid its secret pathways, and where they did not, there were stretches of woods which performed a similar screen. She compressed her lips in annoyance. He was right. Both paths would connect with the Way of Declan, to bring them down onto the great Plain of Femen.

'The point is,' Fidelma said quietly, 'are they hostile or friendly?'

Eadulf said wryly, 'My philosophy is – expect the worst and you will not be disappointed.'

'We need to get back to Cloichín,' she pointed out.

'We *need* to get back to Cloichín,' responded Eadulf with more emphasis.

Fidelma smiled at this, saying, 'In that case, we shall move into those woods to our right and wait for a while to allow them to pass on their way without encountering them. At least we have some daylight left to us. However, it is irritating to be held up like this.'

'If you want to chance it, then I am willing,' Eadulf shrugged. 'Perhaps they are not bandits.'

She only hesitated a moment before deciding, 'No. Now is not the time to take chances.'

She dismounted and led the way towards an area of thick woodland that tumbled down the mountainside. The horses had to pick their way through patches of dwarf willow, the plant that spread its tiny reddish-brown and shiny green branches to no more than six centimetres high. The plants appeared to form a protective barrier to the main lush wildwood that consisted of a mixture of alder, ash and yew. The alder were still hung in the brown, woody cones that would not emerge in colour until the warmer weather. Eadulf could see why these giants rose more than twenty metres high for they were growing close to their favourite habitat of a mountain stream. He felt easier as he and Fidelma moved deeper into the cover of the woods. Yet this was still winter woodland and the cover was not as complete as summer woodland with its canopy of green and high-growing shrubs.

There was a little clearing where Fidelma halted and tethered her horse to a convenient shrub.

'We'll wait here a while,' she announced. 'Then if all is well we can continue on to Declan's Way. Let's hope those riders did not see us, otherwise they might come looking for us.'

Unfortunately, they soon realised that they had been seen, for it wasn't long before they heard the movement of horses and a strong voice calling. The words were very clear in the mountain air.

'Any sign of them?'

A voice above them replied, 'We've come up to the spot where you first saw them. They are definitely not on the path below where we should have encountered them.'

The first voice swore in annoyance. 'But there are no tracks before the point where they could have emerged. I'm coming back to join you.'

There was the sound of a horse with labouring breath moving up the path above them.

Fidelma and Eadulf sat absolutely still, hoping that their horses could not be seen through the bare trees and that they would not make a sound.

The first voice was speaking again. 'Well, if they did not come down the path there is only one thing they could have done and that is they left the path. They would not climb up along here, so my guess is they left it and tried to go down the mountainside. That would be stupid. I know this area well.'

'Why do you say stupid, *túaircnid*?' asked one of the men.

The phrase was an unusual one to Eadulf's ears. It meant 'battle-smiter' but he knew that some professional warriors often used it as a term of respect to their commander.

'Because I know this area,' repeated the first voice. 'I grew up riding my horse in these mountains. Beyond this woodland the ground becomes almost sheer. No horse could move down it without taking a tumble.'

'So that means . . .?' asked the same man.

To his surprise, Eadulf saw Fidelma rise and take the reins of her horse.

'It means,' she called out loudly, 'that we surrender.'

CHAPTER SEVENTEEN

' I thought I recognised Friend Eadulf on the path below us, even though my view was obscured.' The voice that greeted them was familiar and Fidelma had recognised it long before Eadulf had done so.

The grinning features of Enda, the handsome young warrior of the Golden Collar, the élite bodyguards of the King of Cashel, gazed down at them in amusement.

'Well met, lady, well met, Friend Eadulf. But what are you doing in this god-forsaken place – and hiding in that wood?'

Fidelma returned his smile of welcome as he reached out a hand to help her up onto the path.

'We were hiding from you,' she replied cheerfully.

Enda responded in bewilderment. 'From us?'

Eadulf joined them. 'We thought you might be bandits,' he said. 'I spotted movement up on the path above, saw armed men passing and we worked out that your path would intercede with ours. Not wishing to meet with brigands, we decided to bide our time in this wood until we estimated you would have gone.'

'But what made you think we were brigands?' Enda was clearly puzzled by the explanation.

'There has been much bloodshed here these last few days,'

Fidelma told him. 'And it seems there are also bandits around who have burned down the old tavern of Béoán and Cáemell.'

'Is that the one which stands at the far end of the pass before the track divides down the mountain?' asked the young warrior in concern.

'The same,' Fidelma confirmed.

Enda shook his head in perplexity. 'But why? They have been there since I have known this route – an old couple who did no harm to anyone, and the tavern was essential to those passing along this way. Who are these brigands that would attack them?'

'I fear they are mercenaries employed by a merchant.'

'If you know who gave orders to these brigands, then . . .?'

'It is a little complicated, Enda. The law is not so clear. It was claimed that the burning of their tavern was inflicted as a punishment. The old couple have gone to live with a relative far from here and have not been harmed. The man who ordered this act claimed defence under the laws of *ainfiach*, the law on debt . . . he said they owed money to him and would not pay. That he was entitled to reclaim money from them. Before I can act, I need more information and the exact position of the law. At this time, I have other problems to preoccupy my time rather than dealing with this matter.'

'Other problems? This matter sounds important enough.'

'But not as important as the several deaths that have occurred.'

Before Enda could articulate his further query, Eadulf glanced at Enda's companions and asked: 'Are there just three of you? I thought I saw more warriors when I first glimpsed you?'

'You always have sharp eyes,' Enda grinned. 'There is myself and six warriors. The others wait for us at the intersection of the path.'

'But what are you and your men doing here in the mountains?'

'We were on our way back from Ard Mhór,' the warrior explained, mentioning the seaport to the south. It was where Declan had established his religious settlement two centuries before, in the petty kingdom of the Déisi Muman. The settlement had grown into an important abbey and the once-small village had prospered, with it becoming one of the most important seaports of Muman. With its long stretch of sandy beach and caves in the cliffs it had become a good landing place and, indeed, not far from the great estuary of An Abhainn Mhór – the great river which was navigable as far as Lios Mhór and beyond.

'What was happening at Ard Mhór?' Fidelma was interested.

'Oh, we were asked to escort some Gaulish merchant prince and his party who came to discuss business with your brother, the King. His ship was waiting there. A boring task.' Enda shrugged. 'It seems that you are having a much more exciting time.'

Eadulf nodded vehemently in agreement.

'Several times, these last days, I have wished we were accompanied by warriors of the Nasc Niadh, my friend.'

'Is there is some danger?' Enda queried.

'I would say so,' Eadulf replied. 'I have not felt so ill at ease in a long time.'

'And you spoke earlier of deaths? But you say that you do not mean the old couple at the tavern – Béoán and Cáemell? So who *has* been killed?'

Eadulf recited: 'At the last count there have been six murders, one being an illegal hanging, and one abduction plus an attempted murder . . . oh, and a second attempt at an illegal hanging. What's more, Fidelma nearly had a very heavy cauldron fall on her head which could have been an attempt to murder her, but we cannot be certain about that.'

Enda was looking horrified. 'Are you being serious?' he gasped.

Fidelma sighed. 'As much as Eadulf can be accused of facetiousness at times, he is telling the truth. And I am not sure we can count the toppling of the cauldron on me as a specific attempt to murder.'

'And this is happening here?' Enda circled his arm to encompass the surrounding mountains. 'Well, I have only half-a-dozen warriors, but that should be sufficient to seek out wrongdoers in this terrain.'

'We could do with your help, Enda,' Fidelma confirmed, 'but I need you and your men in Cloichín, which is where these events have happened.'

'That small village? I have not been there in many a year. I thought it was a peaceful backwater where everyone was content to grow crops, raise livestock and do not much else.'

'We were told it was supposed to have been a veritable Garden of Eden.' Eadulf's tone was ironic. 'There has certainly been a lot of blood spilt in that garden!'

Enda glanced at his companions, who were immediate with their assent.

'Little need to ask, lady,' the young warrior smiled. 'What would you have us do? After all, your brother is commander of the Warriors of the Golden Collar and you are one of our number too.'

Fidelma was remounting her horse and Eadulf followed suit.

'I'll explain the details as we ride,' she said. 'In practical terms, I need your warriors to keep certain citizens in order. The villagers have allowed themselves to be whipped into a frenzy by certain newcomers, and have even forgotten the law a couple of times. Sadly, a young man was taken and killed by the villagers because he was suspected of the murder of a young girl. Suspected, mind you. He was a *drúth* . . .'

'He was mentally retarded?' Enda was shocked, because the warriors of the Golden Collar were taught something of the law. Often, their role was to enforce the law at the word of the lawgivers. 'How can the death of a half-wit be allowed?'

'I had taken him into custody and while we were pursuing other matters, a mob burst into the local magistrate's house, where he was being held, took him and hanged him.'

'Incredible behaviour,' muttered Enda. 'They must know it is against the law – and that the same law will reach out and punish them?'

'Even more incredible is the fact that a prime leader in these crimes is a religieux, a Brother Gadra who calls himself Father Gadra,' Eadulf told him.

'He was responsible for trying to hang another suspect in the custody of the local magistrate,' Fidelma added.

'Brother Gadra?' frowned Enda. 'The name is not familiar. He should be placed where he can do no harm. Is that our task?'

'It is certainly one of them,' Fidelma said. 'We still have one man in custody. He was the first suspect that this same man, Gadra, stirred up the villagers to attempt to hang. We managed to stop that. Then another prisoner, Dulbaire, the *drúth* I mentioned earlier, who was taken into custody for his own protection, was abducted in my absence. As I said, they killed the poor boy.'

Enda's expression was growing steadily more outraged.

'You say that all this is happening within a short distance from the King's capital? Unbelievable that this person you mentioned, Gadra, is a man of the Faith.'

'I know,' Fidelma agreed solemnly. 'It is unbelievable.'

They came to the conjunction of the Way of the Blessed Declan where they found the remaining members of Enda's command waiting. By the time they were passing the charred remains of the deserted tavern, Fidelma had told Enda the whole story. By now, the young warrior, who had shared many adventures with her and Eadulf, was beyond amazement.

'It is certainly time that you had some backing from the sword arms of my men here. That there is a village in this kingdom which ignores the law and obeys some rebellious priest is beyond my comprehension. Do you think you will be able to resolve the responsibility for the deaths, lady? Who do you think is behind all this? Apart from the priest, that is. Is it this farmer Tadgán, for he seems to have most to lose and much to gain.'

'I think Tadgán has something to answer for. Certainly Taithlech should answer for the burning of the tavern,' Fidelma said. 'I am sure all things are connected and this is my problem, to bring the various strands together into the one rope.'

'What would you have us do when we reach Cloichín, lady?' Enda asked.

'I can't be specific but I think things may happen rapidly and you might have to use force to ensure the peace. I will have to give you orders as and when.'

'By your command, lady,' acknowledged Enda, his smile expressing his delight that there might be some action ahead after the lack of incident during the last days.

It was mid-afternoon by the time they left the mountain road and approached the outskirts of the 'village of the little stones'. They had just crossed the ford through the River Duthóg when they saw a rider approaching from the edge of the village. Enda moved alongside Fidelma, his hand on his sword hilt. She stayed him.

'It is the young magistrate, Fethmac,' she cautioned.

Fethmac halted his horse in front of them. His eyes widened in an expression of overwhelming relief.

'It's you, lady! I saw the horsemen approaching from the mountains, wondered if they were brigands and feared the worst. So I rode out to check and, if possible, to warn the village. There is talk about raiders in the mountains. When I saw the emblems I came to seek their help and then I saw you, lady.'

'This is Enda,' Fidelma told him. 'He is the commander of these warriors.'

'I would bid you and your men welcome to the village, Enda,' the young magistrate said immediately. 'But all is not well.' He turned back to Fidelma. 'There has been trouble since you left for Ard Fhionáin, lady.'

'Trouble?' she frowned. 'More deaths?'

Fethmac shook his head quickly. 'No, thanks be. But Father . . .'

He paused and corrected himself. 'Brother Gadra has been causing more unrest among the people.'

'Yet again! About what this time?' she demanded. 'Are Celgaire and his family safe?'

'For the time being, lady.'

'What do you mean?'

'Celgaire may not be safe for long. You see, Gadra has been attacking you in particular, lady. He is still claiming that Celgaire killed Adnán and his family, and saying that you are protecting him. He couches it in his religious talk.'

Enda let out a profanity. 'Does he not know who you are, lady?'

'He knows exactly who I am,' Fidelma replied coldly. 'That is why he needs to be confronted. He is one of those new religieux who have returned from Rome bringing fresh interpretations, teachings and new laws passed by the councils of the churches which try to overturn our native laws and beliefs.'

The young warrior looked grim. 'Then we should go and pay this man an immediate visit.'

Fethmac hurriedly informed him: 'He already has a large crowd of villagers gathered in the *sabhall*.'

'You mean the old barn that Taithlech lets him use to hold his services?' Fidelma asked.

'Yes, lady. He has managed to collect together a horde of those folk who follow his teaching, especially the women, and those women influence their men. Even Gobánguss is persuaded to support him by his wife, as Lúbaigh is by *his* wife. They are all in the barn. It was futile for me to go in and remonstrate, lady. I know you think I am weak, but I barely came away without injury. It is not only me they threaten, lady, but Ballgel. What can I do? Gadra is even now whipping up their emotions to come and take Celgaire by force from my custody again.'

'Do they know where Celgaire is?'

'Gobánguss or his wife must have told him. My wife and I are in danger. I have a duty to protect my wife and can only do that by surrendering Celgaire to them. Truly, lady, I begin to realise that the role of magistrate is not one that I am fitted for. I feel I must resign.'

Fidelma's disapproving look was enough to show what she thought of this, but she did not waste time in expressing her thoughts.

'You and your men will follow me to this barn,' she told Enda. 'We will go and confront this so-called religieux and try to prevent another killing.'

She urged her mount forward, brushing past Fethmac. With Eadulf on one side and Enda on the other, followed by the half-a-dozen warriors and Fethmac, shame faced, trailing reluctantly behind them, they galloped purposefully forward. Fidelma remembered the way to the great barn without having to go through the village and they soon came to a halt outside it, their horses perspiring.

'Enda, come with me and Eadulf. Bring two of your men. The rest stand ready outside the barn doors.'

Enda signalled to two of his men and they dismounted without wasting time on words. One of the warriors stepped forward to take their horses and the others positioned themselves ready outside the barn doors as instructed.

The big door was slightly ajar; enough to allow them to quietly push through without anyone noticing their entrance. The crowd of villagers was standing facing towards the far end of the barn. As Fethmac had said, there was a large number of people present. Facing the crowd was Gadra, mounted on a wooden crate and haranguing them with dramatic motions of his arms. Fidelma signalled to her companions to stand still.

Gadra was in full thunderous voice. '. . . free because Gobánguss heard the word of the Lord and refused to imprison me at the word of a woman, a woman who tries to assert her authority over you. A woman who refuses to hear the word of the Lord, rejects the Commandments that He has given us. Do you know that Jesus foresaw the evils of the unjust judge? He said that God will hear your cries for vengeance and that, day or night, He will come and take His own vengeance on the wrongdoers. It is written in the words of Luke to ignore the dishonest judge and take vengeance quickly.

'My brethren, I am appointed to bring you the Word and I tell you not to consider those who judge otherwise than in the name of the Lord, for the Lord is with you when you render His judgement!'

There was a movement and muttering from those gathered.

'But she is a *dálaigh*,' cried one woman. 'She is sister of the King. How can we stand against her?'

'How can you stand against the Lord?' Gadra replied sharply. 'What does it say in the holy book of Micah? A judge only judges for reward as the prophet divines for money. I tell you, unless you obey the Lord, this land will become nothing but a ploughed field, the towns and villages will be just heaps of rubble. Death and destruction attend those who claim to be judges and know not the Lord.'

Enda bent to whisper to Fidelma, 'Have we not heard enough, lady?'

'Hear the words of Jeremiah,' Gadra was now shouting. '"From the least in the kingdom even to the King, but especially the lawyers who deal falsely, those who are not ashamed to reject the Laws of the Lord, they are named as an abomination. They shall fall away before the people's righteous anger." Your anger is virtuous and upright in the eye of the Lord. Be not afraid of this woman who clings to a brief, temporal power.

'My friends, the murderer of Adnán and his family is yet unpunished. He hides among you under the protection of your magistrate who has been mesmerised by the harlot that claims power over you. Now is the time to complete the task that the vile creature interrupted. Let us rise and take the evildoer to the punishment of the Lord!'

A number of women at the front had fallen into some type of hypnotic frenzy and were weeping, gyrating, screaming and tearing at their hair.

A man's voice yelled: 'We are with you! Lead us! Lead us in the name of the Lord!'

Fidelma glanced at Enda, then she raised her voice. 'Now is the time. Arrest the preacher.'

For some time confusion and hysteria reigned. Enda, with his two men, swords drawn, pushed their way through the crowd. A shove here. A blow there. A sharp jab with sword points, and they were upon the surprised religieux before he fully comprehended it. His arms were quickly pinioned by the expertise of two warriors.

The crowd was suddenly stunned into immobility. Eadulf had now opened the barn doors and the crowd found the rest of Enda's warriors facing them, with swords drawn and shields in the defensive position. Fidelma and Eadulf had just been joined by a pale-faced and shaking Fethmac, still unsure of his own safety.

Above the hubbub Enda had taken his *adharc,* his hunting horn, and blew several discordant blasts simply to attract the crowd's attention. It had the effect of causing them to gradually fall silent. When they did so, Enda looked towards Fidelma.

'Fidelma of Cashel!' he called, as if by way of announcement.

The crowd turned to her, nervously expectant.

Fidelma encompassed them in a belligerent glance.

'Not for the first time I have found you gathered with evil sedition and murder in your minds,' she said, her voice rising harshly to meet the occasion. 'Not content with your bloodlust in killing one of your own kind, a poor, imbecile lad, who was innocent of any crime, but your thirst for blood has led you to be swayed for a second time to try to murder a stranger among you.'

They stood completely still, like children being caught in some act of wickedness.

'It was Father Gadra,' called a male voice. 'He said it was the will of God.'

There was a rising murmur of agreement. Fidelma held up a hand for silence.

'You mean the will of Gadra, not God,' she said in ringing tones. 'Gadra, if he is even qualified to be a religieux, is now guilty of many crimes. And you, who claim to be less guilty, try to seek absolution, because you were led by him? Are you not adults? Do you not have minds and the capability of thought? You cannot so easily shirk your own responsibilities.'

There was another shuffling and uneasy movement among the people.

At her side she found Fethmac, nervous and uncomfortable.

'What are you going to do, lady? This is over half the village. You can't imprison them all.'

'Half the village is still no match for a full *catha*, a battalion of the King's warriors, should they descend on this ungodly place,' she replied loudly, so that all present could hear. If they could be persuaded to think that Enda and his men were representative of others camped outside the village, they might come to their senses. She stared round into the face of every villager and then said, her voice echoing off the walls of the barn: 'If the warriors are forced to teach this village a lesson, then it is the ultimate sanction on a people who cannot obey their King and the law of the kingdom.'

The gasps of horror among those who overheard went a way to satisfy Fidelma. There were some nervous sobs from the women who had previously been in some hysterical ecstasy as Gadra goaded them. Now they stood, shoulders slumped, heads low, the rebellious spirit depleted.

'I have not yet decided what punishment this village deserves,' Fidelma finally said to Fethmac. 'So I say this . . . all of you will disperse to your homes. You will now carry on with your daily tasks and wait until I have reached a decision. Meanwhile, be it known that Gadra is held as a prisoner, having incited murder and rebellion against the King. His fate will be known once I have announced the findings about those who hold responsibility for the deaths that have occurred here. *Is that understood?*'

There was a mumbling of assent from the sullen crowd.

As they began leaving under the watchful eye of Enda and his men, who had fully bound the angry religieux, Taithlech, the chubby merchant, arrived. He appeared astonished at what had happened but was quickly as officious as ever.

'You cannot do this,' he blustered, approaching Fidelma. 'Father Gadra has my full permission to use my *sabhall* as his chapel to preach his views. It is unlawful to break up a religious meeting and manhandle a preacher of the Faith.'

Gadra, who had been uttering profanities during this time as he stood bound under guard, now started to shout encouragement at Taithlech's intervention.

Fidelma glanced at Enda and simply said: 'Gag him until he learns respect for the law.'

In a matter of moments there was silence and then Fidelma turned to Taithlech.

'Let me correct you. You say he had permission to use your barn to preach his version of the New Faith. Did he also have your permission to call for murder, for disobedience of the law of this kingdom – indeed, a call to rise against the King?'

Several emotions crossed the merchant's fleshy features.

'*Well?*' snapped Fidelma.

'Of course he did not have permission for that, but . . .' the merchant spluttered.

'That is what he was doing and that is why I, and the Nasc Niadh, have put a stop to it.'

A woman had detached herself from the throng and now came across to them and immediately spoke to Taithlech.

'Are you all right, Father? I came here to find you and saw the gathering in the barn, so I stopped to listen.'

Taithlech moved nervously. 'It is all right, child. I was away checking some goods and someone told me that some unrest was happening here. I came as quickly as I could and now the *dálaigh* claims that the priest was preaching sedition.'

'He was using some violent language,' agreed the woman.

'I presume you are Flannat?' Fidelma addressed her. 'You are widow of Díoma, son of Tadgán?'

'I am, lady. I have heard of you from Tadgán.'

'This is my daughter,' the merchant added unnecessarily. 'She is my *banchomarba*.'

'Well, there is no cause for alarm,' Fidelma told her. 'But rather than tarry here, I would return to Tadgán's farmstead as soon as you can – unless you are a supporter of this man Gadra?'

'I am not, lady,' the girl protested.

Leaving father and daughter together, Fidelma went to supervise the emptying of the barn before finally speaking to Enda.

'Go with the magistrate here and find a place to bivouac your men. Make sure it is somewhere where you can keep Gadra in your custody.'

Fethmac was hanging around, waiting to speak to her. 'You said just now, lady, that you would tell the village what punishment they will have to face once you have made your decision about the killings here. But when will that be?'

For a moment it seemed that Fidelma was unwilling to reply, for she started towards her horse, followed by Eadulf. She had mounted the animal when the word *banchomarba* suddenly came unbidden to her lips. She frowned and repeated it more positively. Then she smiled broadly and glanced towards the bewildered young magistrate.

'Fethmac,' she called, 'tell Taithlech that the day after tomorrow, around noontime, I shall require the use of this barn, for a legal hearing.'

'Lady?' The young man sounded puzzled.

'I shall require the attendance of you, as magistrate, for it will technically be your court. Also, everyone of concern in these recent matters must attend. The entire village will be told all they need to know then, for I shall be revealing how and why Adnán and his family were killed.'

chapter eighteen

Taithlech's great barn had been designated as the court in which Fidelma would present her findings to the people of Cloichín. Benches had been provided and Fethmac had summoned all those whom Fidelma had specified for attendance. These were busy arriving, some having to be encouraged by the persuasion of Enda and his warriors.

Gobánguss, the smith, and his wife Breccnat looked slightly embarrassed as they took their seats. Eórann, Breccnat's elderly mother, sat close by, staring about her with a disapproving expression. Lúbaigh, with his wife Fuinche, sat sour faced and scowling at everyone. There was Blinne, the mother of Íonait, who appeared in a furious mood, as if she was ready to physically attack anyone who said the wrong thing. Even Slébíne, the son of the murdered Conmaol, had travelled here, accompanied by Tuama but looking ill at ease and out of place. Taithlech the merchant, with his daughter Flannat, came together with Tadgán. Taithlech looked bored and Flannat just puzzled. They all sat in silence, not talking with one another. To one side, in his own space, was the dour, fleshy faced Brother Gadra, who seemed to be totally uninterested in what was going on around him.

Apparently awed by the company that filled the *sabhall*, and seated apart from everyone, was Celgaire, still looking pale under his dark skin and far from recovered from his recent ordeal. Next to him was his wife Fial, nursing their baby son Ennec. Filling the rest of the barn were many of the curious inhabitants of the village.

What was particularly satisfying for Fidelma was the arrival of Abbot Rumann from Ard Fhionáin, together with his steward, Brother Fechtnach, and the scholar Brother Solam. Fidelma had sent a special word for them to attend. The old scholar came across to Fidelma the very moment they had entered.

'Lady,' he whispered urgently, 'when I walked in, I recognised the man who came to see the genealogy, all those months ago. Now I see him again, for his features are most memorable.'

Fidelma leaned towards the old man. 'Do not point or look in his direction, but could you indicate him to me?' she asked softly.

When the scriptor had done so, Fidelma gave a smile of satisfaction.

'It is the man I suspected it was. My thoughts are now complete. I feel we shall now have justice. Thank you, but keep that information to yourself, Brother Solam, unless I call on you to confirm it as witness.'

A table had been placed before the principal witnesses, behind whom Fidelma and Fethmac were seated centrally. Eadulf sat on Fidelma's left while Ballgel sat to her husband's right in order to act as keeper of the records, a role she often took as the wife of the magistrate.

Fidelma whispered hurriedly to Fethmac and the young magistrate rose and let his gaze sweep across the assembly before them, allowing their whispered conversations to fall silent before he began to speak.

'We all know why we are gathered here. I shall not say anything further than to hand over proceedings to Fidelma of Cashel, who is, as you all know, a *dálaigh* employed with one of the highest qualifications in this kingdom. I shall have no compunction on imposing the maximum fines on anyone who does not pay the respect that she commands!'

He then sat down and Fidelma rose in his stead.

'This is not a trial against one person or another,' she explained without preamble. 'I shall explain the law. This hearing is called One of the Five Paths to Judgement. As a *dálaigh,* or advocate, it is my determination to choose one of these paths to bring about an understanding of what has happened here. I have chosen what we call *fír* – the Path of Truth. Now *fír* is a legal term. In this case, we have no *féchman,* that is a defendant, nor a plaintiff. I am here to sum up my findings of my inquiry into several matters so that they may be taken forward to be judged by the Chief Brehon of this kingdom – if, indeed, they reveal any who are deemed to have transgressed the law to the point where punishment must be accorded. I believe that there are some guilty for such judgement. I must be supported in this by the local magistrate.' She paused and glanced at Fethmac. The young man kept his gaze lowered to the table before him.

'My first duty as an advocate is to ensure that the local magistrate, Fethmac, has my *fírgille,* or truth pledge; this is a sum of money to the value of one milch cow which I put forward as a guarantee that I have made my case without bias and on the facts that I will outline.'

Fethmac cleared his voice but did not rise as he responded: 'It is my duty to acknowledge this pledge, duly passed into my keeping. This establishes the three doors through which truth shall be recognised in this court: the presentation of a firm case, a clear pleading in which response may be given, and also the reliance of the witnesses who may be questioned.'

From the bewilderment on most of their faces it seemed few people had been near a court of law or had any understanding of a special hearing or its conduct. Nevertheless it was Fidelma's duty to go through the procedure.

She was still on her feet explaining matters. 'We shall be considering certain types of murder and wounding today. There will be several things that we have to consider. There is the question of whether we consider, under law, that deaths have occurred by *duin-thaide* or plain murder, or by *duine-orcuin* or manslaughter. There is also the charge of *eisce* or unlawful wounding. In addition, what needs to be considered is the subject of *forcor*, forcible rape; we could include in this sexual harassment, as given in the *Bretha Nemed Toísech* law text.'

This reference drew some gasps from several people, apart from Blinne and Eórann, whose expressions were stony.

'These are among many matters that have arisen in this village and which need to be considered,' Fidelma said, raising her voice a little to break the ripple of muttering among the gathering. She waited for a moment until quiet returned. 'Where do we begin? How do we start? One matter I shall state immediately. Celgaire and his wife Fial, sitting with their baby son Ennec, are innocent parties to all these crimes.'

This provoked an outburst of surprise and even angry objections. Fidelma noticed a cynical smile on the lips of the lugubrious-faced Gadra.

'I shall say it again. Celgaire was illegally accused, taken from custody and nearly murdered by hanging. He was later attacked, dragged from his prison, and nearly burned alive to make it seem that he had escaped because of his guilt and perished in the process. Compensation will be due to him and his family and recompense for the loss of his wagon.'

The mutterings increased to a substantial volume.

'Where is my evidence, I hear you asking?' Fidelma raised her voice again, only slightly but it had the effect of causing them to fall silent. 'The evidence will become clear as I present my findings on the events that have happened here.'

She waited again for an absolute silence. When she saw that she had their full attention, their eyes on her in expectation, she spoke again.

'One of the problems in resolving this has been that there were no witnesses to the actual murder of Adnán and his family, apart from the witness to the murder of his elder, Cainnech. I have had to think carefully on this, for the law says that a person can only give evidence about what they have seen or heard. Because that witness is now dead, and spoke only to myself and Eadulf, I had to weigh the matter in law, to find out if we were allowed to use this evidence, since the witness had been unlawfully killed.'

She stared straight at Gadra but the man stared straight back as if defying her.

'Is it right for me to accept the word of a dead boy and then put it forward here?' she asked as if it were a rhetorical question.

'Not if the dead man was a *drúth*,' Fethmac interrupted, realising whom she was referring to. 'I know enough of the law of evidence to say a judge would not accept that evidence.'

Fidelma did not seem to be put out; on the contrary, she smiled.

'You are correct, Fethmac, if we were pleading in a legal trial. But, as I have explained, this is only a preliminary hearing to discover the truth. It is not a court sitting with a judge. So I am going to use this evidence and for this reason: the law text called *Berrad Airechta* accepts the validity of such evidence at a hearing if there is more than one witness. I was one witness to what the boy told us while Eadulf was the second. Furthermore, the law text called *Gúbetha Caratniad* says that the evidence of a sick man about to die, the evidence of a woman in childbirth and danger of death, or the evidence of a person who does not stand to gain from his evidence, are all permissible. So I will give the evidence of what was told me and with the support of Eadulf as the witness to it. If there is an objection, let me hear it, citing the authorities that overturn my authorities.'

Fethmac cleared his throat nervously. 'I will accept that the law does acknowledge that while indirect evidence is not of itself conclusive it can be taken into account. But I must point out that this is only as part of other factors. The whole case cannot be based on the indirect evidence.'

'I am sure it will be substantiated.' Fidelma smiled confidently. 'So we will start at the beginning.' She paused as if to gather her thoughts. 'Lúbaigh discovered the bodies of Adnán and his family slaughtered on their farm before dawn one morning. He later amended his account to reveal that it was not at first light. It was, in fact, past the time he usually went to the farm to tend to the cattle. The reason was because he had stayed up late the night before, drinking with his wife and the merchant Taithlech.

'Having discovered the bodies, he said he believed the killing had been done by a vagrant named Celgaire who had, he said, been refused work by Adnán. To this was attributed the motive for murder – the vagrant's revenge. Celgaire had parked his wagon near the farm buildings but he and his family had left early that morning, possibly at first light and before the bodies were discovered. When Lúbaigh gave this information to the magistrate, Celgaire's wagon was pursued and overtaken. He was brought back to the village under the custody of Fethmac but, through the intervention of the religieux Gadra, who believes in a law of retribution which I admit has been adopted by some parts of the Christian world, Celgaire was seized and nearly hanged. At that point I arrived and asserted my authority as *dálaigh*.

'So I began my investigation. And the story was more complicated than ever I could have imagined. I will sum up the story as it unfolded to me.

'Adnán was a powerful and wealthy farmer with ambition. He was well respected by most, but not by all. His cousin Tadgán, for example, did not respect him. Indeed, they were rivals for power in this territory. Both were the descendants of Ágach Ágmar the Warlike whose clan had settled here. It had left them with kin-land, that is a form of private property which could be passed on to heirs, either those chosen by a meeting of family elders or, by the same agreement, by the eldest male heir or, failing suitable candidates, by a female heir – a *banchomarba*.'

She paused for a moment or so and then went on. No one seemed to be moving and there was no sound from those gathered there.

'Adnán had two sons. One, the elder, was called Cainnech. He was a youth just come into the age of choice, seventeen years old. We heard that he was arrogant, just as ambitious as his father and with a cruel streak. He was, in fact, a bully. We know that working on the farm was a pretty young girl, Íonait, daughter of Blinne. Cainnech paid her unwanted attention. And then the day came when he forced his sexual ambition on her. He would have been guilty of sexual harassment under the law which, had he been charged, would have resulted in him paying the full honour price of Íonait. But he went further – he committed forcible rape, *forcor*. When Íonait managed to get home that day, her distress and the blood on her clothes spoke for themselves. Íonait did not speak to her mother of what had happened, only telling her that she did not want to work for Adnán any more. Blinne was aware that young Dulbaire followed her daughter about like a pet dog. She immediately leaped to the wrong conclusion. Yet both Íonait and Dulbaire felt an intense but pure affection towards one another. Eórann knew both well and can attest to that.

'Knowing that Cainnech was supported by his family who would not hear a word against him, Íonait plotted her own revenge. She took a reaping hook from Dulbaire, and arranged to meet Cainnech behind the barn late one night. Dulbaire went with her for support. Out of male arrogance, without suspecting the hatred he had inspired in the girl, Cainnech went to the meeting. That was when she killed him, leaving the reaping hook by the body. Dulbaire witnessed the murder and helped her away from the scene.'

There was a shocked outcry from Blinne.

'Are you accusing my daughter of killing the entire family? And if you are saying that Dulbaire did not kill my daughter, then who did?'

'Anyway, it was a cleaver that killed the family,' yelled Tadgán. 'It was found in the vagrant's wagon!'

'No. There were two murder weapons, so it is logical to suspect that there were two killers,' Fidelma responded. 'Íonait killed Cainnech as I said – and with some justification. Then she and Dulbaire left the scene. Íonait went to her own home and Dulbaire to his in order that they could appear at the usual time for work on the farm the next morning. It was just before dawn when the second killer arrived and found Cainnech. Perhaps the idea sprang into this person's mind to take advantage of the killing. Or perhaps the death of Adnán and his family had been planned all along.'

'How do you mean?' Tadgán demanded.

'It was the perfect opportunity to use the cover of Cainnech's killing to be rid of the rest of the family. Since Adnán possessed one of the largest kin-land farmsteads in the territory, his heir would come into a nice fortune.'

Tadgán was now up on his feet, quivering in rage.

'I protest! I know where this is heading. You are going to say that only I benefited because I was Adnán's cousin and this was kin-land. You are going to claim that I butchered my cousin, his wife and younger son to inherit his farm, knowing that I was the senior heir of the *derbhfine*. Lies! Lies! *Lies!* I did not kill him or his family!'

'Yet you would agree that it is a possibility,' Fidelma replied in a mild tone, making the farmer's outburst seem over-dramatic. 'If you were involved, you would have had to employ someone else to do the killing, because we now know when Íonait and Dulbaire killed Cainnech. We also know that the death of the others occurred afterwards. It would have been impossible, given that time, for you to have personally participated. Did you employ someone else to do so?'

Tadgán was outraged. 'I did not! Anyone who says I did is a liar.'

'We shall see.' Fidelma sighed. 'The motive of inheritance was a matter that weighed against you until the arrival of Conmaol of Cnoc na Faille – a cousin of yours, whom you claimed not to know. Do you still claim that?'

'I had never met him.'

'That is not what I asked.'

'All right. I knew there was a vague story of a branch of the family who had settled in the mountains. It was before I was born. I did not even know the details.'

'You were never curious about them? Even though a friend, and someone who did business with you, knew and traded regularly with this relative?'

Tadgán did not respond. After a pause, Fidelma decided to continue.

'Taithlech was regularly trading with the hill people in Cnoc na Faille and he was well aware of this relationship. When news of the slaughter of Adnán's family was announced, Taithlech decided to contact Conmaol and persuade him to come to the funeral and make his claim to the kin-land. I would suggest that the plan to do so had been long in the gestation period. For it seemed that Taithlech had spoken several times to Conmaol about such an inheritance. We have Conmaol's son among us to give witness to that.'

She spoke the last sentence with emphasis, staring at the merchant.

The swarthy merchant rose unwillingly from his seat and glanced round, finding Slébíne. The young man stared back and it seemed that, for a moment, Taithlech would deny it. Then he shrugged.

'Very well. That is so,' Taithlech conceded. 'Anyway, the main point was that Conmaol would have to prove his senior relationship to Tadgán. To do that he had to get hold of certain documents.'

'Where does that leave us now that this Conmaol is dead?' Tadgán called out, still irritable.

'This is a good question,' conceded Fethmac. He was clearly puzzled as he turned to Fidelma. 'If he was senior, then surely his son who sits among us is the inheritor.'

Young Slébíne was now on his feet. 'Am I now being named a suspect in these matters? I want no part of this kin-land, a practice I detest. I did not agree with my father's pursuit of this matter.'

Fidelma noticed that Flannat was staring at her father with a worried expression. Several people in the crowd were murmuring, some asking what it all meant, others still angry at the proceedings.

Fidelma held up a hand for silence.

'The fact is that Conmaol was, indeed, killed on his way back to Cloichín. He was bearing a letter from Abbot Rumann who sits here. He also had a parchment of the section of the genealogy of the family. He set out with these articles but they were stolen from his dead body. I don't doubt they have been destroyed or hidden.'

'You mean these were the documents which proved he was the senior member of the *derbhfine*? That they showed his entitlement to take the kin-land of Adnán and that was why the documents were destroyed?' Fethmac queried, slightly bewildered. 'Is that why you have asked Abbot Rumann and the scholar Brother Solam to attend here?'

Fidelma shook her head. 'The documents proved, as the abbot and Brother Solam will confirm, that Conmaol was *not* the senior member and not entitled to inherit the kin-land,' she replied quietly.

There was an outbreak of confused muttering amongst the onlookers.

Fethmac raised his hands in a helpless gesture. 'So you are still accusing Tadgán, for who else would have benefited by hiding the fact that Conmaol was not entitled?'

All Tadgán could keep muttering was, 'It is lies! Lies!'

Fidelma ignored him. 'There are others listed on the genealogy,' she announced calmly.

'The deaths would benefit Slébíne as Conmaol's son,' Fethmac pointed out. 'He could claim that the documents showed legitimacy and that he should inherit.'

Slébíne was back on his feet, red faced with indignation. 'That's not so. I did not want my father to claim that kin-land. I am happy where I am.'

'Sit down, Slébíne,' Fidelma said. 'If your father was not entitled it also means that you are not. You forget that we have the abbot and the genealogical expert, Brother Solam, with us. They will bear witness to the other name on the genealogy.'

'Are we getting anywhere with all this, lady?' muttered Fethmac. 'I am patient but I cannot see where this is leading. All I am hearing is accusation and denial.'

'Never fear, it is leading to the killer,' Fidelma promised. 'Had we not been assured several times that Adnán, Tadgán and later Conmaol, were the only surviving members of the *derbhfine* of Ágach Ágmar the Warlike we would have had our minds open more quickly. As I have said, the genealogy was stolen because of the name on it.'

'What do you mean?' demanded the young magistrate.

'As a member of the *derbhfine* of Adnán and Tadgán, tell us how your claim stands – Taithlech,' she said as she swung round on the merchant.

CHAPTER NINETEEN

There was a moment of surprise as the merchant flushed and assumed a defensive expression. His daughter Flannat had already lowered her gaze. It was obvious that she knew of the family connection.

'No need to look so concerned,' Fidelma told Taithlech. 'Some people knew you were related to Adnán and to Tadgán.'

'Everyone knew my daughter was married to Tadgán's son, Díoma,' protested the merchant.

'Yet the first time I met Gobánguss, he mentioned that you were Adnán's cousin.'

'What would Gobánguss know?' snorted the merchant.

The big smith turned to him with a look of disgust. 'We grew up together, Taithlech. I have a long memory.'

'Indeed,' Fidelma added. 'You told me so when I questioned you at your house, Taithlech.'

The merchant was shaking his head. 'So what if I am distantly related? We are probably all cousins in this village anyway. What good does that do me? I am not the senior of the *derbhfine*. I am a very distant cousin.'

'But even a cousin can claim kin-land if there is no one else senior,' observed Fethmac with an uneasy glance at Tadgán. The farmer was frowning.

'He couldn't claim my kin-land,' he said, 'unless . . .'

'Unless you and your family were to be removed from the inheritance,' Fethmac said, completing Tadgán's sentence.

'You accuse me of planning to murder my entire family?' The merchant's voice was filled with sarcasm. His daughter was meanwhile looking increasingly uncomfortable and casting anxious glances at her father as if seeking reassurance. 'There must be other distant cousins with closer links than I have.'

'You know that is not the case,' Fidelma replied. 'There is also your daughter's claim.'

'A claim from Taithlech's daughter?' Fethmac turned to her in astonishment. 'I am totally at a loss.'

'So am I,' growled Tadgán. 'I don't understand. Flannat married my son, Díoma, who is now deceased. She has my grandson, but she could not inherit the kin-land.'

'Strictly speaking, no,' Fidelma agreed. 'But she is a *banchomarba* in her own right. She inherits her father's property. Her father has already ascertained he is the senior of the cousins and next in line to inherit your lands, Tadgán. So she will eventually become Tadgán's female heir because of her father and not because of her marriage to your son. I will explain this in a moment.'

'I am confused,' Fethmac admitted. 'Very muddled. How could Flannat inherit? What has all this to do with the initial murders? Are we talking about different killers and victims?'

'Apart from the killing of Cainnech and the unlawful killing of Dulbaire, when people were misled by their prejudice, things have followed a pattern. A pattern inspired by greed and ambition.'

There was now, once again, complete silence in the barn.

'The first act in this drama was that Cainnech raped Íonait. In revenge, she killed him,' Fidelma announced. 'This event set off a series of actions. It gave a certain unscrupulous person the opportunity to have Adnán and his heirs killed. The motive was the kin-land and the power it would bring. The blame was put on

Celgaire because he was in the wrong place at the wrong time and he was a perfect victim because of prejudice. Firstly he was a *ráithech,* a vagrant, and secondly he was obviously a stranger marked by the distinctive colour of his skin. But the clue was that Cainnech was killed by a reaping hook in a frenzied fashion; a crime of passion. Other members of the family were killed with a cleaver.'

'Which we found in Celgaire's wagon,' Fethmac put in. 'You have not forgotten?'

'I have not. Celgaire and the wagon were brought back to the village. That was when the killer made a mistake. He hid the cleaver in the wagon seeking to ensure it was discovered and presenting proof positive that Celgaire was the culprit. However, because it was not the weapon that killed Cainnech I grew suspicious. Fearful of where my suspicion might lead, the killer released Celgaire, knocking him out before he could be identified, and then drove the wagon to Tadgán's farmland. There he set fire to it, hoping to kill Celgaire in the flames. He believed we would all accept Celgaire's guilt and that his death would end matters. That plan failed.'

Fethmac was growing restless.

'You avoid naming the killer. Anyway, only Tadgán had something to gain by this.'

'You have not been listening,' Fidelma admonished. 'As I said, Taithlech the merchant had a great deal to gain.'

'I did not kill Adnán or his brood,' shouted the merchant.

Fidelma swung round to him. 'Not by your own hand, no, but you had the tool to achieve it. There was only one person who had the opportunity to kill Adnán's family. When he came back from the farm and told you that he had found Cainnech's body, and that the boy had been killed that morning, you were staying with Lúbaigh and his wife. Was that by chance or by accident?'

'That is ridiculous!' Taithlech cried. 'I had a late night's drinking with them and was asleep.'

Lúbaigh sat in stunned silence, while his wife Fuinche started to scream abuse at Fidelma until Enda moved across and tapped the woman none too gently on the shoulder with the flat of his sword.

'Lúbaigh had risen at his usual time and went to the farm at first light. That was when he found the body of Cainnech. The farm was not yet roused. He raced back to the cottage and told you. You might have already discussed the idea of getting rid of Adnán and his boys too. In fact, you might have been planning a similar attack for ages. Anyway, you seized the opportunity and had Lúbaigh finish off the entire family.

'Lúbaigh went back to the farm that morning and found Adnán already stirring. He was on his way to the barn when Lúbaigh attacked him from behind with the cleaver. What then? I would say that Abél, the second son, was then viciously slain. Aoife was in her kitchen about to prepare breakfast. She didn't stand a chance. It seemed so easy. He saw Celgaire's wagon already leaving. It all fitted so well. When Lúbaigh told you, Taithlech, that the task was complete, you told him to get back to the farm as if he had just arrived there and discovered all the bodies. He was to send his brother Dulbaire for the magistrate or Íonait, whoever arrived first. They were to tell Fethmac that it must have been the vagrants – Celgaire and his wife – who had committed the murders. The actual hand that carried out Taithlech's will belongs to Lúbaigh.'

Lúbaigh suddenly leaped from his chair and tried to flee from the barn but at a quick sign from Enda, two of his warriors caught him easily and dragged him back.

'The mistake Lúbaigh made that set me thinking was, as I have said, to do with the cleaver. When he saw the wagon being brought back to the village, he found an opportunity to secrete the weapon in the back of it. This was putting too many eggs in the pudding for my taste.'

Lúbaigh's wife Fuinche found nothing to say at the fast-moving events. However, Taithlech was still argumentative.

'For what purpose would I kill Adnán?' he demanded. 'It would be Tadgán who would take over the kin-land. True, I am a cousin but not so close or powerful as to claim seniority.'

'He makes a good point,' Fethmac observed anxiously, turning to Fidelma.

Taithlech was about to speak when Blinne interrupted. 'Are you forgetting the death of Íonait?' she shouted at Fidelma. 'Who killed my poor girl?'

'Lúbaigh had no compunction in killing your daughter and pinning the blame on his poor half-witted brother,' replied Fidelma. 'But that was at the order of Taithlech there.'

Lúbaigh had twisted in the grip of the warriors. 'It's true!' he shouted. 'But Taithlech told me that I must do it. He is to blame, not me!'

'Why kill that young girl?' demanded Fethmac.

Fidelma answered. 'To stop her confessing to the murder of Cainnech and bringing up the question of the two killers. You had not realised that I was already pursuing that matter,' she said.

'How am I to blame for what Lúbaigh did?' demanded Taithlech, sounding desperate now. 'Besides, it seems Conmaol was not the senior to inherit the land.'

'I think that, to put suspicion away from you, you had encouraged Conmaol to believe that he had a senior claim. You did this all the while you were fermenting your plot to seize the lands. That was why Conmaol was angry after he went to see the genealogy at the abbey and realised that you had tricked him: that you yourself stood in senior position. He was shocked and that caused him to steal the genealogy to bring it here as proof.

'Conmaol had the intelligence to realise that with Tadgán's son dead, and your own daughter as his widow, she had the right to be regarded as a female heir. Because her own father had been of the same *derbhfine,* even though a distant cousin, she would have a right as heir once anything happened to Tadgán or her son.

'To stop Conmaol revealing this truth you waylaid and killed him. You probably also destroyed the valuable genealogy. You had seen your own genealogy at the abbey months earlier. Except you did not know that the abbey had more genealogies of various branches of the family, nor that you appeared in them. Your copy was not the only one. Conmaol had gone to Ard Fhionáin and that was when you realised that you must kill him. That was not something Lúbaigh was able to do for you, so that one killing you had to do yourself.'

Lúbaigh had wrestled himself loose from the warriors and threw himself, grovelling, at the feet of Taithlech.

'Do something, do something,' he sobbed. 'I am not to blame alone for the deaths of Adnán and the others. You said you would protect me, you promised.'

Taithlech was now standing, his face a deathly pale. He looked down at the prostrate man and aimed a savage kick at him. Immediately Enda had sprung forward with his sword tip at the man's throat.

Flannat screamed and burst into tears. It seemed, in Fidelma's eyes, that she had moved away from her father.

'*Facta non verba*, lady,' murmured Enda, still resting his sword point against the merchant's throat.

Fidelma regarded him solemnly. 'Your Latin has improved, Enda. Indeed, actions do speak louder than words and confirm all I have said.'

Flannat had risen to her feet and approached Fidelma, saying tearfully, 'Lady, I swear to you that I knew nothing of this. Nothing of what my father was plotting.' She swung round to Tadgán. 'Truly, Tadgán, I speak the truth. I did not know.'

Tadgán was still in shock and barely took in her words. She turned back to Fidelma with a pleading expression.

'I am inclined to believe you,' Fidelma told her, but not in a harsh tone. 'But for the time being, you will have to go to Cashel to be heard by the Chief Brehon.'

Fidelma cleared her throat and turned once more to address those present. 'I have gathered this evidence and presented it to you all. As I have told you, this has been a hearing in search of the truth and not a trial. Taithlech and Lúbaigh will be taken to Cashel to be heard before the Chief Brehon and they will be judged and sentenced accordingly. Flannat will go with her father, to plead her innocence.'

'You cannot take my husband!' Fuinche cried, interrupting the warriors in their task to bind their prisoners. 'Lúbaigh was duped. It is Taithlech's fault. He made him do it.'

'Lúbaigh will not be alone when sentenced by the Chief Brehon,' Fethmac replied with irony. 'As for you, Fuinche, unless you wish to make a statement seeking exoneration by giving your full part in this matter, then you must hold yourself ready to accompany Lúbaigh and Taithlech to Cashel.'

Fethmac looked to Fidelma, saying, 'Taithlech owns property, lady. I presume the Chief Brehon will endorse your judgement. What of that property? Does it go to his daughter as his *banchomarba*?'

'Until all is clear, as magistrate, you will take all Taithlech's possessions into account as a basis for collecting the fines and compensations that will doubtless arise,' glancing across to where Flannat sat, apparently stunned at the revelation of her father's crime. She made as if to rise but Fidelma motioned her to remain seated. 'You will have ample opportunity to show you were not involved with your father's designs against the family.' She turned back to Fethmac. 'The same sequestration goes for the house of Lúbaigh, who also owns the place where Dulbaire lived?'

'He does,' confirmed the young magistrate.

Eadulf shook his head sadly. 'I find the complications of property here very difficult to grasp. I think we Angles have a better system. The senior son always inherits and there is none of this family council and senior members emerging to argue who should inherit.'

Fidelma pursed her lips in disapproval. 'Better? Different, I grant.

To my mind, the worst thing was the introduction of the idea of any private property into this island. I think young Slébíne has the right idea. It was a bad day when the New Faith brought in the concept of absolute ownership, and of private property, into our culture.'

Eadulf shrugged. 'I grant you that the ideas Gadra was expounding were not part of the original Faith of Christ but only tacked onto it when Rome took charge of the Faith and began to base it on Roman law.'

Abbot Rumann rose and spoke for the first time.

'I would agree with Brother Eadulf. It is part of the nature of man that the more we are moved from the original teaching, the more we lose sight of what was intended. Over these years, we have had council after council in the western and eastern churches telling us what the right interpretations of the Faith should be. What was accepted one year becomes a heresy the next year, so now we do not know for sure what the original teaching was and what was meant by it. These new rules from Rome are nothing more than that – rules decided by a council of men. We should always remember that – decided by a council of men.'

Brother Solam had been nodding in agreement. Now he added: 'We do not question Eusebius in his choice of ancient texts that he chose to translate and compile in the book, the *Biblos*, which we accept as the foundation of the Faith. Did he choose wisely, did he translate correctly? That has been questioned by council after council, by scholar after scholar. Who knows what is right or wrong?

'I am reminded of one of the earliest texts that we have in our library. They say it was written when the Christ was still in the living memory of man. It is a work called "The Teaching of the Twelve Sacred Apostles". It is in Greek and therefore called *Didakthé* – The Teaching. Eusebius did not include it because it seems he thought it was much like the Gospel of Matthew. However, by doing that, some important teachings were neglected.'

Fethmac coughed loudly. 'Abbot, Brother Solam. While acknowledging your learning in this matter, we are still a court of legal hearings and not a council discussing the Faith.'

The scholar agreed solemnly. 'I am aware of it. But it related to what Sister Fidelma was saying. May I have your permission to quote the text?'

'Anything that brings some elucidation of matters,' sighed the young man with resignation.

'It exhorts people in the following manner: "Share everything with your brothers. Do not say, 'It is private property.' If you share what is everlasting you should be that much more willing to share things that do not last." So you are right, the concept of this absolutely private property has become a bane in our society and in our law. They were not part of the Faith until the Roman aristocrats made them so.'

Fidelma smiled at the old scholar. It was not truly relevant to the proceedings but it gave support to the ideas of protecting the native law as opposed to those changes that Gadra wanted to see imposed.

Fethmac made another effort to bring them back to the matters in hand.

'Before we dispense with this hearing, lady, there is still another matter we must consider. I do this accepting that all matters will be sent to the Chief Brehon for hearing and judgement.'

Fidelma knew what he was going to bring up. 'I have not forgotten the actions of Brother Gadra.'

At once the religieux folded his arms stubbornly, snarling, 'I do not recognise the validity of this hearing. I will not condescend to answer any questions.'

'In that case, we will not ask any questions,' Fethmac replied. 'The facts are clear.' He glanced at Fidelma, who began to speak.

'The facts are that Gadra led a mob, first trying to hang Celgaire, having illegally taken him from the custody of the magistrate. He then succeeded in influencing a mob to hang Dulbaire, if he did not actually lead the mob. The fact that those he led now have to live with the guilt of murdering an innocent, half-witted youth, may be punishment enough. I hope they think on this and that the memory haunts them in the long dark nights ahead. The action in both trying to kill Celgaire, an innocent stranger in our midst, and the killing of the youth not responsible under law, is against our laws and incurs heavy penalties and the loss of all rights for everyone involved.'

She paused before continuing. 'However guilty the villagers were in doing this, they were misled by one man: a man claiming authority of religion and the laws of that religion. The guilt lies with the man Gadra, who refuses to participate in the legal hearing. As he wants to fall back on his religion as defence I instruct that he be escorted to the abbey of Imleach where he may argue his case before the Chief Bishop of this kingdom and be judged in an ecclesiastical court. However, I can assure Gadra, from the point of view of the civil law, that he is exiled from this territory. I will plead before the Chief Bishop, the Chief Brehon and the King, that he should be exiled entirely from my brother's kingdom.'

Gadra remained seated with arms folded, looking stonily ahead.

Fidelma now looked across to where Celgaire had been seated with his wife and baby.

'Celgaire, come forward, please.'

He did so, nervously, but Fidelma smiled reassuringly.

'I want everyone to know that you, so far as I am concerned, leave here without any shadow on your honour. You will be asked to attend as witness at the court of the Chief Brehon in Cashel but I, not only as a *dálaigh* having investigated these matters, but as sister to King Colgú of Muman, tell you that you leave here with the sincere apologies on behalf of this village and territory for the way you have been treated here.

'After you have given your witness in Cashel, it may be that you will not want to remain among a people who twice tried to kill you in total violation of the law as they killed even one of their own. I think the village now owes Celgaire recompense. At least a new vehicle is due for the loss of his wagon. I say to you, Celgaire, take the documents of your honourable ancestry and the right to be acknowledged in high esteem in this kingdom. If it pleases you, head for Cashel where, if you show them, you will be received in fraternal friendship by the steward of the King and I guarantee you that suitable work and accommodation will be found for you and your family.'

At that point, the burly form of Gobánguss the smith rose and shuffled forward.

'Lady, let me say that we were all misled by the man Gadra who called himself an apostle of the New Faith. We know now that this is an evil man who ignored our laws in the furtherance of his own ambitions. I am afraid that many of us were taken in. So I join you in expressing our shame and apologies to Celgaire. Furthermore, we shall indeed build him a fine new wagon in compensation, and provide it with all the things that he lost.'

Fethmac was nodding in satisfaction.

Fidelma concluded: 'And now are there any more matters to be brought before me, before this hearing is closed and matters sent to the Chief Brehon for final judgement?'

Once again, Fethmac coughed nervously before he said, 'There is one thing that seems unexplained, lady. What of the falling cauldron?'

Fidelma responded with amusement.

'You are right, one inexplicable mystery needs to be resolved. Or rather, needs to be explained. It's what I thought was an attempt on my life by the pushing of the old sacred cauldron off its plinth, nearly landing on my head.'

'I was wondering when you would come to that,' Eadulf observed under his breath.

'As well you know, it is the duty of a *dálaigh* to explain all aspects of the case or at least try to explain them,' Fidelma replied.

'And so your explanation is?' prompted Fethmac.

'Remember this is an ancient cauldron from the time before time. In the time before the New Faith, the cauldron was not only an object with which we cooked food for the community but a symbol of the power of the chief, indeed, even the power of a king. It was the sign of his wealth and his ability to feed his people.'

'We know this.' Gobánguss was puzzled. 'What are you saying?'

Fidelma glanced directly to where Gadra was sitting, eyes closed and taking no part in the proceedings.

'Are you going to help us, Gadra, with the explanation?' she asked.

The religieux opened his eyes and gave her a look of scorn. 'Why should I?'

'Because you already face great charges involving the highest punishment. But if you demonstrate a willingness to help us on other matters it could bear on your punishment.'

Gadra stuck out his chin. 'In the name of the Faith I say – do your worst for God is on my side! I will not plead anything before your pagan court.'

Fidelma shrugged and turned to Fethmac.

'The cauldron was an ancient symbol of our people and a symbol that might be offensive to some.'

There was a growing muttering in the room.

'Offensive?' Fethmac asked with brows raised. 'I don't see how. The feasting halls of the Five Kingdoms are replete with cauldrons. Our stories and legends are full of magic cauldrons. Why should it be offensive?'

Fidelma glanced at Gadra before replying.

'It is not we who think things are offensive. Consider a moment. The village saw this as no ordinary cauldron, a symbol they have lived with since time immemorial. But in the New Faith, such ancient totems, even given by the founder of this village – Ágach Ágmar the Warlike – become witchcraft. This is regarded as the cauldron that was brought from the Otherworld city of Murias. One of the four great Otherworld cities of the De Danaans, the gods and goddesses of the Five Kingdoms. To some it was the original cauldron of the Dagda, Father of All, the Good God. The legend has it that when Crimthann Srem was presented with this cauldron, it had survived a millennium and was originally part of the Magic Cauldron of Murias.'

'This is true,' Gobánguss interrupted. 'That is the story we often told at the village feasting. That is why we raised it on a plinth in the centre of the village, to be taken down only on a special day of celebration.'

'That is also well known, Fidelma,' Fethmac pointed out. 'Everyone here knows it was supposed to have been touched by the ancient deities and they that had supped the broth of the Ever Living from it.'

'Everyone . . . but some strangers only learned it after they had been here a while. And some strangers not in tune with the ancient lore and its concepts might object to it. Those who might take their New Faith to fanatical extremes.'

'What is that supposed to mean?' demanded the young magistrate.

'Why don't you explain, Brother Gadra?' Fidelma suggested when he remained silent. 'No? When you overheard Fethmac explaining the symbolism to me, you realised that you could not tolerate such a pagan symbol. It was an affront, wasn't it, to your interpretation of the New Faith.'

Gadra's mouth was thin line. Had his eyes been weapons, she would have been dead.

'Are you saying that Brother Gadra climbed up to my barn roof and deliberately pushed the cauldron down on you!' exclaimed Gobánguss. 'But I thought we had decided that in no way could it be construed as a premeditated act?'

'I concede that it was merely coincidental that I was passing underneath, then paused a moment before riding on and, by luck, missed the impact of the cauldron when it fell. Gadra did indeed climb onto your roof and used a long pole to push the cauldron off its plinth. His purpose in doing so was not to harm me. I make that clear. But his purpose was to try to destroy what he saw as a hated pagan symbol. It was lucky that I moved just in time, otherwise Fethmac would have been investigating yet another death in this so-called Garden of Eden.'

'Is that the way it happened, Gadra?' Fethmac demanded.

The religieux remained silent.

'Perhaps we should demand compensation to help us rebuild that plinth and repair the damage to the cauldron?' Gobánguss said. Several people murmured in approval of the idea.

Fidelma was sad. 'It could be said that even under the ancient beliefs it would be a sacrilege to attempt to recast or mend the ancient cauldron from the Otherworld. But as for seeking compensation from Gadra, I doubt if he were given several lifetimes he would be able to pay all the fines and compensations that will be his just punishment.'

She paused and looked round at the assembly.

'Then, if there be nothing else . . .? The prisoners will be escorted to Cashel to be heard before the Chief Brehon along with the witnesses. Tadgán remains in unquestioned possession of the kin-land of his cousin and this hearing is closed.'

EPILOGUE

'What made you realise the existence of female inheritance was behind this?' asked Eadulf as they rode at the head of the long column of prisoners and witnesses towards Cashel.

'I should have thought of it sooner,' Fidelma admitted. 'It was staring me in the face once I knew that Taithlech was a member of the *derbhfine* of Adnán's family but junior to Tadgán. I started to question what his motive would be. I was misled by the fact that if Tadgán was, indeed, the *ádae fine*, the senior of the *derbhfine*, the motive of inheritance would not have been valid unless Tadgán died, leaving a male heir in the form of a son or a grandson, albeit not of the age of choice. But the widow of that son and the mother of that grandson was Taithlech's own daughter.'

'This law of inheritance,' protested Eadulf. 'It seems so complicated to me.'

'There are in the *scriptorium* in Cashel the texts of three old poems which are comments on the legal rights of women and the law. You should get old Brother Conchobhar to show them to you. There is one on how Bríg, the female judge, had to correct a male judge on the rights of women. There is another about a woman called Ciannecht who had to present a case for the recognition of her rights of inheritance. Perhaps the most famous of all, which is pertinent to this case, is the story of Seithir. Her father was from

329

Ulaidh and she had married into the Féni in Teamhar. She demanded her right to be regarded as her father's heir, being of his kindred. The law stated that while she was married to a man of another family, she could enjoy the heritage of his land, but when she died that had to be returned to his kindred.'

'I'm not sure I understand this even now.'

'Our case was complicated until I realised that Taithlech was of the same kindred as Tadgán. I was told twice, yet the relationship failed to register because I thought "cousin" was a loose term due to the fact Taithlech's daughter had been married to Tadgán's son. When I realised that he was related, I also realised that Flannat, under the law, could not only live on the lands of Tadgán but, if anything happened to him, she became female heir of both her late husband's lands – and her late father's, too.'

Eadulf frowned. 'Do you mean that with Tadgán out of the way, Taithlech could even have his own daughter killed to inherit?'

Fidelma grimaced. 'Any crime is possible when property creates envy and ambition. However, I am charitable enough to think Taithlech could have been doing this for his own daughter's sake.'

'So you don't think the girl was part of the murder conspiracy?'

'Frankly, I do not. But it will be up to the Chief Brehon to assess the case at the trial.'

'Well, isn't primogeniture a better law of inheritance? A simpler one?'

'Simple but often unjust. Maybe our laws are becoming unjust now. They have become confusing as old and new concepts clash,' Fidelma replied with a shake of her head. 'The old law was easy but it is the alterations that are complicating matters. I disapprove of the new ideas of kin-land coming into our law system; of the idea of private property. Under the old collective ownership and *derbhfine* control, where decisions were taken as a family group, it was a more equitable system. Since private ownership and private inheritance have emerged, we have seen the ensuing tangle of the rights of ownership. This chaos is going to get worse as our laws and values are set at nothing by the alien laws and codes now coming into this land.'

They rode in silence for a while and then Fidelma gave an audible sigh.

'What I really find worrying, Eadulf, is this: could we have administered the law and have truth prevail without the backing of Enda and his men?'

Eadulf smiled thinly. 'Well, I did say several times that we could do with some physical support.'

'Exactly that!' she said firmly. 'Something is changing in people. 'Time was, I could go anywhere and, being a *dálaigh*, not just the King's sister, I was respected and obeyed. Now it seems that will not happen unless I have the sword arm of a warrior behind me. Once, so it was said, no other people respected the law as much as our people. Now, however, they are beginning to openly question our authority. Look at the disobedience and ridicule even the magistrate, Fethmac, had to suffer.'

Eadulf pulled a face. 'You were very hard on him several times,' he said.

'On his lack of knowledge, not on his authority,' she corrected. 'As he grows older and wiser, he will probably be a fine advocate. But I am fearful about how our society might develop, Eadulf.'

'In what ways exactly?'

'When the New Faith came to our shores, we encompassed it because it was little different from the morals of our own Faith. While we had a central, benign god, the Dagda, it is true there were other gods and goddesses concerned with numerous aspects of life. Our deities appeared in triune form . . . just as the God of the New Faith did – Father, Son and Holy Spirit – the Trinity of which Bishop Hilary of Poitiers wrote. And are not the saints of the New Faith, and their concerns for various aspects of lives, just substitutions for the many minor gods and goddesses who had the same role as the saints? That is why our churches still follow the philosophy of Pelagius, for which they are continually condemned when the Council of Ephesus decided to call his teaching a heresy.'

'I can understand what you are saying although I don't acknowledge it,' replied Eadulf, slightly defensively. 'But I agree that there is much that is changing. Anyway, Pelagius was one of your people who went to Rome. Rome now contends that he followed many of your pagan beliefs.'

'I think the real problem arose three centuries ago when the three emperors of the Roman world signed an edict at a city to the east called Thessaloniki. They were Theodosius the First, Gratian and Valentinian. That was the Edict which made Christianity the state religion of the entire Roman world.'

Eadulf frowned. 'I thought Constantine did that?'

'No, Constantine only granted religious tolerance for the persecuted Christians in the empire. He declared that he himself had converted, but many disagree, claiming that he was only being practical in order to get the support of the Christians to bolster his empire. It was a long time afterwards that it was decreed that only Nicene Christianity was to be allowed throughout the empire. All other forms of Christianity were forbidden and those who practised those other forms were persecuted and their ideologies suppressed. There were nearly two dozen different forms of Christianity, from Psilanthropism to Titheism. And of course these and other forms of religion were then all condemned.'

'The point being?' asked Eadulf in perplexity.

'Here in the western islands we still practise the Faith that first came to us and which was adapted for our culture and our views on life, such as Pelagianism. We have not changed, but Rome continually changes with its various councils. Who knows what the original teaching was? It has gone through so many cultures and languages, and has been changed and obscured by all those councils in which new ideas and rules have been discussed and adopted. Does anyone hold the truth any more?'

Eadulf looked troubled as he asked: 'Does that mean that Brother Gadra could have held some of the truth?'

'One thing I am absolutely satisfied about,' Fidelma said with firmness. 'He did not hold any aspect of truth or religion within him.'

BLOODMOON

IRELAND. AD 671.

Sworn by oath to tell no one the reason for her quest, Sister Fidelma journeys to the abbey of Finnbarr to question the abbot. But moments after she arrives, the abbot is found murdered – and the main suspect, a young woman, has fled the scene.

Fidelma follows the woman into the territory of the High King. And before long, rumours begin to catch up with Fidelma, darkening the name of her family, the Eóganacht, and accusing them of conspiring to assassinate the High King.

In a land where she is now a foe, Fidelma's time is running out, and her enemies are closing in. With no other aware of her mission, she has little choice but to face the challenge alone.

**For more information visit
www.sisterfidelma.com**

HEADLINE

NIGHT OF THE LIGHTBRINGER

IRELAND, AD 671.

A man is discovered, murdered, in an unlit pyre in the heart of Cashel. He has been dressed in the robes of a religieux and killed by the ritualistic 'three deaths'.

When a strange woman named Brancheó appears in a raven-feather cloak foretelling of ancient gods returning to exact revenge, she is quickly branded a suspect.

In their search for the killer, Sister Fidelma and her companion Eadulf soon discover a darker shadow looming over the fortress. For their investigation is linked to a powerful text stolen from the Papal Secret Archives, and Fidelma herself will come up against mortal danger before the mystery is unravelled.

For more information visit
www.sisterfidelma.com

HEADLINE

PENANCE OF THE DAMNED

IRELAND, AD 671.

King Colgú of Cashel is shocked when his loyal Chief Bishop and advisor is murdered in the old enemy fortress of the Uí Fidgente. But as word reaches Cashel that the culprit will be executed under new law, a larger conflict threatens.

Dispatched to investigate, Sister Fidelma and her companion Eadulf discover that the man facing punishment is Gormán, commander of the King's bodyguard. Fidelma cannot believe he could carry out such an act – and yet the evidence is stacked against him.

To save Gormán and keep the peace, Fidelma and Eadulf must find the true culprit. As the threat of war looms, the date of execution draws ever closer . . .

For more information visit
www.sisterfidelma.com

тhе sесоnd dеаth

IRELAND, AD 671.

The Great Fair of Bealtain is almost upon the fortress of Cashel, and a line of painted wagons carries entertainers to the occasion. But preparations take a deathly turn when one of the carriages is set alight, and two corpses are found poisoned within.

As Sister Fidelma and her companion, Eadulf, investigate, they are plunged into the menacing marshlands of Osraige – where the bloody origin of the Abbey of Cainnech wreaks revenge.

What is the symbolism of the Golden Stone, and who are the members of the Fellowship of the Raven? Fidelma and Eadulf must face untold danger before they can untangle the evil that strikes at the very heart of the kingdom.

For more information visit
www.sisterfidelma.com

DISCOVER MORE IN
THE SISTER FIDELMA SERIES

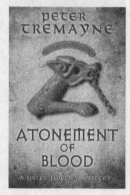

Absolution by Murder
Shroud for the Archbishop
Suffer Little Children
The Subtle Serpent
The Spider's Web
Valley of the Shadow
The Monk who Vanished
Act of Mercy
Hemlock at Vespers
Our Lady of Darkness
Smoke in the Wind
The Haunted Abbot
Badger's Moon
Whispers of the Dead
The Leper's Bell

Master of Souls
A Prayer for the Damned
Dancing with Demons
The Council of the Cursed
The Dove of Death
The Chalice of Blood
Behold a Pale Horse
The Seventh Trumpet
Atonement of Blood
The Devil's Seal
The Second Death
Penance of the Damned
Night of the Lightbringer
Bloodmoon
Blood in Eden

For more information visit www.headline.co.uk
Or www.sisterfidelma.com

HEADLINE